THE OMEGA DETECTIVE: BOOK 2

BLOOD SOAKED
SEA

I0556120

AWARD WINNING AUTHOR

Ken Gardner

Cover Design – Shelly Gardner
Publishing Coordinator & Book Designer– Sharon Kizziah-Holmes

Paperback-Press
an imprint of A & S Publishing
Paperback Press, LLC

ISBN -13: 978-1-970560-05-3

DEDICATION

To Shelly, my wife, and Hunter, my son.

The blessings from God I don't deserve
but will always treasure.

PROLOGUE

Staring into his eyes, Angela quickly understood that reality had left him, and in its place, an insanity that went far beyond simple psychosis. He told her several times that he believed everyone guilty. But guilty of what?

The zip ties holding her wrists to the armrests dug into her skin deep enough to start the blood trickling again. She tried to scream, but the gag in her mouth almost cut her breath off. In fact, Angela nearly died vomiting with it still in place. And yet, he didn't lay a hand on her after zip-tying her to the chair.

She struggled to put a name with the familiar face before he sedated her in front of his truck. When she finally remembered, she didn't want to believe it. Disfigured rage replaced kindness and laughter. Not just a shell of the man, but a gruesome conglomeration of distortion and depravity of humanity on a level higher than those who carried the Beastmark. However, the one on his forehead didn't have a tattoo like the ones suggested by the government. His didn't have symbols or pictures, but words. *Abandon all hope, ye who enter here.* She remembered reading Dante. This man obviously didn't have Christ in his life like he claimed. Like she claimed before the Rapture. A shiver coursed through her body that felt like a winter creek when he spoke. His voice had changed to a low grumble that reminded her of the frightening horror movies her mother enjoyed.

The room felt familiar, but the stress of her captivity made it difficult to recall anything. It didn't help that the only lights in the room came from the computer monitor on an old, cheap metal desk in the corner and the hologram platform just a few feet in front of her. Scanning the rest of the room, she noticed shadowy figures. Maybe furniture, or demons. The shapes ran together like a morbid Salvador Dali dream.

She frantically attempted to talk to him, to build a common ground through shared memories, to remind him they knew one another, but it just agitated him. Angela tried to remind him they went to the same church before the Tribulation began and that his kids attended the Sunday school class she taught. She tried desperately to get him to remember and set her free. If he had only given her the chance to explain.

But she realized that his rage exceeded any rational explanation when he forced the cloth into her mouth, making her lower lip bleed.

Before leaving the room, he restarted the hologram feed from the computer on the desk and paused it. The Antichrist's press secretary came into full view, standing perfectly still with a slight blue aura. He checked the hologram image, nodded, and turned and pointed a large knife at her. "Angela, you can deny it all you want, but the messiah knows you was in on his family's murder. Those people in that church we belonged to are responsible too. But don't worry, he'll send you all to Hell." Then he left.

Angela's panic overwhelmed her when she put it together. He believed the Antichrist's explanation of the Rapture and blamed her for his family's disappearance. But the news had reported at the beginning of the Tribulation that the Antichrist had no living relatives. She needed to free her mouth from the gag. Tears landed on her arm while she tried to work it free of the zip ties. The drugs he injected in her neck kept her weak, and her arms throbbed from the cuts the ties made when she struggled.

Angela stared at the hologram, wondering if he might make her watch the murder theory speech again. He said little when he played it the first time. Just a few grunts that didn't tell her if he agreed with the Antichrist or not. Until he described the murder theory. Her captor nodded enthusiastically when the Antichrist explained it.

She twitched when the hologram came to life. He must've set a timer, she thought when her mind settled.

The press secretary introduced the Sovereign.

"Citizens of the world." The Sovereign's clear, powerful voice filled the dark room. "While working diligently with government scientists to gain a deeper understanding of the event that occurred nearly three months ago, we have made a great, but tragic, discovery from the storm that plagued us a few short months ago. The idea of bloody hail that spontaneously combusted into fire when touching the ground is something that only a science fiction writer can dream up. However, as a witness to the destruction of this extraordinary incident, I needed to understand the actual cause."

Angela remembered hearing plenty about the Antichrist's most recent speech from her underground church leader, and his ridiculous explanation of God's previous judgment.

"After weeks of testing, these brilliant scientists have reported that the culprit of this terrible event is humanity." Audible gasps from the unseen audience made him pause. "The escalating climate changes we have been experiencing since before the murders have rendered the global environment nearly incapable of sustaining the balance necessary for maintaining our planet's delicate bio network. Activists, once considered kooks, protested past governments' feeble attempts to slow or stop this catastrophic chain of events. Unfortunately, they failed to make the world understand the need for major changes in environmental policy. But now, these visionaries will be forever remembered as the greatest sages in human evolution. Then came the murders.

"With the death toll in the hundreds of thousands across the planet, Corpse Patrols were incapable of finding, identifying, and properly destroying the remains before the bodily fluids from decomposition seeped into the ground. These fluids lay dormant, festering into a flammable concoction with the other chemicals placed in the ground across the planet from fertilization and other chemical spills. When the fateful night came, the perfect storm occurred. A meteor shower containing elements never before seen by scientists fell through the atmosphere, caught fire, and hit these fluids, creating a catastrophic firestorm. The reflection of the fire burning these combined components gave the illusion of blood. This new chemical, along with the ash from the fire, began infiltrating the soil, making farming almost impossible.

"In response to this devastation, we are implementing strict environmental laws to clean up our planet and return it to its former glory. Crops will rise from the ashes, much like the beloved Phoenix, to bring hope to the world. Our world. And as a bone heals stronger than before the break, the earth will be stronger when its citizens take their responsibilities seriously."

Thunderous applause from the unseen audience interrupted the Sovereign. Angela rolled her eyes at the ridiculous ideas he spread, which the world bought completely. She refocused on her bindings. Her captor came into the room and stood by the Sovereign and watched.

The cheering subsided, and the Sovereign continued.

"As for the Christian parasites who still claim this false god of theirs is judging us from antiquated laws that no longer apply to our progressive society, I have signed a new law that allows all citizens to collect a reward of ten thousand Earth dollars for the capture or information leading to the capture of a Christian. However, to avoid fraud, the Christian must be alive when turned over to the Peace Forces, who will investigate the accused to verify their treachery before payment is transferred to the citizen's global bank account.

"Do not worry about their fate. For I have decided that only the true subversives will meet their doom at the guillotine. The rest will become useful resources for the cause of peace and rededication to strengthening the planet. Women of proper age will go to breeding facilities to help repopulate the global community decimated by recent tragic events. Suitable parents will adopt their offspring, who will then attend proper global schools, to grow strong in the ways of peace and prosperity. The rest of the Christians are to be sent to regional reeducation centers to eliminate the brainwashing from their dangerous and archaic teachings. When they complete their respective programs, they will help clean up the hardest-hit areas. If they want to blame God for this mess, then His people can clean up after Him." The Antichrist stood still, mouth twisted into a cruel sneer and pointing into the air like a hideous statue.

Her captor looked at her with an ominous smile, but said nothing. The chilling terror that Angela expected to flow through her body never came. Instead, calmness overwhelmed her senses, turning the tears in her eyes from fear to pity. She understood. He had a shattered spirit and mind.

She remembered her pastor's sermon on how God gave dying grace to the faithful under his protection. Letting her body relax, she prayed for the broken man. The slight excitement of seeing her family again surprised her. This isn't how death is supposed to feel. Is it?

Angela prayed for God to speak to him to make him understand his need for spiritual healing.

Once the applause faded, the Antichrist continued.

"As for those impudent Jews who claim that I am Antichrist, my response is that they can claim that these calamities are the judgments of their god. But believe me when I say that they are nothing but sons of sedition. I will deal with them in due time. Until then, pay them no heed."

He stopped the hologram before the Antichrist said another word and walked to the desk. Humming an unfamiliar tune, he dropped the remote control and picked up some things. The computer monitor on the desk flickered as he passed in front of it, leaving just a shadowy outline that shrunk with each step towards her. She knew her time had come when she saw the weapons in his hands, the knife and what appeared to be something resembling a gun. "Angela Hyatt, you are guilty of murder, and I sentence you to hell."

She used her last words to forgive him.

CHAPTER 1

The deep purple predawn sky brightened my night vision optics' view of the South Dakota landscape. But my intentions for this stakeout made the dark sky look bright. Unfortunately, my mind wandered to someone other than my intended target this morning. Thinking about Joy Everhart made my mood match the Custer State Park's landscape, black and bloody. The horrendous stench from the first trumpet judgment's blood and ash became fouler as time passed, like my attitude towards my former superior. Dreading sleep, I rarely had a night without seeing her spitting on Frank's corpse, then smiling and waving at the people like a cheerleader pandering to a crowd. My gut always felt inside out when I awoke. The only calming thoughts came from imagining her lifeless body carrying the .45 caliber SIG bullet I put in her. It comforted me.

Unfortunately, the feeling deep inside chided me for wanting to kill her. But I waited until it subsided. Besides what she did to Frank, she also exiled me to the military to get rid of me under the guise of my need for self-discipline. The thought alone made my jaw muscles ache from clenching too hard. Still, I had to focus on the task at hand.

My squad spent the last two days chasing a Christian Resistance group in Montana faster than I wanted to get ahead of a group of bounty hunters, who already had a reputation of treating prisoners poorly. Intel showed several high-ranking members of the resistance group, and I wanted Tommy to be among them. I had dibs on treating him poorly. He still had Mom's Bible and Dad's prophecy journal, and I wanted them back. I needed them back. He had no right to tell the cleaners to take my personal possessions when he booted me out of the Resistance, and I had every intention of making sure he understood that clearly.

In the early morning, the cave I stared at on the Wildlife Loop Road gave no evidence that anyone lived there. The subtle cave entrance, neatly tucked into the side of a rocky hill that used to be an earthy red, now looked like a bloody rabbit hole with a blackened front yard. A small stand of trees where I sat inside my Humvee held the only greenery in the area.

The personal drone that I bought in Denver before going on my first assignment helped to find potential Resistance locations without having to report my findings. Stretching and shifting in the uncomfortable seat, I tried refocusing on giving them intel of my troops' location and movements, a higher priority. Although I didn't like Tommy, I still felt the need to help whenever possible.

Remembering that it took me several weeks to get used to the smell of the land after arriving at the command center in the Rockies and completing officer training, it still turned my stomach. It took me a while to learn the difference between my stomach churning from the smell or hunger. This time I needed sustenance.

Someone once said that a person can fool their taste buds into believing they put something delicious in their mouth by thinking it's true. That person lied. Pulling an MRE from my backpack, my stomach complained when I opened the powdered eggs and mystery meat, poured water from my canteen to stir the slop that smelled like spoiled milk and tasted worse.

The way the Antichrist dealt with the limited food supply for both humans and animals left nothing to be desired. He began the ridiculous rationing program that gave the lion's share of the food to the wealthy and powerful. The scraps went to the rest, except for the Christians, of course. Although I struggled with God's plan for me as an undercover agent, my place in the Peace Forces meant guaranteed food and drink, however disgusting it tasted. My heart went out to my Christian siblings, then I remembered Dad's journal entry about how God fed them His way.

Chugging the swill, I remembered Mom's home-cooked meals in Springfield, Missouri, and eating at the small diner near Park Central Square. But that made me think of the day of the Rapture and missed opportunities. Then I thought of killing Joy again, but that made the MRE taste worse. So, I cleared my head and focused on the cave entrance. Once finished, I threw the MRE pouch in my bag and planned out what I'd do if I found Tommy in that cave.

A few minutes later, my vehicle, an old Humvee from well before the Trib, rocked violently. The metallic echo from the sharp blow bounced around the hillside. Looking out the driver's side window, I saw brown fur and heard the low grumble of a buffalo. Another strike came from behind. After checking all directions, I realized a small herd surrounded me. Remembering Dad's sermon about how animals will turn on humans in the Trib, I knew the herd's ill intentions.

Each member of the herd had ribs showing. In fact, the two that hit the Humvee seemed out of energy. With my safety in the Humvee assured, I considered my course of action. I didn't want to shoot the animals because I knew that any Resistance members in the small cave might come out shooting. However, the echoes of the buffaloes' striking the vehicle's armor plating already provided proof of life inside the cave.

Two lights brightened the mouth of the cave.

Before looking through my binoculars, a call came through my helmet. Putting it on, I pushed the button on the side of the face mask. Static popped loudly because the entire area became a communications nightmare after the last judgment. An expert said it had something to do with the satellite feed being interrupted by the meteor shower. But I knew the disruption came from the prophesied blood storm of God.

"Yes, Colonel Locke."

Colonel Martin Locke's well-groomed, chiseled face looked grainy on my helmet screen.

"Will, you need to call Colonel Phineas Lonergan, Western Peace Forces Military Command in St. Louis. Use a secure data line. He wants to talk with you about something that's come up in Missouri."

"Can it wait until after the recon?"

"I'm afraid not, soldier. It has a general's order attached to it. Sounds important," he said, using his don't mess with me tone.

"But I'm close to finding them," I said.

He sighed. "This is high priority. Do as you're told, Will."

The screen went blank.

Tapping into a secure ICON line with my Vam, a hologram tablet that attaches to the forearm, I called Colonel Lonergan while checking on the buffalo, who seemed intent on waiting me out. I switched the feed to split screen in my helmet to use the infrared camera mounted outside the Humvee, making sure the two at the cave entrance didn't escape my sight.

"Captain Will Thomas, it's good to meet you." Colonel Lonergan's long face and pointed nose filled half of the helmet screen. "There's no time to waste."

Lonergan's face disappeared, replaced by a video on the screen. A field littered with holes popped up on the screen. The camera operator walked between two of the holes and showed the contents strewn in evidence bags. If not for the past two months of battle horrors, I might've become nauseous. The body parts appeared to be several hands. A CSU tech had arranged them according to their state of decomp. The next hole contained feet, presented in the same manner. Each hole appeared to have one specific body part, like the killer had separated loose change according to denomination.

"I get the point, Colonel." I tapped the Vam to stop the video.

"Police received the call last night. We have reason to believe one of our own may be among the dead." Lonergan's face reappeared. He paused while reading the file. "An arm found in one hole has a military tattoo."

"What do you want from me, sir?" I barely whispered it out.

Anticipating his next words, I knew my time had finally come. Payback.

"I want your help." Lonergan flipped a few pages over the top of the file and squinted.

"Are you ordering me back to civilization?" My heart skipped a beat. The thought of killing Joy overwhelmed my senses.

"No, I just need a little help from your end. You're a famous detective in your past life, and I'm having a turf war with this little insect in charge of the Western Peace Forces police. She's trying to take the case. Says it's her jurisdiction." He ran his fingers through his thick brown hair and frowned. "She struggles with the fact that we are all one big happy family now."

"Joy Everhart." I spat her name out.

Lonergan smiled. "Yep. And from what I've been told, she's an old friend of yours. I thought you'd like a chance to exact some revenge, if only a little."

"Thank you, sir." I took a deep breath to calm my excitement. "She's in it for the glory. Her ambition knows no bounds, and her contacts go way up the ladder." I paused and considered my options. "Tell her superiors it's best if this is a joint investigation, based on the arm, and recommend me. Being a member of the Peace Forces on both sides of the aisle, so to speak, I'd be perfect. We can make her feel like she's in on it, but you can tell her what you want her to know."

Colonel Lonergan's face left the screen as he sounded off a loud guffaw. "Your rank doesn't cover your abilities, Captain. Let me message the general and see what he thinks. I'm just glad you're on our side."

While he typed on his computer, he told me the case covered an incomplete body count due to the extensive holes that covered a twenty-acre field. The heads and torsos remained missing, but the CSU team hadn't covered the entire field yet. Lonergan sat back and stared at me for a long, awkward moment, as if lost in deep thought.

"I'm warming up to the idea of your involvement, Will." A beep came from his side of the feed. Lonergan's face brightened as he turned his attention off screen. Then he leaned forward, his face filling the screen. "And the general agrees. You are to report to me in Jefferson City at the old capitol building. The general wants a meet and greet."

He leaned off-screen again while I tried my best not to act like a spoiled child getting everything on his Christmas wish list.

"General Sokolov has informed me that the powers in the highest reaches of our government believe this is the first concrete proof of the murders our Sovereign talked about. They are already whispering this to the media and letting them spread the rumor of what will become the truth." His sneer sent an icy chill up and down my spine. "When we have all the proof, the Christian insurgents will have no other choice but to acknowledge the Sovereign as their supreme leader and abandon this god of theirs once and for all. And who knows, he might let them live." He clapped his hands and laughed.

The deep feeling gave me a new drive to be part of this. To disprove the Antichrist's plan and keep Christians safe a little while longer.

"See you in a few hours." He saluted.

The screen went blank. Although the other side of the screen kept quiet during the conversation, I noticed movement just outside the cave entrance. The deep feeling gave the impression that I had found someone important. And to play nice.

I didn't understand why the red flags stopped when I entered the military and this deep feeling took their place, but it served me well when I needed to help brothers and sisters in Christ to escape the Sovereign's servants. It didn't come from the gut per se, but from a place inside that made me think of the day I put my faith in Christ. Unfortunately, that feeling made it perfectly clear that God didn't approve of all my plans.

The sun peaked over the horizon to show the red and black landscape between me and the cave. The smell of blood and char reminded me of the similar scent of the bodies from the previous judgments being burned in the factory-style crematorium in St. Louis. Hiding among the few green trees in the area, I realized why the buffalo came to me. Unfortunately for the buffalo, the leaves remained out of reach because the buffalo had stripped the trunks of all bark, low-lying limbs, and leafy vegetation. Several voiced their disappointment with low bellows while looking at what might've been the last meal in the area. Others butted the smaller trees to bring down and get the needed sustenance. But to no avail. They were too weak.

When I refocused on the matter at hand, the Humvee shook violently for a few moments. I checked the buffalo through the window, but they weren't close enough to hit the vehicle. Wondering if the shaking might be an earthquake, the deep feeling reminded me of my duty. I turned off the infrared and saw that the two hadn't wandered far from the entrance, just a quick sweep of the immediate area. Although they didn't seem familiar, I fired up the Humvee to make myself known, eager to find out if my old handler and his outfit hid in that cave.

Putting the Humvee in drive, I slowly pushed my way through the herd. The animals bellowed their displeasure but gave way to the bulk of my vehicle. I felt sorry for the starving buffalo and used the Humvee to push a couple of small trees down to feed and distract them. When they lunged for the much-needed food, I drove to the cave.

CHAPTER 2

Before reaching the field in front of the cave, I saw another figure exiting the cave and directing a flashlight beam in my direction. When I stopped at a safe distance, I put my helmet on and scanned the group, disabling the mic. A court martial offence. However, a tech who owed me a favor taught me how to manipulate the helmets when I didn't want the Beast computer snooping in my personal business.

Without the wind, the stale air inside my helmet made the odors worse. I kept it on to hide my identity and walked the rest of the way. The crunching of the blackened grass made my walk louder than intended.

My anger rose when I saw Tommy's figure in the glow of my helmet screen. I knew that bulky build anywhere. Tommy turned his flashlight off, separated from the other two, and walked back to the mouth of the cave, obviously to warn the other inhabitants.

The other two stared at me while talking like coworkers gossiping around the water cooler, wearing red paint that didn't match their surroundings, acting as if danger belonged to other people. In fact, one smoked while his automatic weapon dangled at his side from its strap. The other pointed his weapon in my direction but acted as though I posed no threat. They must've had sniper cover.

When I got close enough, I removed the helmet but held it so that I saw the screen. The one with his gun on me looked taller and thicker than the other, with a bearing that suggested military. I didn't recognize the other one because he wore a surgical mask.

Probably didn't like the smell. Many people sprayed cologne or perfume on masks to avoid the smell of the judgment. The deep feeling gave me the go-ahead to take a chance.

After taking a deep breath and slowly exhaling, I kept walking toward them. "I'm wondering if you boys took prisoners." I smiled.

The unfamiliar man trained his weapon on my head. "Sorry Mark, but this ain't your lucky day."

Mark, it's been at least three months since I'd heard that term. Christians called anyone a Mark who had taken the Mark of the Beast, a chip implant that guaranteed the carrier a one-way ticket to Hell.

The other took a long, hard look at me. I saw his eyes, shook my head, and giggled.

"I'm sorry, but we can't take prisoners." The masked one looked at his partner. "Check 'em, Henry."

It surprised me that he didn't recognize me. Even in the low light of the sunrise, my face still had to be plain to see. I noticed the helmet registering the one not pointing his weapon at me as a potential non-Loyalist. But I knew him as a close friend. I wanted to talk to him like we used to, but the screen flashed green on Henry.

Henry's dark eyes focused on me in a way that felt deadly. My friend continued to stare at me as if he saw a stranger. Henry's SCAR automatic weapon held steady.

"Drop to your knees," Henry commanded. "Hands on your head. And put down your helmet, Mark."

I did so without arguing. A sweat bead on my forehead streamed down my nose. Meeting Jesus face-to-face crossed my mind. Remorse entered my gut knowing that I hadn't squared things with Him about Joy and Tommy. Then I became angry, knowing that I had unfinished business with them. Laying my helmet in a way that gave me a direct line of sight to the screen, I saw what the green signal meant.

After a sloppy, one-handed pat-down from behind, Henry grabbed my elbow and hoisted me upright. He walked around and gave me the once-over while the other smiled like he finally recognized me. When Henry looked at my boots, I drew my sidearm from the concealed holster in my jacket and shot a .45-

caliber bullet through his brainpan from temple to temple. The echo of the shot coursed through the small canyon as his lifeless body crumpled to the ground.

My friend quickly raised his weapon.

Clay screamed, "Why did you do that? Will, he's a fellow Christian! A brother in Christ!" He ran to the slowly cooling corpse and checked for any signs of life.

"Sorry, Clay." I bent over and picked up my helmet. "He's a spy. My screen flashes green and gives me the info of a friendly Mark."

My old informant's face contorted in disbelief. Then he stood, dropped his weapon and a backpack I hadn't noticed before, took the helmet, and looked at the screen without putting it on.

"He fooled Tommy," Clay whispered, looking at my old handler standing in the cave's entrance, staring at us through a scope mounted on a high-power rifle.

"Sorry, brother. I had no choice. If he got our conversation to his superiors, I'd be dead." I nodded at Tommy, wondering why he hadn't fired when I killed his man.

"No, I get it. But it's still a shock to the system." Clay kneeled beside Henry's corpse. "Maybe he could've believed."

"No chance." I pulled my knife from the sheath strapped above my knee, kneeled, and felt his right wrist. "Unless you know what you're looking for, you'll miss it." I carved the chip from just below the base of his thumb.

"It's the next-gen chip. Isn't it?" Clay stared closely at it. "We haven't got much intel on them. Tommy says they're for the military."

"Yeah. They say this can withstand an intermediate EMP shot and is almost undetectable without the proper equipment." I rolled the tiny chip between my forefinger and thumb. "Good thing I had the proper equipment."

"Yeah, I guess that's right." Clay mumbled, still looking at Henry.

The buffalo bellowed in the distance.

"We'd better get into your cave, or those things will tear us apart," I said.

"No need. We got protection from the animals." Clay looked at the herd.

"Must be nice. We've spent more ammo on animals than people." I didn't consider what I said.

"I know. We lost a lot of people." Clay's frown ate through me.

"So, when did Tommy get you into the Resistance?" I remembered I didn't get the chance to send Clay to Tommy after the last judgment because Joy sent me immediately to the military.

"I came across Daniel preaching near the old Cardinals' ballpark. He's one of the hundred and forty-four thousand. After his sermon, we talked about God, Jesus, and my family. Before I knew it, I fell on my knees asking Jesus to save me from my sinful ways. Then Daniel introduced me to Tommy and even vouched for me." Clay had tears forming in his pale eyes.

Thanking God for making that happen, I turned my attention to the scorched, bloody earth of the South Dakota landscape. Guilt did a lap in my head for not helping Clay like I meant to. But God didn't need me to get a soul searching for Him. Looking back at the cave, I considered how this might affect my relationship, what little I had, with Clay. However, it felt good to hear that Clay had joined the Christian ranks. A real victory for the Kingdom.

"Praise God." I slapped him on the back.

"Daniel told Tommy that I'm good to go after he baptized me in the Mississippi River just outside St. Louis." Clay wiped his cheek and gave a mild giggle with a quick head bob.

"In the shark-infested, bloody waters?" My stomach turned.

"When we entered the water, the blood moved away. And I watched a bull shark head out to deeper waters." He beamed. "Two of God's miracles."

For the first time in a long time, I envied somebody.

"What's that shooting about?" I heard the gravelly voice before I saw the outline of his massive frame coming down from the cave entrance. I started walking towards him.

He had barely said my name before I got in his face. "Where's Dad's journal and Mom's Bible?" I smelled the fresh coffee on his breath.

"Safe." Tommy took a step back. "And being used to help the cause."

"I want my things back, you thief." I put my SIG back in the holster.

"Sorry, brother. No can do. We're using the journal, and I have no idea where the Bible is." He shrugged and slung the rifle.

Wrong answer.

When I entered the Marines out of high school, I took every hand-to-hand class they offered and learned even more during battles, both before and after the Rapture.

Tommy might've seen it coming, but he didn't have the position to stop it. Although I meant the left jab as a diversion as I closed the distance, it still landed flush. Then I landed a straight right at the base of his breastplate. Not to break it, but to knock him off balance. He swatted away my second left jab but didn't see my foot aimed at his groin, but he felt it. Tommy dropped to his hands and knees, where I kicked him in the face.

"Where are they?" I shouted.

Backing up to give one last kick, a new face entered my peripherals. Then he stood in front of me. A kid, no older than twenty, stood between me and Tommy. He raised his hand.

"Peace."

The authority behind that one word brought me to a complete stop, physically and spiritually. The deep feeling made it known that if I took a swing at the kid, I'd be meeting Jesus face-to-face immediately. I relaxed my body and lowered my pulse with a deep breath. The bloody air came across my taste buds, and the MRE in my stomach churned.

"Who are you, and why are you doing this?" I meant for it to be stronger, but the deep feeling held me back.

"My name is Daniel, from the tribe of Levi. And this is my brother and friend. Why are you attacking him?" His voice contained compassion mixed with authority.

His dark eyes matched his hair and beard. He might've been under six feet, but he had a medium, but strong, build covered by jeans, a white T-shirt, and leather sandals that all seemed new. I remembered reading about the clothes of the preachers never aging. Not exactly prophet-looking, but the way he carried himself, paired with his powerful voice, showed that he's the real deal.

Stepping back and collecting my thoughts, I looked at Clay. He picked up his pack and weapon. His pained facial expression made me feel like the bad guy. But I just want to claim what's mine. No harm in that. Right? So why did I feel awful?

The ground shook again, but more violently. Widening my

stance and bending my knees, I adjusted my balance with the shaking earth. The others did the same. It lasted a little longer than before. Once finished, I looked at Daniel.

"The next judgment is being prepared. We are near the epicenter. But fear not. We will be far away when this occurs." The young man's calmness and confidence made me believe him.

Daniel turned around and helped Tommy to his feet. At first touch, Tommy looked like he did before I hit him. Everything inside me raged. "Are you kidding me? Tommy steals from me and gets healed." I turned and ran my fingers through my hair. "Unbelievable."

Then I turned and marched to the Humvee.

"Will, please stop." Clay jogged to catch up with me. "We need to make things right."

"Nothing can make this right." I kept marching.

Clay grabbed my shoulder and gently pulled it. I turned and got in his face, feeling the intensity of my stare. The morning light had increased enough for me to see the consequences of my actions. Clay's wilting look of fear overwhelmed me. I had no intention of hitting Clay, but I knew my body language told him the opposite. Backing away with my open hands spread away from my sides, I turned to the vehicle.

"That's one reason you're no longer welcome." Tommy shouted, walking toward me. "Brother."

I pulled my SIG and pointed it at my former handler and best friend. "It didn't need to be this way, but you stole everything I had. But your special friend doesn't seem to care about that."

Tommy didn't stop walking. When he reached me, he put his hands in the air. "I didn't want this either. But here we are. And you better never come among us again or you'll meet the Savior." The features of his dark-skinned face showed rage.

Ignoring the deep feeling, I thumb-cocked the SIG with full intention of ending Tommy.

Out of nowhere, Daniel stood between us. He spread his arms out as if he wanted to embrace. But I'm not a hugger.

"Stay out of this, kid." I kept looking at Tommy.

"I will not allow bloodshed among believers in my presence." His authority grew. "Your personal effects are not here. You'd just be committing murder."

"You didn't seem to mind." I pointed at the dead spy.

"That is war." Daniel pointed at me. "And you're a soldier of Christ. He sent you to help the Resistance. Thank you."

"God don't use people like me. Isn't that right?" I shook my gun at Tommy. "Not anymore, according to him."

"It's not his call. The Savior placed you where you are to protect the lives of your brothers and sisters. I will talk with Tommy about your possessions, but I believe they are in a place that will help God's kingdom until the Glorious Appearing of Christ at the end of the Great Tribulation."

His words didn't comfort me.

"You're protecting a thief. That's one of the big commandments." I shouted.

"He did not steal. You understood the consequences of your actions. Actions that cost your mentor's life." Those dark eyes drilled into me.

The mental image of Frank's death entered my mind, and I leveled my SIG to Daniel's forehead. "I'm willing to see Jesus now."

A tear hit Daniel's left sandal. "I know you are. The anger in you is unnecessary. We have a common enemy, but it's not each other. As the time of the end gets closer, we'll need each other. But that cannot happen if you cannot let go of your anger and this senseless need for vengeance."

A burning began growing inside. Not an emotional feeling, but a physical fire. I remembered Dad talking about these guys being protected by angels. But I didn't care.

Tommy and Clay had already pulled their weapons and trained them on me.

In that instant, I wanted to die. Let the angel have his way with me, I prayed internally. But I froze as if my body refused my command.

I didn't even see him move or feel him take the gun from me. Daniel took a step back and disassembled the pistol like a highly trained soldier.

"None of you are dying today." His voice deepened, and the deep feeling made it clear that the command came from above. He threw the pieces in different directions, making it impossible to find.

Clay dug into his pack and handed me a Bible. "It may not be your mom's, but maybe it will help until we can get it to you. Once we're done with them, I'll personally bring back your effects."

The feel of the faux leather and onion-peel pages took me back to my youth, when I foolishly ignored Dad's sermon to focus on the cute girls in the church congregation. My rage subsided, and shame replaced it. Along with confusion.

"Please, Will. Trust me when I say that you are an important part of the Resistance. You're needed." Daniel's voice didn't sound like he placated but encouraged.

I looked at Tommy. "You're forgetting something, Daniel. Tommy kicked me out of the Resistance. And I'm not coming back." I walked away.

In the distance, I heard Clay ask his friends to stop me. To make things right. That me being alone put me in danger of Satan's attacks.

But Daniel said, "Let him go. He needs to finish his time in the wilderness. God will strengthen him there. Do not worry. He is almost ready. And we need Will's strength to help us. It is God's will. Come, we must go quickly."

CHAPTER 3

The ancient cargo plane to Jefferson City landed the earliest, and the pilot said it didn't give a smooth ride. However, the discovery of the bodies happened a little less than twenty-four hours ago, which made me late already. Once in the air, the two pilots showed no interest in me, so I went to the back of the plane, climbed into an AAV, an amphibious personnel carrier, and pulled out the Bible Clay gave me. The stowed seats allowed me to lay down and focus on God's book.

Before I unzipped the cover, I tried to pray, but my words fell flat, like they never made it out of the AAV. The deep feeling made me feel undeserving of God's attention by reminding me of my plans for Joy and the way I treated Clay, Daniel, and Tommy. Clay hit the nail on the head when he mentioned my vulnerability from being alone so long. Not only did I lose contact with fellow believers, who I depended on for spiritual guidance and fellowship, but I also stopped praying. And the blame for both fell in my lap.

While in the field, I watched the Beast feed from my helmet screen. The devastation of the judgments and the response from the unbelieving world made me feel ineffective with the feeble information I channeled to the Resistance. Especially since the Antichrist implemented the bounty program. Those needing to put food on the table didn't think twice about turning a neighbor, friend, or family member in for a food voucher or digital currency.

Adjusting my weight to be more comfortable on the uncomfortable AAV floor, I unzipped the cover of the Bible. A few cards fell out of an inside pocket. I saw the beautiful penmanship as I picked them up off my chest. It reminded me of my mother's swooping and elegant style. Something they taught her generation. Not mine.

One card, titled *Stubbornness*, caught my attention. The writer only put the location of the verses below the title, so I looked them up.

"Ye stiffnecked and uncircumcised in heart and ears, ye do always resist the Holy Ghost: as your fathers did, so do ye," Acts 7:51.

The deep feeling agreed.

"But they refused to hearken, pulled away the shoulder, and stopped their ears, that they should not hear. Yea, they made their hearts as an adamant stone lest they should hear the law, and the words which the Lord of hosts hath sent them in his spirit by the former prophets therefore came a great wrath from the Lord of hosts," Zechariah 7:11-12.

My jaw ached from clenching too hard. It's difficult enough to be out of the company of fellow believers, but life feels impossible when God's leading you to verses that call out your sin and there's no one to talk to about it. Although it hurt, I went to the last verse on the list.

"Because I knew that thou art obstinate, and thy neck is an iron sinew, and thy brow brass; I have even from the beginning declared it to thee," Isaiah 48:4-5.

I closed the book and dropped my head. The deep feeling ran laps between my head and heart. Everything from before the Trib until now overwhelmed my thoughts. Joy's face didn't spit. It smiled the pretty smile that caught me off guard. Frank entered my mind, but he chastised me for being petty. Then the memory of Clay's fearful face when I turned on him. All my actions and thoughts accused me of my disgraceful attitude and murderous feelings.

Hating myself for feeling this way, I put the stubbornness card to the back and read the next ones. The guilt and frustration became overwhelming with each entry, which two of the cards had those as titles. However, my desire to kill Joy, and get proper revenge for Frank, became so overwhelming that I fought the deep feeling with every topic on the cards. Even joy, love, and peace sent chills up my spine like the ones I got watching horror flicks as a kid.

The last card, titled *Forgiveness*, made my spirit convulse, remembering Daniel's words. Even the deep feeling made it seem that I didn't need to go to those verses in my state of mind.

Slamming the Bible shut on the cards, zipping the cover shut, and stowing it in my pack, I sat up and closed my eyes. Joy still smiled that cute smile, no matter how hard I tried to remember Frank's execution. The thought of her smile felt a lot like my years before the Trib, chasing girls with my friends, whose thoughts revolved around the end game more than the chase. To get the girl's attention, to get them to notice us, became more of a strategy to get what they wanted. Just like me. Physical contact. We obsessed over hugs, kisses, and more. Especially more. But I didn't want more with Joy. I wanted her dead.

To shut down the deep feeling, I got out of the AAV and looked out a small window. The landscape didn't look any better from the sky. Red and black with spots of green, which reminded me of the smell. My stomach grumbled, reminding me of my morning breakfast and how the buffalo probably ate better than me. Then I planned my first meal in the city. It helped.

Getting back into the AAV and unfolding a seat, I turned my attention to the case. The Vam came to life with a simple tap on the narrow screen. Recent technological advancements still amazed me. The tablet, attached to the forearm without fear of falling off or cutting circulation, had the capacity of a major desktop with the ability to work at speeds not much slower. I connected to the Beast from newly placed satellites. After the destruction of the others, when the skies folded during the sixth seal judgment earthquake, the government didn't waste time replacing them, as if they expected it to happen. In the cities, a Vam easily connected to Wi-Fi nets attached to the cameras and mics on the streetlights and various signage. On the plane, my Vam connected via a satellite link.

The small screen of the Vam might've been good for texting or reading an email, but I needed something more. Any user could switch views to project a hologram above the Vam and see everything in three dimensions or in a flat two dimensions that looked like a desktop screen, or project the screen on a flat surface, like a wall or desk. I sat the VAN on the seat across from me and studied the file using the two-dimensional view.

Going through the initial report reminded me of the old ones I wrote as a rookie with the wrong focal points, and the right ones barely discussed. Just like Joy. The crime scene looked like a hayfield near where I grew up. In one hole, I noticed the bloodied walls. The stains went down at least six inches, guaranteeing no food for the livestock before the end of the Tribulation. Using voice commands, I trained my attention to the left hands. Many had blood stains, except for three, which had no blood stains. A timeline began forming in my mind.

The killer had been doing this for a while. I wondered if he or she started before the Trib. Just after the Rapture, people went crazy. Some looking for their vanished loved ones, others seizing the opportunity to get ahead by either looting, settling scores, or starting a new life using a new identity freshly stolen from someone who had just gone to Heaven. Greed often makes desperate situations worse when people see an opportunity for a quick and easy score.

The CSU report contained little information, and nothing about times of death. They needed time to process. What struck me as odd came from a note attached to the lead detective's report she had recently uploaded. It came from a general from Europe I didn't recognize. He said that the success of the news leaks will help the investigation.

Closing the Vam, I sat back and looked at the ceiling of the armored vehicle. The Antichrist and his bunch wasted no time spinning this. After considering it for a minute, I wondered if they put this narrative together before the Trib began. I remembered Dad talking about how the Antichrist needed all his ducks in a row before the Trib started because of his limited time in power.

The memory of Dad brought about a sense of loneliness that overwhelmed me. Then I thought of Amelia. Over the last few weeks, our messages became shorter, with little interest shown by either side. Before stowing my Vam, I texted her to let her know I'd be in Jefferson City. She quickly responded and asked if I'd be in the St. Louis area for a date. I told her I doubted it because my superiors called me back to investigate the murders. She didn't respond.

The deep feeling didn't approve of my relationship with

Amelia, which I didn't understand. Every time I thought of her, the feeling kept bringing up the verse about being unequally yoked. It's in one of the Corinthians, but without a Bible, I didn't remember which. I knew she didn't have faith, but I constantly prayed for her to meet up with Tommy or one of the Jewish preachers. However, because of my intentions for revenge, it felt like my prayers never reached God's ear. My life felt like the tide. First one way, then the other.

CHAPTER 4

After a short drive from the Jefferson City Airport, I walked into the old Missouri State Capitol, now known as the Peace Forces Western Command Center. Colonel Lonergan met me with a quick salute and ushered me inside to the information desk on the first floor. A lanky man with narrow shoulders, held a gait that showed Lonergan as a military lifer with a Beastmark tattoo on his right wrist displaying a sealed afterlife.

"Will, it's good to finally meet you in person." Lonergan's boney hand reached out to shake.

"Likewise, sir." I shook his hand.

A corporal at the information desk stood and saluted before tapping the scanner screen to begin the identification process.

"Welcome to Jeff City, sirs," she said.

Her beautiful dark eyes gave me the once over. That hadn't happened in a while. It made me feel human again, and a little masculine.

"Thank you." I smiled and winked while holding my ID badge in front of the scanner.

She blushed and returned the smile until the computer beeped us in. I didn't want to leave, but Lonergan didn't notice our wordless exchange.

Leading me to the grand staircase behind the welcome center, a chirping sounded an alert from the colonel's forearm. Lonergan tapped his Vam screen and sighed.

He lowered his voice and stepped into a small alcove with no one around. "You need to know a few things about General

Sokolov. He's a former Russian spy. The most effective in their history, to hear him tell it. After the Sovereign's government took over, they promoted him and sent him here to take command of the military branch of the Western North American Peace Forces. The former general in charge was an incompetent American who deserved the blade. Trust me, I served under him. He became a Christian." He shook his head in derision.

"Did the general have you call me?" I held back from punching him.

"Yes, and no. After the discovery of the murder field, he sent me there when he found out that one victim might be one of our own. When I got there, I got strong-armed by Joy's people, claiming it's their jurisdiction, not ours."

"Sounds like her. By the way, you said that they identified one victim as military."

Lonergan lifted his right arm and pointed at a Green Beret tattoo. "They found a forearm that had a military tattoo like mine. I happened upon it in the case file not long before we talked earlier. After showing the general, he used it to stop the door from slamming completely shut."

Although I hadn't read the entire case file, I considered this new information. She had no right to block the military from the investigation after finding the tattoo. However, I knew about Joy's connections, mainly from what Frank told me about her friends in low and high places outside the government as well.

"After a few rounds with Joy, the general got real frustrated. Then I remembered we had a famous former detective in our ranks." He pointed a thumb at me. "After you volunteered, he thought that with you and the soldier being a victim, it'd be a slam dunk to take over the investigation. So far, he's been making some headway, but it's still an uphill battle."

That told me that Joy's people outnumbered Sokolov's.

Being away from the world for so long, it surprised me that anyone remembered me. Even before the Trib, the public had the attention span of a two-year-old on a sugar rush. When I reported to my unit, half the soldiers didn't realize their commanding officer had solved the most famous case in American history. They had more interest in who the Antichrist believed to be the most eligible bachelor on the planet. Put information at the public's fingertips and they will go to the rich and famous every time. Forget about anything important like the death of a president. That stuff is for the boring people in the world.

"Tell me more about the general. I want to talk to him on his level if I'm going to get assigned to this case."

Lonergan grinned and looked at someone passing who didn't seem interested in our conversation. The colonel didn't seem the type to answer questions rapidly. I liked him already. Too bad he was Hellbound.

"He likes his subordinates to be blunt but respectful. He hasn't been in the military too terribly long, so he doesn't mind certain informalities. Again, as long as you're respectful. Scuttlebutt is that he helped broker the deal for America to be brought into the new government, so he can't be all that bad." He shrugged.

We watched a group of school-age children pass by as their guide, a frazzled, middle-aged man, led them to a painting of the Antichrist. He began telling them the lie about how the Sovereign peacefully negotiated the former USA into the global fold. Lonergan smiled like a proud papa.

"You said something about this being a murder field." I almost forgot to ask.

"This time we got 'em." His evil chuckle bothered me, sounding like a comic book supervillain. "They already have the story finished, and the media started cycling it hourly since I got off the line with you. In fact, I've heard this isn't the first murder field. It's just the easiest one to confirm because there are so many bodies. I hear tell that there have been at least a couple of dozen graves found all over the world. They just had three or four bodies in them. This one has at least a dozen, if not more. They're still digging."

"That doesn't match the count that the media reported after it happened." I shrugged, hoping that he didn't arrest me for treason and send me to the guillotine.

"The way it's playing out is that the murderers didn't have the time or means to bury all the bodies, but they tried to cover the numbers up." He gave a knowing look. "They lied to the reporters and inflated the count."

"I thought it might be a better story for our side with higher numbers."

"It muddles the narrative. They say the numbers are in the millions, but we can't deny or confirm because we can't get an accurate count. With incomplete numbers, their argument has some plausibility. The optics favored them. But finding these murder fields, the truth is closer to coming out, and we can confirm our original count of a little over a hundred thousand."

Optics and facts are something the Antichrist can never line up. Even though I understood God let them believe a delusion, I still struggled with the idea that any thinking human being believed the nonsense dealt them no matter how compelling the Antichrist sounded. However, a colonel in the military who swallowed it hook, line, and sinker stood beside me.

The deep feeling put my jaw in a death grip to help keep Lonergan from questioning my global loyalty. His Vam chirped. He frowned after reading the message.

"General Sokolov's meeting is going longer than expected, so we have a little time to kill." He smiled and rubbed his stomach. "I'm starved. How about a pizza?"

"Sausage and onions." My stomach cheered.

"Just sausage. It's best not to offend the general with onion breath." He winked before ordering on his Vam.

I hadn't laughed like that in a long time. The deep feeling reminded me that even in the Trib everyone needed to laugh once in a while.

After a short wait for the delivery, we ascended the grand staircase to the second floor with a pie and soda each. Lonergan seemed deep in thought, as if trying to come up with the words he wanted to say. He pointed to an elevator. "Go on up to the fourth floor. It's quieter up there. I'll go in and tell his assistant where we'll be, then I'll be up." His demeanor improved when he mentioned the assistant.

Stepping off the elevator, I went to sit in the Senate Chamber's Upper Gallery. The theater seats used to be upholstered in neutral colors and framed in steel painted hunter green. However, the cost of the Trib didn't allow the old state government to keep up appearances. Sitting in one of the few unbroken seats, right behind a white marble column that interrupted my view of the unused senate floor, I took a sip of my drink and let the memories take over.

In middle school, my class went on a field trip to the capitol building as part of a Missouri political science class. We watched the senate debate over a bill to be put on the spring ballot. Not very interesting to a thirteen-year-old overly active kid, but I did my best to stay seated. Although the urge to get up and do laps around the chamber to impress the girls sounded fun, I knew better since Dad came as a chaperone and threatened bodily harm on his only son.

At the end of the session, the state senators tabled the bill until the winter session. Dad said the senators up for reelection in the fall didn't want to alienate their constituency. When I asked what made the bill so important, he smiled and said, "School lunch programs are expensive."

I thought for a second and asked, "Why can't the kids just take a packed lunch?"

Dad giggled at my simplistic view, then he got serious and said, "Not everyone can afford to pack a lunch."

The memory brought regret. I missed my parents and my sister.

With a mouthful of pizza, I looked around at the rest of the floor. Then I remembered that a single signature silenced the American political machine that I helped bring about. The president, now a lowly regional governor of the newly formed island across the Mississippi River, thought he had made the deal of the century. I wondered how he felt now.

With a slice in one hand and the pizza box in the other, I stood and walked into the office area. The white walls still looked pristine and the doors leading to the various offices held their stain well. A sudden jolt of anger consumed me when I saw Joy's name on a brass plate in front of a large set of office doors. Rage filled my body. I reached for my gun but remembered Daniel scattering the pieces across Custer National Park. Then I considered going in there and either breaking her neck or choking her out.

The deep feeling protested and reminded me of the verses from the plane ride. Stubborn, unforgiving, sinner. Looking at the crust and feeling queasy from time spent away from greasy food, I tossed the box in a trash receptacle near me, stared at the nameplate, and sulked like a spoiled child not getting his way. But the more I stewed, the angrier and guiltier I felt. The deep feeling reminded me that murder fell under the big ten too.

With all my conflict raging, I walked back to the chairs and silently prayed. "Heavenly Father, I know my heart's not in the right place. I want justice for what she did to Frank. I won't act like I'm not going to try. If the circumstance presents itself, I'm taking the shot. But for now, I'm willing to work with her to complete the investigation. The one thing You and Dad taught me is to finish what I started, and I intend to do just that. I need your help with the investigation, like the other one. But if you see fit not to, I'll understand. I'm sorry for not talking to you over the last few months. In Jesus name, Amen."

It felt like my prayer didn't even make it to the ceiling. It hurt to think that God ignored me. But I decided on Joy the moment she spat on Frank. The feeling only rooted deeper during my time in the military to where it inhabited my thoughts all day, every day. The deep feeling chastised me for throwing God's plan for me to the wayside. Guilt grew in my chest until I hardly knew what to do. Then I saw Lonergan coming my way.

He nodded for me to follow and led me to a small office near where I sat. A sparse space with an old, small wooden desk, and a chair on each side of the same wooden quality as the desk.

"This isn't my office. It's in the basement. The general is still in his meeting." Lonergan took the chair that faced the door.

The silence lasted too long as Lonergan rubbed the dustless desk with his left hand while nibbling his slice from his right. I knew he'd get around to it, but I let him make the first move out of respect. He swallowed the small piece and finally made eye contact.

"Will, I need to tell you something." He fidgeted in his seat.

"What's that, sir?" Lonergan gave the impression that the news came with consequences.

"I didn't tell you the location of the crime scene because I didn't know how you'd react." He looked at the slice, still searching for the right words.

I kept silent knowing he'd come up with the rights words on his own. The deep feeling gave me the feeling of home, but I wanted Lonergan to say it.

"Someone found the body parts near Springfield." He didn't look me in the eye. "Not far from where you grew up."

It didn't make any sense that he'd keep that from me. I've never been ashamed of where I came from. But he didn't know that. So, I waited silently for him to keep going.

After an awkward minute, he looked at me. "Knowing your…" He hesitated and rolled his hand that held the pizza slice. "Parentage. I thought it best to wait to tell you face to face about the crime scene location to give you the opportunity to react as you see fit without those under your command to witness it. To avoid embarrassment."

He obviously studied my file and read about their spiritual background and service. Those still alive whose friends or family members went in the Rapture became societal pariahs. Regardless of their monetary or social status, people placed them in the lowest class. Those within the government or who had the means to find out which rich and powerful global citizens with this dirty little secret made a great profit or quick advancements. Like it says in Ecclesiastes, nothing new under the sun. I wondered where Lonergan's game for me might end. Did he place me here for his own personal advancement in the military?

"I've made peace with that part of my past." Not a lie, only a misdirection to get him off-balanced.

He frowned for a minute, as if trying to figure out what I just said. Then he raised his eyebrows in comprehension. "That's not what I meant, Will. I'm not trying to hang your parents' past over your head to make you do my bidding. That's what these are for." He pointed at the colonel cluster pin on his shirt collar and grinned.

Stifling a small chuckle, I gave a knowing nod.

He leaned over a bit. "I understand the importance of discretion pertaining to this." He leaned back. "My wife was a Christian. Murdered by my brothers, according to the local police. I can't even return to Ohio because the people I grew up with might try to take it out on me."

Our working relationship needed trust, and he offered it first. I stared at the Beastmark tattoo on his wrist. Nothing fancy, just a rules man. The military frowned on opulence. Although I struggled with his affiliation, I needed allies on that side of the spiritual aisle, considering my precarious undercover status.

"I was in Springfield on vacation when the murders occurred, but KCPD immediately called me back because of the riots. But I went back to Springfield a few weeks later, when we gained control of K.C. to deal with my parents' will and my guilt for things out of my control." I lied. My time in Springfield reminded me of my family and my missed opportunities for a quick trip to Heaven.

After a short, awkward minute of silence, Lonergan finished his last slice, clapped his hands, and rubbed them together. His infectious smile told me that the conversation ended the way he wanted.

"Let's get to it then." He opened a file on his Vam and produced the hologram. A screen full of information shown on both sides of the hologram for us to read without having to sit on the same side.

The gruesome scene still turned my stomach. The killer treated the victims' bodies like a child separating Legos into their proper piles, then burying them for a rainy day. Lonergan pulled up a new report from the CSU stating they had found the torsos. All they had left to find were the heads.

I sat back and stared at the last sentence. Did the killer keep them as trophies?

Lonergan brought me out of my thought with an unsubtle clearing of his throat.

"What's on your mind, Will?" He asked.

"The heads are obviously important. I'm trying to decide if the killer is trying to make it harder for us to identify the victims, or if they're his trophies."

"Trophies are my guess. Everyone knows we can identify the victims with either chips, DNA, dental records, or prints. So, he had to take them for personal reasons."

"If the CSU can get viable DNA or prints from the other parts to make the identifications." I sat up and pointed at the holes. "And if the victims are in ICON."

"They told me that the list of murderers in ICON is comprehensive." Lonergan put his cheek in his hand as he studied the pictures.

After a long pause, Lonergan's eyes widened while his eyebrows raised. "Won't it be great when the Sovereign declares the murder theory is now factual, and he mentions us?" He barely contained his elation.

My mind scrambled to diffuse his joy, but the deep feeling reminded me of my need for discernment and discretion.

CHAPTER 5

Major General Brendan Sokolov occupied the office of the former Missouri governor, but Lonergan said that the general was in another room finishing up a digital conference with the Sovereign's Minister of Reportage, trying to get me assigned to the investigation. Sitting in the opulent office with its amazing wooden walls and golden décor, I noticed the elephant in the room. Awful portraits of the Sovereign replaced the four paintings of famous Missourians. They looked cheap, giving the feeling of what the Antichrist thought about our side of the world.

The general, a tall, plain-looking man who looked perfect for a life hiding in plain sight, walked into his office and grumbled something in Russian while pouring a cup of coffee. Sokolov's piercing blue eyes didn't intimidate as much as he thought. Yet, he stared anyway.

"Captain Thomas, I am glad you are here. I finally received approval for you to join the investigation." He sighed and sipped his coffee before starting again. "It's difficult dealing with this woman, and I hope, with your experience with her, that you can get her to warm up to the idea of a joint investigation without further provocation." He sat in his overstuffed leather office chair and stared some more.

"If you want, sir, I can take the whole thing from her." I sat back in my chair and returned his gaze.

"That will not be necessary, Captain Thomas. It is the Sovereign's desire that the Peace Forces maintain a collaborative mindset for the citizens of our global society's benefit." His smile looked like a grimace. "To show us waving the global flag together might help get more people to accept the loyalty chip."

"And Will is the man who can do just that." Lonergan sat up straight, looking like the class kiss up. "He has my full confidence in finding the killer of the soldier found in that field."

Sokolov didn't look at the colonel. "Is this correct?"

"Yes, sir. But please remember that I've been in the field for almost twelve weeks fighting the enemy." My gut churned at calling fellow Christians the enemy. "My diplomacy skills are a little rusty." As well as my lead investigative skills which only covered one investigation.

The general's deep and raspy laugh sounded like he had allergies. "Then it will be necessary to sharpen them quickly. This little woman is formidable. If a little annoying."

"I remember, sir. And I will do my utmost to maintain a professional working relationship with the Peace Forces police." I smiled as I lied.

"Which brings me to the second point of why I called you here." The general sat straighter and placed his beefy hands on the giant desk made of mahogany. "Counting your enlistment in the former U.S. Marines and your time as a police officer makes you the perfect candidate for a program that has launched in this country. Our illustrious Sovereign will announce the joining of all agencies into a single entity within the year. He believes it is necessary for the public to be protected from potential internal corruption by creating a separate policing sector of the Peace Forces involved to maintain transparency to the utmost." Sokolov leaned forward in his chair and looked directly at me. "With that being said, I am offering you a position in this new sector. It will mean that you have full authority to keep a watchful eye on government officials, those with government contracts, and those who have any contact with government officials. Along with this, you will investigate possible subversives trying to undermine our government and our illustrious Sovereign from within."

Sitting back in my chair, I thought about what he meant. Then it hit me. This is the secret police he had just asked me to join. "Sir, what is the name of this policing sector?"

"Data Retrieval and Undercover Investigations Division or DRUID." He grimaced and shrugged. "I know it is terrible, but politicians do love their acronyms."

"Is that what they call the agents?" I didn't even try to hide my smirk.

"Unfortunately, yes. But it is what it is." He went stoic. "If you take this position, and with your history in the police forces, I need assurances…"

The deep feeling told me to jump at the chance to go even deeper in the government.

"Begging the general's pardon, I am a soldier, loyal to the Sovereign." I lied, holding my gag reflex. "I accept this position and will complete all of my assignments to the best of my ability."

"Splendid." His smile stretched across his well-tanned face. "After this meeting, I will have it posted on ICON. As for this assignment, you will post daily reports to your new commanding officer, Colonel Lonergan, who will send it to me on ICON's DRUID database. And due to your unfortunate time under Commander Joy Everhart's authority, you will let her in on the information that is deemed necessary for her to have. But only that which I allow."

"Sir, I have read his file, and Captain Thomas is a man of great integrity and drive. And from his brief record in the military, I assure you that when he puts his mind to something, it's as good as done." Lonergan smiled.

Sokolov finally looked at the colonel. But the stare felt icy. Lonergan had crossed a line.

Lonergan's posture slumped a little in deference.

Then the general looked at me. "Please stand, Captain Thomas."

I stood and came to attention, hoping to hear the order to let me get started on the case.

He opened his center drawer, retrieved a box, stood, and walked around the desk to me.

"Welcome to DRUID. You are now promoted to major, which gives you full access to vital information in all sectors of the government to complete your directives." He replaced my captain's bars with the oak leaves of a major. "And with your success in capturing the murderer of the former president of the previous United States of America, I am confident that you will capture the murderer whose subversive actions will discredit those infernal Christians and bring revenge for the slaying of one of our own."

Then he and Colonel Lonergan stood at attention and saluted. I saluted back, trying to slow my thoughts. Things spiraled faster than I knew how to react. The wrong response ensured a trip to the blade.

He motioned for us to sit while going to the table behind his desk, poured vodka without offering us any, and said a quick Russian toast after sitting down. He followed it with a burst of air from his mouth and opened a physical file. Old school.

"Before you go, I need to tell you the importance of maintaining the strictest of silence. Anyone not involved in the case, no matter how close they are to you, cannot know what is happening." He stared at me as if trying to decide to let me in on the secret. "Now that you're a DRUID officer, I want you to know that the identity of the perpetrator, whether Christian or psychopath, is irrelevant. However, it is best for the world to see this as a Christian murder burial ground. First and foremost, the public needs to trust the Sovereign and his scientists. There has been plenty of opposition from the Christians about the murders, claiming that their Christ is the one who magically transported the true believers to Utopia." He used air quotes on the last four words. "This crime scene gives us the optics to show that to be a lie."

"Second, the joining of all departments in law enforcement and the military has met with plenty of opposition from within those departments, as well as other political sectors in the world. And many are calling DRUID the secret police, like the Nazi Gestapo. That we are there to trap people and send them to the guillotine. Will, if you can solve the case, we can show the people of the world that we are here to protect them from threats like the Christians. Then they will trust us."

"I'll be honest, sir. I just want to solve the case and make Joy Everhart look bad. Maybe even get her out of our hair permanently. Let those on a higher pay scale worry about the public." I shrugged.

Lonergan giggled. Sokolov smiled and stood.

"Then we are all in agreement." Sokolov said with a prideful smile.

"Yes, sir." Me and Lonergan stood at attention and saluted.

"Congratulations, Major Thomas. Colonel Lonergan, take him

to the depot and fit him with new clothes, weapons, and tech." Sokolov returned our salutes, then shook our hands. "And get me that Christian killer."

The phone on the general's desk rang. He tapped a button while sitting, waving his hand to shoo us away.

Lonergan led me to the parking lot.

CHAPTER 6

Lonergan chewed his thumbnail and frowned in deep thought while driving to the Peace Forces depot. Maybe suffering a little self-abuse for not fully impressing his superior officer. After a few minutes, I broke the silence and started a conversation with my new superior officer to get a better lay of the land. Sometimes, superiors put on a good show until they get you alone.

"I assume, as my new commanding officer, you will help keep Joy and her department at bay while I investigate."

"Yes. The general wants us to be in complete control of the case." He tapped the steering wheel, not completely paying attention. "Being in DRUID has its advantages."

"I've never heard of it until now. So, how new is it?"

"Not very. It's been in Europe since the Sovereign took office. Now that the U.S. is in the global fold, we've been slowly implementing it across the country. Not all the citizens like the idea of the U.S. getting soaked into the global government."

"What are the parameters of my position?"

"You have full authority to complete your assignments as you see fit. Up to, and including, lethal means." His cheek flinched like he held back a smile.

"Lethal means?" I didn't believe my ears.

"Yes. If you find anyone in the act of treason, you have the authority to kill them."

I forgot that the death of the United States had happened only a few months ago. This kind of power doesn't belong to a single person. Then I remembered Joy and came around to the idea. She probably had a secret that made her susceptible to a bullet.

"Major Thomas." Lonergan leaned back, stretching without turning loose of the steering wheel. "You've probably already realized the general used all his contacts to get us into this investigation. But you need to understand that a lot is riding on this. Commander Everhart is pulling every string and lobbying anyone who'll listen to keep us off this case. It feels like she's taking this as personal as you."

"I'm not taking this personally." Even he didn't believe me.

"Sure. Even so, she will scrutinize every move you make to discredit you and get you off this case." He sighed. "I've been around her enough to know that she's been using every high-profile case, including the president's assassination, to climb the ranks of the police Peace Forces. But, Will, you need to know that she wants the whole shebang."

"The whole shebang?" I lifted my eyebrows for emphasis.

"The Peace Forces." He rubbed his chipped wrist. "All of it. And that includes DRUID."

"That's pretty ambitious. From what I hear, no former American is in the highest ranks of the new government. They're even replacing the Americans in this country."

Lonergan sat up and leaned forward. "How do you know this? Not even the media is covering it."

I panicked. The information I received came from a Resistance member I captured a week after my squad entered Montana. "Scuttlebutt. I might've been out in the field. But it still gets to us in the sticks." I internally clenched, hoping he'd buy it. "Out in the field."

It seemed to pacify him as he shook his head. "The one time it's accurate."

Changing the subject, I asked. "What does she know about DRUID?"

"Enough to be dangerous to herself and everyone around her, but she doesn't have the clearance to get the full grasp of it. Higher up positions like hers are in the sights of potential treasonous members. Unfortunately, Sokolov believes she knows more than she's supposed to, considering how she's been able to keep him at bay. But if she gets the whole Peace Forces, she will use the information we collect to weasel her way into the Sovereign's inner circle." He frowned. "That scares all of us in the military."

"How so?" The deep feeling said he didn't like telling the truth.

"She's taken control of things she had no experience with and turning them into a giant circus, with her as the ringleader." He shook his head while looking out the window. "I wouldn't put it past her to go for the Sovereign's position."

His Vam rang. Lonergan looked at the caller id and rolled his eyes. "Her highness." And he put it on the speaker.

"Colonel Lon…"

"I know who I called Colonel Lonegan." Joy's voice sent violent flashbacks through my mind.

"That's Lonergan. There's an R in the middle." His voice deadpanned.

"Colonel Lonergan." She put extra emphasis on the R. "Much to my apprehension, I have received word that the military is now involved in the investigation. And am I correct in hearing that you intend to assign Sergeant William Thomas to this joint investigation?"

"Actually, it's Major Thomas now." Lonergan smiled like a giddy child waiting for what came next.

"Are you telling me that overbearing, insubordinate, sorry excuse for a human being has become an officer?" Her shrill voice made the speaker on the Vam distort.

"That is really none of your affair. And I expect you will be more civil when Major Thomas is in your presence."

The line went silent. I knew she had muted the mic to scream at the top of her lungs like a spoiled brat not getting her way.

"Colonel Lonergan, I have no intention of allowing that man into my investigation." She acted as if she had control.

"To be honest, ma'am, you have no say in who we assign to this investigation. In fact, Will is with me right now. We are on speaker."

I heard her gasp.

"Howdy, Superintendent Everhart." I used my snarkiest voice. "And it's Will, not William. Remember?"

"That's Commander Everhart to you." She screamed.

I imagined how red orange her face became when I got her station wrong. On purpose.

"Oh, that's right. You got a promotion from my arrest."

Lonergan looked like he wanted to join her side. I held up my hands in mock surrender, reached over, and muted the mic.

"I need her this way. She makes more mistakes." I winked and unmuted the phone. "Plus, it's true."

He nodded and winked.

We waited for her tirade to finish before I interjected, "Please have the investigation file updated before I get to Springfield. I don't want to waste any more time than you already have."

"You will report to me first. Then we will go to Springfield together." She hung up.

A face-to-face with the woman I intended to kill might've felt like God had been helping me out, but I knew He had no intention of helping my plan. But under my new position and rank, my chances of doing it increased significantly with little repercussion.

"Sounds like she's good and off balance." Lonergan pulled his sleeve over his Vam.

"It'll work itself out." I crossed my legs, sat back, trying to get comfortable. "Now I have a question for you, sir."

He didn't give a look of confidence. "What's that, Will?"

"What about my security clearance?"

"The highest clearance possible. You can enter any base, police station, and even Peace Forces facilities of other departments. And with ICON, you can have a look at everything. Except the personal files of the Sovereign himself. Not that he has anything to hide."

With the chip firmly planted on him, I had to listen to nonsense like that without puking. Another perk of the undercover job. After letting it go, I needed one more answer.

"Other than the narrative of the Christian conspiracy, why is this case so important?" I paused for effect. "It felt like the general left something out."

Lonergan's grimace said it all.

"A lot has changed in the short time you've been gone." He sighed and scratched behind his ear. "Since we are merging with law enforcement, getting the upper hand over the cops for control is of the utmost importance to the military. They don't think like we do. They still believe in democracy and certain rights that aren't there anymore. To be honest, I'm still getting used to the idea myself, but soldiers know how to take orders."

"This pissing contest seems a little petty. I mean, this case might just be a psychopath with his own agenda, after all." I said, hoping to get more information about the conspiracy.

"It's more than that. This is getting into the social consciousness. The hype surrounding it as a potential murderer's hiding place will draw more people to the Sovereign. He is on the precipice of bringing a peace that this world has never seen." He shifted in his seat. "It'd be great to never have to fire another bullet again. I mean, think about it, Will. To be a soldier in name only. Old soldiers like me never thought we'd see the day. And the Sovereign is making it possible. But we still need to be in control to help him make it happen."

"So, this narrative…" The hairs on the back of my neck stood at attention.

He nodded. "Came from the top of the food chain. The Sovereign has been waiting for something like this to pin on the Christians since the murders happened. And the military needs to be the one to take credit for it to subvert people like Commander Everhart."

"So, whoever solves the case, gets the Sovereign's adoration?" I already knew the answer. "Not to mention the internal power."

"Yep. That and a big fat promotion. And that's why Commander Everhart is intent on doing this herself. She wants to move to Babylon."

"She's working the investigation?" I sat up straight and shouted.

Lonergan grimaced. "Watch the ears, Will. Yes, and that's why I warned you. She'll do everything in her power to discredit you…"

"And take the glory for herself." I sat back and sighed.

Investigating a murder with that meter maid made me think that my plans to kill her needed to be placed officially on the back burner because the entire world would watch, anticipating that the crime corroborated the Antichrist's ridiculous theory. And my superiors had no interest in a petty vendetta overshadowing their narrative.

"Is it too late to back out?" I groused.

"That will never be an option." Lonergan faced front and became rigid. "You are now a DRUID officer, Will. And I have no doubt that you will complete this mission as ordered. We need you to solve this case without her name on the arrest report to keep that annoyance where she belongs, in the police sector."

As a soldier, I had no other choice. "I will make sure of that, sir."

"I am going to Springfield, per the general's orders, to aid you in any way I can. When you finish your initial investigation, come to me. I'll make sure you have everything you need to solve the case first." He went stoic.

My stomach went into knots when it occurred to me. "Am I required to get chipped?"

"Unfortunately, you cannot get chipped. Being an undercover agent, you cannot have the chip in case you get captured or are undercover among non-Loyalists or Christian Resistance." Lonergan gave a doleful look. "I know it must hurt, but we know you are loyal."

I gave a quick internal exhale. Although me and God didn't agree on some things, He still watched over me.

CHAPTER 7

The depot sat camouflaged in plain sight. Lonergan said the military constructed the metal building quickly after the global earthquake to house the weaponry salvaged from the western states that remained above water. Although as large as most massive warehouses, it remained unremarkable.

Once parked, after three checks of credentials with several guards complaining that I didn't have the Beastmark, we entered the building. The industrial shelves held crates with various colored stickers filled with barcodes and no words, so no overly curious onlookers will know the contents. The lack of dust in this area made me think the crates contained valuable items.

Lonergan took me to an office that smelled of fresh paint and stale coffee. He poured some coffee and sat behind an ancient metal desk that had little paint to speak of and slowly sipped. After the moment had passed, he got serious.

"You need to be careful about who you tell about being a DRUID officer. We've had people killed thinking they confided in a friend."

"Will do." I looked around the office.

"And now, the fun part." He set his mug down and reached into a large bin behind him. "Here's your new badge. Keep it with you at all times." He over-enunciated for effect. "Unless you're undercover."

I stared at the badge that looked to be made of titanium. The symbol looked like a tree of some sort.

"That's our symbol. Someone with a higher rank than me

looked up druids on ICON and found that they worshipped trees, particularly the oak." He pointed at the badge. "That has a loyalty chip in it. If you ever leave the service, that's what they'll put in you. It also has advanced GPS, so I can find you if you go missing. You lose that, don't come back. All citizens now know that sign intimately through public service announcements on their ICON accounts and through the media. Flash your badge, and they know you are someone they can't mess with. When you're undercover, put that in the safest location you can find. Get it the second you come out of your mission. If you lose it, I'll have you arrested and sent to the guillotine for treason.

That's almost exactly what Tommy said about the thumb drives. I laid it on the desk when he pulled out a handgun case.

"Here's a new gun. Best of the best. Fifty-five caliber, twenty in the clip, and will destroy a target at close range and can reach distances of three hundred yards with little recoil. These babies came to us last month and let me tell you." He wiggled his eyebrows. "They will do plenty of damage."

The weight distribution felt amazing. It didn't look or feel that bulky. In fact, it looked to be the same size as my SIG that Daniel disassembled.

"There are two hundred rounds in the pack I have here." He pulled a medium size backpack from the drawer and tossed it to me.

I checked the contents. The same stuff I had in my investigator's kit during my time in the police Peace Forces, with four fifty count boxes of bullets. Zipping the bag up, I looked at Lonergan. His opossum eating garbage grin spread across his narrow face.

"I'm guessing you have some more goodies for me." I returned the smile.

"Thought you'd never ask." He stood and walked to a door across the room. "It's a dangerous world out there, my boy, and our beloved Sovereign can't have one of his best and brightest in constant danger without a little protection." He pulled out some clothes on hangers. "Especially the one who helped broker the old U.S. into the global fold."

My stomach knotted up tight. I never considered myself a pawn on that big of a scale. Then I remembered Sokolov telling me that my primary job was to infiltrate groups, like the Resistance, who operate against the Antichrist and send them to a reeducation camp, a breeding facility, or the guillotine. Maybe that's the reason God kicked me out of the Resistance. A traitor against the Lord. Then I remembered Matthew 7. Maybe Jesus never knew me.

"The bathroom's around the corner. Try these on and I'll tell you about them." He handed me what looked like a red jacket, tactical pants, and he reached on a shelf in the small closet and brought down a pair of sneakers.

I struggled to get the clothes on in the bathroom that reminded me of an old telephone booth I saw on television. The toilet and sink looked like the ones from Grandpa's old RV. I had to step out to get a good feel for the ensemble. The jacket had the St. Louis Cardinals insignia across the front, just like my old jacket I left in a storage locker in a Colorado barracks. It had some weight that I knew I'd get used to. The black pants had a few pockets but felt like the same material as the jacket. The red and black shoes looked the same as my old pair, but much lighter.

When I walked into the office, Lonergan smiled and stood, putting his hands on his hips. He asked me to turn around like my mom did when I tried on school clothes at the store.

"How do they feel?" His smile stretched wider. "We had to do a rush job."

"Like you stole them out of my locker in Colorado." I winked.

"Actually, we kinda did." He gave me the once over again. "The boys over at tech needed your dimensions, so they got their people in Colorado to look at your clothes from the barracks and sent the measurements."

"Copied them?" I began doing a pocket search, starting with the jacket.

"Since you're going undercover a lot, it's best to give you something that'll blend into your surroundings. Defunct sports teams are the rage in fashion and, unfortunately, the Cards are never coming back. In fact, the only sport recognized by the government is soccer." He winced when he said it.

"Maybe the Sovereign isn't that great after all." I didn't lie.

"Easy there, buckaroo. That's a blading offense, whether you mean it or not." He winked. "But I understand. Football is my game. In fact, there are some beer leagues forming all over the world for the old sports. They just can't have a professional league."

He sat back down and finished the coffee.

"Now for the fun stuff. What you are wearing is bulletproof." He smiled like the Cheshire Cat.

"Seriously?" I opened the jacket and looked at the lining. Everything seemed normal.

"Yep. It can stop a fifty-five-caliber bullet at point blank range." His smile turned to one of admiration while he studied my reaction. "This is top of the line, straight from Europe. Only for DRUID officers. Even I have a set of clothes made of that material. However, it's like the old Kevlar. You'll still feel it and get a broken bone or two."

"Better than a through-and-through to the chest." I sat down. "Shoes too?"

"Yep. Those too. Once you break them in, you'll never want to wear anything else."

We sat and talked about the action out west. Swapped stories of the fights we engaged in. Then Lonergan got serious.

"Will, I'm going to Springfield to help you in any way I can. We need to discuss when and where to meet. I've never been there, but you're from that area. What's your opinion?" He leaned back, giving me his full attention.

"Where's the Peace Forces headquartered?" I put my hands behind my head.

"Some place called…" He pulled out a wireless keyboard and opened a file on his Vam. "Park Central Square."

"Downtown." It made sense to be centrally located in the city.

"Offices are in what used to be a museum. The prison is in an old department store."

"Heers. What about the rest of the square?"

"A religious center and a food distribution facility."

"Sounds crowded. It might be best to meet further away." I closed my eyes and thought about the layout of Springfield. "How about the Battlefield Mall?"

Lonergan tapped a few times and shook his head. "No good. It took a lot of damage from the earthquake and aftershock. Now, it just attracts drug addicts and the homeless."

Sitting back, I looked at the floor and thought for a minute.

"Why don't we just meet in your vehicle? We can drive around and talk. I'll show you the sights."

He went to voice command and ordered a spacious SUV with highly tinted windows. "I hate cramped spaces."

I looked up, craning my neck. "Do I get one of those fancy Vams?"

"Yep." Lonergan closed his and reached into a drawer and tossed a box to me. "Just like mine. Has all the bells and whistles. Hey, before I forget. The badge?"

I tossed him my old Vam and put it on. The sleeve of my jacket easily slid over it and hid it well.

"There's a small pocket near your collar." He pointed at his own collar. "Your chip is in a small metal case in the badge, and it will detach from the badge to fit in there."

Although tough to pull, the new Velcro finally gave way with the typical ripping sound. Lonergan pushed a tree root on the badge to release the chip case. Patting the Velcro in place, I knew I needed to remember it, or I'd lose about a foot off my six-four stature.

"Just forget it's there, unless you're undercover, and you'll be just fine." His smile returned.

"What if I get caught without my jacket?" I raised my eyebrows.

"Until all the Peace Forces are united, don't." He still smiled, but his tone became dead serious. "Other departments will have no problem sending you to the blade and discrediting us."

Pulling up my sleeve, I tapped the Vam screen on my left forearm. It lit up. *Good morning, Will.* After getting my ID settings configured, I looked up and noticed Lonergan frowning at the screen of his tablet.

"What's the matter, sir?" I asked.

"I'm afraid your old stomping grounds aren't what you remembered." He saw me raise my eyebrows and continued. "Since the storm, the food supply has taken a massive hit. People are struggling to eat even one meal a day. Since we're Peace Forces, we get our daily nutrition, but people are getting frustrated with seeing us eat while they go hungry. In Springfield, there are plenty of incidents where people are protesting at the food distribution facility near Peace Forces Headquarters. Occasionally, it gets violent. Now that the bounty system is in full force, we're hoping that this will abate. But until then, be diligent. Don't let them get to you." He stretched and stood. "You better get going. And please, Will. Don't start anything with her immediately."

I stood, saluted, and said goodbye without promising anything.

CHAPTER 8

Entering Joy's office at the capitol building, I saw a pair of glaring, but beautiful blue eyes that immediately returned to her work on her computer. Marjorie must have quit when she found out that Joy set up Frank. As short as Joy, but prettier, the young woman moved efficiently at her desk and refused to acknowledge me until I grunted. Then she gave an annoyed look.

"Can I help you?"

Her attempt to act like Joy annoyed me. Another puppet.

"Naw, I'll let myself in. Joy's expecting me."

I walked around the desk to the only door behind her.

"You're not allowed in the commander's office." She raised her throaty voice.

I opened the door and found Joy staring at her Vam screen, munching on an apple. The look on her face told me that I hit what I aimed for. Surprise turning to anger.

"Major Thomas, you will wait in my assistant's office until summoned." Her calm voice didn't hide her anger because of her red face.

"I'm not under your command, Commander. We're equals now." I plopped in the comfortable seat across from her and crossed my legs.

"Where is my salute? You are in direct violation of the…"

"Sorry, kid. You're not military. Remember? You sent me there when I didn't bow and worship at your feet."

"You threatened to kill me. And I did you a favor by not sending you to the guillotine." She threw her apple core in the wastebasket under her desk. "And you will respect me when we are in Springfield. Is that understood, soldier?"

Finding it difficult not to laugh in her face, I knew I reached my limit without ending her. Then I noticed it. The one thing that made everything worthwhile. Joy had the Beastmark. Elation flowed through my body. Now I can kill her, and she'd go to Hell guaranteed.

"Okay, but you have to extend the same olive branch. This is a joint investigation, and respect runs both sides of the street." I gave her my best annoying grin.

She sat back and stared like a politician strategizing her next move. Still the same old Joy. When she railroaded me into the military, she lost her hold over me. Knowing her the way I did, she needed my help with the quickly cooling case.

"And none of this protocol stuff. I'm Will and your Joy." I enjoyed pushing her buttons, but she deserved every bit of spite I mustered.

Her smile lit up the room. It threw me off.

"Before we go to Springfield, we need to talk to the superintendent to get an update on the case." She touched the screen on her Vam.

Although she had no power to command me, she had the upper hand in having almost all the information about the case. I let her have it for now. Not that I had a choice.

The Vam chimed and a familiar face popped up on the holograph screen. I almost choked. Karen Evans. The detective assigned to me for a hot minute in the presidential assassination case.

"This is a joke, right?" I asked, sitting up.

"Sergeant Thomas, I trust you've learned some self-discipline and esprit décor in your time in the…"

"Not even remotely. And that's Major Thomas to you, Karen." I ordered.

"That is enough, Major Thomas." Joy shrieked. "You will not demean the superintendent of our fine city. Superintendent Evans is a valued…"

"Kiss up. I get it." I crossed my legs. "Placed her yourself, Joy?"

The redness brightened. But she said nothing. Then took a deep breath and smiled that same smile from earlier.

"How I run the police in this territory is none of your concern. And that includes my professional decisions. Now we need to get down to business concerning the murder scene.

I had to give it to her. Joy took everything I dished out. But I had plenty more where that came from.

"Major Thomas, Superintendent Evans has taken the liberty of putting together an extensive report on the case. With the death of the Springfield Chief of Police, I have extended the jurisdiction and given Superintendent Evans full responsibility of Springfield, not to mention full support, to make the arrest. Forensics, interrogations, and computer-generated models of the crime scene layout and scenarios are at her disposal, and I believe she has come through admirably." Joy smiled and nodded to Evans, who glowed at the attention. "And I commend her for a job well done."

Promoting Karen Evans as the new superintendent didn't really surprise me. In fact, if I'd thought about it long enough, it made sense. Joy needed someone who'd do as told without wanting the credit. At least, not without Joy's consent. And even then, Joy had a natural ability to weasel her way into getting more praise and power. I almost felt sorry for Karen.

Evans looked like she wanted to bust out crying. A perfect little minion.

"If it's all the same, and as you made perfectly clear, time is of the essence. And this grandstanding without an interested or powerful audience is wasting this valuable time. So, if you please, can we get down to business and start the investigation?" I uncrossed my legs.

"Major Thomas, this office is not yours to conduct. And these proceedings are not for your entertainment. We are simply bringing you up to speed on the case and are completing the transition of the case from Superintendent Evans to us." Her annoyingly snarky smile returned, but something seemed out of place. "Please remember that you are not in the Peace Forces police. You are a liaison from the military, and your only responsibility is to report my findings to your superiors here in Jefferson City. I realize that the conversation earlier today might have given the impression that you will be part of this investigation…"

"I'm not sure what you think is going to happen, Joy. But let's make this perfectly clear. Between the three of us, I'm the only one with the ability to investigate this murder. Karen has very few homicides under her belt, none as lead. And you are just a glorified meter maid. And General Sokolov made it abundantly clear that I am not an observer, but an active investigator." I mimicked her snarky smile. "You're here for the glory. I just want to catch a killer. You do your part, and I'll do mine. Now let's see this case file Karen put together."

The screen appeared on my side of the desk, and I almost gasped at the organized mess. It contained nothing new, not even the stuff Lonergan told me about earlier. The rest comprised nonsensical guesswork that made little sense. Frowning at the screen for a moment, I looked through it at Joy and realized what I had missed.

No orange face. A beautiful, natural color that resembled human skin had replaced her old fake bake. I barely knew what to say. My snark left me until I came to my senses.

"This isn't the complete file." I sat back, trying not to stare at Joy.

"Are you saying that my file is incomplete?" Karen's voice had no believability in it.

"I'm saying you're stonewalling me." I folded my arms.

"As I said before, Will." Joy's snarky voice returned. "I will give you the information that General Sokolov needs to stay informed about my investigation. You are just a liaison."

I caught Karen smirk in my peripherals.

"If it's all the same to both of you, I guess it's my duty to inform you I'm not just military. I'm DRUID." I didn't wait for their reaction. "It ought to be posted by now. Have a look."

It helped that the fake bake had faded because I enjoyed watching the color leave Joy's face when she tapped and stared at the screen. Karen gave a slight gasp.

Joy tapped her Vam again. "Vanessa, will you please get the complete hard file for Major Thomas." Joy turned to me with a stoic look, probably trying to figure out a loophole.

After Vanessa gave me the file, I read through it. The only thing new covered the placement of the body parts from an aerial view. It seemed random, but I'd cover that with the CSU.

"Karen, I have to give it to you. You don't know what's going on, but at least you have a useless theory." I clapped the folder shut.

"Will, you will stop besmirching my best and brightest this instant. And I will make it my personal responsibility to have you put in your place. When I solve this crime…"

"Joy, you're in way over your head. This isn't just a burial plot. This is a serial killer we're dealing with, and you need all the help you can get. In fact, it might be best to bring someone else along who knows what she's doing."

Karen perked up on screen and smiled at Joy, who returned it.

"Not her. She's clueless even with a bagful of evidence." I watched both seething. "I meant Jenny in St. Louis CSU. She's still there, right?"

Joy's anger turned to contemplation. "She's there, but the Springfield Peace Forces have a lab filled with competent workers."

"But we need the best. I want Jenny."

Joy sat back, tapping her chin with a well-manicured fingernail. I knew her ego enough to believe she'd allow it.

"I like the idea." She turned to her subordinate. "Karen, have Jenny join us at the airport in two hours. Major Thomas, I will meet you there. I have some things I need to deal with before I leave."

"Yes, ma'am." Karen saluted before Joy ended the video feed.

"I have to report to Colonel Lonergan." I emphasized the R for Joy's benefit.

Out in the hallway, Joy needed the last word.

"Will, it is in your best interest to play nice. I'd hate to make a couple of phone calls and get those pretty little oak leaves removed." Her smile sealed the deal.

I got in her face, staring into her beautiful blue eyes. The deep feeling screamed that I can't kill her. But my rage deafened me to its demands.

"After what you did to Frank, you're lucky that I don't remove that loyalty chip with a fifty-five-caliber bullet." I straightened when the look on her face surprised me.

To see her for the first time, someone might mistake the look as one of surprise mixed with extreme regret or remorse. But with our past, I knew she focused more on the threat.

She surprised me by slouching a little, turning, and almost running for the elevator.

CHAPTER 9

Outside the capitol building, I walked towards Lonergan's car he let me borrow. The meeting with Joy went as planned, and I wanted to drive around a bit to be alone and rethink my strategies. Then I saw her. Amelia's smile lit me up as I remembered the last time I saw her. That night burned in my mind like a fire brand marking a calf. The swirling red clouds made downtown St. Louis look like Dante's dream. However, the inferno of passion I carried for that woman overwhelmed me.

Her gray eyes still captivated me when she looked into mine. Without the wind, her maroon hair kept its shape. My heart went from overdrive to trampled when I saw the Beastmark tattoo on her forehead. The smile that interrupted my thought patterns did nothing to stop my heart from breaking. She'd made her decision.

She ran into my arms and kissed me. Although I despaired, my mind refocused on her lips. Like the last time they met, our lips did all the talking. They spoke a language that didn't need to remind us of the time missed and the miles apart. They simply allowed us to stay in the moment. No matter how brief.

Her voice made the time apart worth every minute. "I wasn't about to miss an opportunity to see you, flatfoot."

"I got in a couple of hours ago." I looked at my Vam to make sure.

She stepped back, frowned, and put her hands on her hips. "And I'm not the first one you talked to?"

"Sorry, babe. But duty called." I pulled her back to me. "And I'll pick you first every time I have a choice."

We kissed some more.

She took my hand and started hustling me towards her car. "We need to get to the restaurant quickly, or we'll be in line all day."

After a terror-filled ride of less than a half mile, we made it to the Sweet Smoke BBQ restaurant. The line trailed out the door. She cursed under her breath and looked at me with somber gray eyes and shrugged.

Needing to look important, I grabbed her hand and walked past the line into the diner. An obscene, plump woman complained until I pulled my DRUID badge. Her round face turned to immediate fear before she turned and tried to start a conversation with the woman standing behind her.

We went to the front of the line and ordered from the menu the cashier nervously handed me. The order came out a few minutes later in brown paper bags and a cardboard holder with our drinks. Sweet tea for me and a diet soda for Amelia. To my relief, Amelia told me she'd pay for lunch and pulled her government ID card to pay. She had the tattoo, but not the Beastmark chip.

Sitting in her car and opening the bag and handing me the burnt ends and fries, Amelia noticed me staring at the tattoo. She waited until pouring the BBQ sauce on her brisket sandwich before confronting me.

"What's your problem?" She asked before taking a bite.

"To ruin such beauty with that." I pointed a fry at her forehead.

She finished chewing and retorted, "The tattoo artist said I look sophisticated. Like a real woman of the world."

"You look like a billboard." I sipped my tea.

"If this is how you will receive me after all this time, you can go back to South Dakota." She shifted her body to face the car in front of us.

"I must not be the first to say something." I grinned.

Her shoulders drooped. "It stinks dating a cop." Then she looked at me and smiled. "My boss said the same thing. She has the chip in her hand. Said it takes away from my professionalism. But I'm having the last laugh. She has to be hand-scanned by the government security every time, and I don't. I just walk past the guard, through the scanning booth, and grin."

"But you're not chipped." I took another bite of the overly seasoned fries.

"I hold my card up. But I'm scheduled for next month. The new chip is out, but it's in short supply. So, I have to wait like the rest." She looked at my forehead and right hand. "You're in the Peace Forces. Where's yours?"

"Can't get it." I shrugged.

"Can't or won't?" She raised her eyebrows, challenging me.

"Both. I just got promoted to major and transferred to DRUID this morning. As part of my undercover duties, I can't get chipped." I bit into the burnt ends that melted in my mouth.

"But you said you won't." Her intense stare said that she still bought the Antichrist's spiel.

"Nope. Don't want to be tagged like a bull in the herd. I'm an individual." I didn't look away.

"No, you're still an American." She returned her gaze to the river.

I shrugged. "If that's a problem, we can end this right now." I took another bite.

The pause lasted longer than I expected. Her haunting gray eyes looked away, but they focused on her answer. Although I knew we had our differences, I still believed we had a future together, even with the tattoo. Praying silently for God to change her mind towards Him, I started a plan to get her to someone like Daniel. She turned to me, her expression hard to read.

"I'm sorry for what I said. You have every right to feel the way you do." Her face went stern. "But I will not be involved with someone who does not see the world the way I do."

"You mean the way the Sovereign does." I wiped my mouth.

"I mean the right way." She tried for virtuous, but the words came out malevolent. "I wish I never wasted the time to come here.

I ignored the last line, giving it to her temper. "The last time we talked, you said we'd wait until we can talk this out. I get it. The government is about to make the chip mandatory, but I still have a bad feeling about it. It seems so..." I looked at people slowly passing us by.

"Perfect?" I heard the hope in her tone.

"Orwellian."

Waiting for the backlash, she said nothing. I turned to see her reaction, but the confusion in her face told me enough.

"I had a history teacher in high school who showed us a

documentary on the Holocaust. He talked about the tattoo the Nazis put on the Jews in concentration camps. It's hard not to compare that to this." I pointed at her tattoo.

"But Hitler was a fascist despot." She put her food on the dash and faced me. "And if you're comparing that maniac to our beloved Sovereign, I will gladly march you to the guillotine myself."

"I didn't say he was Hitler. I'm just saying that we need to be careful. An unchecked government can be a slippery slope. Who knows where it can lead."

"Spoken like a true American. Well, let me tell you something, Major Thomas. That corrupt government needed replacing, and when the President of the United States had enough decency to see that and give it to the Sovereign, the world became infinitely better."

"And yet the freedoms we enjoyed are completely null and void." I showed her my DRUID badge. "And it's now my responsibility to ensure those freedoms will never be observed again."

The look she gave me broke my heart.

"Even England can no longer observe former freedoms without a one-way ticket to a reeducation center. Welcome to the perfect world." I sighed. "Welcome to Utopia."

She put her food back in the bag and drove back to the Capitol Building. "I need to get back. There's a meeting today that I still need to prepare for, and it's a long drive."

"Okay." I didn't apologize, like I needed to.

She put the car in park, got out, and met me in front of it, pulling me into an unsure embrace. "Tell you what. I'll reschedule my appointment until we can talk longer. And you need to get on the case, copper." Her smile melted my breaking heart.

"Sounds good." My smile felt weak.

Our kiss didn't last as long as I wanted. And it didn't have the right words that a couple falling in love needed.

CHAPTER 10

After watching Amelia go, I started walking towards the Capitol Building. But I had no interest in seeing Joy or Lonergan. I needed some time alone.

Stopping in front of the statue of Thomas Jefferson near the capitol's entrance, I began thinking about the last few hours. Starting in Custer National Park gave me the opportunity to show Tommy I wanted my effects in a way that I wanted him to remember. And the opportunity to exact my revenge on Joy made me feel like things were going my way, especially with her having the Beastmark. Now, the case loomed and my argument with Amelia felt like God showed me that I needed to reevaluate the way I looked at life.

After a few minutes of calming my emotions, my mind began focusing on the case. The crime scene made me think the killer didn't hide the victims. Otherwise, he'd have put them in different fields across the area. Although it felt like he discarded them to keep the heads, I tried to figure out why he separated the body parts. The pictures looked like he meticulously dismembered each victim and placed them in their proper hole. I wondered if the killer buried them, dug them up to place new victims' parts, and reburied them, or if he buried them on top of the last victim.

Looking beyond the bronzed Jefferson statue, I noticed the columns of the Capitol Building and remembered the marble came from the Phenix near Springfield. Devon, my friend and baseball teammate, had a distant relative who worked the quarry when they dug out the marble for those columns. I wondered if my friend made it to Heaven in the Rapture. Then I thought about the narrative.

The little evidence we had felt like a serial killer had done this and not a murderous bunch of Christians. It sickened me that the Antichrist had the public fooled in a way that they'd believe anything. I realized the Bible said that God will send them a strong delusion that they will believe a lie, but any thinking human had to realize the ridiculousness of the murder theory. But what Sokolov said about the media turning these killings into a story that supported the theory had enough plausibility to make even the smartest people believe. And it saddened me to be a part of it. It felt like God punished me for being part of it, even though I knew better. He's the forgive and forget type. Unlike me.

Maybe He intended to derail my plan to kill Joy.

In fact, my plan had many scenarios that allowed me to pull the trigger and get away with it. And seeing the Beastmark on her untanned forehead generated an elation that might've made a better person cringe in remorse before the fact. But I felt excited. The deep feeling chastised me for that one too.

Changing from one foot to the other, I stared into the mental void in front of my eyes, ignoring the bronze politician and marble columns. "Vengeance is mine, I will repay, saith the Lord." Romans chapter twelve if I remembered correctly. Then a verse came to me I didn't remember knowing. "To me belongeth vengeance, and recompense; their foot shall slide in due time: for the day is at hand, and the things that shall come upon them make haste." It felt like it came out of the Old Testament.

"I see zat you are collecting your soughts. It can be a profitable veenture in heestoric times like sees. If you considair how our glorious Sovereign helps in all sings, you weel be most successful." The beautiful woman with a bad French accent entered my visual field, sending chills through my entire body. She slid a finger across her forehead to sweep the dark hair from her dark eyes. Her lithe body sauntered to the bench where I sat. If I hadn't felt the evil emanating from her, I'd have begged her for a date, completely forgetting about Amelia.

"I think I've heard about you. That is one lousy accent." I grinned. She didn't.

"Most people enjoy my French." She switched to a mild

Russian accent, which sounded more natural. "And I know everything about the famous Major Will Thomas. Detective extraordinaire." She stood in front of me, blocking the statue. Her deep, dark eyes pulsated with sexual desire and evil.

The deep feeling came to my rescue. I snapped out of her gaze.

"Not Jason Ewing. He said it's terrible." I sat up straight. "And he's right."

She gave a murderous stare. The deep feeling told me to tread lightly. And I actually paid attention.

"Let's get to the real reason I am in this God-forsaken country." She leaned forward. "Joy Everhart has been a thorn in our sides for far too long. She needs to be eliminated."

"Wow, you don't mince words. Do you?" I looked around to see if she travelled alone.

"She is too ambitious for her own good. Ever since she started climbing the ranks of the Peace Forces, she has been insufferable. She is too…" She looked just above me as if searching for the right word. "American."

It felt like she had listened in on my earlier conversation with Amelia. "Too American?" Just saying it brought my blood pressure up, but I didn't let her see it. "We just joined the global community. We might need a little time to adjust."

She gave an amused grin. "We? Are you saying that you have forgiven her for this?"

She raised her Vam and tapped the screen. A hologram of Frank's execution popped into the air above her arm. Instead of starting it when Joy spit, she showed the whole thing. Right up to the moment Joy waved and smiled to the crowd. Then the video changed to a new camera view directed towards me. The camera focused closer to show the look of rage as I bent the fence with my grip.

They had been watching me the whole time. Dad used to say that it's not paranoia when they really are watching you.

My stomach churned with rage. "What is it you want from me?" I grumbled.

Her smile turned to a sneer. "I want to give you what you want. A chance to kill her."

My heart pounded at the thought of doing it. But the deep feeling told me not to trust her.

"What do you get out of this?" I tried to hide my feelings.

"Let's just say that I get a potential rival out of the way. You see, I have my own ambitions, and I will not have them altered by that little pest." The fire in her eyes became unsettling.

"Why didn't you set her up with your assassin?" I wondered if she'd tell the truth.

"That was the original plan, but the little spider crawled through the cracks and set your mentor up to take her fall." She folded her arms in a huff. "I underestimated her. That will never happen again, I assure you."

The rage coursed through my mind. Frank became a pawn between two people playing God with other people's lives over power. Letting the emotion dissipate, I let the quiet moment last a little longer, hoping that she took it for granted that she lured me in, playing on her team.

"Who are you?" I finally asked.

"I am Daria Petrovich, aide to the Commanding General of the Global Peace Forces. My task is to ensure his private projects meet his full expectations." Her arrogance filled the surrounding air. "I get things done."

"Not everything, or Joy'd be dead by now." I knew better than to poke the Russian bear, but I didn't excel at holding back.

She let it pass. I had to give it to her. She knew how to negotiate.

Ewing, her assassin, told me to be careful with her. She kept her promises. A few weeks after his death, I read about his group being captured and sent to a reeducation center. Now, they all have the Beastmark. Although the deep feeling told me to get as far away from her as possible, I chose to become her temporary ally.

"I guess we have a commonality in that we both hate Joy and want what's best for global peace." Everything I said felt right and wrong at the same time.

"And if you do your job as well as you did your last case, I can guarantee that your time as a major will be short-lived." Her wicked smile deepened as she raised an eyebrow. "If you fail in one, or both, it will still be the same short life."

Trying not to look intimidated, I smiled back. "I plan to have a long and successful career and a longer and healthier life."

Her sweet smile returned. "We will meet in Springfield the day after tomorrow. I will find a good place for us to meet. And you will figure out how to exterminate our little bug problem."

The deep feeling did somersaults in my torso when she left.

CHAPTER 11

With time to spare before meeting Joy, I refocused on the case because a solid plan to kill Joy didn't come to mind. That and the deep feeling constantly impeding my planning. It felt wrong, even though she had the Beastmark. Her own ambitious desires of upward mobility in the Antichrist's government had punched her trip to Hell. Is it really murder when she chose against God?

The thought of returning to my old stomping grounds in Springfield brought both nostalgia and a mixture of grief and regret. I didn't hear the black limousine with tinted windows pulling up behind me until I heard the power window rolling down with an electric hum.

"Major Thomas." Hectar's familiar voice made me smile.

"Been a while, Hectar," I said, turning around to see his shadowy figure.

"Too long. It's good to see you made it back unscathed. Please, join me." The hum of the window made me feel like I didn't have a choice.

The car pulled away from the curb after I got settled in the back seat facing the driver. Hectar faced the trunk. He still didn't have a Beastmark.

"Always looking behind you?" I asked.

"It never hurts to know where you came from." His smile still captivated any audience. "Especially where you're going. It's been too long, my friend."

He already knew about my trip to Springfield for the investigation. His resourcefulness still impressed me.

"You're right. It's been a while since we last talked. I missed it." Stretching my legs a little to get comfortable, I had a feeling this conversation meant either vital information or an idle threat.

"As have I." He pulled his mother's Bible out of the console beside him. "I have had no one to talk to about this."

"Not everyone had a preacher for a father?" I grinned. The chess game had begun.

"Hardly. The people I associate myself with had, shall we say, checkered pasts." He patted the Bible.

"I know the feeling. As a cop, I'm surrounded by that type."

His deep, infectious chuckle lightened the mood. "I hope you're not insinuating."

"Hardly. I'm just saying we have some commonalities."

The car turned away from the capitol building.

"Hey, how's everything in St. Louis?" I watched the buildings slowly pass.

"The cleanup is slow but progressing nicely." He looked out the window. "I bought the food truck patio and building an Automat."

"Automat?" I looked back at him. "What's that?"

He laughed a hearty laugh and slapped his knee. "You youngsters never cease to entertain me. I thought you liked old movies."

"I do, but what's that got to do with this?"

"The old Automats are restaurants without servers. There is a wall filled with doors like microwave ovens. You open one by either getting scanned or placing currency into a slot in the door handle, which will open upon approval. Reach in, get your food item and enjoy. You can get an entire meal or an individual dish in one slot." He stared behind me. "I brought it back when thieves began holding up my trucks. The local Peace Forces police got sick of fishing the thieves out of the river."

"I'm guessing you have bouncers to watch for anyone trying to break open these doors."

"No bouncers. I have meal protectors." His smile became evil. "But it works for the less fortunate, like your friend Clay. If someone like him can scrape up enough change or get some money put on their chip, they can at least get something substantial, no matter the size."

"You're a real humanitarian." I chuckled. "Guess you won't

know how successful it is until you get it open."

"I already know because I have opened three. One in Memphis, one in Chicago, and one in the city you're about to visit." His eyes danced while waiting for me to figure it out.

I shook my head and laughed. "I forgot you know everything everywhere. I just caught on to you calling me Major Thomas. They promoted me this morning."

His smile turned into a grimace. "Will, I want to warn you about Springfield. This is just a guess, but I believe you haven't been home in quite some time."

"I went back not long before I came to investigate the President's murder." I tapped my knee in remembrance. "It wasn't the same as before the murders."

"True. It's far more dangerous than St. Louis right now because it's not in anyone's sights in the upper echelons of government. Drugs, weapons, prostitution, you name it, it's there. I ought to know. Over half of it is mine." He tapped his chest. "And now with this bounty scheme the government started, it's getting worse. Bounty hunters are bringing in their own families to get some money. Since the last judgment, food is scarce. With the government hoarding it and passing it out to the rich and powerful, people are doing horrible things to quiet a starving belly. Which reminds me." He pulled a card out of his inside coat pocket. "Here, it's fully loaded to eat whatever you want at any of my Automats. Consider it a small bribe." He grinned when I took it.

"They still got cashew chicken there?"

Whenever I returned to Springfield, I absolutely looked forward to the cashew chicken that became the city's food identity.

"Of course. I obtained the original recipe for it." He laughed. "It's quite good."

Knowing how he got it, at the end of a gun, I changed the subject.

"How's business going with Joy?" I knew the answer but wanted his side of the story.

His eyes rolled slightly. "She's not as active as before. Her little minion, Superintendent Evans, now delivers messages from Europe."

"Speaking of Europe, the French woman is here in Jeff City." I rubbed my knees, acting like it hurt to say it, but not a complete lie. "We just finished talking before you picked me up."

His stare became icy. "You then know that she is my liaison. But why is she here? I thought she went back to Europe after her hired assassin got the blade."

"She wants Joy dead." I held back a grin. "Joy is a little too ambitious for Daria's plans of upward mobility."

"That sounds like Daria." He looked past me into the future. "Why didn't she set Joy up with her assassin?"

"Joy outmaneuvered her. Another reason she wants Joy dead."

Hectar's eyes turned to me. "Will, you need to be careful with this woman. She's the one who helped me take control of the Mississippi. I'm guessing that after her little squabble with Joy is over, I'm next on the list. And anyone who gets in the way will be bladed right along with me. She might work for the higher-ups in Europe, but she wants power and will kill everyone in her path. Word on the street is that she wants to be the Sovereign's number two."

"Sounds about right from our little chat." I tried to maintain a state of calm even though the deep feeling told me I aligned myself with the wrong person.

After a long pause, Hectar tapped the dark window separating us from the drive. I stopped paying attention to the route we took, but I noticed the State Penitentiary. My gut tied in knots at the memories. We turned towards the Capitol Building.

"I will go to Springfield in a few days. There are some things I need to handle in St. Louis before I go. You will need help with her and many of the elements I told you about earlier. And I have my interests to protect from Daria Petrovich as well." His smile returned.

It looked like a plan had formulated in his mind just then and no intention of telling me.

"Before I drop you off, let's talk." He picked up the Bible and opened it towards the back. "The next judgment is going to be supervolcanoes, is it not?"

I grinned when he looked at me over the book. "Sorry, but it's difficult not to be a little nostalgic. I haven't talked to anyone like this since our last conversation. Since I don't have my dad's prophecy journal, I'm not quite sure of the verses."

He didn't miss a beat. "And the second angel sounded, and as it were a great mountain burning with fire was cast into the sea: and the third part of the sea became blood; And the third part of the creatures which were in the sea, and had life, died; and the third part of the ships were destroyed." He closed the book and put it back in the console that instantly locked.

"I remember reading Dad's journal before the blood storm judgment. He believed they'd be supervolcanoes, too." I hadn't thought about Dad in a while, just his journal. He'd agree with the deep feeling about my plans for Joy.

"The research I did shows that the western U.S. has at least three potential volcanoes. Two are now under the water with California, and the other is Yellowstone. If my calculations are correct, it won't have any impact here because the winds are still turned off."

I stared out the window. "But what about the Mississippi? It's now completely saltwater."

Hectar waved it off. "Too far away. I believe the ocean affected by this will be the Pacific. Mainly because many of the potential volcanoes are in the Pacific Ring of Fire. A good name for it, eh?"

"Sounds like you've got a good handle on this one. I think you're right. It might not affect us geologically, but it'll be more food off the table for the world."

The car stopped in front of the building.

"More money for me." He wriggled his eyebrows.

It didn't take much for Hectar to remind me of his mobster ways. All about the money.

At that moment, the car door opened. We shook hands and left it at that.

CHAPTER 12

The dense clouds threatened a deluge when I found the Potter's Field, just across the river from Jefferson City. I had requested Frank's body to give him a proper burial. They buried the executed prisoners in mass graves, and I refused to let Frank be part of the nameless. However, because they executed him as a traitor, they only allowed him to be buried in the potter's field, reserved for those too poor for the expensive cemeteries. Because of my immediate transfer to the military, Marjorie finished the arrangements.

The fields surrounding the Potter's Field mimicked the rest of the country with its blacks and reds with green trees sprinkled about. In fact, the moroseness of the scene made for a truly grim visit, perfect for a cemetery. Although I needed to focus on paying respects to my mentor, the potential mistake I made by teaming with Daria filled my mind. The deep feeling kept bothering me about her. I knew an alliance made no sense, other than our desire to kill Joy. Using my experience with the deep feeling, I ignored it long enough until it went silent.

Will I ever learn?

A concrete barricade blocked the edge of the cemetery to keep vehicles from tearing up the unkempt field. Bloody and charred grave markers stood in perfect columns and rows.

Trying to remember Frank's grave's location, I climbed over the barrier and began counting rows. Marjorie emailed me its placement. Twenty-eight back and tenth from the right with a burned cedar tree at the end closest to Frank's grave. The markers either had the occupier's name or a number. Name meant a poor occupant. A number on a marker showed a criminal. Then I found it.

37265

Not knowing the numbering system used for the graves, I laughed when Clay got the information to me. On an old phone, the numbers spelled out FRANK.

Dusk began its slow takeover of the sky when I noticed someone close to his grave. At first, I didn't recognize the person because they knelt in front of the marker. Keeping my steps light out of respect for the mourner, I walked closer to Frank's grave. Then I recognized the ponytail. My breath, like my movement, became quiet and slow. Wearing a black shirt and pants, I blended into my surroundings.

Joy rested on both knees at the foot of Frank's grave. With her head bowed low, her body convulsed like someone laughing, mocking his resting place. I let my rage overtake me.

She didn't move when I aimed my SIG at the back of her head. But she wasn't laughing.

"I'm so sorry. I didn't know what I was doing. Please forgive me." She sobbed.

"I will never forgive you!" I growled. It took all my control to keep my heartrate down and my gun hand steady.

With redness in her eyes and watery streaks down her cheeks, she turned and glared at me like I had interrupted a private conversation. "I'm not talking to you." She shouted.

Although a little confused, I didn't buy it. Moving around to face her, I put the end of my pistol's barrel on her Beastmark. She didn't flinch. I'd never planned this moment so perfectly. My nervousness didn't contain dread or possible regret, but an overwhelming, almost maniacal, giddiness. Frank's murder was about to be avenged.

"Joy Everhart, you are guilty of premeditated first-degree murder. You knowingly and willingly planned and set up the execution of Captain Frank Malone. And for this, I will execute you." I pulled the hammer back.

"Go ahead. You're right. I deserve it. I set Frank up and watched him die." Her shoulders dropped as she cried.

"You spat on his corpse." I screamed. Then I slapped her.

She tumbled to the ground and shrieked in pain. Rubbing her

reddening face, she quickly stood and faced me, staring up at the barrel when I placed it back on her Beastmark.

"I did. And I'm sorry." She didn't plead for her life. She admitted her transgression and asked for forgiveness.

"I'm not in the forgiving business. I'm in the justice business." The deep feeling protested vehemently, but it didn't stun me like last time. Which confused me a little.

"I don't want *your* forgiveness!" She shouted. Her red face beamed with rage. "You arrogant coward!"

Before I pulled the trigger, a gun barrel tapped me on the temple. Tommy pulled back to a safe distance, sidestepping into view. "She's with me."

"Go ahead. Fire. You know what happens when a person holding a gun with his finger on the trigger gets shot." I grinned. "You taught me that lesson. Remember?"

"I also know that when you kill Joy, those drones will come screaming to kill you when her vitals flatline with her Vam close. Remember?" He snarked. "Wait, you taught me that."

"Will, you don't understand what's going on here." Joy had taken control of her emotions now that she had backup.

"And neither does Tommy." I pointed to the car. "Mine is in the car. When a member of the Peace Forces dies and there's another member present, the drones don't come. The Vam will ding me to explain why her vitals went dead. I'll just tell them I lost her in the woods and can't find her." I nodded to the black and bloody treeline that surrounded the cemetery.

"Thought of everything. Figures." He shook his head and grinned. "You're a good agent now that you're gone."

I glanced around. "Where's your preacher friend? I thought he'd be here to stop me."

Tommy shrugged. "He said I can handle the situation without his guidance. Said I'd do the right thing." He cocked the hammer.

"Unlikely, considering the way you unceremoniously left me for dead and stole my property."

"You ain't dead," he said.

"But that's always been the plan. When Will messes up or becomes useless to the cause, you dump him when he's still deep undercover and let your little girlfriend set him up like she set up Frank."

"That's not how we played it. You know that. I had your back the whole time. If anything bad happened, I'd have you extracted in a heartbeat."

"But you left me to die. That's something bad that had happened." I took the gun off Joy's forehead and aimed it at Tommy. "You wanted me to die."

He slightly bowed his head without taking his eyes off me. "That's the way we did it in the C.I.A. You get burned. You get left."

"But I'm not in the C.I.A. Never was." I frowned when something caught my attention. Something stuck on the end of my barrel. I tilted it up to get a better look.

Joy's Beastmark hung from the end of the barrel.

I turned and looked at her. A red spot on her forehead quickly formed in its place. Frowning, I looked at Tommy.

"She's been with us a couple of weeks. Daniel led her to the Lord, and she accepted Christ at Cardinal's Park." He smiled at her. "She's our sister now."

The deep feeling confirmed it. But I didn't accept it.

Joy wiped her nose and frowned in confusion. "Wait, he's a believer?"

Tommy nodded. "He's one of my best undercover men. Gave valuable intel that saved a lot of lives. Then you burned him by getting that flash drive. I had to cut him loose. Couldn't take any chances that the flash drive might lead your old friends to us."

"It can't be!" Joy's eyes widened. "He's the most evil person I've ever met!"

"Trust me, if it wasn't for his faith, he'd be dead and burning. No one really liked him, Mark or otherwise." Tommy lowered his weapon. "But he'll grow on you."

"Not likely." Joy rubbed her forehead.

"You'll need to let it happen. Especially since you two are working together." Tommy holstered his gun. "Trust me."

Joy took the fake Beastmark off my gun, put it in her pocket, and sighed. "It won't be easy. But if it's the Lord's will, I'll try."

"I'm not much for trying." I aimed the SIG back at her forehead. "You're about to meet your Savior."

This time, the deep feeling intervened. My left arm went numb, and I dropped the gun.

She looked confused when she picked up my fallen sidearm. Then she looked at Tommy.

"Give it back to him. He's whipped. God just showed him he's not going to kill you." He walked up to me and slapped me upside my head. "Nor me."

They walked to Joy's SUV and left.

Humiliation blanketed me as I held my gun in the cemetery. Alone. I holstered it and looked at Frank's headstone. "I bet you're laughing yourself stupid over this," I said, remembering Frank's favorite saying when his wife humbled him in front of everyone.

But I had no ability to laugh or self-deprecate. In fact, I had no one. Clay went to the Resistance with Tommy. Frank died. Then the deep feeling reminded me of Dad's sermon series on fellowship. *No Christian can be an island when God's in them.*

Sitting on the hood of the car, the rain slowly fell. Not caring about getting wet, I tried to think about my next move.

"You need to focus on the case. It's why God brought you back, you know," Daniel said, sitting in the passenger seat with the window down.

I turned and grumbled, "Now you show up. So why me? Why now? I had a gun on your new protégé. Don't you think you need to guard her a little better?"

He motioned for me to get in the car and shrugged. "She has her own guard. I have this deep feeling you need me. It'll be good for you. You're nearly out of the wilderness."

Not knowing what he meant, I went to the driver's side and opened the door. Trying to avoid talking about Joy, I tried to figure out a way to talk to him about Amelia, but my anger made it difficult to focus.

I just got behind the wheel when I realized.

"Hey, didn't I threaten you the last time we spoke?"

"You did, but I knew you didn't mean it." Contentment filled his smile.

I coveted that smile.

Strapping on my seatbelt, I looked at the cemetery.

"You are confused, but you cannot find the answers to your questions with the dead." He rolled up the window. "They can only come from God, the giver of life."

"You led her to Jesus." I didn't know if I felt disgusted or happy. My feelings felt like lightning bolts fingering out in all directions. I got tired of corralling them.

"She'd been searching for God before I met her." His contented smile returned. "Haven't you read her file on the Devil's computer? It's all there."

"I've been trying to keep Christians alive out west." I put the car in reverse and backed out of the parking spot. "It bothers me that you know things that are on the Beast."

"I know. It reminds you of Hectar. He does that to you all the time. I do it in jest. He does it as a power play to remind you of his standing in the world." He paused. "And to let you know where you stand with him."

I smiled as I turned the car around.

"But you already know this, too." His giggle almost made me smile, but my stubbornness didn't allow it.

After crossing the bridge, my anger started to return. The thought of Joy as a spiritual sister threw me off. She needed to die for what she did. Didn't she?

As if on cue, Daniel said, "Jesus never promoted murder to fight against tyranny. In fact, he went against the zealots who wanted to kill their Roman oppressors and make Him king. He always said it's not His time. You are trying to murder Joy for what you believe to be an injustice, but Jesus took her injustice on the cross when she gave it to Him. You must get this murderous plot away from you. It is consuming you so that God cannot use you. If you do not stop, He will take you home." His voice cracked. "It will be violent, and it will be bloody. Just like his coming judgment."

"It's hard to let something go when you know it's right." I scowled at the road.

"Right for God, or right for you?"

"Neither. It's just right. She committed first degree murder, and she got promoted. That might be right to the Antichrist, but not me. Even believers get the blade for murdering someone. It's about the consequences of the sin."

I mistook his silence for acceptance of my argument.

Then he spoke. "There is nothing about this government that is right, and you know it. Although she set Frank up, she realized her sin and gave it to God, who gladly forgave her. She repented. She'll never do it again."

I slammed on the brakes. "Zero consequences are what this government is all about. They only punish the innocent. But what about God's consequences for murder?"

"God told Isaiah that His way are not our ways. We have no right to determine who receives His consequences. You want blood for blood but remember what Christ said. 'Love your enemies.' Put this behind you or it will consume you. Remember, your end will be violent and bloody." He let that sink in. "And besides, she didn't commit the sin against you. She committed it against God and Frank. And I know they both forgive her. You have nothing against her to forgive. You are not her judge. That's why God is against you."

The silence lasted too long. The deep feeling beat me over the head with the truths God gave me through one of His chosen. I fought it by trying to find an argument that justified the actions I planned to take. Just before reaching the airport, Daniel motioned for me to stop.

"I will join you and our new sister in Christ to Springfield. I've been meaning to see an old friend, and you need looking after. But I know no one can see us together for your cover."

Then he wasn't in the car.

Stewing in my confusion, a thought came to me. With Daniel in Springfield, who'd talk to Amelia about Jesus. Being out of the Resistance, I didn't know their situation, and I knew they had no ability to focus on one person without taking the chance of exposure. A deep melancholy overcame me. I cared for Amelia, but it felt like God didn't have any plans to help her. At least, not now.

CHAPTER 13

The private jet felt a little too fancy for my taste, but I figured Joy thought it a little too ordinary. Joy's tardiness gave me hope that our little meeting at the cemetery scared her off, however the hope died when Joy's SUV pulled in front of the general aviation building. Although she looked out of sorts, she still tried to put on a strong front.

"It's only a three-hour drive to Springfield. Isn't this a little much?" I pointed to the plane.

"Probably." She walked to the door. "It will be faster, and we're losing valuable time." She smiled nervously when she turned to use her back to push the door and held it for me. "Let's catch a killer, brother."

My jaw clenched in anger and disbelief. Figuring she meant it as an olive branch, I kept a steely appearance and walked out the door. I fell behind on purpose to consider her calling me brother. It's common for Christians to call each other brother and sister. However, another major problem had to do with the fact that I conspired with Daria Petrovich to set Joy up for the guillotine. The deep feeling overwhelmed me with regret and the desire to right this wrong, which I fought.

Just before reaching the plane, I tabled the deep feeling until I had more information about Joy's sudden faith. When we reached the plane, I noticed Joy's Beastmark back in its original position, like it never peeled off. Although impressed, I knew Tommy's people included former Hollywood makeup artists and tech geniuses. Even in the Resistance she had pull.

We climbed aboard to find Jenny sitting at a small round table at the back of the plane, smiling.

"What's so funny?" I asked while reaching into a small fridge for a bottled water.

"You look comfortable for a criminal investigation." Jenny stood and gave me a hug. "Thanks for letting me get into the field. Bobby's not too happy to find out I'm the first choice."

"Bobby is better suited for crimes in the big city. But you're a country girl." I grinned and winked. "And if you don't like that excuse, I'll come up with a better one later."

She giggled, knowing that I favored her over Bobby.

Joy returned from the cockpit, pointed at my Vam, and sat with us. I stowed the Vam and my jacket containing the DRUID badge in a compartment near the front of the cabin.

"Don't worry about wandering eyes and ears on the plane. This is a safe place, and we can talk freely. The pilot can't listen in and won't come in unless there's an emergency." Joy pulled out a short stack of folders, then smiled at us like a proud mama hen.

Before I could roll my eyes, Daniel came from the rear of the plane carrying a tray of sandwiches and bags of chips. He sat the tray on the table and passed the food out.

"Okay, how did he get on the plane with no one raising an eyebrow?" I asked, trying not to glare at him.

"No one knows he's here." Joy had a matter-of-fact tone.

"I have my ways of getting into places I'm not supposed to." Daniel didn't brag.

I opened the sandwich and chips. Then I looked at Jenny and did the math. She smiled and shrugged. "Hey, big brother."

My heart nearly exploded. "Sister in Christ?"

"Yep." She followed it with a quick testimony of accepting Christ just after the sixth seal earthquake when she heard Daniel preaching in St. Louis near Busch Stadium.

"I didn't realize." I almost knocked my food off the table when I reached over and squeezed her hand. "Some detective I am."

Joy giggled. I had an intense desire to drop her with one punch, but Daniel read my body language.

"Let us pray before eating and discussing the case." He took mine and Joy's hands.

We joined hands and Daniel prayed over the food and for our

success in finding the killer and for God's protection over Christians all over the planet. Then he finished with a prayer of forgiveness that made the deep feeling bring the guilt of how my lack of forgiveness for a sin not committed against me had no place in my heart. Then I thought of Petrovich. The deep feeling made it clear that I needed to get out of my deal with her. But I still didn't know if I wanted out of it yet.

After the meal, Daniel excused himself to rest while we did our work.

"I just received word that the bodies, except for the heads, have been received at the Springfield lab." Joy gave me and Jenny each a folder. "If you look at page three, you'll see that Superintendent Evans has used the ICON database to complete a profile of the killer. I don't think this case will take too long. Especially after we input the CSU's findings."

"Not to be a naysayer, but it can take years to find guys like these. Bundy, BTK, even Dahmer took decades to find." Jenny frowned while reading.

"This seems to be a local who did this. And since the population of this area has the highest rate of disappearances since the murders." Joy's face went red. "Sorry, I'm still new to this. Since the Rapture and subsequent judgments from God, Springfield and its surrounding counties isn't a hotbed of activity."

"Except that the new bounty hunters have been exceptionally active in the Ozarks." I read the report. "We need to pay attention to both fronts. My superiors expect to spin this into the Antichrist's murder theory. If we make any wrong moves, it can mean the deaths of millions of believers. However, if we make it look like we are trying to subvert the Antichrist's regime, we may be on the chopping block ourselves. And Springfield isn't the dead little burg you believe it to be. My source says it's the Wild West out there. In fact, we need to be careful on all fronts."

Joy and Jenny took deep breaths. The reality of their spiritual decisions spilt into their physical worlds. I remember the same thing happened to me when Tommy trained me for undercover work. I felt a responsibility to make sure these two stayed aware of that. Any mistake and we'd see Jesus before His return.

After a long, awkward silence, Joy looked up from the report. "Any thoughts?"

Jenny closed her folder. "It's hard to say from my end until I see the evidence they've collected. If it's alright with you, ma'am, I'd like to go to the crime scene first to get the lay of the land. Try to get into the killer's mind. Then I'll do the same at the lab. Are the techs there on board with this?"

"They'll have to be. Since taking over this case, they know my orders and will comply. I guess you can go, though I'm not sure if it's the best use of your time. We'll go there first thing in the morning. We need some sleep." Joy looked at me. "Will?"

"Yeah, sure." I kept reading the file on what the Beast compiled. "Unless we find the heads, this case may never be solved. I don't care what Evans' report says."

"They're probably trophies. We'll find them when we find the killer." Joy read the report verbatim.

"I don't think so. Few serial killers kept trophies like that. Usually trinkets, maybe a finger or something seemingly insignificant. I think that when we find them, they will give us a better understanding of the killer, but there's still no guarantee that we'll find him before the end."

"How's that?" Jenny asked.

"Look at the placement of the body parts. They're spread throughout the field but still close enough to find them all in about a day. But the heads are somewhere else. Somewhere special. It's as if he hid them for a special purpose." I kept looking at the photos taken by the drone.

"Yes, as trophies." Joy's impatience gnawed at me. "ICON may be the tool of the Sovereign, I mean the Antichrist, but it's still a tool we can use to find the killer."

"It's still a computer. A tool that can be used up to a certain point. Then we'll have to use good old-fashioned police work to finish the investigation. Even Jenny can't completely rely on her testing devices to give her the answers to all the questions. She must consider witness statements and other human parts of the investigation to help create a timeline to allow us to follow the path of the killer."

Although I struggled with Joy's actions concerning Frank's death, I still hated the fact that she believed she had what it took to lead a murder investigation of a potential serial killer. Her dependence on the Beast made it obvious that her skills as an investigator lacked.

Joy's red face indicated her attempt to not lash out. "I am not a rookie, and you will not treat me as such. Even though we are on the same team spiritually, that doesn't give you the leeway to treat me like I'm incompetent."

"Then quit acting like this computer is the end all be all of investigations. We can use it to help, but it will always lead us in the wrong direction because those in power want this crime scene to say what they want it to say." I pointed to page five of the file. "Read that and tell me I'm wrong."

Both opened their files and read with Jenny the first to react. "Wow." Joy followed with the same.

"May I interrupt and ask what it says?" Daniel stood a couple of rows from us.

"The unsub has the psychological makeup of a Christian, making this a mission serial killer scenario. Investigators will find that the burial sites of the body parts follow a rigid pattern of Christian burial methods and are arranged in the shape of a Christian cross or an Ichthus fish. He believes that if he does this, it will absolve him of his murderous ways and to discredit the Sovereign's logical theory of the murders that took place before his glorious ascension to the throne." Joy almost choked out the last words.

The silence in the cabin overwhelmed the group. Joy and Jenny had another large dose of reality in a short time. I didn't like it because they needed to process so much in such a short time. Being the oldest Christian of the group, I knew they needed this extra time, but with a little over five years left, we all had to process quickly. For the first time since I met her, I felt sorry for Joy. The stress outlining her pretty face showed that the crossroads of faith and ambition of her job didn't meet her expectations. Just like me when I rose in the ranks of the police force.

"Will, can we talk?" Daniel pointed to the front of the cabin.

The darkness there made Daniel's outline seem cartoonish. His small stature, paired with his powerful stare, gave me pause. We sat beside each other in the first row, facing the cream-colored wall separating the cabin from the cockpit.

"I guess the reality check is necessary. In fact, I believe you didn't enjoy it like you might have earlier today." Daniel smiled without looking at me. "That is good progress. However, you need to understand that this isn't a replacement for letting go of the past. I know that the Holy Spirit is telling you she does not need your forgiveness for her part in Frank's death."

Frustration coursed through my mind. Joy still needed to pay somehow for committing this murder. Crime needs punishment.

"I feel your anger. It eats at your soul like a cancerous tumor. Remember, God has forgiven you for sins that you have never been punished for. Joy is under the same forgiveness. Give it to God to decide her consequences like He will for you. All you can do is the one thing that will hurt the most." He patted my forearm. "Love her like Christ loves her."

He got up, joined the others, and began preparing them for the hard decisions to come before the Glorious Appearing. He had offered a baton that I needed to take from him and pass to Jenny and Joy, but I sat there arguing with the deep feeling and watched the dark world go by outside the window.

Shaking myself from the mounting regret, I turned and looked at Joy. She had beauty, albeit hidden beneath coply ineptness and overly exerted ambition. She retrieved her Vam, put it on her forearm, and walked in my direction, as Daniel and Jenny cleaned the dinner trash.

"Nice Vam." I tried to sound friendly, which grated me to the core.

"Yes, it is. It has everything. I can go straight into ICON with a simple vocal command. It's also linked to my vitals, blood sugar, blood pressure, and all other medical testing with no need to draw blood. I can watch TV without paying and instantly see anything important in the news or at work." She sat where Daniel sat and leaned on my shoulder while pointing out all the bells and whistles. "And the best part is that if my life is in danger, drones will be sent to stop the person or people trying to hurt me."

Big brother, meet little sister.

But far more deadly.

I didn't show her my Vam which had more bells and whistles. Maybe Daniel's little pep talk helped more than I wanted to admit. The deep feeling tried to get me to feel better about it. But it's hard to get over the past and someone you trained yourself to hate so fast.

CHAPTER 14

Daniel walked off the plane and disappeared into a small crowd at general aviation in Springfield. He told us he'd catch up outside the Peace Forces HQ. We made our way to the oversized SUV waiting for us outside the terminal. Joy told me to drive, since I grew up here.

The drive from the airport to the hotel became a memory lane cruise. Just outside the airport, we passed the road that led to the big cemetery where my father had presided over many funerals. Then we passed the old golf course where Mom's friends unsuccessfully tried to get her to like the game. The black and green trees with the bloody greens and fairways looked more like a PGA nightmare than a weekend warrior's getaway.

Joy put us up at a motel on the north side of the city to get us closer to the crime scene but not too far from the Peace Forces HQ on Park Central Square. The woman at the front desk handed us our key cards with little eye contact, although her beautiful green eyes needed attention. Joy grabbed her leather briefcase and matching wheeled suitcase and went to her suite while Jenny and I went to the opposite side of the building where our single rooms faced the trash dumpsters.

After saying goodnight to Jenny, I swiped the door card and entered my room. A joke of a light barely lit up its corner at the far end of the room. The tattered orangish carpeting, almost smooth from time and cleaning, had the feel of an overused basketball I had as a kid. The king size bed looked like it had seen better days and too many visitors. I heard a spring groan under the weight of my travel bag. Although an improvement from where I slept the night before, the smell of the bison might've been better than the must, the dust, and an unfamiliar odor coming from the AC unit.

Logging into the Beast, I sat at the tiny table in a metal chair older than me. But the brown vinyl covered cushion provided a comfortable seat. I pulled the folder out and started at the beginning. Unfortunately, my mind wanted to think about my day instead. A habit Mom taught me.

The bison may have been the most entertaining, if a little alarming. But I remembered Dad and Mom talking about how the animals of the world will be more aggressive to the point of continual attacks on humans because of fear caused by the judgments and hunger. Dad said the Pale Horse judgment predicts this. I then realized that the bison had every intention of killing me if I stepped out the Humvee. Not so entertaining after all.

My fight with Tommy and confrontation with Daniel and Clay came next, and I let it be a memory without consideration. Then Colonel Lonergan had the potential of being a close ally, but I didn't trust General Sokolov. He wanted out of the country and didn't seem to care who he needed to run over to leave.

Daria Petrovich came next. Before I knew about Joy's faith, I made a deal with her. This woman clearly had deep connections within the government, making her risky to associate with and even more dangerous to line up against. And Hectar will always be Hectar. An enigma.

Then Daniel. I remember Dad preaching about men like him in a sermon not long before the Rapture. They had special, angelic protection. Anyone who attacked them immediately burst into flames and became ash just as quick. Although I admired him greatly, he still rubbed me the wrong way. Mainly because he chose Joy's side and not mine. I knew my heart and mind weren't in the right place. But how do you overcome such overwhelming feelings of anger and guilt? Especially when you're trying to stay on an island.

A soft knock sounded from the door, and Jenny's soft voice barely made it to me. I jumped up and jogged to the door.

"Sorry, but I don't enjoy being alone in a new place. Do you mind if I bore you for a while?" Her shy smile melted my anger.

Opening the door and stepping aside to let her in, Jenny

cheerfully walked in.

"Thank you. But is it okay if we are in a room alone?" Her innocent shrug made me laugh.

"It's all about the optics, right?" I giggled. "Although we aren't dating or married, I think it will be okay. Just don't tell Joy. There's no telling what she might say."

I put my Vam and jacket in the bathroom, turned on the obnoxiously loud exhaust fan, and closed the door. Jenny sat in the other chair at the table.

"Will, I'm struggling with being a Christian. I know that I'm forgiven, but…" She shrugged and put her fingers on her temples.

"I get it. You struggle with past sins." I leaned back and stretched. "My dad was a preacher. A real good one. He said the devil is always reminding us of who we were, whereas God tells us who we are and can be. If God can forgive and forget, we need to follow his example and to do the same, especially with ourselves."

The deep feeling beat me over the head with that one. My stomach twisted in knots. Practice what you preach, hypocrite.

She smiled. "That helps a lot."

After a few minutes of awkward silence, she turned the folder and read.

"How did you get in on the investigation?" She didn't look up.

"One of the forearms has a military tattoo on it. My superiors used it to get me in."

"Oh." She left it alone. "Do you buy all this that ICON spit out?"

I shrugged. "Not all of it, of course, but there is some good info that we can glean. We just need to be smart about it."

"How do you mean?" She raised her gaze to me.

"We need to be careful what information we use and how we use it. The Antichrist will do anything to make this ridiculous murder theory stick. He is clever and has surrounded himself with clever people. They will figure out how to spin this in their favor. So, we must do our best to make it as difficult for them as possible without casting a spotlight on ourselves."

Her shoulders dropped. "Sounds easy." She snarked.

"Same thing happened with the President's case."

Her eyes widened. "I didn't realize it."

"The government hired the assassin, and they paid him with a blade." I felt my eyes gloss in remembrance. "The senator and Frank got set up to fall with him."

"When did you become a believer?" She asked.

"Right after the Rapture." I looked out the window and remembered. "Dad's church is just up the road. Less than a mile. We'll pass it on the way to the crime scene." A wave of regret and nostalgia overwhelmed me. After the Rapture, I only visited our house twice. But I never considered going back to Dad's church.

"I bet your parents are proud of you for making the right decision. Even though it happened after the Rapture." I liked the way Jenny worked on the positive side of difficult topics.

"Never thought of it, to be honest." I shrugged.

"I looked a little at Revelation, and it's too scary to consider. Since I'm a newb and all." Her fearful smile made me feel sorry for her.

"Dad kept a journal of what he thought the Trib might be like. So far, he's been spot-on with everything. It's pretty scary stuff to read, but you need to get into it. These next five years will only get worse before Jesus comes back. God gave it to us to be ready for anything and everything." I fingered the edge of the folder.

"I don't know about you, but I feel kind of alone. Bobby, Ruth, and Evans have the Beastmark, and most of the police do, too. How do you deal with it?" Her eyebrows raised.

"Not very well. In fact, I'm the poster child of don't do it my way." I looked at her. "I harbor a lot of rage. Something God's been working on me."

"I saw a verse in Ephesians the other day." She frowned, "Let all bitterness, wrath, anger, clamor, and evil speaking be put away from you, with all malice."

The deep feeling had a field day with that. I wanted to lash out at her, but I saw an innocence in her I desired.

She seemed to understand my struggle and focused on the folder.

"If I'm guessing right, this is a single killer. What do you think?"

"I agree. Most serial killers are loners. The field feels personal, and dismemberment usually indicates rage. If two or more did this, the bodies would be torn up and not dissected."

"We'll get a better understanding once the local M.E. does the autopsies. Which reminds me. I forgot to ask Joy if they started yet."

"Not in the case file. Another feather in the cap of Evans." I flipped through the folder. "She's more interested in looking good for Joy than doing the work right. Anything for a promotion."

"It's all over HQ in St. Louis. Even the cops don't respect her." Jenny sighed.

"Frank told me that people like her only get in the way. And Joy is the same way…"

"Was the same way. We talked quite a bit today. She's different. I know this probably isn't what you want to hear, but it's true. She seems more focused on getting the case solved. Not to improve her status with the top brass, but she really wants to catch this guy."

"I trust you enough to not go against you. But until I see it…"

"A real Missourian. Show me." She laughed, stood up, and stretched. "I'm sorry for talking your head off. I bet you're exhausted from all that went on today." She made for the door.

"Not at all. It's nice to talk to someone about God. I need it just as bad as you."

She said good night and left.

After a quick shower, I laid on the bed staring at the water spotted ceiling. I needed to get over the anger at Joy, but I didn't want to. I fell asleep arguing with the deep feeling and getting nowhere.

CHAPTER 15

After a restless night, I woke up feeling like I hadn't slept in weeks. Pacing the floor, trying to get my wits about me proved impossible. The case loomed heavy on my mind, but the deep feeling gave the impression that the day would prove to be frustrating. I had only one case under my belt as lead, but I had plenty of experience with crime scenes and investigations during my time as a patrolman. I helped investigate two serial killers in Kansas City, but my role as support personnel mainly covered canvassing neighborhoods searching for potential witnesses. And adding Joy to the mix had the makings of a complete disaster.

The hotel had a small dining room for the continental breakfast. It had four scratch and dent tables, each with four mismatched chairs, and a buffet that looked worse than fast food fare, with one exception: real biscuits and sausage gravy. Something I haven't had since before I made it to St. Louis all those months ago. Being the first guest, I took more than my fair share and left everything else. After praying for my meal, Daniel sat beside me.

"Hello, Will. You look awful." He grinned.

It annoyed me he let the silence go too long, but my stubbornness knew no boundaries. I kept eating.

"That stuff will kill you." He pointed at my plate.

"Better that than him." I pointed at a portrait of the Sovereign hanging over the buffet.

Daniel's joyful laugh made me smile. "That's true."

Joy and Jenny came into the dining room and modestly filled their plates before joining us. Once seated, they both bowed and prayed.

Joy looked at Daniel. "I thought you wanted to keep your distance."

"The cook is outside smoking, and you are the only guests in the hotel right now." Daniel shrugged.

"So, I've been rethinking the case and reading the ICON report, and it got me wondering why it's important to go to the crime scene." Joy buttered a slice of wheat toast. "Especially her. The evidence is at the lab by now, and she needs to get started."

"We need to get a feel for how the killer operates. That field will tell us as much as the evidence. It will help Jenny better understand why the killer does what he does if she gets some dirt under her fingernails, so to speak." I took another bite. Not the best I've ever had, but not the worst either.

"I didn't read that in any of the crime scene investigation manuals." Joy widened her eyes like she struggled to believe someone went against textbooks.

"You can't teach instinct. Either you got it, or you don't."

My dig hit its mark. She took a sip of her overly sugared coffee.

"What's the plan for the day?" Jenny sipped her orange juice.

"After the crime scene, you need to go to the lab and get started. I'd like to get an ID on as many people as possible. And talk to the M.E. to see if he's found how the killer killed the victims." I scooped the extra gravy into my mouth.

"We need to interview the surrounding neighbors. That's investigating 101." Joy didn't look at anyone.

"The local cops will have already done that or will finish it up this afternoon. We'll get that from the lead when we get there." I tried not to roll my eyes.

"Investigators are required to complete interviews for thoroughness and accuracy." She finally stared at me as if challenging me.

"But lead investigators are required to interview persons of interest, suspects, or witnesses. We have none right now. We let the uniformed cops do the preliminary interviews to help us weed out the relevant from the irrelevant. That's in the textbooks, too."

She didn't respond.

I drank the last of my coffee, threw away my trash, and walked to the SUV.

Leaning on the fender and considering my strategies for the investigation, Daniel walked out and leaned on the door beside me.

"You have a plan for the investigation?" His attempt at deescalating the situation fell short.

"Start with the crime scene, put the evidence into a reasonable timeline, and go from there. Nothing out of the ordinary." I shrugged and toed the broken asphalt.

"You seem to have solid instincts for this job."

"It's funny you say that. When I investigated the assassination, it felt like red flags waved in the back of my head when something seemed out of place, or I knew someone lied, or if something connected with something else. But when I went into the military and saw the battlefield before me, it seemed to change to this deep feeling." I hesitated, trying to decide if I wanted to say the rest. "The problem is that the flags only pertained to the investigation, whereas the feeling is always there. Funny how people change."

"That's not just instinct, Will. That's the Holy Spirit revealing things to you. You've allowed Him into your life and He's there helping you. The more you trust Him, the more He will connect with all of you, so long as you let Him. In intense situations, like battle, you are looking for His guidance to survive and win. The Holy Spirit connected with your instincts to help guide you to those victories, whether on the physical battlefield or spiritually against the wiles of Satan. You have a new instinct that shows God is with you, but you need to act on it. I believe He is telling you to get past this petty, vindictive spirit in you and get on with your life. Embrace your new spiritual sister. It will also help with the investigation."

His words cut deep. The deep feeling screamed AMEN with every word he said.

But Daniel didn't know what I had done with Petrovich. Or did he? But the more I thought about it, the more it made sense to keep her close to better understand her plans and strategies. The deep feeling gave the impression that I still needed to tread lightly.

Taking a deep breath, I noticed how the coolness of the morning seemed to have a calming effect on me. The dew on the blackened landscape gave it a ghostly aura. Oddly enough, it looked hauntingly beautiful.

"That conversation back there seems to happen a lot with you two." He put his thumbs in his pockets, letting the other fingers drum his thighs.

"Honestly, if it didn't happen, Jesus will come back that second." I almost grinned.

He chuckled. "It must be difficult to work with someone with little to no experience."

"It's not that her inexperience is the problem. It's the know-it-all attitude. Don't get me wrong, I had the same problems as a rookie, but I never challenged the lead investigator. I knew they had the experience and know-how, otherwise they'd be doing something else. But she has the authority with no experience and still challenges me because of our past. She will try to bulldoze me at every angle of this investigation because we are not in the same department and she's trying to get the glory." I sniffed.

"Maybe she feels threatened by you. When it comes down to it, Will, you are an intimidating man. You're blunt and to the point, and your physical stature makes me feel small. Plus, I know your military background is nothing to be ignored." He sighed and turned to face me. "Will, like it or not, you two are spiritual siblings in a world ruled by the powers of evil. I know God put you two together for a reason, but if you're going to keep with this childish act of vengeance, you'll lose. Remember, violent and bloody."

He turned to walk away.

"Where are you going?"

"To meet my friend. We are going to preach downtown this afternoon. I'm meeting him so we can plan our sermons." He turned, then stopped and turned back. "By the way, the next judgment will take place this week. Remember, it is a burning mountain cast into the sea, turning a third of it to blood."

"The Yellowstone Supervolcano." I stood up straight. "You mentioned it in South Dakota. Will it affect us here?"

"Not like the blood storm. But it will affect your stomach if you like seafood." He turned and left.

CHAPTER 16

Not wanting to cloud my mind with the past, I didn't slow down when we passed my old church. I just pointed it out. Jenny asked a couple of questions, but Joy didn't look up from her Vam. She only looked up once to argue that I took the wrong route to the crime scene. Not paying her any attention, I went the faster way. After passing through Willard, I turned onto Highway 123, then to a farm road that went straight to the Phenix Quarry near the crime scene.

Memories of taking my girlfriend on those back country roads to find a quiet place to make out didn't fill my mind with emotions of young love, but of sinful pleasures that made me miss the Rapture. But her name came back to me. Liberty "Libby" James. Her blond hair and blue eyes matched a curvy figure that drove me crazy. And she liked me. Our dates always turned physical. So, when Dad preached against sex outside of marriage, I tried hard not to giggle or smile. Thinking back to those sermons now, I hated that arrogant kid.

Pulling into the entrance of the crime scene, it looked the same as the rest of the area. A burned and bloody hayfield. The rolling hills had at one time been a beautiful green or gold, depending on the hay crop, until God's previous judgment. It looked to be about forty acres, with a large stand of hedge apple and black walnut trees that ran along the southern border. The trees burned and bloody, members of the unfortunate one-third. It felt and smelled like South Dakota, ash and stale blood.

When we got out, Jenny went straight to the first hole in the field and began talking to the officer standing by it. Joy pointed out the cop in charge and led me to her. She didn't wear a Peace Forces uniform, and her conservative black pantsuit with a yellow blouse made me think she didn't always dress this way. Her dark green rubber boots, most farmers wore during the rainy season, stood out. Maybe she left her good shoes in the car, not wanting them blackened by the field.

"I'm Detective Tara Gallway. I understand you're taking over." She looked at me with disdain.

"Yes, we are taking over the investigation." Joy's red face made me grin.

Gallway lost a little color in her face. "Apologies, Commander. I didn't know."

"Let's get on with the crime scene. Tell us what you know." I didn't have time for the typical brown-nosing after saying something stupid routine.

"The night before last, we received a call from the neighbor." She pointed to the west side of the field. "Said he saw some mounds that looked suspicious. They speculated it to be a stash of illegal contraband because they saw no one digging them in the daytime. One of the local cops came and thought little of it. We have a lot of people hiding guns, drugs, and food out this way. When he dug beside the first mound, he found a foot. Then he dug more and found more. All left feet. Since then, we've uncovered the rest of the bodies except for the heads, which we are still looking for."

"How many victims have you counted?" I asked.

"Eleven." Her demeanor went stolid, like she might know some of them.

"Have you used cadaver dogs?" Joy had been furiously taking notes and never looked up.

"Can't. They are useless here." Tara looked bewildered at Joy.

"The trained dog can detect…" Joy started.

"Nothing with the remnants of the storm still buried in the ground." I finished. "In the field, we had to send back our scent dogs because they struggled to track anything in this muck."

Joy went red again.

"How much of the field have you searched so far?" I asked.

"A little over half. We're hoping to finish tomorrow. We have some more Peace Forces personnel coming in this afternoon." Tara said.

Looking at the end of the field, I nodded towards the trees. "Have you looked there yet?"

"The drone footage shows nothing out of the ordinary. But we've been having trouble seeing anything conclusive because everything looks the same. Burnt." She shrugged.

"We had the same problem out west. The computers struggled to find well-camouflaged people and vehicles. If the killer planted the heads there, he probably did his best to keep them hidden from the air and the ground." I looked at Tara. "How fast can you get there?"

"The path we're taking will make it the end of the line. Probably sometime tomorrow." I knew she wanted to go straight there. "It might be where the killer buried the heads, but we need to keep to procedure. Don't want to be stomping on potential evidence."

"That can never happen, detective." Joy smiled. "It's nice to be around someone who understands and follows procedure."

I let the comment roll off. "Has the M.E. given you any good ideas?"

"Not yet. He thinks this is a dumpsite. No surprise there. But it might take some time to find where the killings took place. That storm a few months ago contaminated this crime scene worse than any I've seen or studied." Tara sighed and stared into the distance. "We may never know what happened."

"We can't let that happen. You will be in support while Will and I take the lead. We value your experience, and I want you to know that we won't overlook your input," Joy said.

Tara's icy demeanor seemed to soften. Maybe Joy had her uses after all.

"What are the locals saying?" I asked Tara.

Tara failed to hold back a grin, then shrugged. "Hardly anything because there's hardly any people around, before or after the murders. Since then, the population has been sparse at best. Now that Walnut Grove's turned into a lake and Ash Grove is a ghost town, you can almost count the population of families in the area on two hands."

"Lake?" I asked in an incredulous tone.

"Crazy, isn't it? After the earthquake and aftershock, Stockton Lake emptied, and Walnut Grove dropped into the ground several feet. Then water came up from somewhere near the center of town, and the newly formed valley filled up. Now it's Lake Walnut Grove." She looked deep into my eyes. "You from there?"

"No, I lived on the north side of Springfield. We went through Walnut Grove to go fishing in Stockton a lot before I went into the Marines." Although we stood about five miles from the old town, I still looked north. "A lot of memories in that little town."

"Let the nostalgia go, Will. We need to get started." Joy's snark brought me back to reality.

"Is the neighbor who reported the scene close?" I asked.

Tara pointed to the onlookers. "I knew you'd want to talk to him, so I arranged for him to be here."

"Thanks." I turned to Joy. "Walk the field with Tara and let her show you where the killer buried body parts. Maybe you can see a pattern."

"I have everything I need in the drone footage." She tensed up.

"Again, get a feel of the land, get a feel for the killer." I walked to the group. "I'll talk to the neighbor."

Joy grumbled and went with Tara to the hole where Jenny stood beside, looking into it and listening to the tech Jenny met earlier.

"Who reported this?" I asked the group.

They pointed to a man in the middle. Nodding him to a place away from the crowd and cops, I quickly walked to beat him to the point. I wanted to see his body language before talking to him. He wore bib overalls with a long-sleeved shirt that might've been white when it was new. He walked with gentle confidence. Nothing guilty about him. But they thought the same about Ed Kemper and look how that ended.

"Hello." I used my friendly tone.

"Howdy." He stuck out his hand. "Timothy Weaver, but everyone calls me Tim."

"Nice to meet you, Tim. I'm Will Thomas." I shook his hand.

"Detective, how can I help?" His slow but determined voice grumbled.

"I'm not a detective, just a military liaison trying to help." I mirrored his voice to let him know I meant no harm when I showed my DRUID badge.

His eyes widened just enough.

"Tell me what you told them." I leaned against a metal fencepost.

He scratched his head, tipping his well-worn trucker's hat that revealed a receding hairline. "The other night, I walked the fence line checking the barbed wire. We had a stubborn calf testing it." He pointed to the clearing near the first hole. "I had stopped to watch the sunset. When I had an eyeful, I turned and saw that mound. I don't know why it stood out to me, but then I noticed another one, then another. Before I knew it, I'd counted five mounds. Now, I knew the owner of this land was one of the murder victims, and he had no family that I'm aware of. And he didn't waste his land digging holes. He grew fescue on this parcel. So, I knew that he didn't make the mounds.

"I figured that a smuggler or someone of that kind had contraband stashed there. So, I did my civic duty and called the police." He turned to the scene and pointed to where Jenny and Joy talked to the tech. "I watched that poor kid dig up that mound. He turned his flashlight on it when he hit something, looked down hard, then vomited by the hole. That's when I knew it had to be something worse than drugs or guns.

"The other police officer asked me several times if I'd seen anything unusual on this land, but like I said, not many people come here during the day that I've seen, and even fewer come at night from what I can hear. But we hear the occasional vehicle driving down the roads." He shrugged and straightened his hat. "Other than that, that's all I know."

He lied about something. But not the murders. The deep feeling led me to believe it had to do with something other than the body parts. So, I let it go for the time being.

"I know you told this several times, but I appreciate it. I'm originally from Springfield, but my dad was a preacher in a church just outside of town near Willard."

"Ozark Mountain Community?" I almost missed his slight grin.

"The very same. I just got back from the west. They called me in to help investigate."

"You're the guy who solved the old president's assassination." He smiled without joy.

"That's why they called. Otherwise, I'd be chasing Christians all over the Rockies."

The glint of anger crossed his face but went away just as fast. Then I knew. He's a Christian. Time for me to back off.

"Tim, if I have any more questions, I'll get ahold of you. Alright?"

His smile didn't welcome. "Anything I can do to help."

We shook hands, and he left. I decided I needed Daniel and his friend to find out if he held back anything else.

Joy and Jenny stood in front of our SUV. After I told them some of what I found out, I asked them what they discovered.

"First of all, these local yokel cops need some retraining. It's as if they've never read a textbook in their lives. Their interviewing methods are atrocious. I mean, they talked to the people more than questioned them like they're visiting grandma and y'all." Her twang left a lot to be desired.

"Easy there, Joy. Remember, these are my people. They're more willing to talk in conversational tones and will give more information without a cop breathing down their necks. City folk are too used to talking to the cops and are more able to give information when given direct questions. You must know your audience. Otherwise, they clam up on you and nothing important will ever surface." I watched Tim lead what seemed like his family over a small hill.

"I guess the brilliant minds of law enforcement never reached the sticks." Her arrogant look needed shoved down her throat.

"They have, but you don't know how to read. Knowing who you're questioning is Interviewing 101." I turned to Jenny before Joy responded. "How about from your end?"

"Not a lot. Just tag, bag, and send to the lab. The CSU tech is taking soil samples from each hole. The interesting thing about this is the killer dug the hole about four or five foot deep, like he knew how many he was going to bury. Then he placed the body part in the hole, covered it with lime and dirt, but just deep enough to save room for the next victim. They are layered instead of being spread out." Jenny's cute face when in deep thought made me smile.

"Does the tech seem competent?" I asked.

"He seems to know what he's doing, but he's too far down the chain of command to know what the higher-ups are thinking. I remember those days. Smart enough to collect but dumb enough not to be part of the conversation." Jenny looked at him like she didn't want him to hear. "But he did say that the M.E. mentioned that these killings have been going on for at least a year. Unfortunately, he didn't elaborate."

"Anything else?" I asked them.

"Detective Gallway came back and mentioned a local business owner near the lake known for hearing the local gossip. I told her we'd question him if we think he's relevant."

"It's something to consider," I said, getting into the driver's seat. "Local scuttlebutt can be helpful."

As I pulled out of the field, I told Joy and Jenny I needed to make a pit stop.

CHAPTER 17

The old church had seen better days with the roof and walls showing signs of damage from the quakes. With all signs tore down or missing, and the steeple ripped off, the church looked like a red brick schoolhouse from long before the Trib. Graffiti covered everything and said horrible things about God and Christians. The worst mentioned Dad by name. My gut tightened wanting to find the scum and send them to Hell. But the deep feeling reminded me that Jesus wanted all to come to faith. Even the scummy ones.

Taking my Vam and jacket off, I motioned the others to do the same. Once far enough away from the SUV, I told them I wanted a few minutes to myself before talking about the case. Jenny and Joy walked to the playground near the entrance.

The smashed glass door had an opening big enough for me to slide through. Knowing there'd be no lighting, I had pulled the flashlight from the back of the SUV. The powerful beam lit the foyer, and the memories overwhelmed my mind. The red carpeting and wood panel walls brought back the past when Dad preached those sermons all those years ago. The overturned table that held an assortment of Bible tracts and other church literature lay on its side with the moldy pamphlets teaching people how to accept Christ as their Savior scattered about.

Entering the sanctuary, where I had the chance to miss the hellish last couple of years, overwhelmed me. Sitting in my old spot, I tried to regain my composure. However, it left me when I thought about how I had acted and ignored God's invitation sitting in that very spot. A feeling of comfort came over me when I saw the wooden cross on the wall behind the old pulpit. An old man, who helped start the church, built it so people saw the cost of salvation. It gave me the hope I hadn't looked for since getting on my knees in Mom and Dad's empty house just after the Rapture. Then I thought of Libby.

We used to hold hands and pass notes on that back pew during the services with Dad preaching those important words. If I only paid attention to Him and not her. I didn't blame her. It's all on me. Plus, she went in the Rapture. At least one of us paid attention to God's calling.

A memory pushed its way to the front of my mind about the day I decided I wanted to marry her during a revival. The visiting preacher had been shaming us kids into staying pure for the Lord, and I knew that ship had sailed for us. But I paid attention when he began talking about marriage. Although he talked more about staying a virgin until the wedding night, I locked onto how he described his marriage to his wife of over forty years. Looking at Libby, I knew I wanted to spend at least forty years with her. Unfortunately, I didn't get the chance to go on one knee and propose like I had planned. A year later, we ended the relationship when Libby went to college in Joplin on a volleyball scholarship, and I enlisted in the Marines when the war in the Middle East broke out and the U.S. sent troops to help Israel.

The deep feeling told me to get over the past and get on with the now. I sat there for a while longer to collect myself before rejoining the others. The walk outside brought me back to reality to help focus on the case.

Joy and Jenny swung on a swing set, giggling like little girls.

"Why did we stop here? Did you think a lot here?" Joy asked while I walked to them.

"This is where my dad preached. I grew up in that church." I pointed at the building.

She slowed the swing.

Standing by them with my hands in my pants pockets, I said, "I'm the first one to swing on that."

"I didn't know you're that old." Jenny laughed. Joy snorted.

"I guess I am. Actually, I helped Dad and Frank build it. They let me be the first."

Joy's smile left. The pain returned. I didn't mean for that to happen. But I didn't apologize. She needed the reminder.

She stopped swinging but stayed seated. Jenny kept going.

"Everything okay?" Jenny asked, squinting the sun from her eyes.

"Dealing with some ghosts of the past." I shrugged. "You guys solve the world's problems?"

"Hardly." Joy said.

I looked around, taking in the scenery that reminded me of the days when I had a chance. "The witness is a Christian."

"How do you know?" Joy challenged. "Only the witnesses, like Daniel, can tell."

"You don't need spiritual eyes like theirs to see what's in front of you." I meant it as an insult. "The way he acted. He kept things general. Usually, that means he knows more than he's willing to give. But when I mentioned chasing Christians all over the Rockies, he accidentally showed his anger. I want to go back to the field, maybe tomorrow, and bring Daniel and his friend to sniff around."

"Why Daniel?" Jenny asked, still swinging.

"He'd get Tim and his people talking. I showed my DRUID badge to Tim to see where he landed. They'll clam up the minute they see us." I pointed at me and Joy.

"Will you have Daniel tell them the truth about us?" Joy asked, wiping dirt from her high heel.

"No, it's too dangerous. But I want to see if he'll talk to Daniel about the case."

"You think he knows who did it?" Jenny stopped swinging and let her feet dangle.

"Not sure. Tim might've already told me everything he knows, but we can't find that out without Daniel."

"Let's get Daniel, go there, then visit the store owner Detective Gallway mentioned at the scene." Joy stood and started for the SUV.

"We need to get Jenny back to the lab, see if the techs have anything new, and get settled in ourselves. Besides, it's best to let Tim and his people stew for a while. Like God, you gotta let the case come to you when it's time." I heard Frank in my voice. One of the first lessons I learned from him. "We'll visit the store owner when it's time."

Joy stood still and stared like she wanted to challenge me. "We need to get some traction in this case as soon as possible. The eyes of the government are on us. The sooner we find the killer, the sooner we can get them off our backs."

"I get that, and I agree. However, cases like these don't get solved fast, if at all." I leaned against the swing support pole. "I want to get this right, and I want to do my best to make it as hard as possible for the Antichrist to use this for his plan. If they spin this right, more Loyalists will become bounty hunters. If we can at least slow this down a bit, the Resistance can get more believers to safety. And people like Daniel and the other witnesses can get more people to the Cross to make their final decision."

Joy looked down in deep thought. "Is it hard for you to remember your faith? I find it difficult to remember that I have new priorities."

"Me too." Jenny stood and dusted off her jeans. "It's like I can't focus on my Christian priorities because I'm spending so much time trying not to get caught."

"Welcome to the world of espionage." I remembered Tommy telling me that. "We can't tell the world about Christ. Our job is to help those who preach the Word, except for the witnesses, by obtaining all the intel we can get to keep them out of harm's way."

"But we're not in the Resistance." Jenny stood by Joy.

"Neither am I." I shrugged.

"Tommy recruited me, but I told him I'd have to think about it." Joy kept looking down and kicked at the burned grass. "After what happened with you, I'm not sure if I can handle it."

"What happened to you?" Jenny nodded at me.

I told her the whole story. Left nothing out. When I got to Frank, Joy walked away. The deep feeling shot a wave of remorse through me for the way I said it. So, I said that she did it before getting saved loud enough for Joy to hear.

"Sounds like this Tommy is hard core." Jenny's eyes widened.

"Ex-C.I.A. Taught me everything I know about spying."

I watched Joy return. Eyes red with regret.

"What was your dad like behind the pulpit?" Joy's soft voice sounded sweet.

But it hit me wrong. "We need to get Jenny to work."

Joy didn't deserve those intimate details yet.

CHAPTER 18

Coming down Booneville Avenue brought back memories of flea markets and antique shops Mom and Grandma drug me through twice a year. The smell of stale dust, musty furniture, and sketchy buyers and sellers invaded my nasal memory of the shop owner who helped me start a baseball card collection that I later sold for the down payment on my first car. Joy and Jenny discussed the Sovereign's speech in positive affirmations in case the Beast picked up our conversation on our Vams.

The parking lot across the street behind the old DMV had a sign claiming it for authorized personnel only. The attendant gave me a nervous side-eye when I used my ID badge to get in and we parked near the corner of Booneville and Olive. As we walked across Olive, I noticed the tunnel that separated the old Heers building and the former DMV, which was blocked by a chain-link fence and two armed guards. The sign above it said BOUNTY ENTRANCE.

"Every city has at least one, now." Joy's face lost color. "From what I've read on ICON, the local bounty hunters bring suspected Christians and non-Loyalists in stock trailers."

"Seriously?" Jenny whispered.

"They make it a spectacle on the local news." Joy led us to the other side of the DMV building. "Sick, right?"

The earthquakes didn't affect the buildings as much as I thought they might, and the central area where the buildings face brought no memories or nostalgia. A bleacher section had replaced the art piece that kids used to play on. They cleared the rest of the area to add more seating, except for the triple fountain. However, the water didn't shoot up anymore. The top fountain had a large stage covering the basin, with two guillotines with blood-stained blades.

Then I saw the small sign signifying that the first quick draw shootout had taken place on the square between Wild Bill Hickock and Davis K. Tutt on July 21, 1865. I told the two that the city used to stage a dramatization of it every year on that day. But I only saw it once when I was ten, and then only by accident because Dad had to get tags for the family car. Dad used it as a teaching moment and said that it reminded him of what the Bible said about nothing new under the sun. Violence struck everywhere at all times.

Joy pointed to the former DMV building. "Jenny, that's where you go. Third floor. Talk to the CSU supervisor, Dr. Chad Taylor. He knows you're coming."

"Get a quick rundown of the scene and what they've found out so far, talk to the M.E., then report to us before you get too deep into your work." I said and winked at her.

Jenny smiled, winked back, and quickly went inside.

"Why did you do that?" Joy asked, while taking me to another corner of the square.

"We need to know things as quick as they come up. And Jenny will need to get over her first impression of new surroundings and coworkers by venting a little… or a lot." I stopped before entering the building in front of me.

"What's the matter?" Joy stopped and sighed.

The Peace Forces HQ didn't have the extravagance of the St. Louis HQ. As part of the square, it felt trapped in its insignificant corner. But I knew the history of that corner.

"It's the old Fox Theater. Dad told me about it. Of course, it was already something else by the time I came around, a museum of some sort, if a remember correctly." I put my hands in my jacket pockets, finally having something to reminisce.

Joy rolled her eyes. "If this is the way you're going to be the entire investigation, I have just one comment. Save it for someone who cares." She walked into the building.

Then I remembered another reason I wanted to kill her.

HQ looked and felt antiseptic. The taupe walls paired with cheap white tile flooring that Joy's heels clacked on gave more of an old doctor's office feel than law enforcement. The desk sergeant barely looked in our direction when we signed in and mindlessly pointed to the right hallway and told us to go all the way down to find our offices. Joy acted as if she had no interest in her surroundings while we passed through the bullpen filled with junkies, prostitutes, and other sundry criminals. The Peace Forces' officers and administrators looked at us for a brief minute and then returned to their respective duties. No one approached us to kiss up or ask if we needed help. In fact, everyone gave the impression of indifference.

We reached a pair of offices that contained the same basic spartan design. A desk, a chair, a filing cabinet, and nothing else. But at least the white walls held no appeal.

Joy looked around and sniffed her derision. "It'll take getting used to for me, but it might be perfect for you." I noticed the smirk.

"Won't be in here long enough for it to matter." I sat my messenger bag on the desk and sat. "Once you get settled, we need to get a game plan together while we wait for Jenny."

She walked out. I heard a bag hit the floor, and a briefcase hit the desk, followed by an office chair's wheels squeaking towards me.

"That was fast." I grinned.

"Like you said, we don't have a lot of time." She raised her eyebrows when she sat. "So?" She opened her notebook and Vam and sat them on the desk.

Leaning back in my chair, I stared at the wall behind her and collected my thoughts. Once a decision came to mind, I opened my messenger bag, put my Vam on the desk, and logged into the Beast.

"The case file is a little lean, but that's to be expected since we just got started. But something's been nagging at me since I first saw the pics and drone coverage. And even more so since everything but the heads has been located." I swiped the screen that floated above the Vam to send the picture of the field on the wall beside us.

"What's that?" She looked at me with a look of innocence that reminded me of most of the rookies I've been around. That and she looked adorable, which threw me for a second.

"What's the purpose of dismembering the victims?" I stood and walked to the picture.

"You mean motive?" She scoffed. "Will, our job is to find the evidence, build a timeline, and figure out who is the killer. Motives are for the lawyers, tribunals, and audiences." She spouted it straight from the textbook.

"No, not motive." I turned the screen. "If there is a pattern, the computer will eventually spit it out. But look at the report."

"The conclusion from ICON reads *Random*." She frowned. "But that's not what the reporters are saying on the news feed."

I shrugged and mouthed, "They're lying."

"So, what do we do about that?" She pointed at the picture.

"Dismemberment is usually one of three signs. The first is to get away with the murder. Make it harder for the police to find the evidence. No body, no crime. But here, all the body parts are in the same section of the field, so he's clearly not trying to hide the evidence. The second is to tell a story or make some sort of point. But the computer hasn't deciphered anything to that effect. So why the dismemberment?" I looked at Joy staring at the computer screen.

"This feels like a lesson, which greatly demeans me." The fire that I despised returned to her. "I may not have the experience of training that you do, but I am a competent cop. Don't play games with me. Do you know?"

I sat back, feeling the same rage as I did so many months ago, which I enjoyed too much. "Honestly, I'm not sure. But I remember reading about dismemberment also being about rage, the third reason. Whether at the victim or society, the killer doesn't believe killing is enough."

"But the computer profile calls the murderer a mission serial killer. He's getting rid of people he finds undesirable."

"That may be true, but most mission killers like to preach their beliefs through the act of killing," I said.

"So, this isn't just a story." She turned her attention to the screen. "It's what, a rage sermon?"

She hit me between the eyes. "That maybe it. Good job rook."

"That's also demeaning." She looked up from the screen. Her green eyes blazed into me, and I loved it.

I stared at her with my best steely gaze. "Get used to it. Until this case is solved, you're nothing but a snot-nosed rookie. And I'll treat you just like Frank treated me."

The pain returned to her countenance, but I wanted her to feel it. And I wanted her to know that as long as we worked this case together, I had the lead. As for our past, I had the high ground.

Jenny walked in and looked for a chair. She walked out and returned with one. Probably stole it from the breakroom near my office.

"I've seen worse, but at least the people are rude." Jenny blew her bangs.

"Territorial, just like someone I know." I smiled and let her rage.

She spent at least five minutes complaining about the archaic machinery, then did another ten on how everyone acted as if she didn't exist until she tossed a stapler at the head of the department, just missing his head.

"So, no new information on the case?" Joy's devious grin drew slowly across her face.

It felt good that I didn't have to hold back my laughter.

Jenny's sheepish smile deescalated her tantrum. "Not much new stuff. It's going to take a while to get ID on the victims. Prints are either scrubbed, or decomp is making it impossible. DNA will take a while for the same reason. But we have a tentative timeline. What's interesting is that…"

"He's been killing since before the blood storm, but after the murders." I said, looking at the top of the desk.

"How did you know?" Joy and Jenny sounded like twins.

I tapped the Vam, put the photos of the holes on the wall, and pointed it out.

"The holes are deep enough to see the red stained dirt from the storm from a couple of months ago. See how the dirt goes from dark red to brown? The depth of the dig suggests the killer has been doing this for quite some time. Plus, not all the body parts are blood-stained. A few of the skeletal remains are clean."

Jenny's eyes lit up. "It's the same with the dirt in between the body parts. In fact, the M.E. told me it's been easier to put the bodies back together because of it."

"And since the owner is a suspected murderer or murder victim, I believe the killer didn't start killing until after the murders." I sat back down.

"What if the owner didn't work his land much?" Joy asked.

"Tim said the land has been used to grow fescue, but not since the murders. If he had people doing the work for him, or if he rented the land, it still proves my point that it had to have happened after the murders, since no one has reported the mounds until now."

"He's right." Jenny jumped in. "The body parts buried last are not red like those at the bottom. They soaked it in, whereas the newer parts show little to no sign of soakage."

"So, he's been at it no more than two years?" Joy started writing.

"Yes, and once we get the victims identified, we might better understand the rage sermon." I sat back and considered it.

"Rage sermon?" Jenny asked.

"I thought the killer might be preaching through the dismemberments." Joy's matter-of-fact tone surprised me. "And he's angry."

Jenny sat back and stared at the pics on the wall. "Interesting. It's like he's trying to get the world to see things his way."

"The problem is that he might have to actually tell us the reasoning, even if we find him," I said. "The same thing happened to several serial killers I read about. They had to spell it out after they went to prison."

"I guess it's time to get back to those fun people." Jenny stood and stretched. "And maybe a round of apologies for the way I left things."

"Don't," I said. "They'll use it against you the whole time you're here. Let them fear you a little. Joy, call them up at the end of the day and put the fear of God in them for treating her that way. That'll get them to fall in line when we need it."

Joy's cocky smile told me she liked the idea. "Sounds good to me."

Jenny blushed. "I'm not sure about this, but I'll follow orders." She saluted.

"Before you go back to work, let's grab a bite to eat. We passed an old Chinese place I've forgotten about on our way here," I said, standing and stretching.

They agreed, and we left.

CHAPTER 19

As a mainstay of the square for as long as I knew, The Riksha Restaurant stood unassumingly on the northeast corner of Olive and Booneville. In fact, Joy said that she didn't even notice it on the way to HQ. The smell of cashew chicken, dumplings, and egg rolls exited the establishment when I opened the door to let the two enter. We looked around to find a place to sit when I saw a familiar face peeking around a corner near the back of the dining area and waving us to him.

Daniel ushered us into a small room with newly painted walls that didn't overtake the smell of the food. We sat at a round wooden table while he closed the door and joined us.

"The owners are believers who turned this into a private room for Christians to talk freely. It is soundproof." He looked around approvingly.

"How did you find this out?" Jenny smiled.

"The friend I came here to see. He'll be here soon. I wanted to introduce you to him." Daniel opened his menu then looked at me. "Will, this is your hometown. What is this cashew chicken I've been hearing about?"

Joy and Jenny frowned at each other like they'd never heard of it themselves.

"It's the official dish of Springfield, like toasted ravioli is to St. Louis. But I don't suggest trying it here. They may not use the original recipe. The place that invented it is still not too far from here. I want to take you there for your first try. I've had just about everything else, and it's good."

The owner came in from the back door and took our orders. Daniel ordered sesame chicken for him and his friend. Joy and I had the general chicken extra spicy. Jenny stared at the menu for a long time and decided on shrimp lo Mein, making me think about the next judgment. Everyone had water, and we agreed to share some dumplings. The owner just nodded while taking our orders and quickly disappeared.

Daniel asked about the investigation.

"Too early to tell," I said. "We're just getting started..."

"Joy thinks the killer is preaching a rage sermon." Jenny cut in like a schoolkid who knows the answer.

Daniel frowned. "I'm not sure I like that analogy. Preaching a sermon doesn't include dismemberment. And rage can only be preached against."

"Sorry, Daniel." Jenny said, shifting nervously in her seat.

"But it's the truth." I cut in. "Many serial killers use their victims to preach their ideology. Either they use the way they kill or the way they dispose of the body to speak to a specific group of people or to society. The ideology of a psychopath or sociopath is their reason for doing what they do. Ed Kemper admitted he told his mother to shut up through the women he killed until he finally shut her up himself. And it's up to us to figure this guy's ideology to find him and get him in prison as fast as possible."

The owner brought in the water and dumplings.

"So, what you're saying is that he uses his victims as part of the sermon by physically showing what he's trying to say to the masses.?" Daniel took a sip of his water.

"Not just part, but it's the whole sermon. And the first thing we know what he's saying is that he's angry about it. The dismemberment is a sign of rage both to the individual and to the group." I put a straw in my water glass.

The backdoor opened, and a large man entered the room. He had a friendly bearing with intense dark eyes, a dark beard, and a thick, disheveled head of hair.

Daniel quickly stood and hugged the man.

"Ezekiel Ben Levi, these are my friends I've been telling you about. Joy, Jenny, and Will." Daniel pointed to each of us. "Guys, this is Ezekiel Ben Levi. My brother in Christ and fellow witness."

"Howdy everybody. You can call me Zeek." His deep southern

drawl threw me, and he must've caught on. "What's the matter folks, ain't you ever met a Jewish redneck?"

His infectious laugh came from deep within.

"Not that I'm aware of," Joy giggled.

"It's a pleasure to meet y'all. I'm originally from around Tuscaloosa, Alabama. Roll Tide!" He looked around as he talked. "We need to say grace, don't we?"

We bowed and let Zeek ask the blessing. The deep feeling overwhelmed my thoughts as Zeek prayed for God's Kingdom, the missions God gave all of us, and that we find the killer quickly. Then he blessed the food and finished with a hearty amen.

We made quick work of the dumplings with little conversation. But before the main course came, we began talking about the Sovereign's speech. Daniel and Zeek controlled the conversation, but I didn't mind that at all, considering their status. Although six more judgments remained before the halfway point of the Trib, they seemed to have plenty of energy to keep preaching to the masses.

"What about the…" Joy pointed at her fake Beastmark. "Rumors around the watercooler are that we'll be required to take them sooner than what the Bible teaches."

"According to Will's father's journal, it won't be mandatory for the public until the midpoint. However, that doesn't necessarily mean that government employees such as yourselves won't be forced to take it sooner." Daniel said.

He looked at me like he expected me to lash out about Tommy stealing Dad's journal, but I held it in. What happened between me and Tommy stays between me and Tommy. And Daniel needed to stay out of it.

Zeek must've noticed Jenny squirming a bit. "Never fear, little sister. God will guide you through that tough decision. Obviously, you will deny the Mark of the Beast, but you will never be alone."

Jenny's tears showed her fear of the blade.

"Joy, talk to Tommy and see if he can get her one of those." I pointed at her forehead.

Joy rubbed Jenny's forearm and gave a reassuring smile. "I'll see what I can do."

"And tell him from me, make it happen, or I'll pay him back double what I gave him last time." I had no intention of letting

Jenny go through what Frank went through.

"That's enough." Daniel almost shouted. "Tommy can only do what he is led to do. If God wants to bring Jenny home to be with Him, there's nothing you or I can do about it."

My rage came out as I pointed at Daniel. "And I'm sure you'll heal all his booboos I give him. But remember, you can't always be around." I got up and went to the bathroom.

After flushing the urinal, I washed my hands. The man in the mirror looked as bad as I felt. Tommy had been a sore subject since the blood storm, but between Daniel, Clay, and the deep feeling, I struggled to maintain a brotherly mindset concerning Tommy and Joy. When I tossed the paper towels and turned, Zeek stood between me and the door. His intensity made me feel small. Although short and portly, he looked me dead in the eyes.

"I've never met Tommy, and Daniel only gave me a little of what happened between you two. But you need to dial it back a little. We're on the same team. We don't have to see eye to eye all the time, but in these times we're living in, we've got to have each other's back." His face softened. "Daniel also told me you've been undercover for a long time and that you've been alone with unbelievers for the last three months without getting to be the new creature God made you when you became a believer. That's got to be hard. And this thing with Joy. Wow! I don't envy you, brother. It's got to be hard to not only call her sister, but to have to work side-by-side on this case. But she's still your sister in Christ. This is difficult to say, but my daddy used to tell me that in situations like this, you've got to get over and beyond it. Otherwise, it'll eat you up from the inside out." He patted my shoulder and walked out.

The deep feeling simply said amen.

CHAPTER 20

Daniel and Zeek quickly ate and left through the backdoor. We finished our meal in thoughtful silence and set up to meet at the hotel, the best place to speak freely. Jenny left first to get started on her part of the investigation, while me and Joy sat in awkward silence until the bill came. She paid, using her Beastmark, which she said felt uncomfortable every time she used it. I nodded and pointed at my badge.

By the time we got to the square, a crowd had congregated near the corner opposite the HQ, near the guillotines. We heard them before we saw them. Daniel and Zeek stood in front of the guillotines preaching. Although their voices sounded calm, the intensity of the words came loud and clear to us from across the square. Joy tried her best not to respond, but her body language agreed with the witnesses. I whispered in her ear not to make too much of a response. She calmed down.

Zeek talked about God's judgments and how the Bible predicted every one of them thousands of years before they happened. He read from his Bible to show where he got the words from, though I believed he had the entire book memorized. He then told the crowd how the Old Testament predicted Jesus' first coming, and how He fulfilled those prophecies, just as God is fulfilling them today. The memories of Dad's sermons covering similar topics made it difficult not to react like Joy had earlier.

Daniel took over and began telling the crowd about God's plan of salvation. How they can avoid the coming judgments if they accept Christ as their Savior and inviting anyone to pray with him.

It reminded me of how Dad finished every service with the plan of salvation, followed by the altar call.

My mind snapped back to reality when the military truck rounded the corner of South Avenue and stopped in front of the two men. A military SUV parked near me and Joy. A captain stepped out and started shouting orders for the men to surround the two and place them under arrest.

"Be careful, captain." Joy said. "You need to know that those are two of those special Christians. The authorities have debriefed us about them."

The oversized man turned and stared at her with ill intent.

"If I want your input missy, I'll ask for it." He shouted.

She didn't miss a beat. "For your information, captain, I am Commander Joy Everhart of the Western Peace Forces, and you will give me all the respect I am afforded. Is that clear?"

He stepped in closer to lord over her. "You are in the police Peace Forces and have no jurisdiction over me or my unit. I will follow the orders given to me…"

Although she stood her ground, her eyes flashed fear for a heartbeat, which enraged me.

"Then you will follow my orders, captain." I entered his personal space and shouted while flashing my badge. "I am Major Will Thomas of DRUID. And you will back down before I place you under arrest for insubordination and whatever else I decide to arrest you for."

Blood left his face as he snapped a salute and asked for forgiveness.

I stepped back and lowered my voice. "Although she isn't military, she has a valid point. Those two are the special Christians that have been popping up all over the world. If you haven't read your emails or talked to someone smarter than a goat, then let me enlighten you. We have lost key personnel to people like them. Our boys get too close, and they get fried crispy. I don't know how they do it and I don't care. But you will tell your men to step back, and you need to assess the situation to avoid any more key losses. Am I crystal clear soldier?"

He saluted, stepped back, and spoke into his mic. "All personnel will step back and maintain a tight perimeter around…"

Just then, a ball of flame erupted near the guillotines. A soldier writhed on the street while the others tried to roll him on the asphalt to quench the flames. But those were God's flames. The soldier died. Joy put her hand over her mouth and darted into HQ. I ran to the scene with the captain on my heels, both of us shouting orders for everyone to stand down.

One soldier didn't pay attention. With a look of vengeance, he stood, prepared his rifle, and pointed it at Daniel.

Getting between the soldier and Daniel. I raised my hands to the soldier and shouted. "Stand down, soldier. This isn't the way to do it."

"Who are you and why are you giving me orders?" He never stopped looking at Daniel.

I raised my badge and shouted to his superior. "Tell your man to stand down, captain. That's an order."

But the captain said nothing. He stood there looking like he wanted to draw his pistol and join the young soldier.

"He killed my brother." The soldier shouted.

Before I said anything else, he sidestepped me and raised his weapon with a finger on the trigger.

I felt the heat of the flames on my face when he caught fire. The other soldiers did nothing, because they knew. I turned and cursed. The two witnesses looked at the burning soldiers with sadness.

"I will have you busted down to private and send you to the Arctic." I shouted at the captain, who stood there in a dumbfounded state.

Not being able to say anything to Daniel and Zeek, I threw up my hands and stormed back to HQ. Before reaching the doors, Petrovich cleared her throat to get my attention. When I started for her, she turned and walked to the opposite side of the square from the scene. I followed. When we stopped, she stared at the smoke and shook her head.

"I thought you said you weren't coming till tomorrow." I really didn't want to deal with her.

"My project finished early, and I felt it necessary to make sure you're doing your best on both of your projects." She sighed and nodded towards the two preachers. "One of these days, the Sovereign will figure out how to destroy those insolent Christian rebels."

"Until then, we need to stop provoking them. Too many dead

already without doing something stupid like that." I snuffed.

We stood and watched while Daniel and Zeek walked away from the dead and continued their sermons closer to the old Woolworths building. People began following them.

"Sheep to the slaughter." The demonic grin on her face spread. "You know, we take names of those who choose that overbearing sheepherder. We get them the next day and send them to either the reeducation camps or to the breeding facilities."

"I heard the Sovereign's speech. Not sure I agree with the latter. It feels too much like farming. Animal husbandry."

She turned and the look she gave almost made me step back. "Are you questioning our savior? The Sovereign has been nothing but patient with the likes of those Jew boys flitting around the planet constantly causing upheaval and confusion among the populace. If you don't show more respect for your Sovereign, I will make sure you will have a meeting with one of those." She pointed at the guillotines.

At that moment, I had an overwhelming desire to pull my gun and end her, but the deep feeling reminded me I needed my cover to help the people she targeted to escape the camps and clinics. I bowed my head in submission.

She turned her attention back to the witnesses. "Have you figured a way to end Commander Joy Everhart?"

"Not yet. But honestly, I'm getting over what she did. Frank was a Christian, and she had every right to turn him in." It hurt to say it.

She shook her head. "To look at you makes me think of a powerful man with proper priorities. But your words are feeble like an old woman. I am looking for powerful individuals who have fire in their soul and ice in their blood. Obviously, I chose poorly when I came to you."

She meant for the attack on my manhood to get me to fall in line, but I didn't play her game.

"If that's your best shot, you need better material. The military drummed the machismo out of me a while back."

"Then how about I talk to General Sokolov and tell him that your parents present a problem? Your past affiliations might make you biased and unstable. Maybe a trip back west will take that out of you, like your machismo. I hear that the land back there is getting quite unstable. Maybe you'd fit right in there. You know, being one with the land." She didn't even look at me.

That's when I knew she needed to be taken out. It's one thing to go after Joy. That had been my plan for a while. However, threatening my life brought my anger to a tipping point.

I let the moment linger, giving the impression that I believed her threat. The deep feeling told me to cut bait and run. However, I needed to keep my new enemy closer. Although I knew my vengeful plans for Joy grew less likely to happen, this woman had no intentions of letting her plans of killing Joy go. I played her ridiculous game.

Standing straight, I towered over her by almost a foot. "I'm not going back." I let a tinge of fear enter my tone.

Her grin needed pushed to the back of her head. "Good. Now we need to figure out the best way to set her up. I will dig into her past and find any weaknesses to use against her. But if nothing comes of it, I need to know you'll take care of her. Remember, she set Frank up. Even though he proclaimed to be a Christian, there's a chance he might've turned during a short incarceration. Otherwise, he'd still be among the living, enjoying the fruits of our glorious Sovereign."

She left.

The idea of being that woman's yes-man soured my stomach. But if that's what it took, so be it. Turning the tables on her might be Joy's only chance. However, the evil emanating from her still bothered me.

CHAPTER 21

Daniel and Zeek finished their sermons while the Peace Forces removed the burned corpses from the street. The crowd of about fifty dispersed. About half left, mostly Marks, while the rest went to the center of the square, got on their knees, and prayed. Daniel and Zeek took their time going from one person to the next, making sure no one left without talking to them. Two from the crowd went and talked to the captain, handing him slips of paper.

About to go back to my office, I heard a familiar sound that took me back to my days living in the Ozarks. A clanking cattle trailer pulled around the square wasn't commonplace before the Trib, but I knew the sound all too well with Dad's church located outside the city limits close to farming communities. The brakes squalled behind the CSU building. Then I remembered the tunnel and walked there to see the process.

It didn't surprise me that a local bounty hunter used this form of transport because of the poor conditions of the area, but it still made me angry that this so-called progressive society had no problem treating people like cattle. But what did I expect from the Antichrist, a minion of Satan?

Heavily armed Peace Forces guards dressed in black fatigues opened the gate from inside the tunnel. The one obviously in charge walked into the tunnel with two in tow. Showing my badge to one guard, I asked for a quick rundown of the situation.

She saluted, then pointed to the sign above the tunnel entrance saying the same as its counterpart on the other side. "Not from around these parts, sir?"

"Just got back from out west. Fighting Christians and non-loyalists." I put my hands in my jacket pockets.

"You know about the bounty on the Christians?" She pushed her brown hair over her ear.

"Yeah, the Sovereign just announced it. Hard to believe this gate got up so fast." I pointed at the tunnel.

"Didn't take long for the captain to figure it out." She pointed across the square at the man I threatened to demote. "Pretty obvious, if you ask me. Of course, an enlisted person suggested it." Her smile showed yellow teeth.

"Of course." I grinned.

"Most hunters escort them to the front door, but that's usually to bring in one or two at a time." She shifted her rifle to a more comfortable position. "There are about three or four who bring them in bulk, like Charlie. He has a crew of five who scour the countryside looking for Christian meetings. He's easily our most successful."

A whistle came from down the tunnel, and the soldier went to a small box and pushed a button. Lights came on in the tunnel. The leader hollered out with his hand raised, and I saw the trailer's brake lights brighten. Four men dressed in grungy camouflage overalls and carrying automatic weapons got out of the truck. Two climbed on top of the trailer and stood at the back edge to stop anyone trying to escape that way. The other two walked on either side of the trailer, cursing at its inhabitants and smacking the sides of the trailer with the butts of their rifles.

"Tell your commander I'm coming up to take a look." I started before she protested.

The commander put a finger to his ear, turned, about pointed at me. "Don't come any farther."

Holding up my badge with one hand, I never stopped walking. "I want to see the contents of that trailer before you unload."

He took my badge and read it. After a quick shake of his head, he spoke into the mic mounted on his collar. "Sir, we have a situation in the tunnel. A DRUID officer wants to see the Christians in Charlie's trailer before we unload."

The captain let out a litany of curse words and told him not to let me near the trailer until he got there to set me straight.

Of course, I didn't stop. Although the sergeant protested, I went around the trailer looking through the metal bars. The fear etched on those faces made me want to pull my gun and lead them out, but the deep feeling held me back by reminding me of the new believers in the square who needed help from people like Charlie. Studying each person, I looked for familiar faces but adjusted my recollection to include age progression because of my prolonged absence. No one talked to me because I knew they heard DRUID when the sergeant reported me to the captain.

"Can I help you?" The voice came from the driver's side door.

An older man slid down the driver's seat of the 4 x 4, his worn cowboy boots lightly clicking on the asphalt when he landed. His red with black mesh trucker cap read "Charlie Caplan Farms." A pistol swung from the left side of his hip holster, old west style, a large knife, maybe a machete, swung loose on the left. A hand too big for his medium build stuck out to shake.

Taking his firm grip, I looked him directly in the eye the way Dad taught me. "Just looking Mr. Caplan. I'm Major Will Thomas, DRUID. I came here to investigate the bodies found in the field near Phenix Quarry.

"Call me Charlie." His dark eyes squinted in the sunshine. "What do these people have to do with the killings?"

"Not sure, but I still want a look. You never know." I gave a quick shrug.

"Can you look when we get them processed, sir?" The captain came from behind and saluted.

"You're already on my bad side, captain. You want to dig a little deeper?" I glared at him.

"I'm sorry, sir. It's not my intention to cross you again, but we're blocking the street." He pointed to the traffic that lined up on Olive.

"They can wait or turn around. Their inconvenience doesn't supersede a murder investigation." I turned to the trailer and looked some more.

"No, sir." The captain walked away without saluting, which I intended to put in my report.

"Charlie, where did you find this group?" I struggled to see inside the dark trailer.

"Up north, near Aldrich." He pulled some paperwork out of the truck. "Other side of Walnut Grove Lake." He pulled a trash bag from the truck bed and opened it to show the Bibles.

"You say you're looking into the killings?" A red-headed young man, face full of freckles, standing beside the trailer asked. Smiling.

"That's right, son. You know anything about it?" I turned my attention to him.

"Nope." He spat tobacco juice on the street and turned his attention to the trailer. "Just don't take my money."

"I'll take whatever I need to solve the case." I kept my voice even.

Charlie glared at the young man. "Pay him no mind."

Looking back in the trailer, I saw a pair of blue eyes I hadn't seen since before the Rapture. My heart both pounded and broke at the same time. Libby James stepped from between two tall men and stared at me. She frowned until her eyes lit up in recognition.

"Will?" She whispered and reached through the guardrails. "I thought I heard your voice but wasn't sure until I heard you say your name." The tears flowed freely.

Trying to hold back my own, I looked at Charlie, who had been giving the sergeant his report about the raid. They heard nothing.

I winked subtly at her. "Captain, get over here." I barked.

"Yes, sir." The captain's sweat started dripping from his chin.

"That girl." I pointed at Libby. "Put her in a separate cell. I want to interrogate her this afternoon."

"But sir, we still need to process her and the others. She may not even be here this afternoon if she isn't in the ICON database." A note of whining in his voice set me off.

"Listen, you insignificant pissant. You've crossed me for the last time. Go to your office and wait until you hear from me. Is that crystal?" I shouted, making sure some spittle landed on his face.

"Yes, sir!" He snapped a salute and disappeared into the tunnel.

"I still get paid for her, right?" Charlie's scowl set me off.

"You'll get what I let you get, no matter how long it takes." I grumbled and waved him off.

He cursed under his breath and yelled at his hunters to finish unloading.

"Sergeant, did you hear what I said?" I turned to her.

"Yes, sir." She snapped to attention and saluted.

"Make it so." I grumbled.

"Isaac, you help this lady get the blonde off the trailer." Charlie pointed at the redhead.

Isaac scowled and patted his gun to intimidate me. When I walked past him, I slammed my shoulder into his. He tripped back a bit, cursed under his breath, and hustled to the back of the trailer. Maybe the military didn't strip my machismo from me. When they got Libby off the trailer, the sergeant cuffed her and had a corporal lead her into the building. I told the sergeant to finish unloading, pointing at the traffic and telling her to make it quick.

"Friend of yours?" Charlie followed me to watch the soldiers work.

"Old flame." I smiled. "But she's from around here and a bit of a gossip. If you catch my drift."

Charlie didn't smile like I thought he might. "Whatever you have to do, I guess." He scratched the back of his neck. "So long as I get paid."

"If she's a Christian." I deadpanned and went through the tunnel to the prison.

CHAPTER 22

Before entering the building, I called Lonergan and told him about the captain. Lonergan asked me what I wanted him to do about it, as if he had no say in the matter.

"Bust him down at least one rank. He got two men killed for his lack of intelligence. He acted like he never read the information on those Jewish Christians who light people on fire." I stood by the door as a cop to enter the jailhouse.

I heard him typing and humming. "Let's see. Nobody important, so that's good. Okay Will, I'll get it done. You're right, this guy doesn't need to be getting our people killed. I'll get him reassigned and demoted."

"Good, he's in his office waiting for the call." I hung up and looked at the building.

Mom and Dad called it the Heers building, after the old department store. Since then, it wore several hats. Now, it's the jailhouse for the Regional Peace Forces.

"Will, what are you doing?" Joy stood at my side as if appearing from thin air.

"Seeing an old friend." I looked down at her.

The deep feeling tried to get me to feel safe with her, but I shrugged it off.

"I heard. Is she cute?" She gave a knowing smile.

"Couldn't tell. She was in a cattle trailer." I shrugged.

She frowned. "That's still sick."

"Agreed. But I also am wondering if she might know something about the killings. Maybe someone in her group might have some information." I sighed and looked up some more. "My only problem is that she might talk too much. If you know what I mean."

Joy raised her arm and tapped her Vam screen. After a couple of swipes and a few more taps, she looked at me and gave me a cute smile.

"No one is watching the cell she's in. So, you can smooch if you want." She giggled. "While you're doing that, I have an important meeting with Superintendent Evans. It will only last an hour."

"Make sure to tell her the case file stinks." I grumbled.

"Will, even though we may agree about some things doesn't mean we agree on everything. Evans is a good cop and an extremely competent administrator." The old Joy came out to play.

"Agree to disagree," I muttered.

I had to show my badge about a half dozen times before being escorted to Libby's cell by a heavily armed guard. He waited for me to stow my badge, jacket, gun, and Vam in a secured locker before opening the door to the room of cells with a swipe of the Beastmark on his right hand. He closed the door behind him and walked to the cell.

"On your feet Christian." He spat out the last word and hit the steel bars with his baton.

Libby slowly rose from her cot. I barely recognized the emaciated body I once lusted after. Her sunken eyes, sallow skin from malnutrition, and brittle hair made me wonder why God allowed this to happen to his people.

"When I tell you to move, you move." He slammed the baton against the bars and swiped his wrist to open the door. Quickly reaching for his sidearm, he started to swing the door open.

I grabbed his wrist and slammed him against the bars.

"Let me make this perfectly clear, kid. I grew up with that woman. It doesn't matter who she affiliates herself to. You will treat her with respect."

His glare set me off. I jerked the baton from his hand and put it against his throat. His eyes bulged from lack of oxygen and his pistol hit the ground.

"This isn't the old American military anymore." I shouted. "I can drop you and probably get a metal for getting rid of dead weight. Is that clear?"

He violently shook. From the lack of airflow or affirmation, I didn't know. Or care.

I loosened the grip and let him suck in some much-needed air.

"Nothing happens to this prisoner, or I'll finish this conversation."

"Yes, sir," He gurgled while I jammed his baton in his gut.

"Get out. I will question her about the murders alone."

He bolted out, mumbling something about reporting me to the captain. I chuckled at the thought of his reaction when he walked into the office and learned of the former captain's fate.

She stood in the same place as if frozen by fear. Her eyes widened like she couldn't find the old Will who had chased her relentlessly until she had finally agreed to a date. I smiled, trying to get her to see I had no ill will. I took off my ball cap and raised my right arm to show her I didn't have the Beastmark.

"From what I hear, not all enemies get chipped," her raspy voice croaked.

I went out the door and found a chair and a bottled water in the breakroom. When I held it out, she stared at the bottle like I had poisoned the water. I opened it and took a sip while I sat.

"If I wanted you dead, I'd just send you to the guillotine." I pointed toward the square.

She took the bottle and downed its contents in a few long gulps. I took it from her and went to refill it at the cooler. When I returned, she sat on the cot sobbing. I put the bottle inside the cell and sat back down. Keeping quiet to let her finish her emotional outburst, I remembered her grandfather's funeral. The only time I ever saw her cry. In all the years I knew her, she never let her emotions or thoughts escape without first considering them.

The faded purple, flower-patterned dress hung off her like a little girl trying on her mother's dress. Her bony arms, strong from playing sports, had earned her a scholarship to Missouri Southern State University in Joplin. A couple of twigs that barely held her upright replaced her long, strong, silky legs. My heart hurt for her.

After ten minutes, I started again.

"Libby, I'm not who you think I am," I whispered. "But I need to keep quiet because there might be ears on the other side of the wall."

She looked at the corners of the room.

"We are safe. These cells are for the interrogations nobody hears about. And as you heard earlier, I won't let them do those kinds of things to you. But we need to talk." I sat and waited.

She let her hands drop between her knees and sighed.

"You're supposed to be in Heaven," she muttered.

"You are too." I whispered.

She looked up, staring through me.

"After all we done, you thought I had any chance to make the Rapture?" She rolled her eyes and rubbed her cheeks with both hands. "I never listened to your dad's sermons or anyone of the Sunday school teachers. Not even my parents. Oh, I had it figured out. Or so I thought." Her tears hit the dusty floor.

"I can say the same for me." I needed to change the subject. The guilt overwhelmed my thoughts. "Where were you when it happened?"

She scooted back on the cot, leaned against the wall, and brought her knees to her chest.

"Jessie called and wanted me to come to her place. Her boyfriend dumped her. We were talking when she looked up at the ceiling and then she disappeared. Poof." Her eyes widened at the last word. "I tried to call Mom and Dad, but they obviously didn't answer. So, I thought I was alone."

"I was at the diner near the square with Jeff. His fork hit the plate when he disappeared. When I saw his uniform on the floor, I knew. Then I went to Mom and Dad's house, even though I knew Jesus had taken them home. That's where I dropped to my knees and prayed for salvation." I looked at my fingers.

She looked up and whispered. "You're a believer?"

"Yep. I'm undercover." I sighed and shook my head in disgust. "Was undercover for the Christian Resistance." Trying to keep my emotions in check, I gave her the rundown of the past two years.

She stood and wiped her eyes. "Wow. My life's been boring compared to yours. I didn't become a believer until after the earthquake. The reason it took me so long to come around was that I blamed you for everything."

"Me?" I grinned.

"Yes, I mean, I wasn't a nun by any means, but you talked me into so much. Or so I thought. Then one night, I listened to this guy named Zeek, and he made me realize no one talked me into anything I wasn't already willing to do. So, I got on my knees and accepted Christ." She smiled.

After a few pleasant moments passed, I asked. "Did anyone from our old church get left behind?"

"Several that I know of." She stood and paced while going through a list of people who surprised me, including the youth pastor.

"He was all out for Christ." I shook my head. "At least, I thought so."

"He took the Mark. Said that if God didn't want him, he didn't want God."

"Wow!" I never thought I'd see the day. His devotion to serving God seemed so real, so spot-on.

She stared for a minute, then asked, "What happened after you got saved?"

"Almost immediately after I prayed, Frank called me back to Kansas City to help with the riots."

She looked up. "Frank Malone? I remember his wife being an excellent cook."

"Claire made it into the Rapture." I had to hold back my anger. "But he accepted Christ before he got set up and bladed."

We let the realization sink in that our losses had just begun.

She came close and got on her knees and looked at the bars. "I want you to know that I'm sorry for my part in you being here. We made a lot of mistakes together, but I am an equal partner in our sins."

"Same for me." I got on the floor in front of her. "Maybe I *am* to blame for our situation."

"You know the truth. We're responsible for our own actions. But we sinned together certain sins that I wanted you to know that I'm sorry to God and you for…" She looked at the bars.

"As am I."

She stood, wiped her cheeks dry, and smiled. "Can you get us out?"

"Maybe you and a couple of others, but not all. Sorry, but I'm still undercover trying to help as many as I can. But I need to tread lightly. If my cover gets blown, too many brothers and sisters get the blade, including me. But right now, I'm investigating the murders over by Phenix Quarry." I looked around to make sure no one had entered the room without my knowledge and lowered my voice. "The Antichrist is going to claim that it's a mass grave from the murders. If he gets the world to believe it, we're all in trouble. So, me and my colleagues, who are Christians, are trying to solve it in a way that discredits his claims."

She raised her eyebrows. "That's a lot to take on, Will. You know the world accepts everything he says, no matter how ridiculous it sounds. If you discredit him, he'll just spin it from a different angle to favor himself and have you killed."

"I know. But if we can throw a cog in the gears of his machine, maybe more people will see past the lies and accept Christ." I reached through the bars and took her hand. "It's worth the risk."

"Don't make me watch you lose your head." Her tears hit the dusty floor.

I needed to change the subject. "Why is everyone so skinny? Isn't the Resistance or Zeek getting you food?"

She shook her head. "Some people in our group are farmers. We did pretty good last year, but the blood storm wiped out our crops. Zeek brings what he can, but the animals have disappeared, and the woods are mostly burned and bloody. What little trees survived don't give us enough. We do the best we can. But we're not connected to any of the Resistance groups. Most of them are closer to the big cities."

I tried to think of a way to get word to Tommy. Then Daniel entered my mind. He'd help for sure.

"There's a new witness in town. A friend of Zeek connected to a Resistance group I belonged to. If we can get you guys out, they can hook you up." I smiled.

She gripped my hand. Her tears fell on my fingers. "Thank you. God has sent you to us in a time of need."

"Don't get too far ahead of yourself. Just one day at a time." I didn't want to dash her hopes, but a little practicality never hurt.

After a few minutes of silence, I asked. "Have you heard anything about the killings?"

She looked over my head and thought. "Not really. Since the announcement, we've heard some rumors about people on this side of the lake. But you need to talk to Bub."

"Bub?" I asked.

"Bait shop owner. He set it up not long after the earthquake formed Lake Walnut Grove. According to Zeek, he knows everything that goes on in that area."

Remembering Gallway had mentioned the store owner, I made a mental note to ask Zeek about Bub, I thought about what I wanted to ask next.

"I think there's a church group near Phenix." She tapped her fingernail on her front teeth like she did when we dated.

"Tim Weaver. The field next to his farm is where he found the bodies."

Her eyes glazed in thought. "Talk to Zeek. I think he knows those people."

"I plan to have Zeek and Daniel talk to. them. I think they know more but are unwilling to talk to DRUID."

"Good idea." She stood. "Will, I'm not so dumb that I believe you'll get us out of here. Only if it's the Lord's will. But thank you for the tiniest bit of hope."

She reached through the bars. We hugged. Memories flooded my mind of the girl I loved. When I left the room, I thought of my new sister and thanked God for letting us meet and get things right. The deep feeling reminded me I had the choice to have the same thing with Joy. But I still wasn't ready.

CHAPTER 23

Making a mental note to talk to Daniel and Zeek about Tim Weaver, Libby's group, and Bub before the end of the day, I stowed my gear in my office and went to Joy's office. Her brow furrowed in deep thought as she studied her computer screen. She looked adorable. While closing the door, I shook my head, not believing I thought that of her.

Joy took a bite of an apple.

"You sure do like those things." I waited for her response before sitting.

She swallowed, looked up from the screen, and offered a surprisingly clean smile. "One a day and all that. Have a good time with your ex?"

We decided on the way back to HQ to talk in lower tones. Even without the tech in the room, we had to be careful of curious ears.

"How'd you know that?" I plopped in the chair across from her.

"Looked her up. You two went to church together." She logged out, placed her apple on a napkin, and took her gear to my office and returned.

She sat and put her chin in her palm. "So, what happened? Broke up?"

"Yeah." I didn't want to give more to someone I struggled to trust. "We went our separate ways after high school."

"That's so sad." She sighed like a little girl. "And now, you two are back together. It's so romantic."

"So romantic." I rolled my eyes. "And we're not back together. A lot has changed since the Rapture. And she's facing a breeding facility."

"Not if you rescue her and disappear into the sunset." Her sugary tone caught me off guard.

"You read too many romance novels as a child, didn't you?" I deadpanned.

"Maybe." She returned her focus to the case. "Will, I've been looking at the drone pics of the field and there's something I wanted to talk to you about."

I sat up. "What's that?"

"Someone said the field only had one way in or out. Right?"

"Tara mentioned it."

"That's not correct. There's another road on the back side of the property that connects to the farm road we used to get there. I didn't see it on the map, but it's in the records." Her cute, thoughtful frown returned as she pulled a drone pic from her desk.

Looking at the image, I said, "It's an easement."

"A what?" She took a small bite of her apple and grinned as if I made it up.

"An easement. It's like a driveway. The farmer probably put it in to subdivide the land into housing plots. It happened all the time when I lived in the area. Farmers wanting to get top dollar for their land." I stood and started pacing.

"But there's nothing else on the drone footage." She looked through her notes.

"He wouldn't put asphalt down until the construction began. It barely looks used." I squinted at the photo. "Maybe a set of tracks there, but it's not been used in a while."

"You're right. The former owner had applied to subdivide the land, but it didn't get approved because of the murders." She looked uncomfortable saying the last word.

"Makes sense," I said.

"The killer probably knew about it. That's why the next-door neighbors heard nothing." Joy picked up her apple, took another bite, and stared at the wall behind me. "It's far enough away and in a lower part of the field to keep the sound of any vehicle down."

I got up and left Joy's office.

Crossing the hallway, I almost ran into another cop, who lurked suspiciously near our door. After giving him a stare down that ran him off, I went into my office and pulled out my Vam. "Tara, Will.

Have you made it to the trees yet? Get in your car and go around to the back end of the land. There's an easement. Check for tire tracks and get a team into those trees. Thanks."

"She didn't know it was there?" Joy stood at my door, face reddened.

"Easy there, kid. We didn't see it until you did some digging."

Nodding at the cop still loitering at the end of the hall, I told Joy we needed some air. The cop shriveled in a desk chair when Joy glared him down and told him he needed to find something productive to do or she'd send him to the landfill to find the rest of the bodies. I grinned as we walked into the square.

We walked to the parking lot, locked our gear in her SUV, and went to an open area near some old train tracks. The motionless, smelly air did little to improve our mood, but that might've been more about the frustrations of trying to investigate with little help. Although alone, we still knew that the mics on the streetlights and signage had the capability of picking up our conversation.

After a couple of thoughtful minutes, I remembered something. "Tim said the owner was one of the murdered. What's the name on the application for the subdivision?"

She blew her bangs and stared at the motionless sky.

"Christopher Penn was the last owner. He's listed as a murder suspect. No known whereabouts. All family were…"

"Murdered." I finished.

"You knew them?"

"One of the most devout families in Dad's church. I'm not surprised they got killed. And I'll bet Tim and his family had many long talks with Chris and JoAnn." I closed my eyes. "If I remember right, Chris gave a prayer request for his neighbors. Said he'd been working on the dad."

"You have an excellent memory." She smiled.

"Chris and JoAnn requested it a lot. Repetition."

After a few minutes of silence, Joy sighed and smiled. "It feels like we're making headway, even though things are going slower than expected from the top."

I smiled. "Didn't take you for the glass half-full type."

"I've been more like that lately." She blushed.

"And not as ambitious." I tested the waters.

"Still ambitious, but in another direction." She looked at the sky and changed the subject. "How do you think the spin doctors will use this?"

"It's a slam dunk for them." Blowing out a breath, I lowered my voice. "I tell ya. I've been going over this all night and day, and I haven't figured a way we can turn this to our advantage. All points of view seem to be useful to them."

"I know, right?" She leaned closer to me and whispered as she slouched. "I've only been a believer for a short time, but I'm feeling the pressure. I can't imagine what it's been like for you."

"I've been on the bench since St. Louis. The only thing I've done was steer my soldiers in the wrong direction or go after nonbelieving militia groups, like the LDM."

She raised her voice. "That was you?"

"Yep." I grinned. "Why?"

"I always read the reports on ICON about what's going on in the U.S. You're the one who took down the Last Days Militia?"

I giggled. "Accidentally."

Her laugh echoed off the nearby buildings. "Seriously?"

Lowering my voice again, I said, "Intel told us that Tommy's people were in Colorado. They had just raided an armory near Denver, and my superiors ordered me to chase them into a trap they set just outside Cheyenne. So, I did a drone recon and found this group about ten miles from Tommy's last known position. I knew it wasn't him because he didn't go through mountain passes. The dangers that the mountain pass presented made me reconsider my attack.

"I called my superior and told him I found the real Christian Resistance group, and that the other one was a decoy. He let me go, and we ran right into the LDM. They had no desire to surrender or even talk. They just started firing when they saw us, and we responded." I lowered my head and focused on my shoes. "The only one left was their leader. Some David Koresh wannabe. He took the mark and is now a religious leader somewhere near Toronto."

"I read that the battle didn't take long." Her interest bothered me.

"Not really a battle. They had plenty of weapons and ammo, but no knowledge of engagement. Don't get me wrong, they did some military style maneuvers, but for flat terrain, not mountains. In the end, they charged up a steep hill. It quickly escalated to a real fish-in-a-barrel situation, a massacre. Me and my people didn't feel all that heroic."

"ICON News made it sound much more thrilling." She stepped back.

"Nothing thrilling about killing." I muttered.

"Unless you're a psychopath."

"Amen, sister."

Her eyes drifted for a while. I didn't interrupt the thought, but I caught myself admiring her beautiful green eyes. A slight guilt bubbled in my gut. I had a girlfriend, but something drew me to Joy at that moment. The deep feeling didn't disapprove either, but reminded me of Dad preaching about not dating someone outside the faith and how the contention broke couples apart. I let the thought pass, still wanting to be with Amelia and not fully accepting Joy. After a few minutes, her gaze returned to me.

"That's how they'll spin it." Her beautiful eyes widened as she lowered her voice. "You're right. There really isn't any way to turn this around. That computer will make the lie sound reasonable to people who want it to be true. I am so glad God opened my eyes."

"Let's talk to Daniel and Zeek before going to the CSU lab."

CHAPTER 24

Joy might not be that tall, but when she got those legs going in power walk mode, I almost had to jog to keep up. She typed furiously on a phone that I didn't recognize. We got in the SUV and waited while Joy pulled out her VAN and manipulated a few cameras to give us privacy.

After a few minutes, the back doors opened, and the two witnesses got in.

"What's up?" Zeek asked.

"Will talked to someone you might know." She turned to face them. "Tim Weaver."

Zeek's smile seemed uncomfortable. "Yeah, I know them. Why do you ask?"

"He's the one who reported the field of body parts." I turned.

"I take food to them sometimes. God even had me heal a couple of fields for them to plant." He wiped his lips.

"You see Libby James much?" I asked.

"Yeah. I'm supposed to see her group next week."

"Not unless you spring them." I pointed at the jailhouse. "Charlie Caplan brought them in this morning."

Zeek punched his knee. "I should've torched him when I had the chance. He's been no good since the Rapture, from what I've been told. A little crazy even. He crashed one of my meetings a while back. Even put a gun to my face. Must've felt the angel about to fry him because he turned white and ran off. His boys aren't much better. They're money-grubbing drug addicts looking for their next fix. They saw him tear out and followed."

Daniel piped in. "Why are you asking about Tim Weaver?"

"I'd like you two to talk to him and his people." Joy pointed at them. "Will thinks Tim held some things back after Will showed him his DRUID badge. But we thought that if you talk to him, it might loosen him up enough to tell us what it is."

Zeek looked out the window. "I'm not supposed to see them until next month. But seeing how you guys need to talk to him, I can get out there tomorrow. It'll have to be at night. You see, I got these shadows and they're easier to lose in the night."

"Good. Let Joy know when you find something out." I started to turn.

Daniel put his hand on my shoulder. "This Libby is a friend?"

I hated how he read me so easily. "Ex-girlfriend."

"We will pray for God to provide her and her people a way of escape." Zeek's emotion came out. A mixture of fear and anger, not like mine. I wanted to storm the castle and kill all who got in the way. He wanted God's will to be done.

The two witnesses stayed in the SUV while we went to the lab.

My respect for Joy had increased, but my old feelings for her remained strong, creating an internal divide. The deep feeling and part of me enjoyed this new wave of trust for her, but the other part of me had strength that occasionally overruled the other two. My memory of Frank's death faded a little with time, and the emotions surrounding it seemed to abate into occasional numbness. But her new faith gave her a bearing that I admired. The old, overly ambitious, self-serving Joy had died when she gave it to God. I needed to turn the past loose, but my stubborn side refused to comply.

We entered the CSU crime lab. Although the building had survived the earthquakes the year before, the room still had cracks in the walls and ceiling. The smell of chemicals and coffee wafted through the air, a reminder of the St. Louis lab. The old machines spun and whirred loudly.

"Can I help you?" A man walked up to us.

"I'm Commander Joy Everhart and this is Major Will Thomas, DRUID. It's good to meet you, Dr. Taylor." She stuck out her hand.

His brown eyes glared at me when he shook her hand. "Why is DRUID involved?"

I glared back. "This is a joint investigation." I already didn't like him.

His face flushed. "My apologies, Major Thomas." He turned to Joy. "Commander, if it is alright, may I speak with you in my office? Alone?"

Joy, always the professional, nodded and went into the office and took his seat. She either kept up appearances, or she didn't like him. Or both. I grinned and looked around for Jenny. They put her in a corner with the ancient machines and an even older computer. Her downtrodden look made me want to interrupt the meeting and put Chad in his place.

"Hello, Major Thomas." Jenny seemed to be on the same wavelength as Joy.

"Jenny, I see they still don't approve of your presence." I sat at the table where Jenny had the victims' right hands lined up.

She whispered, "They don't have a clue. I mean, they have plenty of clues, but they…"

"I get it. The same thing's happening to me. Joy might be the commander, but her lack of experience makes it difficult to do my job." I patted her forearm. "Anything new to report."

"Detective Gallway sent some tire tread pics with the impressions to be sent later, but I'd like to start with the crime scene photos first, if you don't mind." Her exasperated tone set off my anger.

About to go charging into the office again, I stopped when I saw Joy walking towards us with a don't-mess-with-me glare. Chad followed like a schoolboy who just got scolded by the principal.

"Jenny, there's something Dr. Taylor needs to say to you." She snapped her raised fingers to call the CSU techs' attention to her, then turned and scowled at the CSU supervisor.

Chad stepped forward as the techs gathered around him. His jaws clenched in a way that made the Beastmark on his forehead dance a little. "Dr. Lewis, I'd like to apologize for your treatment by me and everyone else in the lab."

"Louder," Joy demanded.

"We have been unprofessional in trying to push you out of the investigation, and I fully assure you of our complete cooperation. Our lab is your lab." His shaky, shrill voice echoed off the walls.

Seeing the angered body language of the techs, I needed to put my two cents in to set the proper tone. So, I stood over him, looked at the crowd, and raised my voice. "You treat my friend like that again and Joy won't get to you fast enough. I'll pistol whip all of you into an early grave." I let my jacket swing open enough for him to see the fifty-five cal.

The blood ran from Dr. Taylor's face, and he whimpered something unintelligible. Then he almost ran back to his office. The techs' frightened reactions made it clear that they got the message.

"That was less than professional." Joy let a slight grin flash.

"You know me." I shrugged and offered her my seat, which she quickly took. "Always the bad cop."

Jenny, near tears, smiled and mouthed a thank you to us.

"Now, back to business." Her old spunk slowly returned. "The crime scene is a bit confusing. Detective Gallway is right. There doesn't seem to be a pattern in the locations he buried the body parts. And I've been working with the DNA as best I can. Unfortunately, the chemicals from the storm and decomp are making it difficult to retrieve usable samples. It seems our best bet is finding the heads and using dental records.

"The best timeline we have is decomp. The only thing that bothers me is that the last victim died around the time of the storm a few months ago. If that's the case, then the killer might either be done..."

"Maybe the discovery of the field made him stop." Joy perked up.

"Possibly, but he might be looking for a new field. Or is still hunting for the next target. What about the timing of the killings?" I looked at Jenny.

"Sporadic. He's still a fairly new killer and may still be perfecting his process." She shrugged.

"So, we focus on what we have." Joy returned to her notebook.

"I still think the heads are the key." She clicked the mouse, and the field appeared. "I've marked where the burial sites are on this drone pic of the field." She pointed at the blue dots on the antique monitor. "The pattern appears circular, but I've been comparing patterns against those in ICON, but nothing has popped yet. To be honest, I don't have a lot of confidence. I believe he just randomly placed them."

"Do you think the heads are in the field?" Joy wrote without looking up.

"That's Tara's job to find them, but I'm not sure. If the killer keeps them as trophies, I doubt it. He'll keep them close to him. If they are a statement, like the rage sermon you guys already discussed, then I think they might be in the field." She shrugged.

"Have you had a chance to look at the tire tracks yet?" I asked.

"Yes, and this is interesting." She clicked the old mouse a few times and brought up the tire tread pics. "The tires are standard tread for older pickup trucks. Unfortunately, they're so common that I can't identify make, model, or year, but I'm guessing it's an older model since these tires haven't appeared on new vehicles in over five years. The interesting part is that they go in only one direction. Towards the tree line."

"There's an easement on the other side of the trees from the burial plots." I pointed it on the pic.

"Detective Gallway should find tracks leaving there." Joy nodded at the screen.

"So, if he saved the heads for last, they might be where Will said they are." Jenny looked up and pointed at the trees.

"If he didn't keep them as trophies, I'd say that's the place to look." Joy looked up from her notebook and nodded.

"I called Gallway earlier, and she's looking there as we speak."

Leaning in to get a closer look, I tried to find any mounds near the trees. Unfortunately, the drone footage showed little. But the deep feeling led me to believe we were close.

I pointed at that spot. "That's got to be where he buried them."

Joy pulled her Vam up and texted Gallway to see if she found anything yet.

"I know this is a longshot, but do you have anything telling us where the killings took place?" I asked.

Jenny's look said enough. "Sorry, too early to tell. My best guess is that they happened indoors. First, because most serial killers want a place where they can take their time and have privacy. Second, because there are no foreign substances on the body parts that suggest it happened outdoors."

"Are the victims all females?" Joy asked.

"No, there's no pattern there. Males and females. Different races. Different sizes. Everything points to random killings." Jenny stared at the hands. "Unless there's something about the heads that triggered him."

"Cause of death?" I asked.

"According to the M.E., stab wound to the neck." Jenny pulled up the autopsy pics of the torsos and focused on the neck area. "See how this part of the neck has a notch in it? The M.E. thinks the killer tried to hide the fatal stab wound when he decapitated the victim. All the necks have the same markings."

"That's about where the carotid arteries are." I pointed at the screen.

"Very good, Will. I'm impressed." Jenny smiled.

"Part of military training. Learn where a human bleeds out the quickest, and you win the fight faster." I stared at the screen.

"There doesn't seem to be any other marks on the torso." Joy squinted at the screen. "What about the other parts?"

"The arms and legs show signs of being wrapped in multiple plastic zip ties. Three or four per limb, by the way it looks." Jenny rubbed her wrist.

"Any material shards to get an ID on the zip ties?" I asked.

"Sorry, we found nothing yet." Jenny shrugged. "But we're still processing. I'll call if we find anything else."

"Thanks." I stepped beside her and whispered, "If anyone treats you bad, let me know."

She giggled. "I will, big brother."

"Okay, I guess it's time to get back to the office. I have another meeting with Central Command in Europe. They want daily reports." Joy stowed her notebook and stood.

"What about supper?" I asked, looking from Joy to Jenny.

"Sorry, I'm working late. I'll grab something from a restaurant on the square." Jenny said.

"I don't know how long this meeting will take. So, I'll grab something on the way back to the hotel." Joy checked her Vam. "How will you two get back?"

"I'll get a ride from a cop," Jenny said. "Unless I pull an all-nighter."

"I'll manage," I said.

"Hey, I heard a couple of techs talking about a diner just down the street. They called it Hamby's. They said it has the best breakfast in town. Let's go there in the morning." Jenny smiled.

"Sounds good to me." Joy returned the smile and looked at me.

"I haven't been there in a long time. And they had the best breakfast back then, too. I'm in." I nodded in agreement, fighting the regretful memories of breakfast with Libby after date night.

"Great, let's meet in the hotel lobby at six." Joy checked her Vam. "I need to get going." She left, but not without glaring at Chad on the way out.

CHAPTER 25

Standing outside the CSU lab building, I looked around, trying to decide what to do about supper and how to get back to the hotel. The smell of burned flesh still lingering in the air made me consider going to the hotel and ordering delivery. Then I noticed a restaurant where the old Woolworths had been, with a sign above the door reminding me of the card in my pocket. The Automat.

"Look at the rich boy getting his fill of the Sovereign's food." A skinny young man with tattered clothes led a similarly dressed group of protesters near the entrance of the Automat.

The small crowd, the oldest looking about twenty-five, carried signs opposing Hectar's place and the government's unfair treatment of the poor. Their anger and hunger stuck to them like the buffalo from South Dakota.

Flashing my badge didn't impress them.

"A cop, a soldier, or a rich man. You still make me sick. The Sovereign promised to get the food out to the public, but what we didn't know was that he meant it for his chosen people." He pointed at his scarred forehead, where he'd scratched out the Beastmark. "And we're none of those. So, we became autonomous."

"Not my problem, kid." I shrugged.

That didn't help. They surrounded me. A few tugged at knives in their pants pockets. A couple of others pulled ax handles from behind their signs. The deep feeling and my training told me to get inside as fast as I could before they had the chance to express their hostility.

Pulling the SIG and threatening them with a trip to the guillotine seemed to slow them. When I reached for the door, I holstered my sidearm and let the leader keep prattling about the injustices of the world. I stepped through the first set of doors of the restaurant door and saw the meal protectors at the door staring at the protestors with their sport jackets open. The small automatic weapons hung loosely in front of their vests. Nodding my approval, and breathing a sigh of relief, I went to look inside.

The smell of the food overwhelmed me, from Salisbury steak to fried chicken to cherry cobbler. The north and west walls looked like stacked microwaves with the windowed doors revealing a cornucopia of freshly made food, from single servings to full meals. Beside each door, a small digital screen showing the price had a place to scan a Beastmark or insert the exact amount of cash or coin. The southern wall had a long bar of drinks, from water to soft drinks to adult beverages. I watched a tall man wearing a blue business suit with a red tie lean over to let the screen scan his forehead mark before dispensing coffee into a porcelain mug.

The simple white Formica tables in the center of the room had chrome molding surrounding the sides. The chairs had seats covered in sturdy red vinyl with chrome metal frame and legs. I looked up at the balcony surrounding the lower dining room. The place looked like an old diner from the movies I watched as a kid with a well-dressed clientele who didn't appear to worry about the prices on the doors. No poor people here. Hectar lied about being all-inclusive.

Getting into line and taking a gray tray with silverware wrapped neatly in a black cloth napkin, I stared at the offerings. The loaded card gave me carte blanche. I took the medium-rare ribeye, a loaded baked potato, and corn on the cob dripping with butter, all surprisingly still hot. I noticed that as soon as I removed a dish and the door closed, another identical meal appeared from a door on the opposite side. Deciding to get dessert later, I went and got a large sweet tea.

With the dining area still full, including the balcony, I didn't know where to sit.

"Sir, the owner of the establishment has invited you to dine with him." A man in an expensive black suit with matching bow tie and clean white shirt pointed me to a small doorway in the corner where the west and south walls met. I mistook it for a worker's door.

The door led to a short hallway with only one exit at the end. When I entered the room, its opulence amazed me. Mahogany walls gave the room an ominous feel. The white marble floor with gold veins shined bright under the silver chandelier. The table had a white linen cloth with gold silverware. A centerpiece with flowers I thought extinct from all the judgments gave an aroma of spring. Hectar sat on the opposite side of the table, hovering over a filet mignon with asparagus tips and rice pilaf, smiling at me like he knew something I didn't. A glass of fine red wine waiting for the first tasting sat above and to the left of his China plate.

Giving the man who led me into the room my jacket and Vam, I asked him to take them out of the room.

"Sorry, they're bugged." Not having to ask if the room had any, I set my tray on the opposite side of Hectar.

"Hello, Will. How are you this fine evening?" He shook my hand when I walked to his side of the table to give him proper respect.

"Doing good considering." When I sat, I took a quick bite of the steak and raised my eyebrows.

"If I knew you were coming, I'd have had the chef prepare something better." He took a small bite of steak and savored it.

I took a bite of baked potato and let the buttery goodness slide down my throat. "You said you'd be here tomorrow."

"Business went faster than I anticipated." He took a sip of red wine. "Have you any leads?"

I knew better than to ask about his business. Maybe he had a meeting with Daria. Not wanting to dig into a sore spot, I kept things cordial.

"Nothing yet. We're just getting our bearings. My CSU tech gave us a couple of possibilities that we'll check tomorrow." I wiped the sweet corn juice from my mouth.

"Serial killers are the lowest form of the animal kingdom. I hope you find him and bring him to justice. There's no room, even in this horrible world for his ilk." Hectar barely contained his rage.

"Of that, we agree." I raised my tea glass in a mock toast and took a drink.

"That and other things, I think." Hectar's cryptic grin always kept me guessing.

Then I remembered. "Daria Petrovich."

He slowly nodded. "A thorn in both our sides. She is on the same level as this killer you are searching for, in my estimation. But she has buried more bodies than him, I can assure you."

"That doesn't surprise me. There's something off with her I can't quite put my finger on. Something evil." I set the glass down.

"Evil is the proper term for her. She's been very demanding these days, and I am struggling to find out why." He shook his head before returning to his rice.

"Right now, she's after Joy."

"And so are you." He looked deep into my eyes, then pulled back from his plate. "Please don't tell me you've teamed up with her. Will, I told you not to do that. She doesn't keep partners. They end up dead. Or worse."

The deep feeling gave a big I told you so.

"To tell the truth, I'm starting to get over my feud with Joy, but Petrovich isn't letting me out of it. And I'm not sure I want out yet." It felt weird shooting straight with Hectar, but I needed a sounding board.

"True. She will never let you out once her claws are cinched firmly in you. But why the sudden change in attitude?" His stare bore into me again.

"Frank is gone, and I can't bring him back. I need to focus on keeping myself upright and breathing. Plus, Petrovich is now the problem. Compared to her, Joy is just a minor annoyance. And since she is Petrovich's enemy, I know that losing her might not be the best for my career right now. We may not be in the same department anymore, but it still can't hurt to have her owe me a favor." I smiled.

His grin spread. "I am impressed. You are learning the ways of the world. Keep your friends close." He raised his glass before taking another sip.

"I know you employ a similar strategy. If it's okay, may I ask that you let me know anything about her concerning me or Joy?" I knew the risk of aligning myself too close with such an untrustworthy man didn't bode well for my potential future, but the immediate situation called for it.

He took another bite of steak and looked deep in thought while chewing. "I will, if you give me information about her ... among other things."

There it was. The extra. No trading information about Petrovich. He wanted more. I expected it, but it still hit me wrong. I stalled a while to get the bad taste of compromise out of my mouth before nodding in agreement.

He smiled. "I am glad we agree."

"However, I will not give you information on criminal investigations concerning your community. I still have my integrity. This joining is of mutual survival against a single person. It goes no deeper than that." I used my best stern voice I learned from Dad.

His demeanor changed. I knew he wanted exactly what I refused to give him. Although he dealt in information, I knew he had an intense pragmatic side. He shrugged, took a bite of asparagus, and stared.

Playing the mirror game, I took a large bite of my steak and waited patiently.

He smirked. "I like the way you do business, Will. And this is an offer too good to refuse."

I laughed at the movie reference. "I'm glad."

"The first order of business is to tell you that Miss Petrovich has been digging deep into your past. I'm guessing your little talk just down the street earlier included a threat using this information. So, I will also tell you she is doing the same with Commander Everhart. It's in your best interest to do some digging on Daria. That way, there will be no surprises when she strikes at your new ally."

"All I can tell you is that Petrovich doesn't seem to include you in her future endeavors. From the looks of things, she has a list, and you may be next on it. After my new ally." I didn't lie, just went with an educated guess.

"Trust me, I will be on top of that list soon enough." His face turned a light shade red.

"My guess is that she hasn't been authorized to eliminate you because of your deal with the government. It's part of her job. And Joy is the more immediate danger to her because the commander is quickly climbing the ranks of the government and may make her irrelevant. Making it personal." I finished my corn to let him chew on that.

"Not being fully in her sights might give me a significant advantage. Would it not?" He took a bite of rice and smiled. "For both of us."

"I agree. With your contacts all over the world, you can come up with the proper leverage without having to hurry."

"Ah, Will. A man after my own heart. You are a gifted strategist. The military has done wonders for your skills and confidence." He pushed his empty plate away. "I tell you what. I will stay in Springfield for a while longer to monitor her movements. And you play your little game with her. Maybe we can get her to make a mistake and blade herself."

I smiled.

Once finished, Hectar offered to give me a ride to my hotel to discuss other business. I put my jacket and Vam in the trunk and got in. After the driver pulled from the curb, Hectar pulled his mother's Bible from the console.

"I don't trust the workers in my establishment. DRUID is always trying to invade my privacy."

Chuckled at the irony, I looked around the leather-filled limo.

"Don't worry about the car. I have it swept three times a day. My driver is a former KGB operative. An expert in bugs." He found the place in the Bible. "The next judgment will be a fiery mountain that goes into the sea. A supervolcano."

"And it will turn a third of the ocean waters into blood."

"But magma doesn't turn water into blood." He smiled like a little kid. "I did a little research, and it's never happened."

"And there hasn't been hail mixed with blood that caught on fire since Egypt, either. According to Dad, only God can do this because He created everything and can change the laws of the universe to make His point."

"And what point is that?" He closed the book and stared at me.

"That He is angry with Satan and sin and wants the world to come to Him and his Son." I shrugged. "That's what Dad believed."

"That's seems to be His point, if I am reading this right. However, I am going to use this to my advantage." His cryptic grin returned. "You see, I have been buying up as many edible saltwater creatures as I can find. I have also purchased several aquariums around the country. My program has been very successful, and when the judgment takes place, I will be ready to cash in."

"Always looking at the world in angles." I smiled. "Glad I have you as an ally."

His deep laugh filled the car. "And I am glad to you, and your father's insights. I missed our biblical talks. I dare not discuss this with even my closest friends for fear that they will turn me in to gain favor and financial reward. But I trust you."

"And I trust you, Hectar."

We both lied.

CHAPTER 26

In my hotel room, I opened my Vam to video chat with Amelia. It took me a while after my shower to plan what I wanted to say, since our last conversation didn't go well. Dealing with my frayed nerves from the day didn't add to the anxiety of talking to her about the Mark of the Beast she wanted to take.

"Hello, Will." Her tattoo became my primary focus.

"Hello, Amelia." I settled in the chair at the table.

"How's the case?" She situated herself on her bed pillows.

"Difficult." I rubbed my tired eyes.

"The news says that you will have it wrapped up within the week."

"The news has no idea how to investigate."

"They get their information straight from the government." Her tone annoyed me.

"And the government gets the information from us. And we haven't reported since we got here." I grumbled.

"I don't get you, Will. You have a great job. You just got promoted, and you're on another high-profile case. The Sovereign and the media have all the confidence in you, and all you can do is whine. I'm starting to think that you're the type who complains if you don't get everything exactly the way you want." The creases from her frown made her look older.

"No one seems to understand that it can take decades to find a serial killer. We're just getting started."

"Maybe you just need to believe that you can do it." Her smile flashed brightly.

"Just not in the timeframe everyone wants." I smiled back. "But that's the life of a detective."

"I have every confidence in you, Will." Her voice softened. "Even when you're living on an island."

"I'd be all in if it was just the two of us." I wiggled my eyebrows.

She grinned and pointed to her tattoo. "That might make this an easier conversation."

"Maybe we need some more time before having this conversation. Implanting the chip still bothers me. I still want my privacy."

"At the expense of your safety?" She crossed her arms and glared. "Although the Sovereign has made great strides to ensure peace and safety for us all, there are still those who want to harm those who support him. We need the peace of mind the chip brings to remind us that we are part of something greater. That and it makes it easier to eat and shop."

"I can take care of myself." I looked at her. "And us."

"But you're not here, right now." She raised her eyebrows as if she won. "Are you?"

I sighed. "No, I'm not. And the implant is still a bad idea. The thought of injecting my body with a tracking device feels like I'm someone's pet or part of a herd." I raised my badge. "This is all the chip I need."

"And I've had enough of this. If I didn't know better, I'd say that you're a sentence away from treason." She glared. "Part of a herd. You need to get out of the past and realize that the chip has progressed humanity in a way that brings everyone closer together by keeping us safe. Just the other day, I read about a family whose grandmother had wandered off, and they found her faster because she had the chip. Maybe if you look at the chip from that perspective, you'd see what I mean. Maybe even find the killer."

"If he's been implanted." I grumbled.

"That's why everyone needs this. See, I just proved how the implanted chip keeps us safe and makes your job easier. How many lives will be saved in situations like the one you're in?" Her cheeks reddened.

"Then I'd be out of a job, and we can go and find that island." I mumbled.

"I've had enough. Goodbye, Will." She reached for her Vam. "And grow up."

After taking some time to cool down from the argument, I finished my night by checking the case file on my laptop. Jenny had nothing new to report. However, she emailed me and Joy to let us know that Chad and his people calmed down and treated her better and thanked us for the support. She then reported on the impossibility of retrieving viable DNA because of the composition of the chemicals from the blood storm mixed with the agricultural products put into the soil and decomp. After logging out, I put my Vam in the bathroom with the rest of the equipment. I wanted some time to myself and didn't want any eyes or ears invading my personal time.

Sitting back in my chair and staring at the dumpsters outside my window, I became painfully aware that the investigation hit its first wall. I shot a quick prayer that Tara and her people would find the heads in good condition for identification. The prayer felt genuine, and God had heard it. As a kid growing up in a preacher's household, we had a Bible study and prayer every night. Dad and Mom taught my sister and me to think of prayer as a two-way conversation. It's not enough to do all the talking, but to listen as well.

With my eyes closed, I calmed myself, cleared my mind, and slowed my breathing. The deep feeling seemed to be quiet for a while, waiting for me to be at my most receptive. Then Joy and Petrovich entered my mind. Fear mixed with regret penetrated my calmness. A plan of trying to set up Petrovich with Joy as the bait crossed my mind but made me anxious. Who am I to play God with Joy's life? Overwhelmed by the feeling that my actions with Petrovich put Joy at risk of the blade, I went to my bedside and got on my knees.

My prayer resonated in my mind. Perhaps the first time I'd shot straight with God since praying for Christ's salvation. I spilled my guts and asked for forgiveness. As if seeing myself in a mirror, I despised the man I became. Even as a believer, I acted like the old Will. Petty, immature, irrational. Finishing the prayer with the request of how to approach this dangerous situation, I sat on my bed and cleared my mind.

The knock on the door startled me. I looked out the peephole and quickly opened the door. Clay stepped into the room, and we hugged.

"What are you doing here?" I asked, escorting him to the table.

He sat and rubbed his legs. "Tommy's got a lot going on in St. Louis. He didn't like it when Daniel called and asked for me to come here. But here I am." He innocently shrugged.

"Daniel sent for you. How come?" I stepped back.

"All he said was that you needed help and to bring this." He pulled out a square, brown leather case from inside his jacket.

He handed Mom's Bible over with a smile. I stared at it while rubbing the leather Bible holder that had her name, and "Happy Anniversary" etched in gold leaf. The zipper snagged in its usual spot but gave way with the second tug. The New King James opened to John chapter three without a book marker, with the sixteenth verse highlighted in yellow. Covering my mouth with my hand, I heard her saying the famous verse. God loved us all.

Clay sat patiently, then he cleared his throat.

"They're almost done with your dad's prophecy journal. Tommy thinks we can get it back to you within the month." He nervously rubbed his stubbly chin then grinned. "Your dad was something else. Our people have been using it to save a lot of lives, both spiritually and physically."

"Good for Tommy," I snarked.

"Good for all of us. Please, Will, let this thing between you and Tommy be done. He needs you. We need you." He sat back, and for the first time since I've known him, his serious tone penetrated. "And you need us. No Christian is an island."

Twice in one night. The words bit deep. Most people might look at Clay and see an ex-junkie who lost too many brain cells to think straight. But I knew different. His past showed me his genuine quality. Husband and father with a strong work ethic. God brought that back.

Thumbing the tabs on Mom's Bible, no snarky comeback came to mind. The deep feeling stayed quiet because Clay made sense. But I didn't want him to make sense.

"There's more Christians in the world than Tommy. Once I get Dad's journal back, I'll be on my side of the world, and he can stay on his side. I don't hate him. I'm just mad at him, and I can be that. But he made it abundantly clear that I'm not welcome back. And I don't want to come back." I zipped the case closed. "Besides, you guys have Joy on your side now. She has more pull and contacts than I ever will. She'll do more with one phone call than I can with two days on the Beast."

The long pause in our conversation made for an awkward start to the new topic.

"So, what's your plans for the rest of the Trib?" Clay's narrow eyes focused on me.

"Survive. Do what I can for Christians from a distance, like I've been doing since the blood storm."

"How's things with Joy?" He seemed uncomfortable bringing in another person he knew I hated.

"Better, I guess." I shrugged, turning my attention to the dumpsters. "I don't want to kill her anymore."

"That's a good start. Means the Holy Ghost has been working on you." His humble smile reminded me of the day I caught him at Ballpark Village in St. Louis. "And you're responding."

"Something like that, I guess." I mumbled. "She doesn't need me gunning for her. She's got enemies." I told him about Petrovich, leaving out that part that I co-conspired with her.

"Sounds like she needs protecting. Maybe a big brother in Christ can help." His smile grew. "Maybe that's why God put you two together."

The deep feeling spoke up, telling me I needed to tell Clay and Joy about Petrovich and me. But I didn't agree.

"Maybe, but this case is going to last a long time. I think Joy will lose interest before long."

"Is the case already cold?" he asked, crossing his legs.

"Almost, but it's a serial killer case, and they're rarely solved quickly."

"Have you found out who the victims are?"

I gave him the rundown, using him like a sounding board.

"Sounds like you need help." He sat up straight, uncrossing his legs. "Maybe your old confidential informant can help."

"Have you been to Springfield before?" I grinned, glad that I had a close friend nearby.

"No, but when I was downtown, I saw an old friend from my using days. She's dealing for Hectar's crew down here now and owes me from the past. She can tell me any rumors being spread.

I'd even wager there's some good information amongst the junkies."

"I'm not sure about this." I scratched the back of my neck. "With Petrovich everywhere, I don't want her to see us together. She might use you to get to me or Joy."

"I doubt she has any interest in an old junkie like me. But if God's ready for me to go home, ain't nothing you or I can do to stop it."

No argument there. I learned that lesson many times since the Rapture.

"Okay, but where are you going to stay?" I asked.

"Daniel told me that Zeek has a place set up for the needy by the big mall. I'll help when I can and stay with them. They're good people. I feel safe around them." He stood and stretched.

"You should. They have guardian angels." I stood.

"You ever see one?" his eyes widened.

"No, but I saw one at work." I walked to the door and checked the peephole.

"It's scary, ain't it?" He shivered. "A few soldiers went after Daniel in St. Louis. They died fast, but ugly. And the smell mixed with the last judgment almost made me puke." He hugged me. "I'll try to make our meetings quiet like. If I have something that can't wait, I'll tell Daniel. He'll get it to you fast."

"Be careful. I can't have another death on my conscience." I whispered, opening the door and nodding.

Clay walked down the hall, hands in pockets, and acting like he'd

CHAPTER 27

Hamby's Diner, about a half mile north of the square, had been a breakfast tradition in Springfield since my parents were kids. The two-story red brick building had a few quake cracks but looked sturdy enough. Jenny beat us there and had a corner booth away from the few patrons. Joy sat beside her, and I sat across from them.

The menu seemed simple enough. I ordered biscuits and gravy with a side of bacon and hash browns. The other two decided on egg white omelets and fruit.

Just after the server brought our water and coffee, Daniel walked in, pulled a chair to the booth, and sat.

I looked around. "What are you doing?"

"Don't worry, they don't see me." He smiled. "I still can't get over being able to do this. People see me, but they'll never be able to describe me. Oh, and you don't have to worry about your tech. We are safe, so you don't have to hide it."

"Cool," Jenny said. "I wish I had that ability at the lab."

"Have they started bothering you again?" Joy's face started turning red.

"No, but they still get in the way." Jenny rolled her eyes. "I think they attended clown school. They bump into each other and bicker over the smallest things. I gotta tell you I miss Bobby. Everything is a well-oiled machine in St. Louis."

I saw the bags under her eyes. "You look tired. Did you pull an all-nighter?"

"I took a couple of naps on the table while I waited for the machines. Long enough to make a difference." Her sleepy smile said different.

"Anything new?" Joy asked, putting creamer and sugar in her coffee.

"No. I tried everything in the book to get some usable DNA." She pushed her bangs to the side. "It's a no go on that and the prints. The killer scrubbed anything identifiable. I hate to say this, but he's good."

The server brought our food and took Daniel's order.

Daniel prayed over the meal, then became unusually quiet when we started eating. Everyone seemed deep in thought. Even Joy stared at her food without once glancing at her phone.

"Are you going to the crime scene today?" Daniel asked.

"A little later. I need to visit Libby." I looked at Joy. "Which reminds me. Is there anything we can do to get her and her people released?"

Joy stared at me, deep in thought. "Not really. I talked to the sergeant, who processed them. All of them are linked to someone Raptured."

"Six degrees of separation. We can make anyone on the planet connected to someone taken in the Rapture." I wiped my mouth.

"That's the problem. If ICON can send anyone to a reeducation center or breeding camp, it'll shoot them over lickety-split." She looked into her coffee mug. "Unless they're believed to be a subversive leader."

That meant the blade.

"What about you?" I asked Daniel, knowing the answer.

"Only if it is God's will. And only if He wants me to be the one to free them."

We sat in silence for a while.

"Sorry, we got off topic. Why did you want to know if we're going to the crime scene?" Joy sipped her coffee.

"We will ride with you if you're going today." Daniel took a bite of cantaloupe.

"You want us to get kicked out of the Peace Forces?" I said too loud, but no one else in the diner seemed to notice. "Or bladed?"

Daniel motioned to the indifferent diners to remind me. "You are safe with us. We just need a ride to this Phenix place."

"Fine by me." Joy smiled. "It'll be nice to have you and Zeek with us."

"Why do you want to see the crime scene?" I wondered.

"We want to talk to the group you asked about." Daniel gave me a puzzled look.

"Tim Weaver. I forgot." I shook my head.

"By the way, why are we going back to the field?" Joy looked up from her Vam.

"I want to find out how far along Tara and her people have gotten. And to see that easement for myself to get a better feel for the route the killer took to bury his victims." I pushed my empty plate away.

"How do you eat that way?" Joy screwed her face. "Do you want to die from a heart attack?"

"We only got five more years, and a heart attack is better than the blade." I smiled.

The hurt look returned to her eyes. Maybe she felt as if she'd never get over Frank's death. Join the group, Joy. Everyone has regrets these days.

Jenny wiped her mouth and asked Joy for a ride back to the lab.

"How did you get here? I forgot to ask," I said.

"Walked. It's chilly, but a pleasant morning." She smiled, looking out the window.

"I need a vehicle." I looked at Joy. "This carpooling is going to be a problem."

Joy tapped on the screen of her Vam. "There will be a truck for you when you leave the jailhouse. Sorry, all out of cars." She grabbed her briefcase and went to pay. Jenny followed.

"Seems like things are going well with Joy." Daniel fished.

"For now. But there might be a problem." I didn't look at him.

"The woman with a bad Franch accent?" He took a drink of water.

"You're aware of her." I said, surprised.

"She's a dangerous woman. She's been around St. Louis for the last two months. Interrogating people I've led to the Lord. Most have disappeared. I'm guessing she sent them for reeducation or breeding."

"She's here."

"I know. I noticed you talking to her yesterday during our sermon. It looked very conspiratorial." He raised his eyebrows while taking his last bite of pineapple.

"She has every intention of killing the witnesses," I said, not wanting to discuss Joy.

"But she cannot do this." He frowned in confusion as if Petrovich already knew their protection from the angels guaranteed their safety.

"She knew the consequences even before the two soldiers died. But she mentioned that the government, meaning the Antichrist, is looking into the possibilities of shutting you guys down for good." I finished my water.

He smiled. "He's been trying since the church began. Surely, he knows it won't work."

"He doesn't have the devil inside him yet. Maybe he's unaware of it. And maybe she's just hoping to shut you guys up and has put all her eggs in the wrong basket." I wiped my mouth.

Daniel sat back and stared at me. I hated when he did that. It felt like an invasion of privacy. The deep feeling felt connected to him and they conspired against me. Or maybe I suffered from acute paranoia.

"Are you two still conspiring to murder Joy?" His face went grim.

I sighed and rubbed my face with both hands. The subject I tried to avoid. It felt like getting called on by the teacher when you didn't raise your hand because they knew you didn't know the answer.

"I tried to back out, but she threatened me. So, I played along to see how she plans to do this. Maybe I can prevent it." Although I had no power in how I said it, I still meant it.

His eyes glazed for a moment. Then he smiled. "That is a good plan. It may be dangerous, but knowing the mind of the enemy can help."

We left the diner and walked towards the square. Jenny called it right. The morning had a crisp feel like something good had either happened or will happen. I hoped for the latter. The city didn't bustle with traffic like the old days. But the numbers of dead and Raptured made for a small population. Wondering if Daniel always looked ready to bust out a sermon in a moment's notice, I let the silence linger till we reached the lot we had parked the SUV.

"This is where we must part. I need to meet Zeek and prepare for our trip." He stopped and stared at me. "Concerning the Petrovich woman. You need to be very careful with her. She is an evil minion of an evil man. Never let your guard down. And never believe you are a step ahead of her. Believe you are always behind. And consider all possibilities. She has."

I took it in. The deep feeling agreed with him. As did I.

Shaking his hand, I said, "I'll follow that advice."

"And follow this piece of advice. Joy is your sister. Treat her well. Love her."

"That'll be difficult." I shrugged. "No promises."

CHAPTER 28

Libby's cell still had a chill to it, and she had nothing to keep warm. She sat on her cot, shivering. My anger hit an unusual high. I pulled the guard out of the room and slammed him against the wall.

"I'm guessing you didn't do too well in school. Am I right?" I knew he smelled what I had for breakfast.

A cocky grin crossed his pasty white face. "I am just following protocols."

Taking a step back and buried my fist deep in his gut. He fell to the ground and expelled his breakfast all over the floor.

"I'll take that as a yes." I stepped back and leaned against the desk. "So, let me spell it out for you. This isn't America, son. I can hit a lesser-ranked soldier without fear of retribution, especially being a DRUID officer. In fact, I can have you, your family, your friends, and the girl you kissed behind the bleachers in third grade bladed for whatever infraction I decided you committed. So, you will get my prisoner a blanket, turn up the thermostat in there, and give her all the food I've ordered for her, or so help me, I will follow through. Is... that... clear?" I shouted, feeling an exhilaration of having a little justice paid to a member of the enemy that I rarely experienced.

He stood, wiped his mouth, and grumbled. "Yes, sir."

"Start with the thermostat, get the blanket and food, and clean up that mess." I waited for him to salute and pass me. "Pronto!" He picked up the pace.

Forgetting that my Vam was in the safe, I called my

commanding officer to get that kid away from Libby. Lonergan sighed when I called him to have the jailor reassigned, but he confirmed the transfer before hanging up. Before entering the room, I texted Joy to make sure Libby and I had no one listening. After she confirmed the room's safety, I stowed my Vam back in the lockbox and went back to talk to Libby.

Libby stood near the cell door, apparently where the vent blew the heated air into the room.

"You didn't need to do that." Her sunken eyes filled with worry. "Yesterday, he said his family is high up in the local government. They are already going to get the captain back and have you facing the guillotine by the end of today."

"I did a check on him and the captain last night." I sat in the chair I had placed by the bars the day before. "One, his family went in the Rapture. He's the only one left. Two, the captain, now a lieutenant, is already on his way to Nebraska to be deployed to Colorado, never to return. Three, he's being transferred to West Texas to watch the desert sands for the rest of the Trib. He'll get his papers in a couple of minutes."

Her tears hit her bare feet. "He didn't treat me good last night. He didn't rape me or anything, but he talked. A lot."

"Don't worry about him." I heard things being slammed in the next room. "I believe he might've already got his orders."

He walked in with a metal tray filled with roast beef, mashed potatoes and gravy, and a large glass of milk. A blue wool blanket folded neatly under his arm. A scowl on his face made the ensemble just right.

"What you ordered, sir. Now, if you don't mind, I have to pack. It seems that I've been transferred to northern Alaska immediately. My replacement will be here in a few minutes." He opened the cell door and handed everything to Libby.

I laughed. "Kid, you really need to calm the cockiness. I told them to send you to guard the desert in Texas. But you must've done more than this to get sent up there."

His icy glare might've put the fear in lesser humans, but not me. Then he turned it to Libby, who shrank a little before collecting herself and glaring back.

"It's in your best interest to leave this room without saying another word, boy. You know there are posts farther north than

Alaska." I leaned back in my chair, interlocking my fingers behind my head.

He cursed under his breath, slammed the cell door shut, and stormed out of the room.

"It's hard to believe that a private has that kind of arrogance." I shook my head.

"As I recall, you weren't much better." Libby grinned with a mouth full of potatoes.

"And the Marines beat it out of me, too." I remembered the old arrogant Will Thomas.

Libby returned to the cot, covered her bare feet with the blanket, and wolfed down the food like it might be her last meal. I let her finish before starting the conversation. Giggling after hearing her belch loudly, I took the tray and watched her wrap the blanket around her shoulders as she sat on the cot again. A brief look of contentment crossed her face.

"I'm trying to figure out a way to get you and your people out of here, but it isn't easy. All of you popped on the murder list. I don't think any of you will face the blade, since none of you are linked to any Resistance activities. But the thought of you in the breeding centers makes me want to kill the Antichrist right now."

Her smile turned grim. "I've heard things about the breeding camps. What do you know about them?"

I sighed, trying to think of a way to make them not sound so terrifying. But I always shot straight with her. "They'll start by testing you to see if you're fertile. If not, they'll immediately send you to a reeducation center. If you are, they'll start getting you into better shape. You'll eat better than what you just had, and they'll put you on a physical training regimen to prepare you for the pregnancy. You will be subject to frequent examinations, mainly gynecological, to make sure you're fertile throughout the entire preparation process. When you're deemed fit, they'll put you in the stirrups and artificially inseminate you. They will monitor you throughout your pregnancy, and after you deliver the baby, they will give a month to recover before being impregnated again. They will either send the baby to the biological father or an adoption family, who will raise the child to love the Sovereign and be a productive member of the new global society."

She let it sink in. "Sounds antiseptic, like a TV commercial. So, what's it really like?"

I sighed. "From what I hear, they treat you like farm animals. Isolate you in individual rooms and play reeducation videos all day, every day. They don't let anyone associate with anyone else. Mainly because they are either Christians or non-Loyalists. The soldiers are known for their cruelty and have raped the women. However, if the rumor is true, the soldiers are bladed. I heard another rumor that they tested the soldiers to be of breeding stock to avoid unwanted pregnancies, resulting in less than desirable citizens."

"Sounds like everything a girl desires." Her chuckle had no mirth.

"Like I said, I'm doing everything I can."

I let the silence last a short while. Libby needed time to process, but time didn't allow.

"How did your church get caught?"

She stared at her hands. "The bounty hunters found us."

"I figured that. But tell me how they did it." I crossed my arms over my chest.

"In the middle of a Bible study. We'd been at it for less than an hour when our lookout rushed in, shouting that we'd been discovered."

"No radios?" I asked.

"No, the walkies worked just fine. We have four lookouts for all directions put in places where they can see the entire area. But the bounty hunters somehow managed to get past our lookouts without being noticed." She furrowed her brow.

"Did anyone escape?" I smelled a spy.

"A few did, but I don't know how many." She looked at me. "You think someone sold us out?"

"Or a plant." I looked at the ceiling, trying to piece this together, but let it go. It had nothing to do with the case.

"You said you heard rumors about the killings." I rubbed my eyes. "Do you remember any of them?"

She stared at the floor in deep thought, then looked up. "Yeah. One of the bounty hunters said he knew who did it."

I quickly looked at her. "Which one?"

Her eyes danced as she tried to remember. "The red-headed one. He said that he passed the field all the time going home. He lives in that area."

Remembering the kid, I made a mental note to have Joy look him up.

"The one you need to talk to is Devon White. He talked to the kid for a while. They grew up together."

I sat. Devon White went to our church. "Why didn't you mention him yesterday? I knew Devon well. We played baseball together on the American Legion team."

Libby came over and sat on the floor beside me. "I can't remember everyone. We try not to get too involved within our group so as not to let anything slip in public or during interrogations. Devon has been with us only a short time. He lived near Fair Play with his parents until they went in the Rapture. He didn't become a believer until last week."

I stood. "I will talk to him."

She grabbed my pant leg. "Please be careful. If the plant's DRUID and in the same room, you might play into a trap. I don't want to see you die."

Touching her hair, I wanted to open the door and take her some place safe. "Keep praying and I'll think of something."

Before going to the other side of the building where the holding cells were, I texted Lonergan to see if DRUID had any undercover agents in the cells. After a brief wait, he texted back that I was the only agent in the area because the government was still recruiting and barely had enough for the major cities. After stowing the Vam, I went to the cells. I tried to think about how to talk to Devon without tipping a scared Christian willing to do anything to escape the centers.

The room had a large cell on each side, both stretched the length of the room. Men on one side, women on the other. Although both cells contained at least forty people, the room still held a chill. And a sweltering smell. Body odor mixed with what reminded me of a stagnant port-a-potty made the room reek. The inmates kept their distance, choosing instead to stay close to the windows where outside air leaked through the cracked plexiglass from the quakes.

With the men spread out, Devon stood out. The once athletic shortstop who had scholarship offers from three Division 1 universities looked like a tragic before picture in the old muscle magazine ads. His once lean yet muscular body looked like too much skin stretched across too little bones. No wonder I didn't recognize him in the cattle trailer.

"Devon White, meet me over in that corner." I kept walking to the far end of the cell and saw two prisoners huddled together. "Get out of this space." I flashed my badge.

After they scurried off, Devon stepped close to the bars and looked at the floor.

"Will, how are you?" He whispered with a rasp that worried me.

"I'm good. Trying to make it the best I can in this world." I nodded, trying to get his attention.

"Looks like you haven't." I raised my eyebrows.

His silence and expression told me he didn't know what to say. This from a guy who got the team running laps and picking rock for talking too much.

"I'm better since the Rapture. Got Jesus in my heart and I'm going to Heaven." His smile, although pathetic, contained contentment.

"You feeling okay? You look sick." I tried not to sound worried, but I failed.

"I almost starved myself. After Mom and Dad got raptured, I felt hopeless. Didn't want to live, really. Then the food ran out. I sat in the front room waiting to die. Then Libby and her friend knocked on the door." He wiped his nose with his sleeve. "I'm eating a little more every day, getting stronger until those bounty hunters caught us. Now, I don't know what'll happen to us."

I needed to get to the point and raised my voice to keep Devon safe from the others. "I've been talking to Libby. She said you heard one of the bounty hunters talking about the bodies in the field near Phenix. What did he say?"

He shrugged and wiped his nose again. "Nothing much, really. He just said he lives near the field and thought one of the locals did it. Said the owner's a psycho, and he buried the bodies before the murders." He shook his head at the reference. "Jill, over there, said she knew the owner. The kid smashed her fingers with the butt of his gun and cursed her out for talking. Then he told his buddy that the son's even crazier. Jill whispered to us later that the owner and his whole family went in the Rapture. Her husband saw it happen."

I looked at the woman Devon pointed out who sat in a huddled mass on the floor, whimpering. The guard in the booth near the entrance glared at her like he dared her to cry some more. Her hand, bloody and bent, looked infected. Thanking Devon, I walked to the guard.

"That woman over there with the broken hand. Why hasn't a doctor seen her?" I nodded my head towards her.

"She's a Christian. What do I care about one of those?" The older man sneered, holding his nose as he walked out of the booth.

I invaded his facial personal space. "She's breeder stock. When she goes to the camp with that hand, the doctors will start asking why we didn't send her to the doctor. Then they'll start an inquiry, and I'll make sure you're sent to a reeducation center to learn the proper S.O.P. Is that understood? We have a population crisis going on, soldier, and we need all the healthy stock we can get."

Sweat beads formed on his forehead. The redness in his jowls might've given the old Joy a run for her money. He wanted to snap back, but he didn't seem stupid enough to cross a DRUID officer.

"Yes, sir." He snapped a salute, turned, and got on the phone.

I looked back at Jill. She gave a nod and a glare. I didn't win any popularity contest with the people in the cells, but at least she'd keep the hand.

CHAPTER 29

The four-wheel-drive pickup waited for me just outside the doors of the jailhouse. It sat high enough off the ground that I stepped up to get in. The gas engine roared to life, making some people around the square either jump or glare at the antiquated air polluter. I went around the square to pick up Joy, standing at the Peace Forces HQ typing away on her Vam. Before getting in, she stowed her tech in the side panel storage of the bed with my gear.

Her smile disappeared when she shut the door. "Bad news. According to my superiors Europe, we have a week to find the killer." She clicked the seatbelt and pulled it tight. "The media is having a field day with the news that ICON leaked, and government officials are demanding regular updates."

We pulled into an alley two blocks from the square. Daniel and Zeek got in the back seat and remained quiet.

"I give my report to Lonergan at the end of every day. How about you?" I pulled through to Campbell Avenue and went north.

"They want three updates a day now. But I'll take care of that, so you can keep your focus on the case." She looked back at the two and greeted them.

"I will still fill Lonergan in every night. That way they'll get four a day. I need to keep Lonergan updated. He's my superior and backup." I nodded in the rearview mirror to them.

"Your backup is a full colonel?" Joy giggled. "You are famous."

Looking at her and feeling my face go red. "Not that lucky. They don't trust me. I have a... reputation."

"I gotta hear this," Zeek's southern drawl echoed in the cab.

"Let's just say that I have a problem with authority." I looked at Joy and smiled.

She went red this time.

"I feel there's history there." Zeek grimaced.

"More than you can ever imagine." Daniel mumbled.

Joy stared out the front window, acting like she wanted to say something. Maybe her newfound faith held her back. I didn't have that gift, but the deep feeling helped when I let it.

The two in the backseat talked the whole way. Mostly about how the witnesses had turned the world upside down for Christ. I thought about Amelia and our conversation the night before. The deep feeling let me know she is close to being lost for good. I shot a quick prayer for God to have her cross paths with one of the witnesses.

About a mile from the crime scene, Joy turned and asked, "Do you guys know when the next judgment will happen?"

They looked at each other without conspiracy. Daniel shrugged. "Within the week."

Joy stared for a second.

I followed her train of thought. "It might buy us some time."

She filled them in on our forced time frame, but they only shrugged more.

"Let us pray on it. But no promises." Zeek seemed to be a straight shooter. Not as cryptic as Daniel.

We passed the crime scene. The search party had made it to the stand of trees, but they had congregated in a huddle with Tara in the middle. I rolled down my window and slowed to listen. She shouted instructions on how to search the trees without contaminating any potential evidence. The two in the backseat appeared troubled.

"You two okay?" I asked, looking in the mirror and speeding up.

"Are all the victims believers?" Daniel stared at the field like he saw ghosts.

"That's what the Antichrist is counting on." Joy said.

"How come?" Zeek stared at the group in the field.

"He's going to call this a murder field. Haven't you been keeping up with the newscast?" I grumbled.

"Not really. We're more interested in reaching the world with the Gospel of Christ." Zeek snarked playfully.

"The Antichrist is spinning this as a murder field." Joy used air quotes for the last two words. "He's trying to use this as proof that the Rapture is what he claims it to be. Murders by religious terrorists."

"I remember you telling me that, Will." Daniel spoke up. "Have you figured a way to derail the story?"

"No, I haven't." I stared at the country road. "I believe there's nothing we can do to change it because the Antichrist has firm control of the media and the internet through the Beast. All I can do is my job." I snuffed.

The feeling in the cab had a hint of defeat. But that's the Trib for you. Even the thought of Christ's return in five years seemed farther out the closer we got, and we hadn't made it to the worst part yet.

Tim Weaver's house lay about a half mile from the crime scene. Joy did some research on the Beast about him to see if he'd ever been on the government's radar, but he didn't show up. Yet. However, after hearing what Jenny told me about the plant I didn't want to drive up and drop off the witnesses for fear that someone in their group might recognize us and turn us in.

Once out of sight of the crime scene, about halfway between it and the farm, I stopped the truck and looked in the mirror at the witnesses. "I'll drop you off here and meet you in an hour at the same place."

"These are good people, if a little paranoid. Which is understandable considering." Zeek's voice filled with pleasure. "Tim's congregation are among my favorites. It took a while for them to accept me into their group, but it's well worth it." He opened the door and smiled before closing it.

Making sure the two made it to the farm without incident, Joy sighed. "I'd love to go and see them. It'd be nice to meet fellow Christians. You know, feel you're part of something bigger. That you belonged."

I knew exactly what she meant because I had that until she helped get me kicked out of the resistance. But the deep feeling demanded I keep my mouth shut. And for once I complied.

A few minutes later, Daniel came back over the hill. I worried that something bad had happened until I saw his smile. I rolled the window down.

"Zeek talked to Tim alone and told him he needed to reveal all that he knew about the murders. He didn't tell Tim that you two are believers, but that he needed to trust that you are doing the right thing by investigating the murders of fellow believers."

"Thanks, Daniel." Joy smiled.

"Tim's on his way to find you at the field." Daniel nodded and walked back to the farm.

Parking the truck at the place we parked the day before, I led Joy to the holes to wait for Tim. I wanted to see the holes with no techs getting in the way to get a better idea of how the killer buried the body parts.

I scanned the area for lime dust. "He must've carried a bucket of lime with him from the truck."

"I figured he'd shovel it from the truck bed." Joy shaded her eyes with her notebook.

"There's only one set of tracks." I pointed at them. "They don't veer off at any point. He walked everything to the holes."

"That would take a while."

"He had all night, and no one close to hear him work. My guess is that he kept the motor running to avoid someone hearing it start multiple times and get suspicious."

A few minutes later, Tim came through the fence and walked our way.

"I was hopin' you'd be here." He dusted off his hands. "I wanted to tell you some more about what I remembered."

I shook hands with Tim and innocently added, "I wondered if you'd forgotten anything since the last time we talked."

Tim looked in the hole by us. "I kept racking my brain trying to remember anything more than what I already told you."

"We know there's an easement on the opposite end of the field from where the killer buried the bodies." I nodded toward the search party.

"Oh yeah. I remember it now. The old man put it there to get his tractor in and out without dealing with the traffic on this road." Tim chuckled, wiping his forehead with his forearm. "Not that there's much traffic on either road. I think he wanted to play with his new tractor and needed an excuse."

"But he applied to make the land a subdivision," I said.

"He applied for the subdivision because at that time it was faster to get the easement."

"Makes sense." I tried a different approach. "We know the killer used an old pickup truck. Unfortunately, those are pretty common in these parts. And I'm wondering if you or anyone you know has seen one that didn't belong to a neighbor running around at night."

"Like I said yesterday. We heard a truck running around, but it's hard to see in the dark even when there's a full moon." He looked at the blue sky. "It's hard to believe that people can do what they do to each other. Especially in times like these. It's not like people are dying at the highest rate in history."

Dad always said that farmers had so much time on their hands that they had a habit of getting philosophical.

"I'm guessing you didn't hear any tractors or heavy equipment working over here at odd hours." I took a shot.

Tim frowned, adjusted his hat, and looked at me. "Now that you mention it. There were a couple of nights that we heard someone working near the field in the middle of the night. But that was just after the first quake. We thought someone was filling gaps in the field. We had to do the same thing. Only we did it during the day."

"A year ago, you say." I sighed. "My forensics tech said that the first body dated to about that same time."

"So, what does that mean exactly?" Tim asked.

"It means I need to have Jenny check the holes again and see if she can get an idea what kind of machine dug those holes." After a while, a thought crossed my mind. "You said that you walk the fence line a lot. Why did you just notice them now?"

Tim's sheepish grin made me nervous. "I thought about that a lot. You see, when the grass is tall and green, you don't notice things like that on unfamiliar land. And that field hadn't been worked since before the murders. When I found the mounds, I hadn't checked the fence since before the big storm. Didn't need to until we had our first calf and let it roam a bit. Staying in the barn too long made him grumpy. But he ran wild, and I had to chase him in the truck. Once I got him headin' in the right direction, I got out to check the fence. That's when I noticed the mounds."

"Anything else?" I asked.

He stared hard at me before shaking his head. "Nope."

I sighed and remembered. "Before we head out. What can you tell me about Bub? You mentioned him, and his name's been mentioned more than once since. Some say he's the town gossip, except the town's underwater."

Tim nodded. "That's a fact. Bub's what you might call a horse of a different color. You see, he's not the sharpest knife in the butcher's block, but he means well. He really only knows about fishing and not much else. But if there's anyone who can give you the best scuttlebutt around here, it's him. People seem to tell him more than they'd tell their own kin. And he's got no problem repeating it." Tim winked and smiled.

"Thanks for your help." I shook his hand.

"If you think of anything else, let us know." Joy smiled.

Tim tipped his cap to her. "I will, ma'am."

We got back to the truck and waited to pick up Zeek and Daniel. As Tim went out of sight, I looked at Tara and her people. They worked diligently and carefully. I admired their tenacity and prayed for God to help them find the heads.

"Where to now, Will?" She asked when the two witnesses got in the truck.

"Bait shop."

CHAPTER 30

Lake Walnut Grove covered the old town without so much as a chimney above the water. The only reminder that a town ever existed was an old red brick house with a black roof at the top of a hill that drivers passed before going down a hill into the town. Now the road dead-ended at the banks of the lake. The house stood in the middle of a hayfield that now had a similar coloring to the new bait shop. Bub salvaged the city limits sign and remade it into the bait shop's business sign. If that's what you want to call it. The green sign with the town's name, with the population scraped out and replaced with the number one in black spray paint, leaned against the house. Above the town's name, a piece of two by four painted white with "Lake" in black spray paint attached. Below the sign, a piece of plywood, also painted white, had "Bait Shop" spray painted. I chuckled at the owner's ingenuity.

"Howdy folks. What can I do ya for?" The chubby, bespectacled man, with a weathered face and a youthful smile, stood from behind a small television sitting on the counter by the chip reader.

"What's biting?" I grinned, trying to win him over early.

"Countin' the bugs, everything." I realized what Tim meant. Bub had mental issues. What they were, I didn't know.

"What are the fish biting on?" I retorted.

His smile widened. "Minnows mostly for crappie. White bass ain't runnin', but they still can't ignore a good chartreuse roadrunner."

"The lake is pretty new, is there many fish in it?" I asked.

"After the water flooded the town, a bunch from the conservation department went to the old Stockton Lake and found fish trapped in small pools. So, they loaded them up and put them here." He smiled. "And the hatchery's been loading the lake up, too."

"By the way, I'm Will, and this is Joy." I pointed to her.

She pulled her badge. "Official business, Mr.?" she raised her eyebrows.

I sighed. She gave me the "What?" look.

Bub sucked in a large batch of air and lost the color in his face. "I'm sorry. I don't know what I did, but I'm still sorry. And I'm sorry for not telling you my name, which is Bub."

"Easy, Bub. We're not here to arrest you. But we do have some questions that some people told us you might know the answers to." I tried not to glare at Joy.

He stared at Joy for a long time trying to figure us out. I had no intention of keeping his fear up.

"Joy, go take a look at the lake. Did you know that a small town is under all that water?" I motioned for her to leave.

Her face reddened, but I leaned into her ear and whispered, "Ask our two friends why a mentally impaired person didn't get taken in the Rapture." She nodded and left.

"She's a nervous Nelly. It's her first investigation, and she gets a little gung ho." I noticed his shoulders relax.

"People are just fooling with ya, sir. I ain't got nothing for nobody, except bait. I ain't smart, like y'all." He tapped the side of his head. "I had a four-wheeler accident when I was young. Fell off and smacked my head on a rock. Hit it real hard. Mom and Dad said I died twice, once in the ambulance, and once in the hospital. But here I am, doing the best I can with what I have left." His bluntness broke my heart. Why did God leave him here?

"You know Tim Weaver up by Phenix?"

"Sure do." Bub leaned a little and put the back of his hand beside his mouth. "He ain't as good a fisherman as he lets on." Then Bub gave a heartly guffaw, slapping his knee.

I laughed with him, glad to be around good people again.

"He said you hear a lot of gossip. So, you must know some things."

Bub sat on a bar stool in front of his counter. I reached for the other one and faced him when I sat.

"Yeah, people don't think I know enough to know what they're saying, but I'm not that dumb." He shook his head.

"Well, I'm looking into those bodies they found over by Phenix. Tim's the one who found the holes. He said the way gossip travels, you might've heard something by now."

His eyes got big. "I heard about that on television. One of the boys from Willard said they got chopped up and spread out. Is that true?"

"Afraid so, Bub." I shook my head.

"That's disgusting. What kind of maniac would do such a thing?" His innocence rang true in his tone.

"The worst kind. But we'll catch him." I winked.

"And send him to the blade." He smiled.

I held in a chuckle. "More than likely, but I'll leave that for the tribunal to decide. What I'm wondering is if you heard anyone talking about it. They may've said something that points us in the right direction."

He leaned back, folded his arms, and looked at the dirty tile floor. "Mostly guesses. But there's not been very many people come here since they found the bodies. Bill Wiggins said he believes that the old government is getting rid of the new government to bring back the good ole U.S. of A." He quickly looked at me. "But I don't mind the new government. They leave me alone, and I leave them alone."

"Sound like the best way to do it, if you ask me." I meant it.

"The Harris's came in yesterday afternoon and said they believe it's a government dump site. You know, to get rid of people that don't agree with the new government. They take them, torture them, and kill them. They need a place to hide the bodies, so no one knows what really happened."

"The Harris's?" I asked.

"Al and Dotty live over by where they found the bodies." His eyes widened again. "I don't think they're against you guys. I mean…"

"I get it. People have said worse things about us. I don't take it personal. We used to say just as much about the good ole U.S. of A." I grinned and remembered Gallway's list of those her people already questioned. "But we haven't even talked to them yet.

They're not home I guess."

He looked at the floor and hummed. "But it's not like them to disappear. They don't wander far from the farm. They fish a couple times a month when the weather's good, but that's about it."

"Thanks," I said. "If you see them, tell them we're looking for them and tell them we don't think they did it. We just want to ask if they've seen anything or anyone different.

"Will do." He saluted and giggled. "By the way, have you found out who those dead people are yet?"

"Not yet. The CSU team is still trying to figure that out."

He nodded. "It does take time. At least that's what they say on television all the time."

Joy came into my peripherals with her notebook out. Bub saw her and grimaced.

"Anything else you can remember?" I tried to keep us on the subject.

He crossed his legs at the ankles and sighed. "Let me see. I can't remember who said it, but somebody said that the bounty hunters are keeping some of the women they catch and selling them to sex traffickers. Maybe one of them did this. You know, they kill someone because they put up too much of a fight or something."

I nodded at Joy, who nodded back and wrote it down. Turning back to Bub, I asked if he remembered anything else.

He remained quiet for a long couple of minutes. "Well, a couple of old boys who used to live in Walnut Grove before the flood said they knew about a strange truck driving all hours of the night in the past year or so. But that was a while back."

That got my attention. "When did they say that?"

"This morning. But maybe they said that's what they heard on television. I don't really remember all that well. I was counting minnows when they said it. That's why I know the crappie are biting on them." He smiled.

It impressed me how he turned the conversation into a sales pitch.

"Wish I had a pole. I haven't fished since before the murders." I stood and prepared to shake his hand.

Bub stood and walked behind the counter. "I can't let ya leave without drowning a hook. Here, borrow mine for a couple of casts." He pulled out a nice rig that already had a chartreuse roadrunner on it. "Try over there by that lone tree. My boat's tied to it. Go about twenty yards on the other side. I've been catching there for a while."

I wanted to tell him I'd do it another time but didn't want to hurt his feelings. Just then, Zeek and Daniel came in the door. The look on their face said that they came on business. The Lord's business.

"Don't mind if I do." I nodded to them and walked out the door.

The hedge apple tree stood, across the road, about a hundred yards from the bait shop with a narrow, blood-red footpath leading to it that smoothed out about halfway there. The water gently rippled at the banks, and my memories carried me back to a time when me and Dad bank fished at Stockton Lake. Before I reached the tree, I felt a presence that made my skin crawl. And she stepped from behind the tree.

Daria Petrovich.

"I wondered when you'd take a break from your inquiry." Her smile seemed devious.

"One of the best places to catch gossip and fish." I nodded towards Bub's place.

"Simpleton had nothing of importance, I take it?" She scowled at the bait shop.

"Don't underestimate Bub. People do all the time, and he gets solid information. In fact, he corroborated one family I want to question." I walked to the place Bub suggested, cast, and reeled in slowly, bobbing the lure the way Dad taught me.

"In my line of work, people like him are nothing but a nuisance. In fact, our Sovereign has been kicking the idea around about euthanizing people like him." She sneered.

"Hitler had the same idea." I flipped the pole and let the lure land near a tree that protruded out of the water a little.

Her face went red. "Are you comparing the greatest mind this world has ever seen to a …"

"Easy there Cruella." I slowly cranked the reel. "What do want anyway?" I fought the urge to shoot her and sink her body in the water.

"I've been trying to find a place where we can talk alone. You do keep Joy on a short leash." She stood next to me.

"How did you get here?" I looked around. "Without being seen."

"There's a farm road on the other side of the walking trail and tree line beside the highway. I followed you here and went over there." She pointed at a line of trees that followed the old Frisco Highline Trail. "I wanted to catch you alone."

Letting the moment pass, I hoped she'd get the drift and either get on with her conversation or leave me alone.

"I've figured out how we're going to get Joy into the open and kill her." Her matter-of-fact tone bothered me.

"You have, have ya?" I flicked the lure near the tree again.

"Oh, it's too good." Her evil giggle crawled all over me. "It's historically motivated."

"I can't wait to hear." I deadpanned.

"It's in your best interest to be more respectful to a superior." Her voice went icy.

"Joy used to say that, too." I reeled and bobbed.

She didn't bite. "You will shoot her at Park Central Square." She drew it out too dramatically.

I sat and thought for a moment. "Wild Bill style?" I shook my head.

"Yes." She laughed. "Did you know that the first quick draw shootout happened right there on that square? I mean the Wild West in that little hamlet?" She slightly bent at the hips when she laughed even harder.

"Remember, I lived here. I'm aware." I sighed at the ridiculousness. "And then you haul me off to the guillotine just a few feet away. Convenient."

"Of course not. I will make it go away. She will threaten you in front of other Peace Forces officers and you'll snap." She snapped her fingers.

"Then I'll be admitted to a psych ward?" I shook my head. "No, thank you."

"No. I'll do the investigation and call it a justifiable homicide. She will threaten to kill your lady friend, and you will respond in kind."

The deep feeling sprang to life, with Libby's face appearing in my mind.

"Libby." I whispered.

"Libby." She responded. "All you have to do is incite an argument over your old flame inside headquarters. Joy loves to threaten people. She does it all the time. When she does, you go outside and wait for her. When she comes out to keep the argument going, you shoot her."

"Sounds simple." I shrugged and cast one last time.

"Oh, and you need to shoot her more than once. You know, to keep up the angry lover routine." She slapped me on the back like an old friend.

I finished reeling in, set the hook in an eyelet on the pole, and reeled it in to tighten the line. "One last thing. If the Sovereign passes a law like you mentioned, you forget Bub exists. That's part of the deal. Agree to it now or it's over." I turned to her.

She looked at me with glazed eyes. "Fine, let the simpleton live. But know that this soft spot you carry might be your ruin. Just remember, I know you have more than one weak spot. I have a file on you thick enough to fill an entire cabinet, preacher's son."

My mind raced to people I've been around. Clay, Tommy, Marjorie. There may have been more, but my head swam too much to get full recall. Did she know about my association with Daniel and Zeek? Then I remembered she had no power over them.

She grinned, took a few steps towards her car, and turned. "After this, you know that we'll be working together for the foreseeable future." Then she left.

Just like Hectar predicted. But she also told me how she planned to end me. She'll find a soft spot and use it to do me in.

After returning the rod and reel and getting Bub's excited account of his new faith, I walked out to the truck. My smile went south when Daniel cut me off before I got to the truck with Zeek and Joy laughing and talking in the truck.

"We need to talk now." He turned and led me away from the truck and house.

When we stopped at the bank, he stared at the water, thumbs in his jeans' pockets.

"That woman you met with over there." He nodded at the hedge apple.

"You noticed that, huh?" I shrugged.

"Will." The authority he had at the cemetery returned. "She's the same one I saw talking to you at the square."

"Yeah, she's under the impression that I belong to her. She's high up in the Antichrist's government. Someone who makes sure things get done on schedule." I chose to leave the other part of the conversation out. "And she's been assigned to make sure this case gets the results the Antichrist desires."

"I'm not surprised." He paused like he didn't know how to tell me. Then he sighed. "That woman is demon possessed."

"How do you know that?" I felt my eyes widen.

It felt out of the blue, but it didn't surprise me.

"I saw it." He pointed at the tree again. "It's one of God's gifts. I can see it in people."

"Why didn't you see it at the square?"

"Preaching and praying with new believers is more important." He didn't brag.

Letting the moment drag out for a long moment, I let the information soak in. I had just made a deal with a devil. The deep feeling chastised me for being foolish and undisciplined. My desire for revenge led me to the opposition. Blinded by my rage.

"What did you two talk about?" It wasn't a question.

My humiliation and pride got in the way. "Something I will take care of in due time."

CHAPTER 31

When I turned towards Phenix instead of going towards Willard, Joy gave an inquisitive look.

"Look up the Harris's. Al and Dotty, although I'm not sure that's their real first names. I want to know if they are in ICON."

Slowing to a stop near the crime scene, I waited for Joy to finish her search. Daniel and Zeek kept quiet. Joy brought the hologram up. A couple, who looked to be in their late forties appeared. "Bub's right. Albert and Dorothy Harris live near the field. Been there over twenty years, but they don't have a criminal record." She frowned and tapped her Vam. "Charlie Caplan's crew brought them in last night, but the Peace Forces released them for lack of evidence. They refused the chip but didn't declare themselves Christians either. In fact, they should be home by now."

"Let's talk to them." I put the truck in drive and stepped on the accelerator.

The Harris's lived in an old farmhouse. Built sturdy, the two-story house showed no signs of damage from the quakes but had a pinkish hue from the blood storm. An old mixed breed dog that looked more retriever than terrier slowly wandered to the truck and sniffed when I parked.

A man and a woman came out on the porch sporting holstered forty-fives. Each one's right palm rested on their pistol's grip. They looked haggard from the previous night, with the look of people who had no intentions of returning to the docks. I didn't blame them.

Joy flashed her badge.

"We're with the Peace Forces. We wanted to ask you a few questions about the bodies your neighbor found just up the road." I nodded in the right direction. "Wondered if you can give us a few minutes of your time."

The man looked at the woman who slightly rolled her eyes when he looked at her, but they still invited us up on the large wrap-around porch. Joy opened the door of the truck and pretended to put something in it. When she shut the door, she walked beside me and whispered. "Free agents."

It surprised me she knew the jargon of the Resistance. But it certainly helped to know that for the questioning.

Al looked like a typical farmer, broad shouldered and broader midriff. Dotty, too, looked like a typical farmer's wife, a thin stature that hid a great strength obtained from years of hard work. I introduced myself and Joy to them. The couple nodded for us to sit.

"Not sure we can be of much help. Didn't even know about the bodies until after your people found them. We just got back from town. Stupid bounty hunters." Al grumbled. "And why is the Commander of the whole territory looking into this? Don't you have investigators?"

Deciding to talk about the case first, I ignored the bounty hunter frustration.

"The police around here don't have much experience with this kind of investigation." I sat in an old green and white lawn chair closest to the couple. "Tim Weaver said they heard a vehicle at night in the field on the odd occasion. Have you noticed anything similar?"

"Nothing comes to mind." Dotty's dark eyes bore a hole through Joy, who didn't sit. "I'm the night owl in this house. And that field's too far for us to hear anything when we're outside. Near impossible when we're inside, which we always are when the sun goes down."

Joy's body language made for an unwelcoming presence. "Have you noticed any unusual vehicles at any point in the last few months?"

Al stared at the truck for an awkward minute. "Nothing too out of the ordinary. Just your usual farm equipment and pickups.

That's a nice rig you got there. I thought you big city folk only drove electric." He screwed his overly tan face in derision.

"I'm from north Springfield. Dad and Mom raised me right." I smiled.

They chuckled. I motioned for Joy to sit in the white wrought iron patio chair near me. But she stood firm. They stopped and stared. I sighed.

"Tim's good folk, but he's off. If you get my drift." Al leaned forward and looked me in the eye for the first time. "Him and those people have different ideas than that Sovereign fellow over in Europe."

Dotty shook her head like she didn't care to live so close to Tim and his people.

"He's the one who called the police. We'll be looking into him and his people, so don't worry. If there's something illegal going on over there, we'll find it out." I gave him a nod of confirmation.

"You said you and your wife were captured by bounty hunters." Joy said. "Care to elaborate?"

They scowled at Joy like two feral animals. I wanted to send her to the truck for jumping the gun. But, since she started the topic, we might as well dive in.

"Charlie Caplan is a greedy, self-absorbed..." Dotty held her tongue when Al placed a comforting hand on her knee.

"Yes, the bounty hunters brought us in. But you knew that already." Al frowned.

The deep feeling had me ask. "We just came from talking to Bub at the Bait Shop. He said he heard rumors of bounty hunters not turning in people to sell to the sex traders. Since you've been around them, I wonder if you saw anything."

"They didn't listen." Dotty looked sharply at Al.

He bowed his head. "The people who interrogated us. We told them that Caplan and one of his cronies took a young woman from the group and drugged her." He ran his hand through his greasy brown hair. "The bounty hunters attacked us on our early evening walk. You know, enjoying an after-dinner stroll. They just pulled over and snatched us without asking for our ID's. Said they didn't care who we were, just wanted to see if we popped in the computer and collect on us. They put a gun to Dotty's head before I could put up a fight. When they opened the side door of the cattle trailer, the red-headed kid pulled out a pretty woman, and zip tied her wrists together. After they closed the door, I saw Caplan and the boy take her to the front of the truck. Caplan pulled a hypodermic needle and injected her. She went limp, and they put her in the back seat of the truck."

"It might be in the report. We just talked to Bub ten minutes ago." I looked at Al. "What about the others in his crew?"

"In a second truck. Caplan told them to go on to Springfield after they tied us up. They'd already left when this happened. At the docks, they must've covered her up because none of the police said anything when they walked around the truck."

"Looks like we need to look into this Caplan." I stood and stuck out my hand. "Thank you both for your cooperation. If you can remember anything concerning the murders, please notify the Peace Forces."

They both stood and shook my hand but didn't say goodbye to Joy.

When we got in the truck, I started it and looked at Joy.

"You need to work on your people skills." I threw the truck in reverse and pulled out of the driveway.

"We needed an intimidating presence. You sat there and chatted with them. They needed to know the hierarchy of the interrogation." She folded her arms and glared.

"There's no reason to intimidate them. They are potential witnesses."

"And potential killers. You need to consider that, Will." Joy turned her head.

I blew out a long breath. "They aren't killers. Just paranoid country folk."

"And you know that how?" She turned to me. "Oh, I forgot. These are your people."

"That and I'm a real cop. You need to get back to your desk and have some more meetings." I didn't care that we had an audience. "And you're not intimidating."

"I cannot believe what I'm hearing." Zeek almost shouted to get over our voices.

"Welcome to my world." Daniel rolled his eyes.

"You are siblings in Christ. Where is the love? Where is the compassion?" Zeek held out his hands.

"Where is the respect?" Joy glared at me.

"You'll get it when you act like a real detective and not this mystery drama cinema crap. When are you going to follow my lead in the investigation? I have the experience, the training, and the understanding of a seasoned veteran. Learn from me." I stopped the truck to finish this ridiculous conversation.

"Your experience? You have one case under your belt." Joy's face beamed red.

"As lead. But I have over thirty cases as a support officer. I watched some of the best investigators in the world and learned everything I could to be a better detective when I got my shot. What about you? Where's your experience? Where's your training? Where's you know how?" I turned and faced her.

The redness abated. Her shoulders slumped a bit. Those beautiful eyes stared at me like a wounded animal ready to make its last-ditch fight. She turned to the window and said nothing. Her finger covered her mouth like she wanted a sharp comeback that stung deeply, but the words never fully formed in her mind. Or did she show restraint?

Daniel sat forward and patted her shoulder. "Although he could've said it more tactfully, Will is right. You need to trust him." Then Daniel looked at me with a fierce stare that made me uncomfortable. "And you need to give her more respect. God has placed her in an influential position in an unholy government, much like Daniel in the Old Testament. Now that she is a believer, her position is precarious at best. She needs your support. I will not try to force you two to hug it out, but I ask that you get over this petty bickering and resolve the big issue between you two."

"What's that?" Zeek asked.

"Frank," Daniel said.

I turned on Daniel and shouted. "And I'm in that same unholy government. And the next time you mention Frank, I'll burn trying to knock you out."

"And I'll be thankful to rid myself of the millstone around my neck." Daniel lunged like he wanted to hit me.

Zeek grabbed his friend, and shouted, "That's enough. Both of you."

Zeek pointed to a tree in an empty field and sounded off like a drill sergeant. "Time to pray."

The three kneeled by the tree and prayed. I sat in the cab and stewed.

CHAPTER 32

After deciding on lunch at a diner in Willard, I kept to myself on the drive there while the others focused on Bub and praised God for the new addition to His Kingdom. Zeek's prayer meeting calmed the attitudes, and Daniel changed the subject to Bub. Joy's smile stretched so wide across her face that it looked almost painful. Zeek and Daniel gave her tips on how to better deliver her testimony more succinctly, just in case of eavesdroppers. Feeling like the only one who didn't forget what just happened, I did my best not to let my temper flare. Let them enjoy the moment. I'd give her the wake-up call soon enough.

My mind kept struggling with the deep feeling about Petrovich. I needed to come clean to Joy and the two witnesses, but I didn't want to alarm them and make a dangerous situation worse. The deep feeling disagreed vehemently.

The lunch rush had already ended at the Better World Diner. We sat in a booth in the far corner. The server, a diminutive young man who displayed his Beastmark on his right wrist among a sleeve of violent tattoos, took our drink orders. While he made the drinks, we looked at the menus and discussed Bub's conversion. What bothered me about Bub didn't stem from not wanting him to become a believer, rather from the possibility that he might accidentally spill the beans about Joy, which might lead them to me.

"Why did God leave Bub down here? He's obviously mentally impaired, yet he's here when others like him went in the Rapture." Joy reached for two packets of artificial sweetener for her iced tea.

"He has the capacity to know right from wrong. So, he can understand sin and its consequences. Those taken are innocent because they did not have this capacity," Daniel said.

Then I remembered Dad said the same thing when a congregationalist asked him the same question about her daughter with Downs Syndrome.

The young man brought our drinks and took our orders. Burgers and fries all around.

A few quiet minutes passed by while we waited for the food. The others either left me to my thoughts, or maybe they decided to cut me out of their little group. Fine by me, I needed some quiet time to work on the case. While I mentally put things I learned from the day into different timelines, the cook walked over to us and tapped my shoulder.

"Yes, ma'am?" I asked.

The white-haired cook stood with an abbreviated bow from osteoporosis. Her white towel, filled with sweat and grease, dangled from her hand.

"You look familiar. Have you ate here before?" She flipped the towel over her shoulder.

"Actually, I have. Now that you mention it. It's been a long time, but I remember this place used to have the best pork tenderloin sandwiches in Southwest Missouri." I stared for a second before remembering. "Nell Dinwiddie. It's me, Will Thomas." I stood and gave her a hug. "What happened to Nell's Place?"

"Will Thomas, if wonders ever cease!" Her raspy laugh took me back a decade. "My son runs it now. Thinks the new name will draw in the right crowd. I just fill in when I'm needed."

"Well, that does it. Change the burgers to tenderloins for all of us. And make them like you used to." I winked.

"Oh, we still use the same recipe. Jimmy said that we can't change everything." Her laugh brought happiness and sorrow to my heart. She went back to the kitchen.

Nell used to be a member of Dad's church. I looked hard but never saw a Beastmark on her person. Maybe she still had a chance.

I sat and looked at the two witnesses. "What do you say? Give her the old one, two?"

Their faces sagged with regret. Daniel shook his head. "Sorry, Will. She's already made her mind up. She'll remain a Free Agent. Never committing to one side or the other."

Fighting off the desire to scream at him, the deep feeling reminded me that Dad preached a sermon telling us that God will never give up on us until we have completely decided against Him. Then he backs off. She's as good as burning now.

Zeek, sitting next to me in the booth, patted my shoulder. "Sorry, brother. I've met my fair share of them, and it still bothers me. I argue with God all the time, but I know that He'll never force Himself on anyone."

Another pause in the conversation helped me to resolve the fact that although many people accepted Christ during the Trib every day, those who didn't still staggered the imagination. Especially considering they watched Bible prophecy being fulfilled right in front of their eyes. Amelia came to mind.

Daniel broke the silence. "How's the investigation coming?" He nodded at the plates on the service counter while Jimmy retrieved a tray to put them on.

"Not as good as I'd like." Joy sipped her tea.

"Me neither." I mumbled, playing with the straw in my soda.

"How come?" Zeek asked, sitting back for Jimmy to lay the plate in front of him. "Sounds like you got some good information."

"Until we get the victims' identities, we can only follow leads. Like we've been doing. Unfortunately, we have no names to use in those conversations. People seem to do better when they have a name to bring up any memories." I slathered mayo on the bun and placed the tomato and lettuce on the golden meat before closing the sandwich, taking a bite, and forgetting my bad mood. Fond family memories will do that.

"Finding the rest of the bodies will be of great help, too." Joy cut her sandwich with a knife, took the small bite, and raised her eyebrows in confirmation.

Zeek wiped his mouth. "I thought they could get DNA from just about anywhere on the body."

"They can, but the blood storm makes it almost impossible to get accurate DNA samples," I said with a full mouth that Mom slapped me in the back of the head for in the past.

"So, it is blood." Daniel smiled. "Why isn't that in the reports, I wonder."

We giggled.

"Joy's right. When we find the heads, we'll have a better chance of getting their identities through either dental or facial recognition on the Beast." I sipped my drink.

"Once we get that, we can get a more accurate profile from the computer." Joy gave up on the knife and fork routine, picked up the sandwich and took a big bite.

"I thought the police didn't profile anymore." Daniel dipped a fry into some ketchup.

"Oh, no. The computer is very accurate with profiling. In fact, five years back, some believed that it might even replace humans. But that fell flat. It can give some indications of the criminal, but it cannot pinpoint the actual perpetrator," I said.

Joy wiped her mouth. "This is delicious."

I nodded and winked. "Nell's is the best."

"Why thank you, Will Thomas." Nell sidled up beside me and put her hand on my shoulder. "It took me a while, but I remembered your daddy, which led me to remember you better. You old scallywag." She winked at Joy.

"Why do you call him that?" Joy's face perked up.

"This one here's your classic PK." She giggled. "That means preacher's kid around these parts."

"That means what exactly?" Daniel smiled.

The deep feeling prepared me for the big revelation. It hurt more than helped.

"He's a Grade A hound dog. Never met a cute girl he didn't like." She nudged my shoulder. "And he chased plenty of them. Caught more than his fair share, too." She laughed even louder than before.

"Is that so?" Joy giggled.

"Oh, yeah. Right up until he met that girl. Oh, what's her name?" Nell looked at the dirty, tiled ceiling. "Lizzy, Tilly, something like that." She waved it off.

"Libby James," I said.

She backhanded my shoulder. "That's it. I almost completely forgot about her. She was a pretty one for sure. Cutest girl in the county, if you ask me."

"I liked her a lot." I nodded and took the last bite of my sandwich.

"And she was head over heels for you, too. Her and her family came in here all the time before the murders. She never talked about anybody but you." Nell noticed an elderly couple come into the diner and turned her attention to them. "Sit anywhere you like. J.J. and tell Thelma we have her favorite ice cream for dessert." She leaned over and put the folded towel beside her mouth. "Poor dear is deaf as a post." Then she walked to them.

Feeling the redness leave my face, I still stared at my empty plate.

"Going back to the case, we have another problem that's come up." I dipped a fry in some ketchup.

"The bounty hunters." Joy's anger came out.

"What about them?" Zeek asked, holding his sandwich with both hands.

"Bub told us, and the Harris's corroborated, that Charlie Caplan is keeping some of his catches and selling them to sex traffickers." She raised her voice.

"That's disgusting." Daniel's face reddened.

"And illegal. One of the few U.S. laws that's still on the books." I wiped my mouth. "If we can catch him in the act, I'll put him behind bars."

"And I'll have him bladed." Joy thundered.

Nell and the two customers stared at us in fear.

"Sorry, Nell." I nodded to them. "Folks."

They side-eyed us before going back to their conversation.

"Maybe we need to talk about this without an audience. They will start gossiping. Then we'll never stop the crank phone calls." I pushed the plate away.

"I agree, Hound Dog?" Joy laughed.

"How about we take all of this outside?" Daniel grinned and took a last drink.

Joy's Vam rang to bail me out. After a grunt and a couple of uh-huhs, she stood and hung up her phone. She lowered her voice. "They found the heads. Let's go."

After Nell brought our check, I noticed Zeek looking at me. He nodded to the bathrooms and walked into the men's room. I waited a full minute before going in.

He stood at the urinal, staring at the wall full of vulgarity about easy women and toilet humor. I took the one on the other side, leaving an empty one between us.

"Can we meet tonight?" He whispered. "Just the two of us."

Knowing I had a lot to do, I wanted to bow out, but the deep feeling demanded I go.

"What's up?" I asked.

"Something down deep wants me to talk to you."

"Okay."

"Meet me at the hotel by your truck at nine." He zipped up, flushed up, washed up, and left.

I did the same.

Joy paid Jimmy while I walked out with the witnesses.

"We'll leave you to your business." Zeek squinted at the sky.

"How will you get back?" I asked, standing next to the truck door.

"Back to where?" Daniel smirked. "We go where we're told. Haven't you figured that out yet?"

"We're going back to Tim's place and stay for the night. Too bad y'all can't come." Zeek waved and walked to the road.

"After Bub, I'd like nothing better than to hear you boys preach," Joy said.

"Me too, but God has us where we are for a reason." I grumbled. "We can drop you off. We're going back to the field." I opened the door.

"We've been seen in public with you enough, Hound Dog," Daniel laughed and caught up with Zeek.

CHAPTER 33

Joy bailed me out by staying on her Vam the entire ride to the field, but I knew she had no intention of keeping quiet about my past. Between that and the blowout, I wanted to get away from her for a while. But that's difficult when she's my partner in an intense investigation. I knew it might get worse.

We parked in the easement this time after seeing a group of Peace Forces near the trees. Before we got out, Detective Gallway met Joy at her door.

"Commander Everhart." She waited for Joy to get out.

"Jenny called us. You found the heads?" Joy pulled her sleeve over her Vam and nodded to the other officers.

"Yes, and it's not what we expected." She turned towards the group but kept her attention on Joy. "They are individually buried, and the heads are in bags."

"Individually?" I asked out loud but meant it internally.

"Bagged?" Joy's eyes widened.

"Yes, but here's one of the interesting things. There are twelve heads." Tara nodded her head towards the trees.

"But the lab confirmed eleven from the body parts." Joy frowned in confusion.

"Maybe the killer snuck in after my people left the first night and buried the head to keep the most important part of his process going." Tara tried. "Maybe backed his vehicle into the easement to keep up appearances."

"Sounds as good as any." I shrugged. "Post a twenty-four-hour guard for the next few days just in case."

"What's the other interesting thing?" Joy asked.

Tara still acted like I didn't exist when she started walking. "Two more things. One, the killer buried them facing south. The other thing you'll have to see for yourself."

We passed the group of Peace Forces officers. Faces that seemed both grim and nauseated stared back.

Two rows of shallow graves, six in each row, a head in each hole. They were buried in order judging by the differing levels of decomp. From a skull to a head that had limited decomp, the gruesome graveyard gave a timeline. And all faced south. It meant something to the killer.

Joy walked around, looking at them individually. I decided this to be a teachable moment.

"Thank you, Tara. We can handle this for now. If we have more questions, we'll let you know."

Her glare at being dismissed didn't bother me. I did the same when it happened to me as a young cop.

After she joined the others, I looked at Joy, who had already opened her notebook and began sketching the graveyard.

"What do you see?"

"Heads." She snarked.

"I'm going to treat you like Frank treated me when I popped off. If that's all you see, then you need to go back to civilian life." I put my hands in my jacket pockets.

She frowned harder without taking her focus off her drawing. "I see heads that are severed at the neck with what I can only assume to be a very sharp instrument of some kind."

"Very good. What else?"

Her deadpan look reminded me of St. Louis. "I'm not a rookie."

"Yes, you are. You have no experience in murder investigations. I'm trying to help." I sounded gruffer than I intended.

She stared for an awkward moment, then looked at the freshest head. "They're a mixture of male and female, and we know there are no sexual markings on the bodies in the lab. There are no matching features like hair color or facial features, or race. So, the killer is conveying a message of some sort, like the profile told us."

"Without using the profile, how do we know that?" I walked around the graveyard, facing south, went to one knee to take a closer look.

"I'm not sure." She mumbled. "Does it have something to do with the arrangement of the heads? Nice, neat rows and all." She chewed the top of her pen, shifting focus to her drawing.

"That's part of it. What's the rest?" Something caught my attention.

She finished drawing and looked at me. "South is important."

"That, too." I put on latex gloves I had in my pocket. "What's the most important?"

She sighed. "I don't know. They're in a different part of the field?" She asked instead of saying it outright.

"Are you asking or answering?" I gently swiped the bag of the one that seemed to be in the middle of his killing spree timeline.

"Answering." Her meek tone made her cute.

"Then yes. You're right. The fact that he not only dismembered them but also separated the body parts tells us only part of the story. It's the separation of the heads from the other body parts that is the actual story." I leaned back and saw the CSU van pulling into the easement, with Jenny riding shotgun. "South is tricky. We may never know the answer to that part of the sermon."

"And what's the sermon?" Joy turned the page and put pen to paper.

"That's part of the mystery." I turned and said, "Hello, Jenny. How's it going?"

"Fine." She put her tackle box down and started gloving up.

I stared at the makeshift graveyard and remembered something I needed to ask her. "Did you find out what the killer used to dig the other holes?"

"A backhoe with a narrow bucket. And before you ask, I have no way of knowing where it came from or who owns it. But I believe he dug the holes at one time. These look like he used a shovel."

"That sounds right." I murmured, disappointed that it was another dead end.

"How's things on your end?" Jenny asked while focusing her camera for the first picture.

I stood and looked at the trees. "We had a lot of dead…"

Staring at the trees, I noticed some of the scratched-up trunks. I side-stepped away from Jenny, and the words came into full focus.

Each tree had a letter. Four letters on one level and five letters on a lower level. My blood chilled. The letters spelled out.

H E L L
B O U N D

Nine trees. Nine letters. One loud, rage-filled message.

Jenny and Joy didn't ask. They came to my side and stared.

"What does that mean?" Joy began sketching the scene.

"We now know why the heads are facing south." I looked at the heads. "He's preaching to them. Making them face their eternal sentence."

CHAPTER 34

We left the scene to Jenny and the CSU tech. Tara dismissed the others, after taking statements from the ones who found the heads. Joy seemed to understand that I did a lot of thinking and left me to my thoughts while she messaged her superiors the news. I'd already texted Lonergan. The killer's message bounced around my head, but no matter what angle I used, nothing seemed to make sense except for one obvious factor. The killer didn't preach to the world. Otherwise, he'd put the sentence in a public place for all to see. Everything revolved around the victims.

When we got to HQ, we agreed to meet later because Joy had a meeting with her superiors. I went to my office, closed the door, and let the case ruminate in the back of my mind. It helped when I took my focus from a task that overwhelmed me. Like taking a deep breath before plunging into unknown waters.

Knowing Lonergan expected more than a text, I gave the highlights of the day and left it at that. I'd give him the detailed account later. Then I scratched an itch that niggled itself into my brain thanks to Hectar.

When I spied for the Resistance, I took times like this to dig into the Beast and find information that kept Christians alive. Although my time with the Resistance had ended, I still looked for information and passed it indirectly to the Resistance or changed orders to ensure their safety when I led troops out West.

Now, I stared at the screen for personal safety from Daria Petrovich.

Wondering about my clearance as a member of DRUID, I

decided to dig into the Beast deeper than I ever dared. However, the deep feeling gave me the urge to keep my first search brief, so the AI didn't flag me as a spy or threat. I entered the case file and began reading the reports with information I already knew and adding minor details to show I'm an active member of the investigation. Then I noticed that Jenny had some pictures already uploaded. I didn't need to see them again, since the gruesome memory still haunted my mind.

Remembering some things Lonergan told me during my debriefing of my new position, I felt more confident in looking at similar files I read when I spied for the Resistance, believing that these files fit my DRUID position. I sat in front of the screen, trying to decide the best course of action before plunging into the depths of Petrovich's profile. Using the six degrees of separation to my advantage, I used Joy to complete the breadcrumb trail. She knew an embarrassing part of my past. I felt justified in prying into Joy's past to gain a little leverage if she overstepped.

Much to my surprise, Joy had Christian missionary parents.

My emotions went in a thousand different directions as I read on. They planted a church in Peru, preaching the Gospel to the indigenous tribes of the north. They hadn't been there very long when they sent Joy to a private boarding school for missionary children. Near the end of her sophomore year, the school expelled Joy for bullying a boy until he attempted suicide. She went to live with an aunt and uncle in Missouri and attended public school where she excelled, graduated, and went to a Missouri college, majoring in criminology. Returning to Missouri and entering the police academy in St. Louis, she climbed the ranks of the city's police force on the administrative side until the Rapture, then used the loss of high-ranking officials to jettison up the career ladder. She had no strikes against her. I wondered if she either had them expunged or deleted them herself. After all, she only became a Christian just a few weeks ago.

The file had an attachment that caught my attention. Clicking on it, I immediately wished I hadn't. Daria Petrovich's name headlined what appeared to be a list of known associates. This included Hectar. The file showed the hierarchy of Hectar's criminal empire. First Daria, then Hectar, Franks, and so on. Daria made this list to set Joy up if the situation required it.

Having a clear path, I typed Daria's name into the Beast and found her file buried amongst the top names in the Antichrist's government. Originally from Georgia, Russia, Daria attended a university in Moscow, then joined the lower ranks of the KGB. Her slow upward mobility made me think I had wandered into the wrong file, but a note in the file brought everything to light. Placed in the KGB by the Antichrist before he took power, she spied for him to help bring the Russian government into his control. In fact, Daria delivered the order for Russia to invade Israel in their ill-fated attempt to bring God's chosen into the Antichrist's control. But God intervened, and the Antichrist had to win them over via the promise of rebuilding the Temple. Then I remembered Dad's journal mentioning the Gog passage in Ezekiel predicting the event.

Anger slowly built in my gut thinking of Tommy stealing Dad's journal.

Daria's invaluable service to the Antichrist's top official proved her worth as his person who got things done. He sent her to the U.S. to secure Hectar's mob and ensure the treaty signing, which I knew. However, I didn't know that Hectar had a pre-selected time to die. In fact, the Antichrist himself answered an email from her asking for permission to kill and replace Hectar. He wanted Hectar in place until either he messed things up or until his appointed time came. After some digging, and mental arithmetic, I learned that the end of Hectar's tenure will come after the final trumpet judgment when Satan enters the Antichrist's body.

Sitting back with this new information, I considered how best to use it for mine and Joy's benefit. The deep feeling pointed out that Hectar, still a free agent, needed protecting until he made his ultimate choice between God and Hell, unless he's like Nell. Not wanting to give it to him too late, I thought about killing two birds with one stone. Tell Hectar and have him help Joy take Daria's place. If what Daniel told me was correct, and I knew he didn't lie, Daria Petrovich and her little demon needed sent to their chosen destination…Hell.

Switching back to the case, Charlie Caplan's face came up on the screen, but his file didn't have much. He grew up in the Southwest Missouri area, inherited the family farm, and received his bounty hunter's license on the first day. The details of the rest of his life were obscure, at best. The file read like he and his family kept off the grid. He also didn't have a list of known associates outside his crew, a band of drug users and low-level criminals. None of them had ties to human trafficking.

Sitting back, I considered how anyone can stay out of the Beast that easily. He needed to be watched. Great, I thought, something else to add to the list. But stopping a low life like him needed to be a higher priority.

Before logging out and talking to Joy, I looked up my sister. Still off grid. I shot up a quick pray for her. Maybe a witness found her and got her to believe. Maybe she already died. Maybe I needed to let God handle it.

CHAPTER 35

Joy waved me in while her meeting wrapped up. It sounded like one of those meetings that everybody said something, but no one said anything. Her demeanor reminded me of the class kiss-up. She complimented everyone without sounding too much like a brown-noser and saluted before turning the Vam off and placing it in the new safe behind her.

"The safe is safe from prying eyes and ears." Her infectious smile made the situation seem lighter.

"And no bugs?" I whispered.

"None," she said aloud. "Checked for them myself."

"I hope you're good at it." I sat back in the chair and crossed my legs.

"I learned it early in the game. A former superior of mine at the beginning of the Trib lost her head to Daria Petrovich."

I took a moment to let that sink in. "Isn't she the one who gives you the messages to give to Hectar?"

Her cold stare told me everything I needed to know.

"Hectar tells me things." I smiled and shrugged innocently. "We have a rapport."

"I'm guessing that you two have been buddies since the case in St. Louis." She widened her eyes when she used buddies.

"We have a rapport," I said.

"What do you want?" Her sigh told me I hit the right button.

"I've been skimming through ICON and found a little bit about your nemesis."

She looked up at me quickly. "And why do you call her my

nemesis?"

"Not me. Hectar." I put my hands on my head. "He said you've been wanting her position for a long time now."

She opened a desk drawer, pulled out an apple, and took a bite. She stared at me the whole time she chewed. It might've worked on rookies and suck-ups, but I had plenty of time to wait her out.

"She seems to think that, but I know no one can replace her." She took another bite.

"Because she's been there from the beginning."

Joy took a quick look at me with a mildly surprised gaze and finished chewing. "You have a lot of knowledge of Petrovich."

I knew I hit a nerve. Joy never said a person's name without their rank included.

"Actually, I just found out. While you were talking about money spent, I did a little digging." I stopped because I didn't want to say too much.

The deep feeling did laps in my gut, demanding that I tell Joy everything, but I resisted. I wanted to deal with Daria myself.

Joy pulled two napkins from her desk drawer. One to sit the apple on, while she used the other to wipe the juice from her lovely, full lips. She leaned forward and looked at me. The concern she showed melted her arrogance.

"Will, you need to be careful what you look up in that system. That AI technology is on a level that no one will ever comprehend, ever. If it thinks you're about to compromise any of the Sovereign's plans, you will be bladed for spitting in the park."

I smiled nervously. "I know what I'm doing. Remember, I've been spying on that system for over a year. And I have one of the highest clearances in the government. If Petrovich sees my searches, and I know she's looking, she'll see that I looked at the case file and my search for my sister. She'll either think I'm bored or doing my due diligence. Either way, I'm safe."

"For now, but be careful." The tension left her face, and she grabbed her apple. "Have you found your sister yet?"

"No." I looked down to avoid showing my disappointment. "She's been off grid for a while."

"That's a good thing. She's found a way to slip through the cracks. Maybe she's a Resistance member doing great things for the Lord." Her infectious smile returned.

"She's a nonbeliever. The last time I saw her, she said that she had no use for a God that doesn't exist."

"Keep praying. I'm sure that she'll change her mind when the next judgments come." She threw the core in the trash and wiped her mouth and hands. "And I'll add her to my prayer list."

The gesture overwhelmed me. She said it like it a seasoned Christian veteran, not a snot-nosed rookie. Then I remembered her family.

"Appreciate it." I tried to sound genuine.

"You said that you looked at the case file. Anything new?" She leaned back in her chair.

"Nothing yet. It'll take Jenny and her bunch a while to get the heads identified. The profile on the computer is still vague. But I don't really believe it, anyway." I snuffed.

"Why not? I know what it's used for, but it's still a valuable asset in law enforcement."

"The profile shows a young man did this. But I'm not buying it. Things are different from before the Trib began. People are acting and thinking different. I believe the killer is middle-aged. He's taken some time to consider his sermon, took his time to pick the field and scratch out the letters in the trees, and I believe he did this before starting the murders. A younger man might not take the time for all this setup." I smoothed my pant leg.

"That's interesting. In fact, I have one problem with the profile." She sat up and put her elbows on her desk. "It says that the killer has low self-esteem, but I don't buy it. I think he has a messiah complex. Take it into consideration that he is sermonizing. He's sending those people to Hell personally, meaning he gets to decide who goes. He believes he has this power and wields it like a despotic deity. That isn't low self-esteem, that is pure ego."

I grinned and pointed at her. "You might make detective yet, Commander."

She blushed and smiled, looking beautiful. My gut slightly wrenched in guilt for thinking it, considering the state of my relationship with Amelia.

"I checked on Caplan, but there's not much. His crew, however, is a band of small-time miscreants. We need to set an undercover officer on him and see if Caplan hangs himself and his crew."

"I'll see if the locals have anyone to spare." Joy checked the clock on the wall and stretched. "It's getting late. Care to join me for dinner?"

It took me off guard. Did she just ask me out? Then my better senses came out. Of course, she's hungry.

"Ever had cashew chicken?"

CHAPTER 36

Leong's Tea House smelled like it did the first time I went there as a kid. Their famous cashew sauce, which gave Springfield a food identity like New York pizza and Kansas City barbecue, wafted into my nasal passages and started my stomach to growl. On the way there, I told Joy a little about the restaurant's history and how it put Springfield on the foodie map. Then I raged a little when I told her how Hectar took the restaurant. She listened politely and let me travel back to my past before the Trib.

Joy went to the restroom to freshen up while I waited to be seated. The dining room had an intimacy that I didn't remember, making me uncomfortable with the woman I had recognized as my archnemesis just a few days prior. A quick flash of my badge—and name-dropping Hectar—made the hostess squirm until she recognized my name from my only case. She led me to a small room near the back of the restaurant and asked for an autograph, my first and hopefully last, before closing the door behind her.

When Joy returned to our corner table, her makeup made her eyes sparkle and her smile dazzle. The dim lights accentuated the candles on our table which took the intimate feel to a level that disarmed me. I had to remind myself that this was a professional dinner and not a date, though the ambiance made it difficult to ignore her beauty. The linen-clad tables, the understated flowers all felt too intimate, especially with Joy sitting across from me, her demeanor more relaxed than I'd ever seen. My pulse quickened, a mix of nerves and guilt curling in my stomach, reminding me of Amelia and the fragile state of our relationship. I deliberately straightened my posture, made a plan to keep the conversation focused on neutral topics, and determined not to allow my thoughts—or my actions—to wander into territory I'd later regret.

"This room is ... cozy." Her beautiful smile widened.

"It's good to have a rapport with the owner." I sheepishly grinned. "And this room is safe. Hectar appreciates solitude."

"I'll bet." Her judgmental look made me uncomfortable.

We ordered the house specialty and two sweet teas. While the server went to put in our order and get our drinks, we settled into something we hadn't done before. Relax in front of each other.

"Is it alright if we don't talk about the case?" I wanted to decompress for once.

"Not at all. Sometimes it's good to put it in the back of your mind so your subconscious can work on it. I'm a big believer that we can sometimes get in our own way if we don't take time to be our other selves. To be who we are when we're not cops." She sat back to let the server place our drinks in front of us.

"What did you do before all this happened?" Joy took a sip of her tea and raised her eyebrows in curiosity.

"After high school, I went into the Marines. Did my four years fighting in Iraq and Iran as a special forces recon specialist. After that, I went to Missouri State University on the G.I. Bill and majored in criminology. Then the police academy in Springfield. After that, I was hired by the KCPD. Then the Rapture happened, and I worked the riots. Then St. Louis, where we met." I looked up from my tea. "You?"

I knew her backstory from the Beast, but I wanted to hear her version. Computers, although highly intelligent, have no concept of telling a good story from the main character's point of view.

She blushed. "I know you don't think I'm a real cop, but I went to school at the University of Missouri-St. Louis, where I received my degree in criminology. I also went to the academy there and went to work for St. Louis P.D. I started as a uniform, but I knew I was better suited for administrative duty. My mentor in college recognized my gift for it and suggested I take the necessary classes. Once I did my time on the streets, I started pushing pencils and filing paperwork. Then the Rapture happened, and the jobs opened up. I climbed the ladder quickly. The rest, you know."

"What about your time in the missions' fields?" I asked.

She didn't respond the way I expected. Her eyes began filling before looking at her tea glass, pain enveloping her body.

She took a few calming breaths before answering. The deep feeling stopped me from letting her open the old wound. "I'm the youngest of four and the black sheep of the family. Daddy and Momma didn't approve of my decisions in Peru. Momma homeschooled us while Daddy preached the Word of God to the tribes in northern Chile. My two brothers and sister did everything right. They followed my parents in missions when they grew up. The boys lived in Africa and my sister married a missions major and followed him to Eastern Europe. But they're all in Heaven now. And I'm not. Which is exactly what they expected from their little prodigal." She dabbed her eyes with a napkin. "I'm guessing you read that in my file."

The server brought our supper and Joy remembered to put in a to-go order for Jenny. We said nothing until about halfway through. Joy kept her eyes on the food and only looked up to find her glass.

"I'm sorry I dug too deep in your file. I didn't know the circumstances," I said.

"It's alright. You're a detective. It's what you're made to do." She took another bite. "This is quite delicious. I'm glad you suggested it."

"If it means anything, my sister was my parents' favorite. She blew up her high school graduation party by announcing her atheism and breaking their hearts. But they still preferred her over me." I pushed the chicken around on my plate.

"Because of your reputation?" She kept her gaze on her plate.

I struggled to answer the question because the truth hurt.

"Yeah." I took a drink. "Dad had to explain away a lot of my teenage years to members of his congregation. Especially the deacons. Several people threatened my dad's job because of the rumors that flew around. People like Nell always exaggerating never helped either. I had girlfriends, but not the numbers that came out. In fact, I had exactly three girlfriends in high school. But to hear them talk, I had a new one every week. Mom found out that the first girl I dated my freshman year started the rumors after I broke up with her and dated her rival, which I didn't even know they hated each other. Then she talked about our sexual exploits.

Again, never happened. Although I'm not an angel, I never considered sleeping with her on account that I had every intention of saving myself for my wedding night like Dad preached." I shrugged. "But intentions have a way of being left behind. Not that I'm proud of it."

She sighed. "Look at us. A couple of sad sack black sheep trying to run away from our pasts."

We finished our meals in silence, letting the attempt at normal conversation pass.

She pushed her plate away, took a last sip of tea, and looked at me, sizing me up. I let her while I finished up and wiped my mouth.

"What are you thinking about?" I asked.

"Libby." She sat back. "Your last girlfriend before the Rapture. Right?"

"Yes." I shrugged. "Since then, I focused on staying alive and not my social life."

"Oh, right." She nodded. "Are you trying to get her out of jail?"

"I'm working on it, but Daria Petrovich is being a pain about it."

She frowned hard. "I didn't know you knew her that well."

"She's been sniffing around the case. I think she's reporting it to her higher ups. You know, the stuff that doesn't get in the reports."

"What's she been saying to you?" The old Joy made an appearance.

Although the deep feeling demanded that I give full disclosure, I had no intention of giving it.

"A lot of questions about my investigative techniques. More like she's questioning my abilities." I shrugged. "I think she wants to take over the case."

"She's good at that. Trusts no one to do the job." Joy stopped abruptly and stared as if trying to decide what to divulge. "I know you know that I've been her messenger to Hectar. I tried to keep my distance from him since my promotion, but she insists I keep my role. It's as if she wants to keep me under her thumb."

"According to Hectar, she looks at you as a rival for her job." I paused but said it, anyway. "I think she wants you replaced."

"With whom, and what will happen to me?" Fear filled her

voice.

"Not sure." I lied, not wanting to exacerbate her anxiety. "But she does want a more faithful follower."

"You mean more faithful to her." Joy crossed her arms.

"That's the picture Hectar painted. But that's fairly old information. He told me this in St. Louis. We didn't really talk about your relationship with Daria until here in Springfield."

"Hectar's in Springfield?" Her eyes widened.

"He owns this place and the Automat. I went to eat at the latter and he invited me to his personal dining room there. We chatted about old times, and he took me back to the hotel."

"Did he peck you on the cheek?" She groused.

I chuckled. "Listen. Hectar trusts me. His information helped solve the president's murder. If he can help with this case, I will accept it."

Her rage finally came out. "I can't believe you trust him. After all, he's a mobster. He does nothing without considering his profit."

"No, I said he trusts me. I know all about his so-called empire. He's so powerful that he takes orders from the Sovereign. If what I read on ICON is true, he won't be in power for long." I tipped the glass to my mouth and let a piece of ice slide in.

She looked confused. "I read everything there is to know about Hectar, and there's nothing about his days being numbered."

It hit me, but I didn't want to say it. "I have higher clearance than you. It's in there."

She sat back. Her eyes bugging out. The truth hitting her hard.

Then she whispered, "DRUID."

I smiled. "Yep. Sorry about that, I really am, but we have to play the cards God deals us. This lets me be more help for Christians than I've ever been."

She let the sentence disappear in the air. Her ego just took a massive hit. She needed some alone time. I got up and went to the bathroom to let her have it.

When I returned, she had already paid the bill and stood by the exit holding Jenny's food. Her demeanor felt defeated.

The truck roared to life, but I kept it in park. I turned to her, trying to help.

"Listen, I know how you're feeling. When you sent me to the

military, I thought my days in law enforcement were over. But God opened a new door to get me back into the game. I know He has a plan for you. Just trust Him."

"Let's just go to the hotel." She whispered.

I put the truck in reverse and backed out.

CHAPTER 37

Joy jumped out of the truck before I put it in park and entered the hotel without so much as a good night. Zeek got in after her and told me to drive to the crime scene. I didn't ask why because I trusted him. We kept silent the entire trip. The deep feeling brought the plans of the government spinning the case into a religious statement to dissuade people from choosing God's path to mind. Pulling into the field, I realized that, like Hectar, they might be trying to use the Bible to their advantage. As if God never considered that when He inspired the writers of the prophetic texts of the Bible. That's taking arrogance to a new and ignorant level. Just like Hectar.

The night sky seemed to have fewer stars. Of course, the sixth seal judgment made some go away. I sat, waiting for Zeek to start the conversation, with the windows down, missing the breeze. The noises I remembered when I lived in the area didn't exist in the Trib. Bugs, dogs, and the occasional coyote call let a person know that it's bedtime. Now, the dead silence overwhelmed the landscape. I began wondering how the killer felt in these conditions when he buried the victims. Did he mumble his sermon here or at the place he killed them? Or both? The deep feeling revealed that he never stopped preaching in his mind.

Zeek finally got out, pulled down the tailgate, and sat. I followed suit, and we stared into space a while before he broke the silence. "Have you noticed that there don't seem to be as many stars since the Trib began? Like the universe is standing farther back to avoid the punishments God's puttin' on us. You know, getting as far from us so it doesn't get caught in the crossfire."

"Sorry, I've been caught in my own kind of crossfire." I grunted. "I remember when the sky folded up. The scariest moment of my life, spiritually speaking. Even though my faith in God was new, I still felt insignificant."

"I bet the next scariest thing was the loss of your mentor." Zeek still stared into the heavens.

Under any other circumstance, I'd have yelled and threatened. But Zeek's words knocked me off balance. Although Joy railroaded Frank to the guillotine, the hardest part of that scene popped into my brain. Frank singing his revised version of *The Old Rugged Cross*, ready to go home. However, Joy became my sister in Christ the moment she believed. God forgave her for everything. My jaw clenched from the realization that I had to get over my past with Joy like God got past hers and mine. He forgave me, but I needed to let Frank go to get on with what little of my life I had left.

"Is there something I can do to help?" Zeek finally looked at me.

"I'm trying to get past my anger with Joy. I know what she did to Frank has already been forgiven and that I have nothing to do with it. And that I need to let it go. The deep feeling has been working on me for a while now." I gripped the tailgate and looked at the darkened ground.

"The deep feeling?" Zeek asked.

"Daniel believes it's the Holy Spirit. Or maybe a mix of my instincts and the Holy Spirit. Mainly because it helps me with a case. But it's more than that." I scratched my cheek.

"That's a special thing, Will. It means that God is part of you on a deep level. That's why you refer to it as the deep feeling. You need to trust it. Follow it. Cultivate the relationship."

"Easier said than done when you're as stubborn as I am," I chuckled and looked at the ground.

"You're preaching to the choir, boy. Too many people believe that just because I am a chosen witness, I am immune to the problems all other believers cope with. I'm still human and subject to the same problems, no matter how petty, just like anyone else. The other day when those soldiers confronted me and Daniel. I knew our angels were protecting us, and knowing my ticket to see the end of the Tribulation was punched, I still hesitated and felt fear. Even when those soldiers died, I wanted to run and hide. But the deep feeling strengthened me to stay the course." He sniffed.

"Just like Elijah." I smiled.

"Did you hear a sermon on that?"

"My dad's last sermon I attended was on fear, and he used Elijah as his example." I looked back down, trying to avoid eye contact.

"My family was on vacation in Jerusalem to see the homeland when the Rapture happened. That's when I realized that my best friend in Alabama was right about Jesus. So, I put my faith in Christ, and God led me and the other witnesses to a soccer stadium where two of them began teaching us the Bible and how to reach the world with the Gospel of Christ. I met Daniel there, and we immediately felt a connection and became instant friends. I now believe that God paired us together for times like this. He knew we'd cross paths more than once."

"You mean the Two Witnesses?" I looked at the ground trying to remember their names.

"No, those two ain't coming for another year or so. The two I'm talking about are in my group." He smiled at my ignorance.

"Then Dad was right." I chuckled. "The way the two now are being talked about, I thought for sure they were the two. But Dad said they wouldn't come until just before the halfway point."

"Daniel told me about reading your dad's journal. God gave him a powerful mind and a strong faith. Daniel never stops talking about that book. It's as if God showed your dad everything that will happen to us. I thank God every day for the people in Heaven who paved the way for people like us here on Earth." His eyes glazed in remembrance.

He shook his head to get back to his story. "Anyway, on the second day of the training, the leader of my small group told us about Elijah and his experience with the prophets of Baal. He said to learn it well because we'd experience it in our time in the field. And he was right. And it does help. I have to face the enemy and never run away knowing that God always has my back. Just like you needing to face your past with Joy and quit running from God's blessings." He looked back up to the windless sky.

The long pause signaled the end of the conversation.

"I think I need to have some time alone with the Lord." He patted my knee, slid off the tailgate, and walked out of sight.

Sliding off the tailgate, I took a knee by the truck near the victim's burial sites. The darkness kept them hidden, but I felt their presence and the need to catch their killer. Then I thought about Zeek's words. Getting on both knees and bowing my head, I prayed and let go of my desire for revenge. The deep feeling reminded me that letting go of something isn't a onetime action. It must be a daily decision.

Getting up from the prayer, I noticed Zeek leaning on the side of the truck bed with his forearms resting on the edge, like a good old boy after a hard day's work. "Feels like God's got a few things straight with ya."

"Something like that. But He's still workin' on me." I grinned at the old song reference.

Zeek whistled that tune all the way back to the hotel.

Getting out of the truck, thanking Zeek before he left, and getting my gear, I heard someone clear their throat. In the corner of the building, I noticed a shadowy figure with hands in their pants pockets. Recognizing my friend, I nodded at the building and went straight to my room without closing the door. I hid my gear in the bathroom again and waited for Clay to come in.

"Hey buddy." Clay shut the door behind him, slipped off his coat and took a seat at the table.

Before we settled into the conversation, he snuck a peek from behind the curtains.

"Are you being followed?" My heart rate increased.

"No, but you can never be too careful in our line of business." He let the curtain go and smiled at me. "Hectar's up to something."

"I had dinner with him last night. I got the same feeling myself."

"He's been asking around about that French woman, Petrovich. Got some good information."

"Your source from St. Louis?" I asked.

"One and the same. She said that Hectar found out that Petrovich is working unilaborly or something." He frowned at the desk, trying to come up with the word.

"Unilaterally?" I asked.

He snapped his fingers and pointed at me. "That's the one.

Although I'm not sure what it means."

"It means she's working without orders from the government. Nobody's telling her to do what she's doing."

Clay sat back and stared at me. "Is that good or bad?"

"It's definitely good for us. It means the government isn't involved in this particular activity. She's assigned to make the case go faster, but she isn't assigned to do the other." I scratched my cheek and thought for a minute. "It means that her problem with Joy is personal. She means to kill her."

"Does she know about Joy's faith?" Clay's eyes widened with concern.

"Doesn't matter to her. She's only interested in killing Joy. How she will kill her isn't that important. In fact, I think the blade is Plan B."

"How many plans does she need?"

"Plan A is to have someone else do it. Someone she needs to fall in place. Plan B is the blade." I sighed, feeling the impending doom looming over my head.

"Who do you think she'll get to do it if she can't?"

The deep feeling erupted inside me to tell Clay the entire story. But the less Clay knew, the safer he'd be from people like Daria and Hectar.

"I'm not sure," I lied. "Why is Hectar interested in this?"

"My friend says that he's sick and tired of getting told what to do by her. And that he wants to take her position in the government. Start giving the orders himself." Clay grinned. "Since you two are buddies, it'd be nice to have someone with a little pull to help out."

"Don't trust Hectar. He's only out for Hectar and no one else. Our relationship is tenuous at best. We use each other for information that'll get us ahead and that's it. I'd never call on him in tough times. He might sell me out to get a better deal." I pushed my finger against my chin. "In fact, Joy's the best person for what your people want. She's a sister in Christ and deep in the Peace Forces. She'll be more than willing to help the Resistance."

"More pull than you? You're DRUID." His shock surprised me.

"I've only been in it a couple of days. Joy has been building her inside relationships since she joined the police. I can't compete with that." I grinned at my change of attitude.

"Sounds like you're getting along with her." His smile reminded me of a teenager insinuating a budding romance.

"She's growing on me, but I still don't trust her any more than I trust Hectar. She's a believer, no doubt, but a leopard doesn't change their spots." I snuffed, not really believing it myself.

"But God can turn a leopard into a lion if He chooses to."

The deep feeling agreed with Clay.

"And if God is changing your mind about Joy. He'll change it about Tommy." His matter-of-fact tone bothered me. That and the deep feeling agreeing with him.

"Not yet." I shrugged. "Maybe not until we get to Heaven."

"I'll keep praying for the both of you." His faith impressed me.

"What have you heard about the bounty hunters?" I asked.

Clay looked at the ceiling and sighed before responding. "She said that Hectar ran several of the crews, but not all of them. In fact, since Hectar showed up, a few of the independents either disappeared or joined up with Hectar."

"That's quick work. But I guess I'm not too surprised. He's quite ambitious." I took a moment to consider it. "Disappeared, huh? I think I need to have another meal with our local mobster. It seems that he hasn't told me everything."

"Surprise, surprise." Clay laughed. "A mobster lying to a cop. It must be the first time."

"Alright, alright. I meant I didn't read him good enough last time." I took my turn peeking out the window. "Sounds like there's good money in bounty hunting."

"To be honest. If I hadn't got saved, I'd probably be making money hand over fist down here hunting the Christians myself. Of course, I'd have overdosed on that much smack. Then I'd be burning." His infectious smile of gratefulness overwhelmed me.

"I'm glad you'll never get that chance." I smiled at my friend.

We spent the rest of the time talking about our pasts and what happened when we separated after the St. Louis case. For the first time since the Rapture, I felt normal. Like the world outside that hotel room didn't exist and two buddies shooting the bull. I felt human again.

"Any orders before I go?" Clay stood and stretched.

"Hang around the Automat. Hectar owns it and will be there quite a bit to eat. See if you can't find something more about why he's so interested in Petrovich."

Although I knew the main reason, Hectar had a reputation for having more than one ulterior motive for his movements.

"Here." I pulled out my wallet and gave Clay some cash. "Eat there. It'll look more natural."

Once Clay left, I read from Mom's Bible. The verses of stubbornness I read on the plane didn't bite as hard.

Checking the time, I hurried to get the Vam to video chat with Amelia. I didn't look forward to it.

"I was wondering if you wanted to talk with me." Her beautiful gray eyes looked sleepy.

"Sorry, I had a lot happen today." I changed my clothes out of her sight.

"I heard you found the heads." She smiled. "It's the second lead in tonight's news."

"The second?" I sat down and adjusted the Vam to see her better.

"Yes, one of those stupid Jews fried a group of priests from a global church in D.C. near the old White House." She snuffed. "I can't wait until someone puts them in their place."

"It might be awhile. We had a couple of Peace Forces soldiers die yesterday from two of those preachers. My first time seeing it up close." I shook my head. "Gruesome."

"The Sovereign said he's working on something that will end them all soon." She smirked. "I hope we get to see it."

According to the Bible, everyone will see the Antichrist kill the Two Witnesses who hadn't shown up yet. Only God will raise them a few days later. I wanted Dad's journal even more.

"It's best to keep your distance." I worried for her safety, physically and spiritually.

"Not a problem. The little Jew here in St. Louis hasn't been screaming at us for a couple of days."

"That's because he's one of the two down here."

"He's following you?" Her face lit up. "Why don't you shut him up. You are DRUID."

"I don't think that makes a difference." I chuckled.

"Tell them about your autonomy." She snarked.

"I don't need this right now." I tapped the Vam and Amelia disappeared.

CHAPTER 38

Waking up the next morning seemed harder than usual. It felt great to be on good terms with God again. My talks with Zeek and Clay did my soul good. However, the chat with Amelia stung deep. Even in the Trib, a person needs a good day or two, and I hadn't had a streak that long yet.

After a short prayer session asking for help in all areas of my life, I got ready to face the day. The case still loomed, but I had confidence that the killer had little chance to stay hidden, even in this country. Daria Petrovich felt less of a threat and more of a pest. And Hectar seemed more like a memory than a current event. Standing in front of the window and looking at the new day, I knew that this short-lived moment needed savoring because the real world waited to slap me upside my head.

The others sat at the table when I walked in for breakfast. Their laughter sounded good as I loaded a plate full of biscuits and gravy. When I sat with them, their welcoming smiles gave me peace and a sense of fitting in I hadn't experienced since before the Rapture.

"Morning, Will." Zeek grinned. "Just talking about last night."

"Looks like you two had a successful evening." I sipped my powdered orange juice.

"I know you guys are in a precarious position, but you need to understand how your work is being used to add more souls to the Kingdom of God. Remember that Jesus said that some plant the seed, some water it, and others gather its harvest. Other than Joy's harvest yesterday, I want you to know that your part in this is so important. Without that kind of safety in the last days, I doubt that we'd have as many opportunities to reach the ones we have for Christ as we have in the last few days." Daniel smiled. "I love you, brother."

Knowing he meant the ambiguous apology for me, I nodded my apology back. I raised my glass and smiled. It felt good to have some recognition for our work, and I believed that God knew we needed to hear it. The kind words built on my already growing confidence.

"Wish I could've been there, from what I hear." Jenny shrugged while loading her fork with stale scrambled eggs.

"Speaking of, how's the investigation going?" Daniel asked.

Jenny shrugged. "We didn't get the evidence to the lab until one in the morning. I'm on about two hours of sleep."

"When can we expect the IDs?" Joy buttered her mildly burned toast.

"Not until tomorrow at the earliest. It'll take all day to get the DNA collected and processed." Her eyes drooped from exhaustion.

"What about dental impressions?" Joy bit into her toast and frowned. "Won't that be quicker?"

"It might if the skulls had any teeth." Jenny pushed her eggs around with her fork. "The killer removed them. But since he bagged the heads, we'll be able to pull DNA samples. Once we processed the paperwork and uploaded all of the pics, we called it a night. So, I can't say with any certainty that we'll be able to get it all done today."

The table remained silent for the rest of the meal. The news of the teeth removal took me into the case. Obviously, the killer removed the teeth to make it harder to identify the victims. But some killers collected prizes from the kill.

"What are you two planning for the day?" Zeek asked.

"In my meeting yesterday, my superiors told me to investigate the bounty hunting system here in Springfield. I told them about Caplan possibly selling people to the sex traffickers. They want me to find out if it's true and arrest him and the red-headed kid." She grimaced like she felt the same pressures that I felt. "But don't worry about Tim's church. I will send all leads in a different direction."

"Please be careful. I know your intentions are pure, but I don't want you facing the blade so soon after your conversion." Daniel leaned back.

"Don't worry, Danny boy. I'll train her right." I smiled. "Me and Tommy aren't buddies anymore, but he taught me the ways of spy craft."

"But the one you're training caught you." Daniel scowled. "And don't call me Danny boy."

I shrugged and took another bite.

"Well, teacher. Since Jenny and her crew will take a while to ID the bodies, help me with this new investigation." Joy batted her eyes and grinned.

"I can start by giving you some information I learned last might." I leaned in. "My source tells me that Hectar has several bounty hunter crews on his payroll. And I plan to have a long talk with him about it."

Joy's eyes bugged out. "Who is your source? You never mentioned having one down here."

"I'm from down here. Remember?" I looked at her and smiled. "I know a lot of people."

"Like Nell?" Joy asked. "And don't get me started on your hound dog past, stud." She laughed.

"I missed way too much." Jenny leaned her elbows on the table and put her chin in her hands. "Spill. Stud."

"Will has a past." Joy squealed.

Jenny squealed. Zeek and Daniel guffawed.

I rolled my eyes.

"Apparently, he likes women a lot." Joy put too much emphasis on the last word.

Jenny lowered her eyes at me for a second. "I can see it."

"See what?" I became defensive.

"You're a smart man with a good job." She looked at my face. "And I'd swim in those eyes for a day or two at least."

Everyone at the table laughed but me. My face had to be redder than Joy's darkest fake bake.

Once the laughter ended, Daniel got serious. "Listen, Zeek and I have been praying and the Holy Spirit revealed to us that the next judgment will happen any day."

"The supervolcanoes?" I asked.

Jenny gave a surprised look. "How'd you guess?"

"Dad's journal. I can remember bits and pieces. Of course, when I finish with Tommy, I'll be able to read it for myself." I clenched my fists.

"Anyway, the volcanoes will erupt sooner than the scientists are predicting. It won't affect this area like the last judgments, but we will feel the eruption. It'll feel like a small earthquake. Around here, the marketplace will experience the effects. Saltwater seafood will be nonexistent for a while until they can ship some into the areas that aren't affected. And even then, only the rich can afford it." Daniel's eyes seemed distant, like reading from a cue card.

"We'll have another new West Coast. The Yellowstone volcano will tear that area up." Zeek stared at his empty plate. "Many will die because they won't listen."

"How did Tommy get your dad's journal?" Jenny asked a good question at the wrong time.

"He stole it." I tried to keep my rage to a minimum but failed.

"Will, you need to get past this. Your father's journal is saving lives. Both spiritually and physically. It might be your property, but the words in it are from God, and He is using it for a greater purpose." Daniel hit the table. "Give it a rest."

"Remember what I said about your little angel? It still stands." I stood, tossed my plate and plastic ware in the closest receptacle, and went to the truck and thought about how the tide can change fast in relationships.

CHAPTER 39

Instead of going to my office, I joined Joy in hers to start looking into the reports we heard about bounty hunters keeping some of the people they catch to sell to human traffickers. She logged onto her Vam using a wireless keyboard and put the screen on the wall while I put mine on the opposite wall.

"I will pull up a list of the local bounty hunters and cross reference them with the lists of those they captured. You work on who is working for Hectar." Her gaze never left the screen.

"Yes, Ma'am."

Her cute giggle caught my attention. It still bothered me that I noticed things like that with Joy while struggling in my relationship with Amelia. The stark differences between the two made me question my tastes in women. Amelia, the British bombshell, checked all the boxes, both physically and intellectually, that drew me to her the first time I met her. Joy, on the other hand, had a short but well-built body and looked more cute than gorgeous. Her intelligence only became noticeable when she began shedding the ambition and self-aggrandizing. But, then again, the glaring difference came spiritually. Then I remembered what Daniel and Zeek said about Nell. Maybe Amelia had made her decision. The thought overwhelmed me, and I refocused back on the new case.

We worked for a while before sitting back at the same time.

"Anything yet?" She stretched and yawned.

"A few people who seem the type to take orders but not give them. Just the way Hectar likes it." I yawned. "You find anything interesting?"

"I didn't realize how many Christians and non-Loyalists live in this area."

Then I remembered the day before. "What about Charlie Caplan?"

"We already established that Charlie Caplan was the first bounty hunter in the area. He started hunting the day the program started." She began inputting into the Vam. "In order to get a better understanding of his operation, I need to do a full analysis of those he captured. Run a full list of the people he received payment versus the ones released without payment." She sat back to allow the Beast to do its work.

She frowned.

"What?" I asked.

"If Caplan is doing this, why didn't he take Liberty James. She's pretty."

I put my hands on my head and looked at my screen. "The only thing that makes sense to me is that she needs some time to get her full beauty back. She's looks malnourished. Caplan wants top dollar, but he probably doesn't want to invest any time or money in them. Chances are too high of little to no return on investment."

"That makes sense. And is very infuriating." Joy returned to her screen. "He's by far the most successful in the area. One of the local Peace Forces commanders wrote that it's as if Charlie has a sixth sense for this profession."

I stared at the wall. The deep feeling made me think about this ability.

"He may have been a church member before the murders. I remember one of Dad's sermons that talked about people who act like believers but won't be taken in the Rapture, like me. He said that many will fall to their knees and become true believers, while others will become angry and go their own way, like my old youth pastor." I sat up. "Check his list of Christians caught and see if they have any specific church affiliations."

"Why is that important?" Joy asked.

"In order to find a way to stop him, we need to figure out how he's finding them. My old church used to keep a directory and roster of the church members. If Charlie went to church, he'd know about them and is probably using them to find Christians.

Tommy once told me that when the Beast went online, it invaded all computers linked to the internet. That includes churches."

"Interesting." Her cute frown returned as she typed. "I'll take the list of Charlie Caplan's captures and cross-reference them with church rosters in the area. And at the same time see if Caplan is on any of the rosters."

"Good thinking." I smiled.

She giggled. "And you say that I'm not a good investigator."

"You definitely impress me." I laughed. "Maybe I am coming around."

Her smile melted my icy heart while those green eyes penetrated deeply. Then I remembered the deep feeling's warning about daily occurrences of forgiveness. I shot up a quick prayer requesting forgiveness and noticed Joy's focus, appreciating her capacity to apply new lessons quickly.

"It looks like he didn't belong to any churches, and here is a list of his captures. Unfortunately, ICON doesn't have very many church rosters in its databases." She pointed at the image on the wall. "However, all the people he captured are Christians, not one non-Loyalist. So, it gives us a potential method of capture. But how are we to figure out if he is using these rosters and directories as part of his hunting process?"

"Print this out." I widened my eyes to let her know I wanted to talk to her without computer ears.

She nodded and printed three copies of the list before logging out. I logged out of my Vam and put all the tech in the safe while Joy retrieved the printouts.

"I wonder how the Beast knows who did or didn't get Raptured. Even without very many church directories and rosters in the databases, how can it spit out list after list?" I sat and took the list she gave me.

"Like I said, this AI is beyond next generation. Maybe it's learning how to determine living Christians and those taken in the Rapture based on lists made by the corpse corps." She took out a highlighter and looked at the list.

I rubbed my chin. "Frank said the Beast can anticipate audience reactions and respond by creating news stories that drew them closer to the Antichrist. Then he said that it will take the same lists and turn them against the Resistance."

"Wow, I didn't realize how much he understood about the Beast." Her eyes filled with pain. "I really underestimated him."

"He always caught me off guard with stuff like that." I did something unusual. "I wish you could've known him like I did." It felt right to say it.

She gave a sympathetic smile. "I know how hard it is to lose your mentor. Mine died in the line of duty, a shootout with a drug gang. They had automatic weapons and loaded her car. She took refuge behind it, but you know how that goes. A car can't stop all the bullets." She turned her focus back to the screen.

"Did you help catch the ones who did it?"

"The shootout ended with all the gang members killed. They were high on meth and had no interest in being taken alive." She sighed back tears. "I was at a conference in Chicago when it happened. Networking."

"I'm sorry for your loss." I looked at the list of Charlie's captures.

Staring at it for a long time, the deep feeling kept telling me that there's a pattern. But I didn't see it. Frustration covered my mind in a film of memory that remained fuzzy.

"What's with the third copy?" I pointed at the one sitting between us.

"It's for the Resistance." She pointed at the one she held. "I'll give it to Daniel to give to the local Resistance. Maybe it will help."

Joy began highlighting the vital information. Her thought patterns impressed me. Tommy will have a good one.

While she did that, I returned to my list. It bothered me I didn't see the connections. The deep feeling reminded me to slow down my thinking and focus on the details. Something I learned from Frank. Patience might've been my strength, but slowing down wasn't.

"What are you looking for?" She put the lists in her briefcase.

"I'm missing something, so I'm slowing down to take a closer..." The names stood out. "Wait one minute."

I grabbed her highlighter and marked familiar names. My past began overwhelming my thought patterns. Emotions began rising. Anger and pain swallowed me whole.

"Will, what is it? You look like you're going to kill somebody."

I looked at her while I tried to regain my composure. "We need to go to local churches."

CHAPTER 40

Before the Trib, Springfield embraced the old cliché of a church on every corner. I drove in a circular pattern and widening the pattern after each circle. Instead of looking for a set number, we kept the search to a couple of hours to give us some time to check the lists against Charlie's captures. In that time frame, we collected over a dozen rosters and directories. Returning to the square parking lot, I parked the truck in the shade of an abandoned building. We unbuckled our seat belts but didn't immediately start checking the lists.

"What caused you to think of this?" Joy asked, looking at a directory.

Reaching over and turning a couple of pages in her directory, I found a picture and pointed it out. "Casey Jensen went to my school. A year ahead of me, as I recall, and a real hellraiser. I'm not surprised he missed the Rapture."

"I knew a few of those from my past, too." She rolled her eyes.

Perusing my list, I got a better feel for Caplan. "There are a few others I noticed on the lists. I think this is the best way to prove he uses directories and rosters to find these people."

Joy's eyes widened. "He goes to the addresses for the family and stakes them out."

"Exactly." I sighed. "It's a brilliant method."

"And infuriating." Joy pointed at Casey's picture.

"Amen, sister." I grumbled. "Caplan needs to be stopped."

"As well as Hectar's crews." She kept looking at the directory.

"Yep." I started mentally preparing myself ready for my next meeting with the mobster.

Joy looked at the building, her eyes gazing into another place. The white noise of the distant traffic matched with the hum of an HVAC unit on a nearby building nearly put me to sleep until Joy broke the silence.

"Were you good in school?" She looked at me. "I mean, did you get good grades?"

"Average, I guess." I looked into her deep blue eyes. "Mostly Bs to keep playing sports."

"What sports did you play?" Her tired grin looked good on her.

"Baseball and football." I returned the grin. "And you?"

"Oh, basketball. I played center for my team." She giggled.

"Funny." I chuckled. "I mean it. What extracurriculars did you participate in?"

She turned her focus to the building.

"No sports, obviously. But I was in JROTC. I wanted to be an officer in the military. But that didn't happen." She trailed off.

I wondered if it had something to do with the boy she bullied into attempting suicide.

"What's it like to be in the missions field?" I shifted to a more comfortable topic. "We had plenty of missionaries speak at Dad's church, but the kids rarely talked to us. They mainly hid behind their parents."

"There's a reason for that." She sighed. "Kids are cruel. Once, I had a church brat ask me if I understood English. He talked slow and loud like it helped if I didn't speak the language. Others teased us for having out-of-style clothes or being so poor that we had to beg churches for money or something trivial that only public-school kids believed to be important. We hung around our parents because they provided a barrier between us and the jerks."

"I never talked to any of them, even when they spent the night at my house. Mostly because they were here today, gone tomorrow." I looked at the building to see what she found interesting. "But mostly because I had homework to do. You know, Sunday night cram session before Monday."

"Not really. After I left Peru, I went to an all-girl boarding school that specialized in missionary kids." She looked at me and frowned. "What are you looking at?"

"Trying to figure out what you're looking at." I kept looking at the building.

"Nothing. I'm just looking at the building." The giggle she let out made me feel good, calmed the stress. "Didn't homework interrupt your hound dog ways?"

"Even hound dogs have to do homework because they're chasing girls the other forty-six hours of the weekend." I chuckled.

She let the silence last a bit too long. "Peru is beautiful. The jungles, however, are not friendly. I didn't get along with my siblings, and the wildlife seemed to hate me. So, I got shipped off to boarding school."

"How was that experience?"

"Four point oh every semester." She smiled. "I've never been a hound dog."

"There's a moral to that story."

She giggled. "Yeah, don't chase boys and you can get all this." She motioned to the building.

"Wasn't there an all-boy boarding school near yours?" I asked.

She went silent for a minute. Her instant somberness filled the truck cab.

"No, but the town had a public school. The townies looked down on us because they believed the students came from rich backgrounds, which we most certainly did not." Tears formed in her eyes. "But there was a boy, Luke, who I liked and liked me. However, his parents had no interest in their son dating one of those girls from the other school."

"The other school?"

"It was a poor, small town. They didn't believe their children needed to rub elbows with the likes of us rich kids. Our faculty tried to get them to understand our situation, but the townies never believed them."

"Did you and Luke sneak out to see each other?" I gave a sly smile and nudged her elbow with mine.

"Once, but his parents caught us and threatened me. There was another time when my school's basketball team played theirs at my school. We went behind the gym during the game and talked. When his father caught us, he pushed me down and slapped Luke. After threatening me with the police, he grabbed Luke and left." Her tears landed on her collar.

"I saw your file. It said that you bullied a boy into attempting suicide. But it sounds to me like that it didn't happen that way." It felt like the deep feeling took control of my mouth.

Joy covered her face with her hands and wept. The deep feeling gave me the impression she needed to work it out externally. I put my hand on her shoulder in support.

She grabbed a tissue from her bag and composed herself. Her deep blue eyes surrounded by a red rim made me feel terrible for bringing up such a painful subject.

"Luke tried to commit suicide that night. His parents tried to have me arrested for bullying him, but the police found a letter telling all the terrible things his parents did to him." She took a couple of breaths. "Both of them went to prison, but somehow their claims got into my file. Interestingly enough, it didn't get in there until after I started taking orders from Petrovich."

"Is that when you moved and went to public school?" I asked.

"Yeah. And I didn't nothing to attract attention to myself. I just put my nose to the grindstone." She wiped her cheek.

I thought about Petrovich. It's one thing to think you know the depths a person might take to get their way. It's something else when you see those depths become reality. Daria Petrovich and her little demon had no compunction about destroying anyone in their path. They needed to be stopped before they killed Joy.

"Maybe you should replace Petrovich." I winked at Joy.

"I never thought I'd see the day I'd win you over."

"Oh, you're totally the lesser of the two evils." I snarked.

"Oh, totally." She punched my arm and laughed through the tears.

Then I realized Joy had more to offer than I let her show to me before.

Much more.

"Thanks, Will. That's been on my mind for a while. It helps to get things out sometimes." She focused on her tissue.

"You're welcome, sis."

CHAPTER 41

Jenny texted Joy and asked if she had the time to come and see her in the lab. We hustled to the lab to find Jenny surrounded by the same people who earlier had treated her poorly. Now, they acted as if she had been part of the team for years. Jenny looked less stressed and even a little happy.

The lab supervisor stayed in his office, but not without peeking through the blinds. The others saw us and went back to their stations.

"Hi guys. How's it going?" Jenny smiled and leaned on the table with the heads lined up.

"Working on another project until you called." Joy sat her briefcase down. "Do you have the IDs already?"

"Not yet. We found some usable DNA, but it'll take a while to get all the DNA collected, so we're hoping maybe tomorrow morning, afternoon at the latest." She turned to her computer and brought up a picture of what looked like a Beastmark chip. "And we found these."

"Are all the victims Loyalists?" Joy pulled out her notebook and began writing.

"Not necessarily."

I went around and looked at the screen. "These aren't loyalty chips." I folded my arms and leaned against the table behind me. "But they look familiar."

Jenny smiled while she waited for us to take a guess. Joy just wrote.

"Farm chips." I whispered.

"Ding, ding, ding. We have a winner." Jenny playfully punched my shoulder.

Joy came around and looked. "The killer put them with the skulls?"

"On them." Jenny produced the evidence bags with the chips. "Or in them. The heads that are still intact had them where the loyalty chip is normally injected." She pointed at her forehead just above the bridge of her nose. "The bags of the ones not intact still had the chips mixed in with the decomp."

"What does that mean?" Joy asked, not lifting her head from her notebook.

"The killer might be the one who put the chips in the victims," I said.

"Why might? Isn't it obvious that the victims had the chips before getting killed?" Joy asked.

"Not necessarily." Jenny took over. "He might've killed them because they had these chips and not the official ones."

"Why would anyone put a different chip in their foreheads?" Joy giggled and finally looked up.

"Criminals have been trying to bypass getting the loyalty chip, but still wanting to get the benefits associated with it." I turned and looked at Jenny.

"This might be a Loyalist who found out about this group and took matters into his own hands. A vigilante." Jenny handed me an evidence bag with a chip.

It had an identifying number too small for me to read. Larger than a Beastmark chip and more cylindrical where a Beastmark chip had the shape of a grain of rice, so the skin of the forehead or right hand grew more naturally around it. A cow or some other farm animal didn't care about looks or minor annoyances.

"I'm guessing you did a background check on the chips and have a suspect for me to arrest?" I smiled, knowing she didn't.

"Sorry, Will. It's not that easy." Jenny gave a pouty look. "The truth is, I've had trouble tracking down the chip manufacturers and selling points. ICON only found three chips that were made two years before the murders. The rest must be older."

"Did you find the name of who purchased them?" I asked, already knowing the answer.

"Yes, but there are three names because the chips were sold in different towns around the area. But every name is on the murdered list. Meaning…" Jenny raised her eyebrows for one of us to finish her sentence.

"Someone stole them from the original owners." Joy said. "Probably during the looting that took place after the murders."

"Ding, ding, ding." Jenny sounded.

After the Rapture, thieves ransacked the houses of those believed missing. In fact, someone burned Mom and Dad's house to the ground after I left for Kansas City to fight the rioters doing the same thing.

"Were the chips inserted postmortem?" Joy asked.

"On the ones intact, no. The others we believe the same." Jenny took the bag from me and put it back with the others. "It's part of his killing process."

Jenny brought up the pics of the burial sites, both before and after the removal of the heads. The words on the trees came to mind, and I tried to figure out what all this meant. Then I thought about the sermon. With this new information, the killer's message might've had something to do with the Antichrist and his government.

"What are on the chips?" I asked.

"You mean the information?" Jenny saw me nod and went on. "Unfortunately, I haven't had the chance to see what's on them because of the software. These old things come from different manufacturers. Three from what our computer guy saw, but the companies no longer exist, and their software is obsolete. ICON doesn't recognize it yet, but I believe it'll crack the code by the end of the day, tomorrow at the latest."

"Okay, how about T.O.D.?" Joy asked.

"The newest one is two days. The oldest is a little over a year." Jenny pointed the two out.

"It happened after the murders." I mumbled. "The killer might've had a traumatic experience stemming from that event and begun a killing spree of his own."

"That maybe it," Jenny said. "Or he might have started when the government introduced the loyalty chip and formed a psychotic bond with it and/or the Sovereign."

"How about cause of death?" Joy asked.

"A knife." Jenny shifted her gaze to her commander. "I believe it did double duty like the M.E. said. Killing the victim and dismembering the corpse. And it's a big one. But not a machete. That's too big. Maybe a Bowie knife."

"What's the difference?" Joy looked up.

"I'll tell you later." My stomach rumbled. "I'm hungry. Can I buy you two a bite to eat?"

CHAPTER 42

Joy and Jenny seemed confused about how the Automat worked, so I gave them a crash course. Once they got the hang of it, they quickly selected their food and drink, complaining about its inconvenience. With the lunch rush over, we went to the balcony and found a table in the corner with no nosey neighbors. After a quiet prayer, we spent the first part of the meal eating. Even without words, I felt part of something important for the Lord, unlike my time in the west where the loneliness overwhelmed me with paranoia and revenge filling my every thought. These two sisters in Christ opened feelings of self-worth and priority inside me I hadn't felt since I lived with my parents. No words, but plenty of like-mindedness.

While we ate, I noticed the slight crowd noise dissipate and looked over the edge. Zeek and Daniel had walked through the door. They split up and took the two tables closest to the door. The people at these tables must not have had Beastmarks. By the looks on their faces, they had no intention of dismissing the witness in front of them. Obviously, they had seen or heard what happened to the soldiers and didn't want to be fried crispy their own selves, so they listened politely. Returning to my meal, I sent a silent prayer for the boys and the ones they witnessed to for the Lord.

After refilling our drinks, I opened the conversation with something that occurred to me while eating.

"I wasn't raised on a farm. How do the chips get inserted?" Joy asked Jenny.

"Farmers use an oversized syringe. The farmer pinches the skin, lifts, inserts the needle, and pushes the plunger." Jenny mimed out the sequence.

"Sounds painful." Joy sipped her diet soda.

"Never asked an animal if it hurts." Jenny smiled.

"These are large chips. Growing up, my family had a German Shepherd that the breeder had chipped. She showed us the chips she put in her dogs, which are like the ones in the victims. That's one big syringe." I sat back in my chair.

Jenny frowned and sipped her soda. "My grandparents had a beef cattle farm. As I recall, they used an injector that looked like a gun to my inexperienced eyes. They used the handle to push the syringe in and pulled and trigger that pushed the plunger down. Maybe the cow's hide is tougher."

"What are you thinking, Will?" Joy asked.

"Just curious about the last minutes of the victims' lives. The killer tied them down, injected them, and then killed them. But Joy and I have been talking about the killer's message lately. With this new information, I'm getting a little confused. The perspective is a little muddled. If we look at it one way, it falls apart. If we look at it another way, the same result. Either we're missing something, or the killer is so unhinged that we'll never in a million years guess what he's saying." I took a long draught of my root beer.

"I say it's the latter." Joy repositioned in her chair. "But that's just me not wanting to overthink it and make a mistake."

"I hear ya," Jenny said.

"If this killer is as methodical as it appears, he's put something on those chips that may make the sermon clearer. Maybe the sermon itself."

"Why is the sermon so important?" Joy asked. "Now that we will have the IDs soon."

"Sometimes we can get some evidence pointing to the killer from what he's saying in his sermon." I looked at the young man bussing a table with the Beastmark on his forehead and whispered, "Hell Bound."

CHAPTER 43

By the time we reached the lab building, Zeek and Daniel had returned to the square. They walked to the front of the global temple and began preaching. Jenny went inside, wanting to watch them in action but knowing her job came first this time. Joy said she wanted a better view from HQ, but I knew she wanted a place that made her look uninterested. Smart. I stayed put and watched.

Zeek led off by quoting Revelation. "Fear God and give glory to Him; for the hour of judgment is come; and worship Him that made heaven, and earth, and the sea, and the fountains of water." He didn't shout, but his voice sounded like he stood next to me.

The head priest of the global temple flew out, followed by temple guards and lower priests. His gaudy, red silk robe flapped in his wake. The rest of the temple emptied onto the street to see the spectacle. By the time the priest and his entourage reached the two witnesses, Zeek had finished quoting the last book of the Bible. Before he moved on, the priests tried to shout him down.

"How dare you bring reference to this archaic, intolerant deity you serve? He is nothing but a blight on the human spirit." He turned to the crowd. "We are a people far too evolved to consider anything from the antiquated teaching of bigots like these two and their kind. Our Sovereign has shown us the way to peace both in the heart and throughout the universe. It is a weak mind that takes these lesser men seriously. It is a perverse heart…"

"Enough!" Daniel didn't look like he shouted, but his voice echoed off the buildings like a hurricane.

The priests cowered, their legs wobbling like an earthquake had started. Then the priests collected themselves, circled the two witnesses, and started chanting in a language I didn't recognize. It sounded like something from a movie. Zeek and Daniel stood still, looking unimpressed. The priests moved in unison, looking like an old country music line dance. They increased their volume that distorted their voices. The two stood perfectly still, then looked up and closed their eyes. This had no chance of ending well.

I felt an evil presence standing beside me.

"Hello, Daria." I sidestepped and looked at her. "Enjoying the show?"

"This is about to get good." She sniggered. "The high priest in Babylon found an ancient text describing a way to get rid of Jewish annoyances like them. It goes all the way back to Nebuchadnezzar. The high priest practiced it on a few Jews, and they died instantly. Watch and know that we control this world and not those Jewish wannabes and their pathetic God."

This went on for over ten minutes before the high priest shouted the last word. They stopped their dance and turned to Zeek and Daniel, who didn't open their eyes. Those not taking part began moving back from the scene, as if they knew what came next. The high priest loudly chanted one last time. Once finished, all the priests pulled a dagger from inside their robes and raised them above their heads.

"Hear me." Zeek's voice thundered louder than Daniel's. "Do not presume to that your pitiful gods of old have any power against the chosen of the Mighty God, Father of Jesus Christ whom you reject. You know the consequences of your actions. Do not follow through on your intentions or face the fire of Hell."

The high priest screamed, followed by his entourage, and they all lunged at the two witnesses. A vortex of fire, emanating from the two, scorched the priests, who screamed in pain. Feeling the heat from across the square, I took a step back. The fire intensified, turning the priests into ash, and stopped as fast as it appeared. The molten daggers glowed bright red among the remains.

"Maybe they didn't say it right." I deadpanned. "Or maybe that report wasn't accurate."

Petrovich's face reddened with rage. "It won't be long before the Sovereign unleashes the full weight of his rage on people like them. And I will laugh at their remains being scattered in the wind." She crossed her arms and shifted her weight to one foot.

"What wind?" I asked.

Either she had read the Bible or just guessed, except for one fact. The coming Two Witnesses in Jerusalem will die at the hands of the Sovereign, but none of the one hundred and forty-four thousand. But I thought it best not to correct her.

After cursing at them under her breath for a while, she turned her attention to me. "How is the investigation going? Will the Sovereign be able to make his announcement soon?" Her arrogance annoyed me.

I crossed my arms. "We just found the heads last night. CSU needs time to make the identifications. And your bosses have ordered us to investigate bounty hunters selling people the caught to human traffickers."

"Your people need to understand expediency. We are on a strict timetable and need to get ahead of people like those two. These murders are the blessing needed to rid the world of them. When faced with facts, they will skulk back into the hole they crawled out of. We will get rid of them, and the world will become everything the Sovereign desires. Sex slaves are not as important as the Sovereign's agenda." Her fervor increased with every word.

"I can't promise anything except that we'll keep working until we find the killer. Once we get the IDs, we can analyze the victims' commonalities, then we might break the case. But until then…"

"What about the profile you got from ICON?" she interrupted.

"Just that, a profile. It gives us an idea of the killer, but it doesn't give us the killer."

"ICON is the most advanced AI this world has ever seen. The chances that it has even one detail wrong are astronomical. You are not doing your due diligence, Major Thomas. It might be in your best interest to use all the resources available to you. This old school wait-and-see attitude is reprehensible." She let her arms drop to her sides. "Maybe General Sokolov made a mistake putting you on this case. A quick call from me…"

"Have you ever investigated a murder? No? I didn't think so. So, here's what I'm thinking. Why don't you stay on your side of the road, and I'll stay on mine? Comprenez-vous?"

The smirk that appeared on her face needed pushed to the back of her head.

"Oui." Her body unclenched. "When do you plan to follow through on the plan to eliminate Joy? I won't wait much longer."

Knowing that she acted unilaterally, I poked the Russian bear. "Which do you want faster, the end of the case or Joy dead? Right now, the case has sped up. Killing Joy will just hinder it. And I don't like putting cases on pause."

The redness returned to her face. "I don't care what you like. You need to multitask without losing time. Be like a computer. Work them both as efficiently as possible."

"Speaking of ICON. Do you have the authority to have someone as high on the food chain as Joy killed? You're not much higher than her from what I read. I doubt you can work unilaterally on something like this." I stood stock still to give her the impression that I did my homework, too.

Her left hand began trembling, then it spread up to her shoulder. Her face started screwing into a rage that caught me off guard. I almost felt the demon inside her wanting to jump out and kill me. I considered making a dash to the witnesses and let them turn loose on her. Then the anger subsided just as fast. Dealing with her would be far above my spiritual paygrade. The deep feeling kept me calm, reminding me I never traveled alone.

"That is none of your concern, Major Thomas. You are to do as you are told." Her voice cracked a bit. "Just remember that I'm the one person you don't cross. Joy will die with or without you. If you don't follow orders to the letter, I will go after everything you hold dear, starting with your job. But just before I kill you, I will kill that retard at the lake you seem to have taken a liking to and everyone else you love."

She turned and left.

CHAPTER 44

Once Daria disappeared around the corner of the lab building, I turned my attention to Zeek and Daniel. Many of the people who watched the deaths of the priests walked away, most sporting a Beastmark. The rest stayed and prayed. Then I felt another presence standing beside me.

"Amazing." Hectar's awestruck gaze never left the scene. "I've heard of this happening but never witnessed it myself."

"It happened yesterday with some Peace Forces soldiers. Not far from your Automat." I nodded towards his restaurant.

"That happened before I arrived. My staff told me all about it." He shook his head. "This God of theirs is... formidable."

It felt like his mind started wrapping a little tighter around the truth.

"How can I help you, Hectar?" I maintained my gaze at the center of the square.

"Will, how are things?" His easy tone helped calm me down.

"Could be better. Could be worse, I guess." I shrugged, putting my hands in my pants pockets.

"Sorry, but I overheard your conversation with Petrovich." He tsked. "Not a good idea to cross a woman of her temperament."

"She's demon possessed." I took a chance, but he needed to know.

Hectar let a long, awkward moment pass, recalculating a lot of things.

"I can't tell if you're joking or not." He frowned.

"You see, the shorter of those two praying with that young

woman?" When Hectar grunted in the affirmative, I continued. "He's from St. Louis, as you know. He's also one of the one hundred forty-four thousand in that book and sees things we cannot. He's the one who confirmed it."

This pause lasted longer.

"You know that young man?" Hectar finally talked.

"We are on speaking terms. Although we are not on the same page ecumenically speaking." I hoped the half-truth threw Hectar off.

"I see." He cleared his throat. "And you trust him?"

"Their reputation doesn't include deception." I shrugged.

Hectar chuckled. "That I agree with. But the other might be an exaggeration. No?"

"No. He meant it." I gave a little more. "He even knows about Daria's plan to kill Joy."

"And why does he care?" I felt Hectar setting me up.

"I believe he cares about everyone. Including me." I shrugged. "And you."

"Why you?" He asked.

"I'm not chipped." I knew Hectar and his fishing ways. "At least that's what he told me."

"Makes sense. The book says that those with a chip have no chance in the afterlife."

"I remember Dad saying that." I agreed.

Just then, an ambulance pulled into view, and the EMTs came out and froze. The two witnesses allowed them to collect the ashes. Then Zeek told the crowd to turn away from the false global religion and follow the true God. Daniel and Zeek continued praying with the ones who stayed.

"You need to know that I'm not going after Joy anymore." I turned to him. "I've decided it isn't in my best interest."

"I understand." He nodded. "But that doesn't go along with Petrovich's plans, I'm thinking."

"That's why she left in such a snit. She moaned, groaned, and threatened me before she left."

"Just be careful. I'd hate to have wasted all this time building this relationship. If you die, with whom will I discuss the book?" His grin barely registered on his face.

"Maybe one of them." I motioned to the two witnesses.

"Too dangerous for me." He chuckled.

We watched as the EMTs argued over how they wanted to bag the remains.

"Amen, brother." I grinned.

Before Hectar walked away, I remembered we needed to talk.

"I've been hearing that bounty hunters are holding back some of their catches and selling them to human traffickers. Are you aware of this?" I asked.

Hectar sighed. "It is a business, and I'm a businessman. It just makes good business sense to follow the money. Kind of like many of your investigations."

"This is unacceptable. I will not be in league with someone with these low standards." I raised my voice enough for him to get the drift.

"I am sorry, Will. But this area of my business is not under my direct supervision. My associate, who recently joined my community, oversees that area. If you need to discuss the matter with him, I can make the arrangements." He sniffed.

Knowing Hectar as well as I did, it did me no good to dig any deeper. So, I poked the bear from another angle.

"They say that Charlie Caplan is the number one bounty hunter around here." I tried to get a rise out of him.

"If you put all of my operations together, he's not." His confidence returned.

"So, you're saying he's not in your sights yet?" I hoped I knew the answer.

"You have no cause for concern in this matter, Will." Hectar looked at the witnesses, who looked to be making progress with the potential new believers. "You need to focus on the case and that infernal woman."

"The case is slow, but it's progressing. And the woman is never out of my mind."

Hectar leaned in like a friend about to spill some gossip. "What if we got her to attack them?" He pointed at Zeek and Daniel.

We laughed and let the moment draw out. Then something crossed my mind to discuss with Daniel.

"Before I go, you need to know that the volcanoes are about to erupt. My sources out west tell me that Yellowstone is getting volatile." He patted me on the shoulder. "The military will wait until the last minute, if they move them at all. I am glad you are here."

Watching Hectar walk away, I knew he meant what he said.

CHAPTER 45

With the events at the square still fresh, I knocked on Joy's door to tell her about it. For the first time since I'd known her, she had undone her top button. She looked tired, like a newbie still learning how to time-manage the difficulties of a case. A tired smile crossed her face when I sat across from her. Something inside me, and not the deep feeling, wanted to kiss her. The guilt invaded me for thinking something like that. I had a girlfriend.

"Did Daniel and Zeek do well out there?" Her smile broadened.

"You didn't hear?" I asked. "The priests came out of the global temple and confronted them."

Joy sat straight. "How did that go?"

"Not too well for the priests. They attacked the boys. First with chants, then with knives." I noticed the intensity entering her face. "They all burned. The EMTs are sweeping up their ashes as we speak."

She tensed up. "Wow."

"The good news is that they prayed with at least fourteen people." I smiled.

"That is good news." Her body seemed to relax.

I thought about not mentioning it, but as my partner, she deserved it. "Petrovich approached me while it happened."

She stared at me. I didn't get a good read.

After a few moments, she responded. "What did she want?"

"To talk about you." I sat back, unwilling to tell her everything. "She really has a problem with you."

She took a deep breath and let it out slowly. "You need to know something. Before becoming a believer, I had high ambitions. I wanted to be the first American in the Sovereign's central leadership and in control of the Peace Forces around the world. But Petrovich got in my way. She figured out my plans, put me under her thumb, and is trying to keep me in St. Louis indefinitely."

"But she doesn't have an official position in the government. From what I understand, she's one of those people who worked behind the scenes."

"You're right, but she requested that I be one of her people to do the dirty work in America. At first, I thought that someone else pushed the button on this, but my sources confirmed she acted alone." Joy crossed her arms.

"Do you know why she did that?" I asked.

"I didn't know until after the first earthquake when she came to St. Louis to make sure Hectar didn't pose a threat to the Sovereign's plans for America. He did some things that the Sovereign didn't approve. She came into my office and began barking orders at me. I resisted, and she took offence. Then I got a call from my superior to follow her instructions to the letter." Joy looked at the ceiling. "I'll have to admit that my sources grew by working for her, and the favors owed to me are far greater than I ever dreamed. Now, she has it in for me because I'm more powerful."

"That's not a good thing." I sighed.

"No, it's not." She closed her eyes and whispered, "My time on this earth may not be as long as I wanted, but at least I know where I'll end up."

The silence stood in the room like the grim reaper waiting for his orders.

The idea of Daria Petrovich killing Joy enraged me. I'd never allow that woman to kill my sister in Christ. If Joy went down, I'd go with her. The deep feeling patted me on the back for the sentiment. Now I had to figure out how to protect Joy and get rid of a demon possessed woman.

After a while, I changed the subject to something equally depressing.

"After Daria left, Hectar approached me." I watched her reaction.

"Speaking of, I need to get a message to him. Daria still treats me like a messenger." She sat up and began writing a Post-it reminder. "He needs to make sure the Automats get finished in Canada. He's running behind."

"They are interested in his restaurants?" I asked.

"Will, the government, for all intents and purposes, own Hectar. He can't do anything without their permission. In fact, the top brass looks at him as a manager, not a mobster." She grinned and shook her head as if I said something ridiculous.

"He definitely doesn't see it that way." I grinned, wondering if Hectar knew it.

"He should. They handpicked him for the position." She looked up. "Why do you think they send me to give him orders?"

"Maybe the Sovereign didn't spell it out for Hectar, because he clearly views you as a government liaison and the Sovereign is a politician."

"You said his time is coming up. Maybe the Sovereign lets him think that to keep him happy until he has Hectar killed."

I shifted the focus. "Anyway, he told me that his sources reported that Yellowstone is getting volatile."

Joy turned around in her chair, opened the safe, and grabbed her Vam. After a few taps on the keyboard, she stared at the information.

"Reports came this morning that the caldera has pushed the land to the breaking point. We can expect the eruption any day now." She tapped some more. "In fact, the other supervolcanoes in the world are getting close to eruption as well. Most of the scientists are predicting an extinction event if they all go at once." She returned the Vam to its quiet place and whispered, "Isn't it fascinating that this is secondhand information? I mean, we already got this info from Daniel and Zeek, who get it from God."

"I never thought of it that way. But I am glad God is in control. If not, we'd go extinct."

"Amen brother. But we need to get back to the case." Her eyes sparkled, then went to her normal volume. "What is our next move?"

I sat back. "Until we get the IDs and the info on the chips, there's not a lot we can do."

"What about Caplan?"

"Well, we know Charlie is probably using church rosters to find his next catches. And he separates the ones he intends to sell from those he turns into the Peace Forces. Have you gotten a tail on him and his crew?"

"I asked Gallway, and she assigned two to follow him. They won't report until tomorrow since Caplan mainly works at night." She stretched her neck.

Staring at her, without looking at her, Dad came to mind.

"I'd like to get a directory from my old church. To see if anyone I know is on Caplan's list."

"Okay." She stood and stretched.

CHAPTER 46

The sanctuary of Dad's church smelled the same, like mildew and urine mixed with decomp. Joy put a handkerchief over her nose until she got used to it.

"Why do we need one of these directories? Don't we have enough already?" Joy acted like she already knew the answer but wanted to hear it anyway.

"From the time I entered the KCPD to the Rapture, I didn't attend a church. Mom said they had a lot of people who joined after I left. I'm wondering if any of those people are on the list you printed." I righted the overturned table that once held stacks of directories, bulletins, and other church information.

Vandals had ripped all of them up. I sighed and ran a hand through my hair. Facing the pulpit, I knew where to look, only I never wanted to enter that office for the rest of my short life.

"What's the matter?" Joy asked.

"They kept the extra copies of the directories in Dad's office." I felt the blood leave my face.

"There must be strays somewhere else." She looked around and pointed at a door. "How about downstairs? The Sunday school classes must've had some. I know my old church teachers kept at least one in their room." She walked towards the door to the stairway.

"It'll take too long. Even if people didn't vandalize them." I went to the one at the right of the stage.

"I'll go with you."

"Thanks, but I need to do this alone." I kept my focus on the door. "You know, face your past. Why don't you go back to the truck?"

"Okay. But let me know if you need anything." I heard her footsteps leave the foyer.

Staring at the opening of the short hallway beside the choir loft, my mind returned to those days when I went to get Dad on game nights. He was always immersed in his sermon studies. I hated those books. They kept him away from the selfish little brat of a son, who didn't understand the importance of his work until after the Rapture. Daniel's words haunted me. I held a grudge against Tommy for stealing my past. I still acted like that selfish brat.

The last of the three doors on the right contained memories I didn't want to face. After we stopped the riots in Kansas City, I forced myself to go see the family house, but it had burned to the ground. I believed I had already faced my past until I came back for the investigation. Looking at the church the first time we went to the crime scene, I knew I needed to face my entire past. But I still wasn't ready. Is anyone?

The door hinges squealed when I opened it, just like it did before the Rapture. Dad never greased it because he said it helped him focus on the person coming through it. Although he took his studies seriously, his relationship with his congregation came first. Always God's shepherd.

Much to my dismay, the vandals left the office untouched. The putrid smell from the sanctuary hadn't invaded this room. The faint scents of old books and Dad's cologne remained for me to remember the godly man who prayed for a son more interested in the opposite sex and sports than a God who loved him.

Shutting the door and walking behind the desk, I ran my hand over the cheap fabric office chair that Dad claimed to be the most comfortable chair he ever owned. The indentation in the seat, the worn armrests, the wheels that barely moved. I dropped my head in deep regret for the shame I brought to my family. The PK.

The hound dog.

I stared at the desk where Dad had written the journal. The desk calendar, filled with appointments, reminded me of how long he'd been gone to the day. The lamp that always needed a new bulb every few months. Everything had a value that I didn't appreciate until now.

Pictures filled the walls, displaying Mom and Dad's lifetime of service. Deacons, teachers, and other church members with arms around Dad and Mom, smiling proudly. However, the gut punch came when I saw me and my sister's baptism pictures. Both gasped for after Dad had lifted us out of the cool water. Dad's face elated at the knowledge that his whole family had made their decision for Christ. Regret ran over me like a tank on the battlefield.

Slowly, I sat in the chair and let it groan under my weight. I put my head in my hands and let my groans fill the room. I missed my parents. Mom's powerful presence in how she kept Dad on schedule, pointing to the desk calendar to remind him of meetings and appointments and prayer requests. Unfortunately, their children's presence only brought memories of complaints or us begging for money.

A hand slowly touched my back. I quickly turned and saw Joy crying for me. She knew my pain.

Wrapping her arms around my neck, she hugged me from behind. I patted her forearm and realized that I had straightened things out with God but not with her.

"I'm so sorry." I whispered.

"It's okay." Joy's voice cracked. "But you don't need to face this alone."

"No, I mean, I'm sorry for trying to kill you." I tensed and turned, preparing for her reaction.

She wiped her eyes, smudging her eye makeup. "It's okay. I understand."

"How can you? I came back to kill you, not to investigate these murders. I've been planning it since I went into the military." It felt good to admit the bad, but the worst hurt more.

"I get it. I killed Frank." She wiped her eyes. "I deserve your hate."

"But I pulled the trigger." I looked at her with widened eyes and nodded. "At least I tried to, but something held my finger back. I tried my hardest, but my arm went numb. And it's not enough, but I'm sorry."

Joy looked surprised. Then her face went blank. She reached into her purse. Maybe for her service weapon. I let her do what needed done. To do to me what I deserved.

My breath came out slowly when she pulled out a travel pack of tissues. She pulled out a couple with a confused look.

"What, did you think I was going to shoot you or something?" She giggled and wiped her nose.

Chuckling nervously, I sat. "Can't blame you if you did."

"I forgive you. These are dangerous times we're living in, so I guess it makes sense that we act foolish, too." She wiped her nose again.

The deep feeling stopped me when I wanted to tell Joy about Daria's plans and how I volunteered to help her. Confusion coursed through my mind. Why is it stopping me now when it had been badgering me since I began plotting with Petrovich? But I remained quiet, believing that it had a good reason.

After another hug and apology, I remembered why we had come to the church and began rifling through the drawers. Under a Bible prophecy book, of course, I pulled out the last directory the church put out before the Rapture. I wiped off the dusty desk and opened the book. Using my finger to guide my eyes across the pictures, I found the first name on the list.

"You got a Sharpie or something?" I asked Joy.

She reached into her purse without looking and pulled one out.

"Impressive." I grinned while taking the lid off.

"Thanks." She returned the smile. "But are you going to tell me why this is important?"

"I tried to figure out why Charlie's list is so important, but it didn't come to me immediately." I paused to cross out the ones who I knew had been Raptured.

"They went to this church?" She sat in the chair across from me.

"I'm not sure, but I didn't see anyone from this church on his list that I remember. Get your list out and cross-reference those who went to this church." I patted the directory. "Since we're waiting for Jenny, let's get started on this directory. We can do the other churches later. If we don't get any good leads with this one."

She went to the truck to retrieve her list, returned, pulled out a highlighter, and spread out the pages.

"We can do this quicker together." I began reading names out of the directory.

It took an hour.

"Well, that's it." I sat back and stretched.

"Well?" She folded her arms and raised her eyebrows.

"Inconclusive." I sighed. "Libby and Devon are the only ones from this church Caplan caught."

"You didn't say their names." She looked at the list.

"We weren't in that directory. I had already moved to Kansas City. Libby joined a church in Joplin, where she had a job. Devon walked away from the church not long after high school. But Caplan still caught them. Maybe because he saw another person in their group in a different directory or roster."

"Sounds like we need to get working on the lists." She looked at me.

Leaning back, I looked at the ceiling. "I believe if we found the rosters of the churches in the area where Missouri, Arkansas, Oklahoma, and Kansas meet, we'll probably have the same results." I pointed to the directory on my desk. "My guess is that Caplan is working one or two rosters at a time. He's just getting started.

Joy stared at the directory. Her expression changed. I leaned forward and saw the picture of my family. All four of us. Mom used an old photo of the family. She never stopped hoping and praying for her kids and staying proud of her progeny no matter the circumstances. Mom and Dad smiling, my sister sneering, and I gave my pathetic tough guy stare.

"You have a beautiful family." She whispered.

"Yeah, a great mom and dad and two punks." I sat back hard and sighed.

She quickly changed the subject. "You know that if I report this, the government will use this as a template to track down Christians all over the world."

"If they haven't already."

"I've been reading up on the bounty system, and this is unique. Caplan's system looks simplistic. Everyone should do it this way. But I'm afraid that if I look this up on ICON, it will pick up what I'm checking and add it to the procedure." Her unease stretched across her face.

"Again, if it already hasn't. As I recall, the computer has been doing similar searches since it went globally online."

"So, why isn't it part of the S.O.P.? There's nothing in it that tells bounty hunters how to find Christians." She sat back, not taking her eyes off the picture. "And I've been trying to understand the need for the bounty system. It's old fashion."

After a few minutes to consider it, I thought about Dad's journal. "The judgments."

"What about them?" She asked.

"It's almost impossible to collect the dead and ID them at the pace the judgments have been coming while chasing the Christians. It's a fool's errand to do this on a global scale, even with a mega-computer like the Beast." I put my hands behind my head. "But to do it locally with non-Peace Forces personnel is far easier, especially with the lack of Peace Forces applicants."

"Thus, the bounty hunter system." She shook her head. "They do the heavy lifting for us. But I still don't understand why we don't use Caplan's system more.

"I have a feeling that hunters like Caplan keep things close to the vest to keep the competition at bay." I thought for a minute, then smiled. "Unless Hectar finds out about it."

"I wonder if he already knows. From my meetings with him, he's pretty sharp when it comes to making money."

"I need to talk to our friendly neighborhood mobster and see if he knows. Maybe even give him a heads-up to gain a favor from him."

"But Will, that will put the Christians in more danger." She sat straight.

"True. But I need to find out what he knows." I smiled. "And we need to get this information to Zeek. He can gather all the directories and get the local underground churches to keep away from those addresses. That'll put a damper on the process."

We spent a few silent minutes in deep thought before Joy spoke up.

"I'd like to talk to your friend, Libby."

I sat up. "Why?"

"I wonder if she saw anyone getting separated from her group when Caplan's crew captured them. Maybe she can help us save time with the directory search."

"That's a great idea." I smiled while closing the directory to get her attention. "We might make an investigator out of you yet."

CHAPTER 47

Before we went into the jailhouse, I thought about Devon and talked Joy into moving him into the cell next to Libby. She called in and had Devon moved by the time we reached the cells. I checked to make sure no one stayed in the office next to the cells while she checked for bugs. When satisfied, we joined the group.

I pulled up two chairs where the two cells met, and the two prisoners followed suit. They seemed to be doing better. Prisoners didn't get the best or the most food in jail, but it must've been more than they had in Aldrich. It wasn't enough food to put on any weight, but their skin and eyes still looked brighter.

"Hi, I'm Commander Joy Everhart of the Peace Forces." She watched as Devon stood and walked to the opposite side of his cell. "Don't worry, I've checked, and no one is listening to us."

"Devon, she's good people," I said.

He turned and stared.

"The right kind of people." I hoped he understood.

He hesitated, then came back and sat.

"Can you get us all out of here?" Libby almost pleaded to Joy.

"I'm sorry, but the size of the group is too much to release without suspicion being placed on us."

"Save your own necks." Devon shook his head and snorted.

"That's right. We're the ones with our necks on the line every day. You just got in the game. Welcome to the real jungle, Devon." I grumbled.

His shoulders dropped. "Sorry, man. Just hoping"

"I get it. But we're trying to figure out a way to get you two out now and maybe get the others later. But not before they get reassigned." Joy took her notepad out and started scribbling. "It's the best we can do, unfortunately."

"But it's something." Libby gave a weak smile.

"I'll take anything right now." Devon nodded.

Joy smiled and looked at Libby. "Will tells me you two dated before the Rapture."

Libby shrugged and grinned shyly. "For a while, I guess."

"Two years, three months, and two weeks." I grinned. "But who's counting."

Devon laughed. Joy giggled. Libby rolled her eyes.

"Was he a good kisser?" Joy asked, fluttering her eyelids.

"What's that got to do with the case?" I grumbled.

"Just breaking the ice." Joy smiled innocently. "You know, casual talk to get the witness comfortable."

Now I rolled my eyes.

"Yes, he was good." Libby giggled.

"Just good?" Devon laughed. "You told me you're the best, Will."

Everyone but me laughed.

"Okay, that's enough ice-breaking. Let's get on with this." I shook my head, trying to hide my grin.

"Now, we have some more questions for you two. With so many ears in the other cells, I thought it best to bring Devon here to ask them." I sat back and settled into the uncomfortable chair.

"Thanks, Will." Devon settled in his chair. "The tension is high in there. Everyone believes we're all going to the guillotine."

"No, not now," I said. "That won't come until after the halfway point of the Trib, which is still a little while away. The Antichrist is still using our people for work details after reeducation. Except the fertile women, who will go to the breeding centers."

Libby shivered at the thought. "Barbaric."

"Amen, sister." Joy lifted her eyes to Libby.

"What do you want to know?" Devon sat up and leaned his elbows on his knees.

"How many people do you remember from our old church?" I asked.

The two inmates looked at each other and shrugged.

"A few, I guess, but it was a pretty big church." Libby turned to me. "Besides, I moved to another church before the Rapture."

Devon nodded in agreement. "And I walked away when we graduated."

"But your parents still were. I'm hoping that you might recognize names your mom and dad might've mentioned." I nodded to Devon to let him know the same went for him as well.

Pulling out the directory, I opened to the pages with the family pictures, hoping it might jog their memories. I turned the book around, so they saw the first page.

"Do you recognize the ones that are circled?" I pointed at them.

They leaned into the bars and stared. Devon pointed at a few he recognized, but Libby remained silent. I turned the pages for almost an hour. Libby recognized some, Devon recognized others. It helped that they didn't travel in the same circles until recently. They smiled when they saw their friends and relatives crossed out, knowing Christ had taken them to Heaven.

When we reached the last page, I asked, "Since the Rapture, do you know of anyone's whereabouts?"

They stared at the back of the book, looking into their memory banks. Then they looked at each other.

"You have one in the other room." Devon began. "Jill's one of them. Her family went in the Rapture while she attended college."

"How's her hand?" I asked,

"The doctor came in and gave her an injection, a few stitches, and a temp cast. Then he chewed out the guard for not calling him sooner." Devon giggled.

We sat quietly for a few minutes while Joy finished writing. I struggled, deciding if Libby and Devon needed to know how Charlie hunted.

Joy finished and looked at me. Her eyes brightened, and she turned to them. "Do you know anyone in the hunting crew that apprehended you?"

They looked at each other. Devon slowly shook his head. "Not really. I've heard of Charlie Caplan as a bounty hunter, but the guys with him didn't look familiar."

"Although..." Libby tapped her finger on her chin. "That redheaded kid sounded familiar. His voice reminded me of someone from before the Tribulation."

Taking the directory from Joy, I wondered if I'd missed

something. I also talked to the two hunters, but they didn't seem familiar to me at all. Then again, I didn't try to remember them, since this investigation had nothing to do with the other case.

We poured over the pages at a slow pace, still tearing up when passing over family, friends, and memories. Our bond with our unbelieving lives filled those pages. A bond that kept us out of the Rapture. Then I caught a glimpse of a picture of Dad baptizing a new believer, and I had to walk away to compose myself.

"Tyler Warner." Libby pointed at a picture. "Mom didn't like him because she said he went to church for the wrong reasons. But that was after I moved to Joplin."

"I remember him now. He seemed like a pretty good old boy. But he'd turned into a nasty little booger when they caught us." Devon leaned back. "He's the one who hurt Jill."

Libby handed the directory back. "Sorry, but after the Rapture, I didn't cross paths with many from the old church."

"Neither did I." Devon shrugged.

"I have one last question. Libby, you mentioned to Will that you heard Caplan holds some women back to sell to human traffickers. Did anyone try to separate you from your people when they took you to Springfield?" Joy asked.

"No, but Tyler looked at Jill really hard for a while and brought Caplan over to look at her. He shook his head, mumbled something, and they walked back to the truck," Libby said.

"Probably because she had plastic surgery just before the Rapture. Nose, eyes, chin. I heard her testimony last month. Said her vanity kept her from believing," Devon said.

Joy wrote it down, then closed her notebook.

"If you remember anything more, tell the guard to send for me. Do not tell them anything." I stood, hugged Libby, and shook Devon's hand. "And keep praying. We all need it."

On my way to the truck, I tried to put the new information in a definable order in my mind.

Before starting the truck, Jenny's face appeared on my Vam screen before I answered it.

"Hey, Jenny. What's up?" I put it on the truck speakers.

"Hey, Will. Is Commander Everhart with you?" She sounded stressed.

"I'm here. What's the matter?" Joy obviously noted Jenny's

tone.

"Chad is on a rampage. He has this woman in his office who's pushing all of his buttons. Everyone's on edge and snitching on each other already." Jenny's stress increased.

I looked at Joy and mouthed, "Petrovich."

Joy frowned, like she didn't believe me.

"Does this woman have a bad Franch accent?" I asked.

"You know her?" Jenny sounded incredulous.

"Yeah, but don't get too stressed over her. She's more bark than bite." I lied to calm her.

Jenny breathed deeply.

"Attagirl," Joy said.

"Thanks. I needed that." Jenny's voice went back to normal.

Petrovich overstepped on a level she didn't understand.

"Anyway, ICON translated the messages on the chips and it's creepy." She took another breath. "It's the same message on all of them. No variance or deviation. The message is 'The messiah has avenged the OMCC murderer' followed by 'Romans 12:19'"

"What does that mean?" Joy asked.

"Vengeance is mine; I will repay, saith the Lord." I remembered the verse just a few days before coming back to St. Louis. When I planned to kill Joy. I wanted to be God's revenger for what she did to Frank.

"It sounds like the killer has a messiah complex." Jenny muttered. "The psychologists put it under the narcissistic personality disorder."

"Messiah complex. Good call." I pointed at Joy.

Joy grinned.

"Does the computer say what OMCC stands for?" I asked.

"There is a very long list. The email I sent you has the ones the computer says are the most relevant." I heard Jenny click a few times before mine and Joy's phones dinged.

I called up the list and looked at about a hundred spelled out anagrams. The deep feeling gave the impression that I didn't need to waste my time focusing on them.

"Try religious anagrams." I closed the file. "He's using religious text and wording. He's trying to send a message from a religious point of view."

Jenny clicked some more. A minute later, our phones dinged

again. Scrolling the list, I got the feeling that this direction had more merit. When I finished perusing, nothing jumped out.

"Anything on the IDs yet?" Joy didn't look up from her list.

"Not yet. We have the DNA collected on all victims. However, ICON gives an ETA for all IDs sometime tomorrow." Her stress returned. I heard some discussion in the background. Petrovich's proximity to Jenny put all three of us on edge.

"Why don't we meet for supper?" Jenny whispered, meaning she needed to tell us some things that didn't need to be heard by the others. "Two of my new friends invited us to the bar on Walnut about two blocks from where I'm at."

"We'll pick you up in front of the lab in thirty minutes." Joy checked her watch.

"Sounds good." Jenny quickly ended the call.

Before telling Joy my revised plans for checking Charlie's list with the rosters and directories we'd found earlier, my phone played the Peace Forces military march.

Lonergan.

"Yes, sir." I didn't put the call on the truck speakers, thinking he'd say something derogatory about Joy.

"I haven't had an official report from you going on two days, Will." Lonergan's stressed out voice quivered. "The general is not a man who waits."

"Sorry, sir. An informant came to me last night, and we talked into the wee hours, and I forgot."

I gave him the rundown of what had happened the last two days and wrapped it up quickly to avoid confrontation.

"I'll let the general know but get it in writing tonight. Email it to me before I go to bed." His threat didn't go unnoticed. "By the way, I'm coming down tomorrow instead of today. I don't know if you heard, but two of those Jew preachers killed the priests in your area."

"Saw it happen." I cut in.

"Then we have more to discuss than just this case." He mumbled. "I'm bringing their replacements."

I smiled. "When can I expect you, sir?"

"After setting up and securing the new priests, I will eat at the Global Temple. Let's meet in your office at thirteen hundred."

"I look forward to it, sir." I tapped the phone to end the call and told Joy about my meeting.

"Good, I have a meeting then. We can meet when we're both done with our meetings." She giggled while she buckled in. "Let's eat. I'm starving."

CHAPTER 48

Jenny rushed into the truck before I got it stopped.

"Go." She latched her belt.

"What's wrong?" Joy asked as I pulled out of the square on Walnut Street.

"That French woman is having a conniption fit in there. She's blaming everyone for the slowness of the investigation. She got on her phone twice and told whoever she called Chad is so incompetent that he needs to be checked out for potential connections with the Christian Resistance, even scratching his tattoo to make sure he had a chip." Jenny's face contorted like she tried not to cry. "And she bawled me out for not having one at all. I told her I've been busy trying to solve cases, but she said that she's going to get me kicked out of the lab for good if I didn't have it the next time she saw me."

"I have had enough of that woman." Joy pulled out her phone.

Putting my hand on hers to stop her from dialing, I reminded them that Petrovich is powerful enough to get away with anything she wants. We pulled into the back parking lot of the bar and said a quick prayer for protection and calm minds and spirits.

The Tabletop Bar welcomed guests with e-cigarette vapor collecting like clouds on the wood plank ceiling, strong smelling alcoholic beverages, and the new country music that seemed more ready for the dumpster than The Grand Ole Opry. The glossy black walnut bar stretched across the right of the entrance. Alcoholics started early around here, I thought. An empty stage looked like a dusty conversation piece in the back. The wooden tables in the middle made me think of the old diner we ate tenderloin sandwiches the day before.

One thing that stood out of place came from the far end of the bar where Zeek and Daniel had made themselves comfortable. The patrons they witnessed to seemed content to let them talk, so long as the two Jewish preachers didn't do something foolish like stopping them from their dutiful drinking.

"I'm surprised they're not on the stage preaching." Joy giggled while we sat in the corner by the stage opposite Zeek and Daniel.

"They save that for the square." I motioned for the server.

The cute server, dressed in a cowboy shirt and boots, and tight-fitting blue jeans, brought us a menu and took our drink orders. She frowned when she left because we ordered nonalcoholic beverages. Drunks must tip better.

"I don't mean to bring up a sore subject, but what did Petrovich want?" I thought I knew the answer but wanted it confirmed.

Jenny sighed and rolled her pretty, green eyes. "It's like she wants to take over the case. She even tried to tell me how to do my job. Said that the contaminates in the ground aren't really blood and that it's just poor science to believe otherwise. I brought up the samples from the body parts on the computer and proved it. She said that I am betraying the world with my incompetency." Jenny's eyes filled again.

"Sorry, but I needed to know. The top brass has sent her to speed up the investigation because the Sovereign wants to make the announcement ASAP. Or sooner. She's no good at it, but she doesn't care about people, just results. Which will be her undoing." I stared at Zeek and Daniel. "I will deal with her in due time. But until then, I'm afraid we need to be patient."

"She's all over Will, too, to get him to announce what the Sovereign wants him to say and that the government will come out with the facts when they're complete." Joy rubbed Jenny's forearm.

"I've seen her every day since I got back from the west." I sat back to let the server set our dinks on the table, and we gave her our orders.

Sirloin and baked potatoes for all three of us.

After she left, Jenny sighed. "What do you think about the message?"

Joy shrugged. "Haven't had the chance to consider it yet. Will?"

"The killings are obviously a sermon. He has the messiah complex, referring to himself as the Lord by using the Bible reference." I took a long draught of my soda. "Hell bound scratched on the trees builds on that delusion that he has the ability to send them to Hell."

"But he called them murderers. Doesn't that indicate that he agrees with the Sovereign?" Joy wiped the table with her napkin.

"Not necessarily, because he hid the victims. If he agreed with the Sovereign, he'd have drug the bodies to the global temple or even Peace Forces HQ, took credit, and collected the bounty. But he didn't." I paused when it occurred to me. "He's not preaching to the world. He's preaching to the victims."

"You think so?" Jenny asked.

"What if he agrees and disagrees with the Sovereign? If he has a messiah complex, he disagrees with the Sovereign. By sending the victims to Hell, he agrees."

"Way to cut the baby in half." Jenny frowned.

"That's disgusting." Joy twisted her face.

"It's just an expression." Jenny giggled.

"It's King Solomon." I mindlessly mentioned.

"Lets' get back to the case." Joy sipped her water with two lemons.

"If I'm a betting man, I'd say the killer had someone die in the murders and lost it. Then he connected the victims with the murders when government made the announcement. So, he called the victims murderers too." I noticed Zeek and Daniel changing listeners.

"He killed them for revenge because a relative or friend got murdered?" Jenny tried to be careful with her words in the public place.

"The verse he used tells us that. But, more importantly, he believes he has the power to send them to Hell." Joy looked from Jenny to me. "But a messiah delivers people. Who does he think he's delivering?"

"I don't know. Maybe he thinks he's delivering the world from them. Maybe he doesn't want the guilty to be sent to reeducation or breeding facilities." I thought this guy's really straddling the line.

After the meal, I dropped Jenny back off at the lab but didn't leave until she text-confirmed Daria had left. Before getting the all-clear from Jenny, Joy remembered that she forgot to take a report with her from the office. I took advantage of the alone time and thought about the sermon the killer preached to the victims. The message made little sense to me when I took in all the information we'd found. He referred to himself as Lord.

Dad used to preach that Jesus Christ, the actual Messiah, delivered people from their sins and reconnected the broken relationship between God and humanity. I remember reading in college about how historical figures referred to themselves in similar manners, delivering their country, race, or cult from oppression and to a better future. And Jesus predicted there'd be those calling themselves messiah during the Trib. But Joy's right. What's this guy the messiah of?

On top of that, he scratched Hell Bound on the trees beside where he buried the heads. The thought of a messiah killing and sending people to Hell didn't play right. All the messiahs I read about promised to lead their followers to utopia. Many cult leaders killed their followers to take them to a far-off, perfect place. Jesus always talked about Heaven but didn't murder His followers. I struggled to believe that this killer had a following because no one knew about him.

Watching Joy returning to the truck in the gloam of the day, I noticed her smile. It looked like she'd had a great day the way her face seemed to glow in the fading light. Then I got to thinking about Bub.

"What?" Joy asked when she closed the door.

Realizing that I stared at her awkwardly, I refocused.

"Did you do a background check on Bub?" I asked.

"Yes, but there's nothing interesting." She shrugged. "He lived in Walnut Grove all his life."

I interrupted. "Parents?"

She pulled her notebook from her briefcase and looked. "Andrew and Paula Anderson."

Wishing I had the directories, I went through the names in my memory from Dad's church. Then I remembered them. Some called them part-time members.

"Why is this important?" Joy asked.

"His family went to Dad's church. I remember they didn't attend regularly. But I remember that they always asked for prayer for their son, nothing specific." I trailed off, trying to remember more.

"Ashamed of their own son?" Joy sounded judgmental.

"Maybe. I remember Dad putting a prayer chain together about the time of the accident. They lived in a different school district, so the name didn't stick. In fact, I don't even know Bub's real name." I shrugged.

"Jonathan." Joy piped in. "Jonathan Anderson."

"I want to go back and talk to him. Find out if he remembers Dad's church and its members. I also want to talk to him about his family. See if we can connect anything to the bounty hunters." I blew out a deep breath. "Who knows? Maybe he's heard or remembered something since the last time we talked to him."

"Do you think he might be the killer?" Joy's eyes widened.

"I'm not sure if he's capable of something that deep. However, anything's possible."

A long pause in the conversation made me notice her perfume. She wore nothing bold. Always something subtle. A hint of flowers mixed with vanilla. My enjoyment of that and her company caught me off guard. My attraction had grown considerably since I began working on getting over my misplaced anger with her. Her company felt right. Then I remembered Amelia, whose company I lusted for, and felt guilty.

"We need to check the directories and rosters. I remember some families jumped from church to church to get handouts, money, whatever the church gave. Maybe Bub and his parents attended several churches."

"We can get to them tomorrow. I'm ready for some sleep." Joy stretched.

"I'll start going over them tonight." I looked at Joy. "I want to see Bub first thing in the morning." Then I looked at the directory of Dad's church.

"You got a bad feeling?" Joy asked.

I reached for the directory and stared at the cover.

"Ozark Mountain Community Church." I muttered, then repeated it louder to hear myself say it and connect the letter to the words.

"Why is that important?" Joy asked.

"OMCC. Don't you see?" I showed Joy. "It's the name of Dad's church!"

She took the directory. "Will, you may be reaching." She logged onto her Vam and looked at the list Jenny sent us.

"We can't go any farther until we get the victims' ID. But I believe the victims are members of Dad's church. He's killing people he went to church with before the Rapture because he blames them for his family's disappearance. He bought into the Antichrist's theory and is getting his own brand of justice. The murders might've unhinged him enough to believe he is a messiah bringing justice to an unjust world."

"He's distorting the truth." Joy looked at me with intensity coursing through her face. "We need to find this man and stop him."

She wanted to bring him down, and I understood why. The killer will never stop hunting Christians. If we can't stop the Antichrist, we can at least get rid of a false messiah.

CHAPTER 49

When we returned to the hotel, Joy offered to help look at the lists to shorten my time and help me get more sleep. I agreed but needed to post my reports to Lonergan to avoid any more trouble from Sokolov. She looked at her watch and said she wanted to change and we'd meet in the lobby by the old hotel restaurant that, according to the front desk clerk, went out of business before the Rapture.

Finishing the reports and kneeling for some prayer time, I found myself a little nervous meeting Joy in the closed restaurant. It didn't make sense for me to be this way. Just two colleagues getting some work done. Her perfume kept invading my memory, and her smile disrupted my prayer. I even asked the Lord about my attraction. But He gave me silence, meaning I knew the answer.

When it comes to the boring parts of investigations, the top two rules are comfort and snacks. All I knew about Joy's tastes involved apples, water with extra lemon, coffee and iced tea, both extra sweet. Me, on the other hand, loved snacks. Salt and sugar. I brought the few snacks I had in my room. Chips, packaged cookies, and a six-pack of my favorite soda. On the comfort side, I wore my unused gym clothes. Police academy t-shirt, baggy black coaching shorts, and orange running shoes. Assuming her comfy clothes included the top button down and slip-on loafers, I didn't think too much more about it.

Joy had the documents, so I entered the restaurant with my bag of goodies and reminded a nosey night auditor of my DRUID status. I settled into a dusty circular booth with a large round table.

The chip bag crumpled loudly when I opened it.

My full mouth opened when I noticed Joy walk in. She wore a yellow tank top and black shorts, all form fitting. She filled them out right. Her flip-flops lightly slapped against her heels as she walked. Her pretty little feet sporting a high-end pedicure. She put her dark hair in a neat bun that lightly bobbed with each step. I stood like a nervous teen and gawked at my former boss, who I'd planned to kill just a few short days ago. Cute or adorable didn't describe her well enough. Joy gave Amelia a run for her money in beauty. And beat the British bombshell in the other categories I found desirable.

My phone vibrated. Amelia had set up a video chat.

I ignored it and turned my phone off.

Joy's face lit up when she saw me stand. A shy smile crossed her face.

"Why the chivalry?" Her eyes twinkled.

Like an idiot, I stood silent for a moment before answering. "I've never seen you out of uniform before now."

I wanted to slap myself for the implication.

She blushed and did a little twirl with her arms wrapped around the paperwork like a schoolgirl. "Well?"

"You look comfortable." I stammered.

"As do you, Major Thomas." She winked, slipped out of her shoes, slid across from me, and sat crisscross.

Sitting down and mentally chastising myself for being a total doofus, I offered her a soda and pushed the chips towards her. She popped the top of the can and sipped the soda but waved off the chips.

"I'm a popcorn girl. But the soda is good and cold." She pulled out an already popped microwave bag of popcorn from her briefcase.

"Cookies?" I pulled them from my bag.

"Maybe later." She looked at the package and smiled. "Ooh, the good stuff."

"Nothing but the best." I looked at the paper. "You're the expert with paperwork. Where do we begin?"

She glared at me for a moment before I caught on. "I mean, you're the organized one. I don't even take notes until the end of the day because I take that long to organize my thoughts."

Her smile melted my anxiety. "It's okay, Will. We all have our strengths. Maybe I can teach *you* something. Rookie."

I spread my arms in acquiescence. "I'm all yours."

Her leer made me realize what I just said. Knowing the red of my face must've reminded her of a stop sign, I made a mental note of putting a fifty-five-caliber bullet in my head at the end of the case.

Spreading the paper clipped stacks into a neat line, she looked at them like she wanted to ensure their proper order. Her frown when focusing stood out as a beautiful reminder of her bookish qualities I found attractive. The scent of her shower soap reached me. It didn't feel fair. She didn't know my growing attraction to her, yet I started fantasizing about kissing her. It threw me off how the fantasy grew more intense than any I had with Amelia.

"Here is your copy of Charlie's list." She pushed it to me, giving a cute grunt when she reached her farthest. Trying to act nonchalant, I quickly made up the distance. "I began separating the churches according to denomination and location, but then I thought that it really didn't matter. So, I just split the stack evenly." She shoved a stack to me, this time using the highlighter she took from behind her ear.

It took everything I had to focus on the stack and not her. Then I noticed that she kept Dad's church for herself. She put it at the top of her stack. When she noticed me looking, she put it to the side, blushing again.

A little after midnight, I rubbed my eyes and looked outside. The sight of I-44 reminded me of the countless trips to and from church when we crossed the bridge over the interstate. The old highway used to be a major artery connecting both sides of the county, but now had no traffic, not even an eighteen-wheeler taking a load back east.

"What are you thinking about?" She broke the trance.

"It's hard to work this case. I'm home, but I'm a complete stranger." It's the most open I'd been with Joy.

"I know the feeling. I mainly grew up in the boarding school out of state after Peru, but St. Louis is the place I identify as home. Every time I drive through the city since my conversion, I feel disjointed from it." She looked outside.

"You ever consider taking a vacation to Peru?" I asked.

She giggled. "No. I only lived there a few months before getting shipped off to boarding school. My family visited me in the States while on furlough. I visited them just once in high school and felt nothing for the place. I was glad to see my family, but the rest didn't really matter to me."

"I'm sorry I never asked. Did all of your family make it in the Rapture?"

"As far as I know. I check ICON occasionally, but their names still register as 'Murdered'" She took a sip of soda. "And now I'm glad."

"I'm glad for you." I stretched and looked at her overly organized stacks. "Anything yet?"

"Plenty. I fully believe Caplan uses these to find them." She stared at one of the directories. "But no Andersons."

"I'm having the same results. It appears that the Andersons only went to OMCC." I sighed and stared at the overly highlighted list. "I don't think we need to go into it anymore. It's too obvious."

"We don't have a lot left. Why don't we finish it to be thorough?" She yawned.

Not wanting to leave her, I agreed. We dug back into the lists. About 3am, I noticed movement coming from the restaurant's outside exit. Reprimanding myself for leaving my SIG in my room, I slid out of the booth.

"Bathroom break?" Joy didn't look up.

"No, just stretching my legs." I didn't want to alarm her if it turned out to be nothing.

When I reached the door, the movement stopped. The blackened shrubs on a bed of reddened mulch chips separated the building from the sidewalk that led to the front parking lot. The first vehicle on I-44 caught my attention.

A fist slammed on the window of the door before I saw him. I heard Joy squeal. Clay's terrified face appeared beside the fist.

Opening the door, I felt Joy's presence standing beside me.

I turned and saw Joy trembling, still in her bare feet. "It's Clay."

She stopped and looked at Clay. "I don't know you."

"I'm an undercover informant for Will," Clay said, walking farther into the restaurant.

She looked at me.

"This is Clay, my C.I." I motioned for her to follow him.

"I remember you telling me he worked for you in St. Louis." She went to the booth and slipped into her shoes.

They shook hands.

"I'm sorry for scaring you, Will, but this is important." He rubbed his face like he did when he used drugs. "Real important."

It bothered me to think I sent him back to his old life to fall off the wagon. The deep feeling calmed me.

"What is it?" I asked.

"Zeek and Daniel sent me to tell you that the church in Phenix got captured by Charlie Caplan's crew." Clay rubbed his face again and fidgeted.

"Oh no," Joy whispered.

"Where are they now?" I asked

"At the docks. They haven't unloaded yet because the guards won't answer the phone."

Joy had already collected the paperwork. "Let's get dressed and get down there." Her commander tone in full tilt.

"We'll take you to the square and let you off out of sight." I walked to the hotel entrance.

Clay grabbed the snacks and sodas. "Can't take any chances. See you later." He darted out the door he came in.

CHAPTER 50

The docks had a single streetlight that did little to show the full picture. Charlie's trailer backed up to the loading dock didn't give me much of an idea of how many people he'd captured. Joy's red face gave me pause. I grabbed her shoulder and slowed to a stop.

"What?" Her face lost its softness from the hotel with a hardened resolve I knew too well.

"We need to be careful. Those people are scared. If we get too emotional, something might slip about our affiliations. That's all Daria needs to eliminate you." I kept a low tone.

"But they are our people." She whisper-shouted.

"And they know the times they live in." Daniel appeared out of the shadows.

"We need to get them out of there." She looked at Daniel. "And I'm the one who can do it."

"At what cost?" Daniel raised his eyebrows. "To save a handful of people and endanger thousands more? I'm sorry, but you cannot go there and show who you are. God is not ready to take you home yet. You have important work still yet. I'm sorry."

"But not me." I stormed off.

"Will." She shouted.

"Working awfully late, Charlie." I tried to use a calm tone.

He looked around at me with a scowl. "Nighttime's the best time to catch these people."

Looking at the trailer, I stopped next to Charlie.

"How many?" I asked, hoping for a low number.

"Twenty-seven," He snarled.

My anger spiked when I went around the trailer and found Isaac's arrogant grin taunting the group.

I walked up to the trailer to make sure Tim's group had been captured. A few faces looked familiar from the first time I talked to their leader. Although I noticed Tim, he kept to himself. Probably scared I'd march him to the blade myself.

"Oh, no, you don't." Isaac grabbed the back of my right arm and tried to swing me around. "You almost cost us a bounty last time. I don't care who you think you are, lawman."

My mind went straight to my combat training. Spinning the opposite direction that he tried to direct me, I brought my left elbow to his face and broke his nose. He immediately stepped back as the blood started gushing. I finished the spin with an overhand right and planted it firmly on his exposed jaw. He crumpled to the ground.

"Don't go any farther, lawman." Charlie aimed his sawed-off shotgun at my face.

The thought of seeing Jesus right then didn't sound too bad. I grinned. Charlie frowned.

"And you will never point a loaded weapon at a DRUID officer." Lonergan came out of the shadows with his pistol resting against Charlie's temple.

Charlie turned loose of the shotgun and raised his hands when Lonergan grabbed the barrels. A look of rage flashed on Charlie's face before regaining his composure.

"I have a good mind to take you up to the private cells and discuss how things are in the new world." Lonergan's rage covered his face as he thumb-cocked his weapon.

"Thanks, Colonel, but I think Charlie's learned his lesson." I looked at Isaac, still out cold. "And I think his employee needs medical attention."

Lonergan holstered his pistol and nodded Charlie to Isaac. Charlie kneeled by his quarry and shook him while placing a dirty bandana on his bleeding nose. Isaac moaned.

"Seems like these bounty hunters have a thing or two to learn about how things work." Lonergan smiled.

"We're all transitioning." I returned the smile while rubbing my knuckles.

Just then, Joy showed up. She looked calmer than before. I

hesitated. My mind went into overdrive. She needed to go back to the hotel. Looking around for Daria or anyone looking too interested in Joy's presence, I put my hand in my pocket and held the SIG.

"Colonel, I'd like to see the prisoners. I want to make sure the hunters treated them well. After the incident with the woman and her broken hand, I am writing a request to my superiors that we withhold all bounties for excessive violence. We don't want to develop a reputation for allowing potential breeders and future citizens to be handled inappropriately through the new bounty program. There have been reports of bounty hunters injuring people beyond medical help. As you know, we're in a population crisis, and the breeding program is one of the Sovereign's most important." She walked to the back of the trailer.

Lonergan shrugged, but not before giving a questioning frown. I knew Joy had over-explained, and Lonergan now had something on her.

She ordered one of Charlie's boys to open it and had the Christians line up along the tunnel wall. With her Vam, she notified the night guard that they needed to come out immediately. The jailhouse doors flew open, and five guards and their commanding officer poured out.

"Captain, I'd like to know why these prisoners have been waiting?" She walked to him, flashing her badge.

"Sorry, ma'am." He stood at attention. "I just arrived. Trying to get myself situated. No one told me that a new shipment already arrived."

"We've been calling for over twenty minutes," Charlie hollered while helping Isaac to his feet. "We've never waited more than ten before. Sounds like a piss poor start, Captain."

"I'll be the one talking to my people." Joy turned, face red. "You take care of your people."

Charlie muttered something and helped Isaac to the truck. Looking at Isaac, I saw eyes that didn't focus well. I clocked him pretty good.

Joy turned on the flashlight on her Vam and began looking at Tim's group. When she shined her light in his face, Tim bowed his head in what looked to be a silent prayer. Joy looked at the rest, who followed Tim's pattern. The way she held herself gave the impression of composed power, but I knew better. Her entire body language told me she was trying hard to think of a way to get them out of there.

Asking the deep feeling to help her understand, I knew she treaded dangerous waters. Especially with Petrovich and her people lurking in the shadows.

"Commander Everhart, may I have a word with you?" I asked.

"What are you doing, Will?" Lonergan turned away, so no one heard his thoughts. "Let her blade herself."

"And let valuable breeders potentially get released?" I whispered. "I learned in the field to pick my battles. If Petrovich finds out we stood around and did nothing, she'd personally march us to the guillotine."

"Good thinking. It's nice to have someone thinking clearly this time of morning." He yawned.

Joy followed me across the street into the parking lot, away from prying ears. She stood, crossed her arms, and shifted to one foot.

"You need to be careful." I started in a low tone.

Her face stiffened into a frown. "I am the commander…"

"Yes, I know. But you need to remember that we have to be careful when it comes to our people." I paused when I realized something. "Did you forget what we know about Charlie and the red-headed kid? We need to get in that truck. Maybe some poor woman is in the back. Plus, Lonergan is taking mental notes. If you turn any of them loose, it can be a career killer. You need to think long term." I tried not to console, but to keep her focused.

"You're right. We do need to search the truck." She relaxed and wiped her eyes. "But I need to help them." I heard a crack in her voice.

"They're in God's hands now." I paused again. "Charlie took Isaac to the truck. I'll look in on him to check the cab. You need to let the captain take over and walk away."

"This isn't right." She rubbed her face.

"Welcome to the game." I looked to see if anyone watched us and whispered, "It sucks, but like Daniel said, we can't sacrifice thousands for a few. We need to let God take care of them. Trust me. If He wants us to do something, He'll make it crystal clear."

Her shoulders dropped as she nodded in defeat. Then she

hugged me. I wrapped her in my arms, not wanting to let go.

When we got back, Joy ordered the guards to take the group in and process them before leaving.

While she did that, I went to Charlie, as he checked on Isaac without much emotion, like he didn't want his worker bleeding all over the front seat. I went around and opened the driver's door and leaned in.

"How's the kid?" I did a quick scan while Charlie focused on Isaac.

"Be better if you didn't break his nose." Charlie looked at me with contempt. "Probably got a concussion."

"He'll live." I grumbled before closing the door.

No one in the cab. I walked around the front of the truck and looked at my commanding officer.

"Major Thomas," Lonergan said. "We need to talk in your office." He motioned for me to follow him.

CHAPTER 51

The desk sergeant appeared to be the only person on duty. Lonergan flashed his credentials before handing over the shotgun and telling him to process it. The sergeant put the shotgun under the desk and returned to his paperwork. Lonergan had all the signs of a tired soldier. His gait slow, head slightly drooping. And yet he kept the bearing of an officer, even when no one looked at him but me.

"Not that I'm ungrateful for you bailing me out with that bounty hunter, but what are you doing here this time of night?" I sat in my chair while Lonergan sat across from me. "You said we'd meet this afternoon."

"Those priests are maddening." He rubbed his tired face with both hands. "They wanted to get here ASAP, and they didn't take no for an answer. On top of that, they're demanding military protection twenty-four seven. And the new high priest is commanding me to get rid of these Jews. Like I have any desire to burn." He groused.

Staring at his Beastmark, I knew that time for him grew closer every day.

"Doesn't the global religion have their own guards?" I asked.

"Since those Jew preachers started setting everyone on fire, no one will volunteer to guard the priests, and the ones they had are either dead or deserted."

After a long pause, Lonergan got to business.

"But why did you go to the dock?" I asked.

He sighed. "The temple stinks. They've been sacrificing since we got here." He looked at the ceiling. "And the chanting. I can't sleep."

"Get a hotel."

"They won't let me until I get a protection detail assigned to them." His red eyes flared.

"I read your reports and am worried that you're taking your time. I read your record in the police, and it said that you're the patient type. Will, I made myself perfectly clear the first day. The Sovereign explicitly ordered an immediate resolution of this case so the media can release the full story to discredit the Christians." He raised his eyebrows and rocked a little. "Did we choose the wrong man?"

It took everything I had not to go off on my superior. "Sir, no one can do any better than what I'm doing now. The lab just found viable DNA. They're hoping to get the results sometime today. When they do, I'll have a clearer picture of the victimology of the killer. Then, maybe, things will get rolling in the right direction."

"I saw that in the case file. But you don't realize the pressure we're getting from the top. General Sokolov is getting calls in the middle of the night. The Europeans don't care about time differences. They just want results. And when the general doesn't sleep, I don't sleep." He yawned.

Sitting back, I thought about the day. "The best help you can give me is keeping Daria Petrovich away from the investigation."

His face lost all blood. "Daria Petrovich?"

"The one and only. She went into the lab yesterday and started barking orders like Joy. Is there any way the general can get her out of our hair?" I asked.

Lonergan sighed heavily and paused. "I haven't heard that name in a while. She doesn't leave Europe much. In fact, I didn't even know that she's in the country, let alone Springfield. But it tracks. With the government having so much riding on this investigation, it makes sense they'd send her to make sure things go quickly and smoothly."

"So, you're saying that you can't do anything about her?" I used my incredulous tone to get him to flinch.

He did. "General Sokolov *won't* do anything. Will, you've got to understand. Daria Petrovich makes people disappear. What little the general told me about her keeps me up at night when I hear her name. For her to be here now just goes to show the importance of the case. The Sovereign wants this to happen, and he obviously sent her here to make it so."

"What if this has nothing to do with this narrative?" I needed to hear it.

"They've already written this narrative, and it's finished. All we need for you to do is finish the case. No matter who did it and for what reason, the public will know the truth." He sat back with a contented grin. "And I'm glad for it. The Christians have needed to be put in their place for millennia. This is a historic time, Will. We are the spear tip of one of the greatest movements in history. Politics and science are putting religion in its place. The Sovereign is taking all three and merging them into one. He will leave anyone behind in the dark who refuses to join us. The Sovereign is the light."

I desperately wanted to pull my SIG on him. The deep feeling reminded me of what I told Joy earlier that night. God put me there to help His kingdom, not my ego.

"Why are we even doing the investigation?" I snuffed.

"To make sure the facts follow the narrative." His icy stare angered me. "And the narrative is the truth."

"And if it doesn't?" I returned the stare.

"It will." He smiled. "I promise you it will. The Sovereign sees things, knows things. It's like he understands on a level a mere mortal cannot fathom. It's like he's a god."

A chill ran up down my spine. I didn't expect this kind of talk for another year or two.

"As an investigator, I can't promise anything except this. I will follow the evidence and develop a timeline." I stood and walked to the door. "And I will catch the killer. No matter what narrative any outsider claims. You may not like it, but that's who I am. If you don't like it, it may be in your best interest to take me off the case and put someone who will follow your narrative."

"You just justified my choice. Will, we need someone to get this case closed completely. Let the Sovereign do his job, and he will let us do ours."

"Thank you, sir." I saluted.

He stood and returned the salute. "By the way, I tried calling you when I got in earlier. You didn't pick up."

"Sorry, sir. Working on the case at the hotel." I pulled my phone and turned it on.

"I want more daily reports. Three minimum." He walked to the door. "I have to go back to the temple." He groaned and left.

"Yes, sir."

I shut the door behind him.

My phone dinged, and I saw that Amelia sent seventeen texts demanding my attention and to call her, no matter the time.

She picked up on the second ring. "I'm beginning to wonder if you're playing around with another woman."

I paused, wondering if she had more sources than Daria and Joy.

"Will, I'm kidding." She nervously giggled. "I know you're working. Always working."

"Yes, I have. They found the heads, and we should find out the victim IDs today." I breathed an internal sigh of relief.

"Sounds like you need some sleep."

"Yeah, I might." I grumbled.

"I can tell you're not going to be much of a conversationalist, so I'll let you go." She sighed. "I just wanted you to know that I moved my chip appointment to next month."

"Great." I didn't mean it. In fact, I didn't know what I meant.

"Get some sleep." She sounded annoyed. "Maybe we can have a real talk tonight."

She hung up.

CHAPTER 52

Feeling the exhaustion overwhelming my body and mind, I went to the Automat for a little breakfast, iced coffee, and wound licking. The purple sky showed that dawn approached. My mind tried to come to terms with my failed attempt to derail the narrative. The world had no desire to understand the power the Antichrist had over it. As a spectator, my guts churned over the fact that I had no chance of making the facts useful. Then I wondered about my part in the case. It still felt like I was helping the wrong side further its devilish schemes. As a believer, I felt the need to fight the Antichrist and his government with every cell in my body. And yet, everything I did seemed to further his hellish agenda. Entering the self-serve restaurant, a wave of self-pity overwhelmed me.

After pulling out an order of biscuits and gravy and pouring a glass of iced coffee, I turned to find a place to sit. Hectar stood near the door to his private dining room and motioned for me to join him. I wanted some alone time, but I knew he had something for me that helped us both.

We sat at his fancy table and ate before greeting each other. The meal filled, but licking my wounds made me forget to taste it. Coming out of my haze, I noticed Hectar's Vam brightly lighting his face. He kept the screen to himself, making me think he had important business taking place that I didn't need to know about. Although I knew Daria watched his every move, I figured Hectar had ways around her when he needed it.

I wiped my mouth after taking the final draught of my cold

coffee. Waiting for Hectar to finish his business, I decided not to talk to him about how he fit into the new world.

"Will, I see you are waiting for me to start the conversation." He smiled as he closed his Vam screen. "That's awfully polite. It makes me think you have a lot on your mind."

"Is this room secure?" I asked.

He gave the Vam to his server, who immediately left the room.

"It is now." He had a note of defeat in his voice.

"Your rival has captured another house church." I hesitated, not sure of the timing. "I don't know what you know about him, but he uses church directories and rosters to find his prey. I think he uses one of his guys to infiltrate and learn the church's safety protocols before their raid."

"I had a feeling that it was something along those lines." He leaned forward. "That is vital information. You must be in a lot of trouble to give me such delicate data. You want something."

"Putting something in the bank for later." I whispered.

He slapped the table and chuckled. "You are starting to play the game well. It is a pleasure to watch a young man take the lessons he's learned and apply them."

I let my grin give me away on purpose. "Now I need to learn the best time to cash it in."

"It will present itself, and I believe you will see it and act properly." Hectar sat back with a contented look.

"I doubt you brought me in here to see my progress." I motioned for the server, who had reentered the room, for more coffee. "What can I do for you?"

Hectar paused for a long moment. Something he excelled at. "Like I said before, you're the only one I can discuss this with." He pulled out the worn Bible he inherited from his mother then hid it again when the server reentered the room.

"The supervolcanoes." I muttered while the server put my coffee in front of me and left again.

"Yes. My sources have confirmed that Yellowstone is about to erupt, and several on the planet will follow." He opened the Bible to the back. "I've been doing my homework. It's unlikely that we'll feel the full effect of the actual eruption. Maybe a minor earthquake. But, because there is still no wind, the cloud will only spread in the direction of the explosion."

"That's good because I read a prediction from a top seismologist about the effects of a super eruption. Any air current would spread the ash, and nothing would survive." I took a drink.

"God seems to know what He's doing." Hectar focused on the book.

"He knows exactly what he's doing." Daniel's voice took us off guard.

Hectar scowled at the server who just ran into the room, with gun drawn and looking perplexed.

"I have a way of making an entrance." Daniel smiled as he sat beside me.

Hectar motioned the server to leave the room.

"And you are correct. Hectar is it?" Daniel asked. "The judgment will begin tomorrow."

"I'm guessing you don't need to read this." Hectar pointed to the Bible.

"I have hidden His words in my heart." Daniel's smile didn't mock. "And your mother will be glad that you are taking it seriously. But you need to understand that knowledge is not enough. You need faith."

"I have faith in the right things in life." He looked at me. "Will, Daria Petrovich is gunning for you. It is official. She has taken over the case and will have you eliminated. But I cannot tell if that means death or transfer. In any case, your time in DRUID will be short-lived."

Waiting for Daniel to take over and change the subject to Hectar's faith, I started working on a plan to get Joy, Jenny, Devon and Libby out of the city and somewhere safe. However, I noticed a lull in the conversation. The two men looked at me for my response.

"I don't matter. My fate seems to be decided already." I knew both men understood the meaning. "If I die, so be it. But I have some business to take care of before I go."

Daniel's smirk confused me. "So be it." He stood and left.

"Before you go out in your blaze of glory, you need to know that Petrovich turned your friends loose. Liberty and Devon. I think she is planning to use them as bait to set a trap." Hectar sipped the last of his coffee with a satisfied puff of air.

I stood. "We don't even know who the victims are. How can

she believe she can draw out the killer with people who may or may not be targets?"

Hectar sighed. "Not the killer. You."

Remembering her threat, I charged out of the Automat.

CHAPTER 53

Outside the restaurant, I noticed a couple of priests preparing the guillotines with four armed military guards watching them. Then I heard someone familiar clear her throat.

"Hello, Will. So good to see an employee of the government take time to have breakfast when a case of this level needs tending." She sauntered to me while I gathered my thoughts. "You and Commander Everhart have dropped the proverbial ball, and it is up to me to clean up your mess."

"Why did you turn Devon and Libby loose?" The deep feeling warned me about her true intentions.

The sneer she sported ignited my rage. "The bounty hunting crew that captured your friends had brought in several groups that day. One we had to release because they turned out to be a family who gladly took the loyalty chip. However, we cannot connect those two with any of the Christian groups because the hunters can't remember. So, we let them go."

I knew my look of confusion entertained her. It didn't track.

"Okay." I tried to calm down, but my mind spun. Where did Libby and Devon go?

"Besides, we have bigger fish to fry than two insignificant wretches. And your lack of progress has required me to make a decision." She entered my personal space. "I am having you transferred, at the behest of your general, to Wyoming in two hours. You will be part of a team to protect volcanologists strategically placed to make sure the Yellowstone supervolcano doesn't erupt."

"You can't stop a regular volcano, let alone a supervolcano." I whispered through my teeth.

"You don't know if you don't try." Her arrogance stretched across her face.

"What about Joy?" I asked.

"Commander Everhart has a date." Her eyes danced in pleasure. I frowned. "With who?"

"Her? She's never been kissed before in her life," she chuckled. Petrovich nodded towards the guillotines.

The deep feeling tried to stop me, but my rage took control.

Mustering all my venom, I leaned into her ear. "I know what you have inside you. And I will take you both out. You have no idea what I can do."

She stepped back, the rage she had shown the day before returning. "Place this man under arrest for threats against the Sovereign."

I didn't notice the four uniforms slowly surrounding us. All four pistols were aimed at my head. I toyed with the idea of taking her out before they pulled their triggers, but the deep feeling brought me to my senses. Live to fight another day.

Besides, I needed to help my brother and sisters.

Somehow.

CHAPTER 54

Standing in the same cell Libby had occupied, I sat and stewed. As the day progressed, my rage kept building. The awareness of my rapidly approaching demise gave me reason to consider a violent jailbreak. I began planning to draw in the guard, new to the jailhouse, and overpower him. I stood to call him in but felt a familiar presence.

"Hello, Daniel." I sat back down.

"Will." He sat on the other side of the bars.

"I don't believe God sent you to free me." I looked at the floor.

"Nope." He leaned in to catch my attention. "He sent me to help you calm down."

"Calm down!" I shouted and stood. "Petrovich is about to kill Joy and has probably already killed Libby and Devon. And you want me to calm down?"

Daniel's voice didn't waver. "You cannot control anything but yourself and how you respond to the situation in front of you. That is why the deep feeling sent for me. You showed your hand to Daria Petrovich. You will not make it to Wyoming, where God will have spared you from His judgment. She plans to have you executed under the guise of treason."

"And Libby, Devon, and Joy? What about them?" I ran a hand through my hair and paced.

"God can take care of us all." He knew he quoted Dad.

Between the deep feeling and Daniel, I felt my anger slowly subside. Then, fear replaced it. I finally found someone in Joy who related to my undercover life. Someone I now cared for.

"Joy is a wonderful woman. Libby and Devon are great people as well. If our Father takes them home to be with Him, who are we to rage?" Daniel shifted in the chair. "I cannot count the number of people I have cared for who have gone home. The hurt is temporary, a sign of imperfect reasoning."

I turned and looked at him. "You're saying they're as good as dead?"

He frowned. "We all are in this imperfect body." He then smiled. "But we have life from God and are safe from the second death. That is the victory over the grave."

"And I'm just to accept it without a fight?" I leaned forward and put my hands on my knees. "It's not how I'm made."

"You must always fight. Fight sin. Fight criminals. Fight against the forces of the Antichrist." He stood. "But you cannot fight death."

Sitting on the cot like a second stringer, I considered what he said. Fight the Antichrist.

Petrovich?

Something Hectar said made me think. "Have you ever cast out a demon?"

"The Holy Spirit did through me. Why do you ask?" Daniel's body language told me he already followed my train of thought.

"What happens to the person when it happens?" I stood.

"In some cases, the person will become fatigued to the point of passing out. They also experience physical disorientation. The other symptoms are random, according to the person's physical disposition. Mentally, they all struggle with confusion. Some are glad to be rid of the filth, while others become infuriated and become violent. Again, according to their mental disposition."

"And the demon?"

"Cast into Hades until the Great White Throne Judgment when they are sent to the lake of fire." Daniel's scowl returned. "I will not be your spiritual hitman."

"Unless the Holy Spirit tells you to do it." I smiled.

He disappeared.

Praying for a way to stop her and the killer, I heard the door from the next room open.

"Release this man, now." Joy's voice echoed off the walls.

The guard ran to the cell and opened the door, saluting me.

Joy walked into the room. "Will, we have a killer to find. Guard, leave us alone."

He saluted and hustled out the door, closing it behind him.

Wanting to hug her, I kept my composure. "You need to be careful. Petrovich…"

"Is our problem." Joy's brow furrowed. "She's on a rampage because I cashed in a favor from her superior I'd been saving for such an occasion as this. To show my friends are as powerful as hers when you add God to the mix."

"I bet you didn't think you'd use it for me?" I gave a weak smile.

"Until a couple of days ago, I'd have helped her slam the blade across your neck." The corners of her mouth turned up a bit. "Maybe saved some saliva for your headless corpse."

She didn't bait me. She just tested the waters.

"And I would've deserved it." I patted her on the shoulder, trying to hold back, but I scooped her up into a hug.

She let out a deep breath. Nothing more to be said.

"She's after you. The preparations for the guillotines are for us, I believe." I felt fear in my voice. "She baited me into threatening her, so she can call it treason."

"We need to find the killer. It will stop the blade from dropping. If we get the credit, the higher-ups will have no choice but to stay the executions."

"She'll take the credit." I sighed. "You know it."

Joy smiled and patted my forearm. "I have far more favors than the one. Let's grab something to eat and figure this out. I talked to Jenny a little while ago. They're close to getting the DNA results. She'll call us when they're ready."

CHAPTER 55

Stopping the truck in front of the place I'd been avoiding the entire case. I got out and led Joy into the diner where I'd been eating when the Rapture took place. But I'd been closing my past's doors on everything else, so why not here? The place still smelled greasy, with a side of onions.

The counter where we sat that day had open spaces, but I chose the booth by the front window that had no one close. I still heard the fork hit the plate when my friend went to Heaven. Before I picked up a laminated menu from behind the napkin holder, Joy smiled and scooted over. Zeek and Daniel sat.

"I'd say something about being seen in public, but I don't think it matters now." I complained.

"Not that anyone can notice." Daniel elbowed me.

"Wish I had that power now." Joy stared at the menu.

Zeek's look of concern covered his face. "Daniel told me what's been going on. I'm sorry for the both of you." He reached for a menu. "Is this a last meal before you disappear into the sunset?"

"We're not leaving." Joy sounded determined. "Daddy always taught his children to finish what they start. And finish strong. The killer is still out there."

Zeek shot a look at Daniel, who said, "You guys know we get our information as God intends. He doesn't tell us everything. And we have received nothing. It might be in both your interests to light out, find Tommy, and fight the Antichrist with him and his people."

"Oh, ye of little faith." I chuckled. "It sounds like…"

"We care for you." Daniel interrupted. "And our faith is strong."

Zeek grinned. "Don't take it personal little brother. I think Will here is having a bit of fun at our expense. You know, to lighten the load."

Daniel grunted and returned his focus to the menu.

The owner came over and took our order. Burgers and fries for all. When he left, Joy leaned in.

"I think we need to go back to Aldrich. Libby and Devon may go back there to get their things and leave."

"I'm not even sure they're still alive." I sighed. "Petrovich seemed sure of it."

"Why kill them? It doesn't make any sense." Joy leaned back.

"She's been threatening me since we got down here. I'm not doing what she tells me to do. Now I'm paying the consequences." I knew I sounded defeated, but I still needed to focus on what I could do right now.

"Be of good cheer." Zeek smiled. "I know you will find them and catch the killer. I had a dream last night that you will find all of them in a place of worship. But I'm not sure if it's the same place of worship."

"Church." My hopes increased. Dad's church came to mind. It is a place they both knew well. And Libby knew great hiding places we found when we didn't want to get preached at by Dad.

"Your church?" Joy asked.

"It's as good a place as any to start." I looked at her without seeing her.

"I'll check my Vam to see the movements of all the Peace Forces officers. Maybe I can catch a break and locate where they took Libby and Devon." Zeek stood to let Joy out.

"The judgment will happen sometime tomorrow." Zeek changed the subject.

"Yeah, I got that from Daniel and Hectar's conversation earlier." I looked out the window to make sure Joy made it safely to the truck. I put my hand in my pocket and held the SIG.

"She is safe for now." Zeek looked at me. "You can let the weapon go. Petrovich isn't in the area right now. I saw her leave."

"She didn't travel far. Probably went to the hotel to arrest Joy." I snuffed.

"Why arrest Joy?" Daniel's concern caught me off guard.

"She used a favor to get me freed." I looked at the paper placemat with weekly specials. "They've been rivals for a while. Even before Joy's conversion. This one tipped the scale."

"Oh." Daniel groused.

Zeek looked at Daniel. "It appears we have a long, hard prayer session ahead of us today."

"I'd appreciate it." I mustered as much emphasis on it as possible.

"Will, I know you have this problem with revenge. But you need to keep it at bay. It does nothing but cause trouble in ways unfathomable." Daniel's concern touched me.

"I took your advice into account. My revenge is now focused on the demon possessed woman. If I get the chance to kill them, I will. Sorry, not sorry. But I need to do something about her to protect my people. And I have a funny feeling I can't count on you two. Not that it's a bad thing, just a thing." I baited them into showing their cards.

Daniel left the table and went into the bathroom.

"He struggles with you." Zeek chastised me. "You are important to him because he feels responsible for you. When you lose your temper, he prays for you. He wails out to God for you. There are times I join him. It's as if God has this amazing plan for you, but you're too busy acting suicidal. And going after that demon possessed woman is suicidal. She has one of the strongest demons I've ever seen in a human. And trust me, I've seen plenty since the Rapture."

"It's because she is higher up in the government. Go to Babylon, and I'm sure you'd get the wits scared out of you." I saw Joy leave the truck.

Zeek grunted an affirmation as he scooted over to let Joy in.

"Sorry, Will. There's too much movement to lock down a location on them. But I know they are alive because I think Petrovich is keeping them close to hold them over you until you're taken care of." She leaned back to let the owner set the plates in front of us.

His gaze appeared zombie like, but I knew he only saw what needed to be seen.

Daniel returned. His emotions easily noticed.

About halfway through the meal, Joy's phone rang. After a couple of yeses, she hung up and wiped her mouth. "They have the IDs."

We stood and left. Zeek and Daniel stayed to finish their meal.

CHAPTER 56

The look on Lonergan's face told me he didn't know about my release. He lorded over Jenny, who looked to be near tears.

"Colonel Lonergan, it's in your best interest not to intimidate my friend." I invaded his personal space but whispered my threat, so he'd keep his standing in the room.

He took a step back, blood leaving his face. "General Sokolov didn't tell me you've been released."

"Good thing. You may be my superior officer, but like I said, she's my friend." I grumbled. "Apologize."

"Sorry, ma'am." Lonergan lowered his head. "I was out of line."

Jenny took a deep breath. "Here are the names of the victims." She handed me and Joy copies of the list. "I haven't had the time to use ICON to look for commonalities. I will do that…"

"No need." Joy frowned, looking at the list and retrieving the church directory.

I pointed at one of the names. "Jason Dunham was in the Marines. It was his tattoo that got me on the case."

Jenny pointed at another name. "Angela Hyatt is the head without a body."

"She used to teach Sunday School for kids." I remembered her fondly.

"They are all from the church Will used to attend." She flipped to the roster and used her finger to find all the names. "OMCC."

Lonergan leaned on the table to see. "What does that mean?"

"It means the killer is among Charlie Caplan's crew." I stared at the list. A thousand memories consumed my mind.

"Why Charlie Caplan's crew?" He asked.

"Because he's the one using directories, like these, to find Christians." Joy closed the book. "Are you thinking what I'm thinking?" She looked at me.

"Isaac." I still stared at the list. "He carries a Bowie knife."

"So?" Lonergan stood straight.

Jenny said, "We proved that the murder weapon is a large knife, probably a Bowie."

Joy turned the booklet around for Lonergan to see Isaac's picture. "He knew the people he killed. Retribution for the murders."

"That's the punk you knocked out last night, Will." Lonergan smiled. "Looks like you will close this case today."

"We can get a location on Isaac." I looked at Jenny. "He's chipped."

Jenny nodded and turned to her computer. Her fingers flew over the keyboard.

One of the techs came over and set a file on the table, clearly eavesdropping. "Hey, there's that bounty hunter. I didn't know he went to church." He pointed at the picture of dad baptizing the new member.

Charlie's smile stretched from ear to ear as water streamed down his cheeks. Dad laughed. Although older, I had to look hard to see Charlie's face in the one I'd seen on the docks.

"Caplan's in on it with Isaac, but they're not selling captives to human traffickers. They're using the bounty hunter business to find people from the church. They catch a group of Christians, compare them to the church directory, and set aside the members to kill them." I sat hard on the stool.

"Jenny, pull up Charlie's and Isaac's ID chips." Joy ordered.

Charlie and his family must've joined after the professional photographer did the family pictures for the directory. However, Mom took all the pictures of the baptisms. Knowing her, she rushed it to the printers to make sure he didn't feel left out. I just knew what Dad told me, always bragging about Charles's spiritual growth and how he never missed a service with his family. Obviously, something went amiss. As for Isaac, they must've crossed paths after the Rapture, agreed that the church killed their families and friends, and began killing the former members of OMCC together for revenge.

Considering a request for support, I chose to go it alone. No telling who took orders from Petrovich, and Joy needed to block my request for the same reason.

"Charlie's at his house." Jenny turned and looked at me. "But Isaac's chip is offline. He might be out of range if he's deep enough in the countryside, and a satellite will take hours to reposition. I just checked, and his current address is the same as Charlie's."

"I'll go look for Charlie alone. You guys find a way to locate Isaac." I realized something and looked at Jenny and Joy. "And the rest of the crew. If one of them believes he's some kind of messiah, they may all be followers."

"I'll call you when they do and meet you there." Lonergan looked at me. "It's the least I can do. And while I'm waiting, I have a call to make."

I ran out the door.

CHAPTER 57

It took almost thirty minutes to get to Caplan's house. Situated in the middle of a farming area west of Willard, Charlie's two-story farmhouse had a detached one-car garage, and an outbuilding. He had his hunting truck and trailer parked near the outbuilding with an electric Cadillac SUV parked in front of the garage.

Not noticing any movement inside or outside the house, I pulled my SIG out just in case I needed it. I went around the house and checked the truck and trailer first. The smell of body odor, vomit, urine, and feces inside the trailer infuriated me. Charlie kept captives overnight. In the truck, nothing seemed out of the ordinary, except the blood in the front seat, which I assumed came from Isaac's nose. Before closing the door, I noticed a faint smell of flowers and strawberries. Perfume.

Sniffing all over the cab, the scent led me to the back seat. It looked like it sat a little higher than other trucks I'd ridden in. Running my hand under the seat, it felt solid, like a metal wall. I felt the crevice between the seat and backrest and found a brand-new seatbelt. When I pulled on it, a latch released, and the seat popped up from the back. The perfume originated in a homemade compartment under the seat. Charlie kept prisoners in there to take to his kill space. It had the capacity to hold two, maybe three small people.

After texting a pic to Joy and Jenny, I went to the Cadillac. The gold SUV had all the bells and whistles associated with the company's reputation. Charlie made a lot of money capturing Christians.

After checking the empty garage and outbuilding, I approached the house, which had been had been white at one time, but since the previous judgment, had a pinkish hue that made it look like an old dollhouse. The cracked concrete steps led to a porch in similar condition. Looking through the large picture window, I noticed top-end furniture and tech. I guessed that Charlie's next purchase might be one of the empty houses on the rich side of Springfield. Testing the door handle, the front door eased open without a sound. I checked the living room according to my training, keeping silent, just in case Isaac and Charlie lurked about.

My room-to-room search on the main and top floors garnered nothing. Going down the steps by the kitchen, I pulled my flashlight. The unfinished basement appeared to be empty, but the deep feeling warned me that something looked out of place. The military issue flashlight lit up the area, and I felt someone's presence. I checked behind the hot water heater and furnace, nothing. The same under the stairwell. Going to the back of the room, I noticed a smell that reminded me of the night before. Isaac's cologne. I knew without looking under the tarp in the back corner that the killer had hurriedly placed a body under it.

Feeling the blood leave my face, I stepped back. Two headless bodies lay side-by-side under the tarp. Isaac's bloody clothes made it easy to identify his body, but the advanced state of decomp with a generous portion of lime covering it made the other body unidentifiable. Then I remembered the bodiless head. He didn't have time to dismember and bury the bodies, but he must've buried the woman's head after Tim had called in the mounds.

Charlie may have been the killer, but I still didn't know if anyone in his crew helped him.

After texting Jenny the pics, I went upstairs to look for Charlie. After clearing the rest of the house, I took my time trying to find anything suggesting Charlie's whereabouts. Staring at the leather couch, I noticed a booklet on the end table beside it.

The OMCC church directory. Sitting down, I flipped it open. He had marked each page like a grotesque checklist. From what I made out, Charlie had written H or M over the faces in the pictures. I tried to figure out the meaning. Looking at the victims from the field, I noticed all had the H. Then I found the page with Charlie's baptism. He mangled Dad's face with something sharp and put a red M over it. A narrative unfolded that told me the meaning. The M stood for murdered, and the H meant Hell Bound.

Pulling the phone from my jacket, I tapped Joy's number.

"Will, are you still there?" She asked.

"Yes." I whispered, finding the photo of Bub's parents, I shot up from the couch. "I need you to locate Charlie's chip." I flew out of the house to the truck. "I need his location now."

"Okay, I'm putting you on speaker. Colonel Lonergan is with us."

"Hey, Will. Can you confirm Charlie Caplan is the killer?" Lonergan asked.

"Not fully. It might be him and his crew. I need to know his location." I fired up the truck and roared onto the farm road.

"Will, we found the crew. They are nowhere near your location. Haven't been anywhere near Charlie's house since the bounty program began, according to their chip GPS." Jenny said, still typing. "They must just work for him."

"I'm having my people pick them up." Lonergan's voice trailed off, mentioning something about letting the general know the situation.

"Will, this is Jenny. I have a location."

"He's at the bait shop." I drove to Lake Walnut Grove at top speed.

"How did you know?" Joy asked.

I told them about the directory and how Bub's parents had an M over them, but Bub wasn't in the picture. However, underneath the pic, Charlie put a small Post-it with Bub's name on it. It had no letter on it.

Yet.

CHAPTER 58

When I reached the bait shop, Joy told me that Charlie had already left, and his chip disappeared off the satellite feed. Charlie knew how to circumvent the GPS feed in the rural areas. Tommy once told me that the Resistance found some people who knew how to scramble a chip from being detected by the Beast satellites. This information, like all illegal info, must've spread across the globe.

The shop had an eerie feel. The aerators, keeping the minnows alive, bubbled through the air. Crickets from the holding bin added a muffled chirp. But no Bub.

"Bub?" I hollered, knowing he'd already come out from the back if he heard the doorbell when I crossed the laser eye.

The empty backroom confirmed my fear. Turning to go out and search the banks of the lake, I noticed an old CCTV monitor under the service counter. I found the system in the backroom with a larger monitor that looked older than me turned off. The screen slowly came to life when I tapped the space bar and found the mouse under a stack of fishing magazines. Bub had the program password protected.

Not having the time to mess around with it, I called Jenny and asked if Bub connected his computer to ICON. While waiting for her, I looked out the front door but didn't see Bub's boat anchored to the tree like last time. Hoping he was fishing and praying another quick prayer of protection for Bub, I returned to the monitor when Jenny said she found it.

"Put the feed on the monitor, go back about an hour and find the last time Bub appeared on the camera feed." I sat in the broken office chair and waited impatiently.

I heard Joy gasp. "Will, look."

The video showed Charlie entering the bait shop, looking at tackle boxes, acting like an interested customer. Bub came out and greeted him. The ancient system had no mic. My guts twisted in knots as I watched the brief conversation. The body language told me that Charlie had invited Bub to go fishing. At first, Bub turned him down, waving at the shop and pointing at the clock. According to the timestamp from the video, Bub had just opened and acted like he expected customers at any moment.

Charlie persisted. His charming smile sent angry chills through me. Then Bub laughed and grabbed the pole he let me borrow. Charlie let Bub lead the way out the door. But not before he looked at the camera and smiled.

Cursing out loud, I ran out the door with my SIG drawn. The calmness of the lake helped in seeing any ripples made by Bub's boat. The deep feeling gave me a sense of calmness, like everything had worked out according to God's plan. I stopped to take a deep breath, felt calmer, and resumed my search. The black grass crunched under my shoes. The only green trees in the area caught my attention, and I found a cove nestled amongst them.

"Will." Joy hollered through the phone. "What's going on?"

"I'm looking for Bub." I struggled to keep my breathing regulated.

"Tell us what's going on." Joy's concern rang through the phone.

Tied to one of the green trees, the empty boat only held Bub's open tackle box. I started looking around, my guts knotting up again. Bub's innocent laugh came to mind.

That's when I found him. Not wanting to see the full picture, I slowly walked to the bank about twenty yards from the boat. Tears fell on my SIG when I saw Bub's headless body.

"Will?" Joy's shaky voice broke my heart.

She led him to Christ. Prayed with him when he made his decision. Celebrated when he became a believer.

"Bub's gone, Joy." I barely got out.

Her sobs made me aware of her surroundings. "Joy, I need you to go to your office and find where Petrovich sent my friends.

They went to Dad's church, and I'm afraid that if Charlie found out about Bub, he might figure out Libby and Devon."

"Okay," she whispered.

"Jenny, keep an eye out for Charlie. Let me know when he surfaces."

"Will, this is Colonel Lonergan. Stay there, and I'll come get you." He sounded like a colonel.

"Won't be here, sir. I think Charlie might be burying Bub and Isaac in the field."

I hung up and ran for the truck.

CHAPTER 59

The easement had no new vehicle tracks. The field had no new holes. I knew I needed to stick to my strength and wait for Caplan to make the next move.

But not this time. Not with people that I loved in danger of this psychopath.

Pacing around the trees, I struggled to understand the deep feeling. Before finding Bub's body, I had this overwhelming feeling that God had everything under control for Bub. That I'd find him hurt, but he'd spend some time in the hospital before returning to the bait shop and resuming his life. But that's not how it happened.

"Hello, Will." Daniel stepped from behind the tree with the H on it.

"Why am I not surprised you're here?" I took my hand off the SIG in my pocket.

"You're struggling with confusion." He stepped closer to me.

"You know. For once, I'd like to tell you something that surprises you." I went to the truck, opened the tailgate, and sat on it. "And why are you here?"

"Trust me, it's not as fun as it sounds." Daniel chuckled when he sat beside me. "And I go where God sends me."

"And I need you?" I asked. "Then tell me where Charlie is."

"I don't know." Daniel stared at me with dark eyes filled with compassion. "But I am here to tell you that the Holy Spirit blessed you with the feeling of calmness to let you know Bub is in Heaven. His pain from Charlie didn't last."

I nodded while squeezing my knees to hold back angry tears. "He's home."

"Amen, brother." Daniel wiped a tear from his face. "What stinks about being who I am is knowing that most of the people I lead to Christ will end up the same way Bub did. I stopped counting the believers going to the guillotines for the cause of Him who loved us first when I hit triple digits."

The moment lingered longer than I meant. "I'm sorry for treating you the way I've treated you lately. I've felt alone since I went to the military. Even with the deep feeling, I never figured out my place in God's kingdom or this world. It felt like He punished me for what happened to Frank. I figured He put me in the west to die in the next judgment." I wiped my nose on my sleeve. "A failure to the end."

"Not a failure." Daniel raised his voice in rebuke. "Will, you have helped more people than I can count. Not just Christians, but those who have not given their lives to Christ yet. You have slowed the enemy in ways that allow us to reach out to the lost in this lost world."

"It's hard to celebrate when you're alone." I mumbled.

Daniel lowered his head. "No Christian is an island. No matter how alone you feel. God is with you. It hurt me to see you suffering in South Dakota, but the Holy Spirit held me back because you needed to understand some things about Him on your own. Now, I feel led to tell you that God still has plans for you in this world."

"And Joy?" I needed to know.

"Her, too." He put his hand on my shoulder. "I'm not sure what that plan is, but I know it is going to be fantastic. Keep fighting the fight."

"And Petrovich?" I didn't look at him.

"If God wants her time on earth to end before the conclusion of the Tribulation, He'll do it His way. If you are part of that plan, so be it. Just don't go looking for trouble."

My phone rang. When I put it to my ear, I felt the truck lift. Daniel disappeared.

"Will, Joy." She sounded tired. "I did a little digging and found out that Petrovich had Libby and Devon dropped off at our hotel. I think she wanted to use them to make you look like a member of the Resistance. It feels like she had several plans to send you to the guillotine."

"Call the hotel and see if they're still there."

"Already did. They said a Peace Forces car dropped off two young people earlier. The officer threatened them to not leave, but they walked off the property anyway after he left. In the direction of your old church."

"Maybe they found a good place to hide." I thanked her and hung up.

Then I prayed.

CHAPTER 60

"Will, Lonergan. Are you at the murder field?" He asked.

"Yeah, but Charlie's not here. I'm waiting to see if he pops up here or on ICON." I swung my legs to avoid numbness setting in.

"Until then, all I can say is congratulations, my boy. The general is about to call. He wants to congratulate you himself. He's telling his superiors that you solved the case. She can't take the credit." Lonergan's voice beamed.

I knew he meant Joy and not Daria.

"Sir, the narrative isn't right. Charlie Caplan is a chipped bounty hunter. A loyal global citizen." I fought the futile fight to do my due diligence for Christ and fight the Antichrist.

"Doesn't matter. He attended church before the murders. We now have it in his file from the church directory you showed me. He might be loyal, but his past came back to bite him. He tried to resolve it by hunting the people that used to be his friends and failed." Lonergan's laugh annoyed me. "We didn't even have to lie. The truth is on our side, kid."

Just then, he got quiet. After hearing a couple of taps on his end, I heard Sokolov's voice. "Go ahead, sir."

"Congratulations, Major Thomas. You have done a great service to the people of this planet and, most importantly, your Sovereign." Sokolov's voice sounded triumphant.

Trying not to vomit and dealing with the enormous guilt of how the Antichrist might use this to kill more Christians, I remembered what Daniel said about God's plan for me. I simply said, "Thank you, sir."

He sounded like the Beast had already taken control of his voice. "You and Colonel Lonergan will get time off to give some interviews to let the people know that DRUID is on their side. Protecting them. It will do more to bring the peace our Sovereign has been so diligently working towards all these years."

"Sir, I have a question," I said.

"Go ahead." Sokolov's trepidation bothered me.

"I don't know if Colonel Lonergan has had the time to talk to you, but Daria Petrovich tried to take over the investigation. She even had me arrested and threatened to have me bladed." I let out a little whine in it to sound like a little boy running to papa.

"She is a parasite. I will deal with her later. Just make sure you two get to St. Louis when you finish the paperwork."

"But sir, we haven't caught the killer yet." I didn't want to anger him. Much.

The silence threw me off. I figured he'd poo-poo the details.

"Colonel Lonergan has guaranteed that this Caplan will be in cuffs by the end of the day. And I expect no less." His tone turned violent. "Is that clear?"

"Yes, sir," Me and Lonergan said simultaneously.

"I will get off here so you can close this case." Sokolov's feed ended.

"Will, you still there?"

"Yeah." I slid off the tailgate to stretch my legs.

Just then, I got a text from Jenny. "Hold on, sir."

Jenny said that Charlie popped for a second on the satellites. As I stomped to the truck, I remembered the call.

"Sir, Charlie just popped. I need to go get him."

"But, Will…"

I ended the call.

CHAPTER 61

The parking lot at Dad's church had no vehicles when I pulled in. Feeling like another wild-goose chase, I sat in the truck and looked at the building. No movement.

Thinking about the case and the evidence we collected, I tried to piece together the timeline. According to the ding on his chip, Charlie killed people from the church at the church. He caught them and chipped them, then... I got on my Vam and video called Jenny.

"Is he there?" She asked, sitting in front of the camera.

"No. But something came to me. Can you track those animal chips you found on the heads?" I asked.

"Yeah, but what good will that do?" I saw her eyes widen. "Of course, the rest of the batch." She began typing furiously. "Give me a minute."

I got out, checked my SIG, and put the Vam on the hood of the truck. The deep feeling put a panic in me. Then I remembered Libby and Devon.

"Will, the batch is in the same place Charlie's chip popped. At that church." She stared at her screen. "There are four chips live." She looked at me.

"I'm wondering why he made them go live." I zipped up my jacket, chastising myself for not putting my protective pants before leaving the hotel the night before.

"I believe he has to do that to put the message on them." Her eyes widened. "They just turned off."

"He's in there." I looked at the church. My rage hit an all-time

311

high. He killed people in my church. "Have you heard anything about the rest of the crew?" I needed to be smart about it.

"Before he left, Lonergan said they'd been secured." Jenny sounded jumpy. "Will, be careful."

"Thanks, I will." I stopped the feed.

Four chips live. Libby, Devon, Isaac, and Bub.

Going into the church, I knew Charlie didn't have his kill room on the ground level. But the basement was the perfect place to hide him and his victims for as long as he wanted. No one went to church anymore, and the way the first floor looked, it'd been quite a while since anyone else had been there.

The church had two sets of stairs to the basement. The main staircase in the foyer led to the basement hallway, and the second set of stairs, by Dad's office, went into the chapel where the youth held services on Wednesday nights.

I knew the classrooms weren't good enough for old Charlie. His sermons needed a sanctuary, and the youth chapel filled that requirement. I went to the stairs by Dad's office, doing my best not to make any noise for Charlie to hear.

I told the deep feeling that I had no intention of letting Charlie live through this. With the blade far enough away, he'd get a well-deserved bullet. My bullet.

The deep feeling gave nothing. I knew better than to take that at face value.

His ways aren't our ways.

Fighting off the nostalgia of going down the steps of my past, I kept to the wall and shut the door to let my eyes get used to the dark before going the rest of the way down. I knew, from experience, that the cheap door to the chapel didn't have the strength to keep me out. However, breaking it down might've lost me the element of surprise, but my friends on the other side needed help.

Before I reached the door, I heard Charlie's voice as he preached.

"You almost got away, didn't you? But the messiah sees everything." He shouted. "I didn't see you in the picture because you weren't in the picture. Just like the other one. But I knew your parents."

Checking the knob and finding it unlocked, I slowly opening

the door, I checked the areas in my line of sight. From my limited vantage point, Charlie had emptied the room of the pews, and they sat in the only chairs. Without knowing if Charlie had anyone else in the room, I needed to be careful, since I had no backup coming.

The room had a couple of lights burning. One was on a table in the far corner that looked like a monitor, and the other was a battery-operated camping lantern at his feet. The smell of lime and human decay overwhelmed my nostrils.

"Your sins against the messiah are not forgiven." Charlie raised the tip of his Bowie knife to his face and let it lean on his cheek.

A couple of agonizing moments later, Charlie stood and went to the table. With his back to me, I military crawled through the door to see the rest of the room. The darkness made it hard to see if anyone else lurked about. A stack of folding chairs by the door provided cover for me to further assess the situation.

"Your part in the murder of the messiah's family is reprehensible and must be vindicated with a just punishment." Charlie sharpened the knife on a whetstone.

He then prattled on about the Sovereign being right about Christians killing their own to prove that Jesus had returned. Charlie's body began bobbing. Then I realized he needed to go the bathroom.

Charlie put down the knife. "Gotta go. Even the messiah must heed the call of nature."

That got my attention. Charlie believed himself to be a messiah. After he left the chapel, I hustled to Libby. Before I got there, I noticed something that turned my stomach. On a small desk beside the table, three heads stared at Libby. Isaac, Devon and Bub's lifeless faces looked at her with strained features and dried blood on their foreheads. The fake messiah's mark.

Then I walked around the chair and saw her lifeless eyes staring into the dark side of the room. A small stab wound in the side of her neck, blood covering that side of her body, and the chip implant in her forehead. All of my emotions hit me at once. But before I had the opportunity to react to the scene, a blast threw me to the ground beside her. White hot pain shot through my torso into my extremities.

The jacket did its job, but I dropped the SIG, which landed on the other side of Libby. With little options I raised my head over

Libby's lap and looked at the false messiah. Then he glared.

"You're that DRUID guy who broke Isaac's nose." He glared.

I grabbed my side and winced.

"Major Will Thomas and you're under arrest for capital murder."

Charlie frowned and scratched his head with his .45 pistol.

"And for using my dad's church to do it in." I cursed at him.

"Will Thomas?" He stared for a minute and laughed. "As I live and breathe. The preacher's son. I can't believe I missed it both times we talked. Course, I never met you or your sister. But your daddy flashed pictures of you two all the time." He grinned and walked towards me with the pistol aimed at me. "And you didn't get murdered. So, that makes you a murderer." He raised his Bowie knife.

I tried to move to the other side of Libby to get the SIG, but he saw it and cut me off with a slice to my left thigh that went deep. My shorts quickly became soaked with blood.

"Charlie, why are you doing this?" I asked, gripping my leg to slow the bleeding.

His face twisted into an evil grin. "Justice." He picked up my gun and pointed it at me.

"What did these people do to you?" I wanted to keep him talking while I made a plan, but nothing presented itself.

"They murdered my family. The other messiah said so. The Sovereign." He pointed at me. "And you're just as culpable, being the preacher's kid."

"Where's your family's bodies?" I asked, getting my bearings a little better.

"None of them told me. They took my family and now they won't tell me where they are." The pain in his face caught my attention.

"But dead people don't talk." I moved closer to Libby. "If you kill them all, they can't tell you."

He walked to the desk and pointed at the church directory. "There are plenty of them." Then he pointed the knife at me. "And you are now the messiah's public enemy number one."

He came at me. The speed caught me off-guard. He missed with the knife, but not the .45. White hot pain filled my left shoulder and radiated through my body. Before I fell, I landed an uppercut that sent him backwards.

He looked at me, rubbing his chin. "Good one, kid. Haven't been punched like that in a good long while. But you can't stop the messiah."

"Who died and made you messiah?" I sat up and glared at him.

He dropped the knife and gun to his side. "Didn't you know? There are many messiahs. Check the history books. We've been around a long time. It's just my turn."

"I don't think the Sovereign will agree with you."

"Oh, him? We're a package deal, you know. He brings the peace." He raised the weapons. "And I bring the justice."

My focus waned. The loss of blood made things fuzzier. "Then why am I arresting so many people?" I chuckled. Between the pain and the blood loss, the room became hazy. I figured when I awoke I'd be face-to-face with Jesus. The real Messiah.

"Good question. You see, some people need to be jailed, others need to be dispatched publicly to help prevent crime." He walked towards me. "But others just need to go to Hell."

The next swing of his knife nearly caught me off guard, but I dove behind Libby and vomited from the pain.

Charlie shouted, "Vengeance is mine, saith the messiah. I will repay."

Before I blacked out, I heard another voice coming from behind Charlie. "Freeze, don't move."

Then I heard three shots.

Then all went dark.

CHAPTER 62

The earthquake woke me the next morning in a private hospital room. It didn't last long, but it rattled me pretty good. The lights flickered, and the alarms went off in the hospital, but they didn't last long either. As if someone anticipated it. My window faced west. The ash cloud billowing and belching its way upward, took up most of the skyline.

Then Libby's lifeless eyes entered my mind. Although I felt guilty for her death, the deep feeling assured me of her place in Heaven.

A throat cleared startling me. Colonel Lonergan sat in the visitor's chair near the door.

"Not as bad as the scientists predicted." He gave a sympathetic smile. "How are you doing, Major Thomas?"

I looked at my newly bandaged shoulder and felt my side. Then I lifted my cover and saw that my leg remained attached. "Been worse, I guess."

"The doctor says you will heal just fine. She wants you to stay a couple of days before transferring you to St. Louis. There's a nasty little virus going around that can do a number on its victims." He raised his hands a little. "It's not deadly, if that's what you're wondering. But it isn't any fun, I can tell you that. Corporal Williams got it and…"

"Not to be rude, sir, but." I pointed out the window to change the subject.

"Remember our little talk about the west?" He lowered his voice while scooting his chair to my bedside. "It blew earlier than the scientists predicted."

"Obviously, sir. But what is the status of the region?"

"From the reports, the west coast just got closer, if you know what I mean." He looked at the plume and scratched his head. "And several more around the world blew at almost the same time."

"But they just happened." I mumbled, still trying to get over the anesthesia.

"Actually, they happened earlier today. It took a little while for the percussion wave to hit us."

"Wait, I thought they said only Yellowstone was active." I asked, trying to look dumb.

"They got it wrong. There hasn't been an official count as yet, but the reporters are saying at least twelve." He looked at me. "And this is highly classified, which you are now allowed to know. The lava coming out of them is turning the oceans surrounding them red."

"Like that storm we had a few months ago?" My thigh and shoulder throbbed, but I didn't want to request any pain meds in case it hurt my chances of leaving a little early.

"I'm not sure. But now that you mention it, it does remind me of it a little." He grabbed the TV remote and turned it to the news.

A map of the world had small red triangles placed all over, including three in the U.S. The clicker at the bottom of the screen streamed the names of cities affected by the eruptions. The map soon disappeared, replaced by aerial shots of the oceans. The tag line just above the clicker said that the Sovereign's top scientists believe the eruptions stirred up the ocean in a way that caused a giant red tide. They are now calling it the Red Tsunami because small, red tidal waves crashed into the shores of the countries where the supervolcanoes had erupted.

"As if we needed anything else." Lonergan shook his head, then muted the television. "The scientists are getting an earful from the Sovereign because they can't figure out why this is happening and what the long-term effect will be on humans and the environment."

"This is incredible." I shifted to a more comfortable position.

Lonergan looked at me with satisfaction. "General Sokolov is very pleased with your handling of the investigation and how things ended. The news is playing the Sovereign's announcement while covering the eruptions." He pointed to the sky outside the window.

Looking at the eruption, I asked. "What happened in the chapel?"

Lonergan's sheepish grin told me enough. "When I heard Jenny tell you that Caplan was at the church you grew up in, and that you had no backup, I used the GPS on your chip and made a beeline there. When I walked into the chapel, I saw Caplan standing over that poor girl. I smelled cordite in the air and saw you on the floor. Caplan took a step towards you, and I yelled for him to freeze. But he didn't. So, I put three in his chest."

"Thanks, sir." I didn't like the idea of owing him like that, but God works in mysterious ways. "And I need to apologize for our dust up in the lab. My stress levels were high, and Jenny is a friend of mine."

He waved it off. "Water under the bridge. I get stressed my own self."

We watched the plume that seemed to be suspended in midair without signs of movement. It just hung there as a reminder of God's displeasure with sin.

"I guess Joy's little moment in the spotlight is less than fifteen minutes this time." I tried to get more information about my sister in Christ.

His laugh brought the nurse in to tell us to keep it down.

"Commander Everhart is getting her *five* minutes, but in a different way." He raised the remote, turned the channel to the Peace Forces Network, and unmuted it.

Surrounded by armed guards, Joy walked into the Jeff City Penitentiary. Reporters, with Vams pointing at her, shouted questions about treason and espionage. My heart fell and my anger rose. The headline said that they caught her trying to free Christians and used government resources to further the Christian Resistance's agenda.

"She used her sources to get me out of jail." I grumbled. "Unlike you."

"Petrovich claimed she had irrefutable proof that you threatened her and several other high-ranking officials." Lonergan sat back and stared at me. "Sorry, Will. But I will not stand for that."

"Not until I hand the killer over to you on a silver platter." I rubbed below my biceps. "Then everything is all copacetic."

"It's the nature of the beast. Welcome to the new world." He waved it off. "Which reminds me."

I let it go, since he just forgave me.

He pulled out his Vam and tapped the screen. "I need to get your statement." He sat it on my tray, tapped the screen again, and spoke into it by giving the standard information. Names, the date, topic, etc. He then nodded for me to begin.

I started my statement by telling the events leading up to Tim Weaver reporting the mounds.

Charlie Caplan must've witnessed the murder of his family and caused him to become mentally unhinged. When he heard the Sovereign's explanation of the murders, Charlie took it upon himself to take out those responsible for the death of his family. As a member of the Ozark Mountain Community Church, he took his copy of the church directory and found those who remained alive. After killing a few of them, he found out about the bounty bunter program and profited from his vigilantism. However, through his psychosis, he believed himself to be equal to the Sovereign to the point of referring to himself as the messiah.

I'm sure ICON correctly diagnosed the reasoning for the dismemberment and burying of the body parts in the fashion he did. However, the burial of the heads pointed to the sermons he preached to the victims. The chips and the Hell Bound sign near the location he buried the heads pointed to his mental state. In my confrontation with him, he talked about how he needed to punish the victims for the justice of his family. He believed to be an equal messiah with the Sovereign, going so far as to compare their work for bringing world peace.

Ironically, he recruited Isaac, a former member of Dad's church, to help him overpower his victims with a syringe filled with a drug that rendered them unconscious. Caplan killed Isaac when he took him home to treat the wounds I gave him, probably using the fight to steer attention away from him when Isaac turned up missing.

Then I talked about how they captured their victims. I left the gruesome scenes for when I wrote the complete report. Also, I purposely held back everything about Hectar for my own personal agenda. He still maintained value for me.

I tapped the screen to stop the recording. "I'll be more specific when I write my report, but this will keep the general happy until then."

Lonergan sat staring at the Vam and chewing on his thumbnail. I let him work it out.

"Anything on Petrovich?" I asked.

"She's in St. Louis raising holy hell to General Sokolov, claiming that you and Joy deserve nothing less than the blade. She's batting five hundred, but she wants both of you. It won't happen because we gave you full credit for closing the case. Your name is too much in the public eye for her to gun you down now." He frowned. "But it might be in your best interest to steer clear of her for a good long while. If it's possible. Who knows, maybe she'll find someone else to torment and forget all about you."

"Not likely. She isn't the type to forget anyone who crosses her and gets away with it." I sighed, thinking about Joy.

"Which is why General Sokolov is sending you to Texas for a while. When you're released from the hospital, you'll report to South Padre Island to do some recon on Christian Resistance groups operating in the gulf. It's the farthest away from here he can get you without leaving the country."

"I'm not afraid of her, sir. I'd like to go back to St. Louis and keep investigating homicides." I tried to keep my tone level.

"I understand, but Petrovich is gunning for you, and the general doesn't want to be caught in the crossfire." Lonergan looked like he didn't agree either. "Once she leaves, I'm sure he'll call you back."

"Yes, sir," I grumbled.

"Will, if you hadn't already got one a few days ago, I'd put you in for a promotion. However, all I can say is well done. You've done your military and your Sovereign a great service." He stood and saluted.

Wincing as I saluted, I secretly wished he didn't choose to be Hell Bound. He was one of the good people who made a bad choice.

The television, still covering Joy's arrest, made me think about a way to break her out of that prison. The night I saw her for the first time as a woman and not some overly ambitious brown noser trying to climb the ladder entered my mind. Although I had strong feelings for Amelia, something about Joy seemed more natural. Maybe I'd been away so long that I latched onto the first beautiful woman who crossed my path. Maybe Amelia and I aren't meant to be.

Maybe I needed to consult the deep feeling.

EPILOGUE

Much to the chagrin of the doctor, I left the hospital to go see Joy. Lonergan protested the entire trip to Jefferson City. He said that by visiting Joy in prison I might as well kiss my DRUID appointment goodbye. He reminded me of how much I hated the former commander. But nothing he said stopped me.

Before dropping me off, Lonergan gave me one more chance to walk away from the visit. If he knew the truth, he'd have walked me to the cell next to Joy to await my execution. I declined and told him I'd see him before I left for Texas.

The two days before visiting the prison didn't generate anything interesting other than me avoiding Amelia. For Joy, however, the whirlwind increased with each passing hour. While I fought Charlie Caplan in Dad's church, Petrovich contacted her superior's superior to get permission to arrest Joy and have her executed. On my way to the hospital, Daria led Joy out of her office in handcuffs.

I later found out the priests prepped the guillotines in an attempt to intimidate Zeek and Daniel into leaving the city. Their efforts, however, had no effect on the two witnesses, who kept preaching with complete confidence. Daniel left the next day for St. Louis with Clay to meet Tommy who had plans to smuggle Christians to the island section of the old United States across the Mississippi River.

I had to threaten the warden and two guards before being led to death row. Joy's joke of a trial lasted only an hour before being found guilty and sentenced to death. My expectations of Joy's defeated mental state didn't prepare me for reality. Her smile lit up the room of cells for the soon to be executed. I chalked it up to her keeping up appearances to show Daria she hadn't won.

My heart broke because I never came up with a plan to spring her. Every idea I had come up short. Praying didn't seem to help because I asked God to break her out the way He did with Paul and the other early church members. The deep feeling kept telling me that God put Joy exactly where she needed to be. But I didn't agree with God.

She stood near the bars, wearing the standard orange jumpsuit, when the two guards patted me down one last time and gave threatening looks. I replied by threatening their careers. When they left, the head guard of the cellblock walked me the rest of the way to her cell.

When I saw the state of her cell, I turned to the guard. "Am I mistaken, or is this cell not up to global standards?" I invaded his personal space.

"The prisoner has everything she needs. Nothing more." His glare fell short.

I pushed him into the wall and put my cane across his throat. His eyes bulged.

"I am Major Will Thomas of DRUID who just cracked the biggest case in this planet's history. Commander Joy Everhart is my partner and an integral part of that investigation, and you will treat her with the utmost respect in her last hours on this planet. Is that clear?" I shouted in his face.

"Yes, sir." He squeaked.

Letting him go, I restated my order to bring her cell up to regulation after our meeting and to not be disturbed. He sprinted out of the cellblock, no doubt to report me. I drug the chair at the guard's desk over to the cell and sat. Joy pushed her cot near me and plopped on it.

"Hi, Will. It's nice to see your old self going against someone other than me." Her grin lightened my anger. "You look like you need to be in the hospital."

Warmed by her concern, I played it off. "I've had worse."

Opening the bag I brought in, I pulled out a sandwich from her favorite St. Louis deli with a pickle spear, potato salad, and an apple. She squealed with delight.

"This is much better than the last meal I ordered." She unwrapped the extra lean pastrami on whole wheat with extra mustard and took a bite and rolled her eyes. "So good."

Pulling out my ham and hot cheese on rye with mayo, I left the rest in the bag. "Agreed."

According to the schedule posted in the guard's office, Joy's execution didn't take place until five the next morning. I had every intention of spending the entire time with her. She didn't deserve to be alone.

We didn't talk until we'd finished our meals. Joy saved her apple. I ate my cookie.

"By the way, these cells aren't being monitored. I made sure of that." I winced changing positions.

The warden had no choice by order of General Sokolov. A favor I called in.

She sat with her back on the cinderblock wall and stared at her cute bare feet. "I'm in desperate need of a pedicure." She rubbed her toes.

I grinned and shook my head. "Only you can think of something like that at a time like this."

"I have to think of something to keep my mind off this place. But I'll be out of here in the morning." She pulled her knees tight and hugged them, still staring at her toes.

My anger and guilt ripped my heart in two. Daria and her body bunkmate will soon die at my hands.

"I'm sorry I can't do anything to help." I whispered.

"That's alright. I appreciate the thought." She smiled when she turned her head and laid it on her knees. Her deep blue eyes mesmerized.

I didn't see Amelia in St. Louis on purpose, nor did I talk to her on video chat or text. Joy came first. I'd deal with Amelia later.

"Did you hear about Caplan?" I asked, trying to change the subject.

"Only that Lonergan killed him while being arrested."

I told her the whole story. She didn't like the idea that I owed Lonergan for bailing me out. Then she gave condolences for Libby and Devon. I did the same for Bub. She wiped her tears on her sleeve.

"I'm just glad we know where they are and that we'll see them again soon." She returned her gaze to me. "Very soon for me."

The awkward moment drug on.

"What about Petrovich?" She widened her eyes as if it had just occurred to her. "Is she still after you?"

"Probably. Lonergan told me she's in St. Louis demanding Sokolov have me arrested and bladed alongside you. He said when the general asked her reasons, she refused to say. She just threatened to have him bladed in my place if he didn't fall in line." I shrugged.

"I wonder why she isn't saying anything."

"She doesn't really have a case. I threatened her, but no witnesses. It's her word against mine. And my fame is overriding her standing in the government. That will be short-lived unless another high-profile case comes to St. Louis."

"I'll pray for just that." She winked.

Butterflies did laps in my stomach.

"Any other time in history, I'd say that I hoped not. But in the times we're living in, I'll agree, so long that it's a Mark who's been killed." I winked back.

Her smile made the situation bearable.

"I heard the supervolcanoes went off as Daniel predicted." She looked at me with anticipation.

"They sure did. The Sovereign's scientists are scurrying because they promised two things. One, Yellowstone will be the only one to blow. Two, it won't affect anything because the area had been evacuated. I checked ICON. Twelve blew and about a third of the oceans are blood red. Dead sea life is landing on the beaches and coastlines as we speak. Ships of all sizes can't make land because the crew is sick or dying. But, of course, that's not the narrative the Sovereign is using. He claims the eruptions are smaller than expected and that the oceans will make a full recovery within the year."

"Yeah, right." She snarked.

"Agreed." I smiled.

After a few quiet minutes, I said, "By the way, Sokolov is sending me to Texas."

She stared at me with that politician look. "It's a good plan. He's protecting you from Petrovich and himself. I know I don't want to be caught between you two. But I will miss you."

"And I'll miss you." I didn't lie.

We spent the rest of the night talking about the case and our lives before the Trib. The topics came naturally. Nothing forced. Just two friends waiting for the inevitable morning. At about, the warden came in with three guards. It took everything in me not to take them on and help Joy escape, but reality set in when I stood and felt the pain shoot into every corner of my body. Joy slowly stood and walked to the cell door.

The warden brought his arm up and turned on his Vam.

"Joy Everhart, you have been convicted of treason and other sundry crimes against the people of this planet and the blessed Sovereign." He paused.

My heart sped up. Just a week before, I had dreamed of something like this, but now I begged God to free her.

"However, the appeals tribunal has overturned your conviction and acquitted you due to a lack of substantive evidence. You are free to go." His smile felt more like a grimace.

The cell door opened, and Joy slipped into her prison sandals and sauntered out. My jaw dropped, whether from disbelief or delight, I couldn't tell. Didn't care.

She walked up to me with a sultry grin. "Daria Petrovich is powerful, but my contacts run deeper and higher than hers."

"I will never underestimate you again."

"Make sure of that." She put her hand on my face. "And the next time you see Daria, give her this." Joy stood on her tiptoes, wrapped her hand behind my neck, and pulled me down to her.

The kiss made all my pains go away. Her moist, soft lips pressed hard against mine. I pulled her close, not wanting it to end. When we separated, she put her cheek on mine and whispered, "Pray for me. I used all my favors to make this happen. Next time, I'll be kissing you goodbye."

She walked to the warden and took the Vam he held out.

Before exiting the room, she turned and smiled. "Oh, and please inform Daria that I have been kissed."

After nodding and watching her leave, I sat back down, rubbed my sore leg, and thanked God she was on our side.

ACKNOWLEDGMENTS

To God goes all the glory. His blessings go beyond measure. The family He gave me and the path He put me on is a daily testament to His love that surpasses my wildest dreams.

To Shelly, who also made this beautiful book cover, and Hunter, whom I love so much. Thank you for your love and support. To Mom, my biggest cheerleader and herald. I can never express my love and appreciation to any of you.

To those who have gone on to heaven before me. I look forward to seeing you and telling you how much you mean to me for all eternity.

Thanks to Sharon Kizziah-Holmes of Paperback Press for helping make this book a reality. You've always been a great blessing.

ABOUT THE AUTHOR

Ken Gardner is a Christian, with an inherent interest in Bible prophecy, and an active member in two writing groups. He graduated with his MFA in creative writing from the University of Southern Maine in 2018. While recovering from COVID-19 in November 2020, Ken decided it was time to get serious about publishing. Since then, he became an award-winning writer of short stories.

Ken lives in southwest Missouri with his wife, Shelly, son, Hunter, and German Shepherd, Tank. Sports are a point of great distraction, especially, the St. Louis Cardinals, college football, and the NFL draft.

www.ingramcontent.com/pod-product-compliance
Lightning Source LLC
Chambersburg PA
CBHW060514180626
46817CB00002B/358